The interloper extended his hands forward, rubbing them together as he did so. With his arms straight before him, he turned his palms out toward his target. A ball of fire the size of a large melon soared toward Raftennon, who calmly looked on as the familiar blue glow flickered around his body. The unnatural flames crashed into the unseen barrier, mere inches from the young man's face. The fireball dissipated, leaving Raftennon unharmed.

The apprentice reached into another hidden pocket and began reciting another incantation.

"Drendaymônân symlôvaeelyay karnayjemô sreeznôvlanaee milônel revétômanaylâsim!"

The intruder frantically rummaged through his own spell components to counter this unexpected attack. Before the man could manage to grab whatever he was searching for, an unseen force pushed him against the wall and pinned him there, unable to move.

"Again I ask; who are you, and why are you attacking me?" Raftennon began to walk toward the unknown interloper but stopped when he heard a sound at the door of the private quarters. The entry was empty, the door firmly shut.

"Ventrâllaynus imânilsülan ferbaysylôsay myrnayfôrtrâllesis bynmâlloovaryan drenlôhaylan." Raftennon turned back to his trapped assailant to see the effects of the man's incantation. The dark-clad man lowered his arms and took a step forward, despite the force Raftennon thrust at him. The apprentice intensified his concentration, adding more strength to his invisible shield, but still the man passed through it as if it were not there. The energies that were supposed to immobilize the man simply dissipated as soon as they touched him.

ALSO BY MARC LABELLE

Knightfall

A WOMAN'S SCORN

TRIALS OF THE CHOSEN
BOOK ONE

MARC LABELLE

LUPYNE BOOKS

Map created by Marc Labelle using
ProFantasy's Campaign Cartographer

Lupyne Books
1-140 Railway Street
Sturgeon Falls, ON P2B 3B1
Canada

www.lupynebooks.com

ISBN-13: 978-0-9949314-0-5
ISBN-10: 0-9949314-0-9

10 9 8 7 6 5 4 3 2 1

DEDICATION

For my brother,
who ordered me to write this story,
not knowing I had already begun the labour.

Author's Note

The books in this trilogy are linked to my first novel, *Knightfall*, through two of its secondary characters. Because of this relationship, you will meet all the primary players from that story in this one—eventually. You will relive Ravenna's tale from a different point of view. Those incidents she and her friends did not experience will be revealed.

I tried my best to align the events as accurately as possible, but I am a man constantly trying to better his works. For this reason, those who have read *Knightfall* may notice some discrepancies. I apologize in advance for any confusion that occurs.

I do wish to warn you of a specific change. It is in regards to the eye colour of the aforementioned characters. I will not reveal the discrepancy here, for I do not want to ruin any part of the story for the reader, but I want to ensure you know it is intentional. It is a minor adjustment in appearance, but one I felt compelled to make.

Only those owning one of the first two editions of *Knightfall*, published by either Lulu Publishing Services or Eloquent Books, need to heed this warning. All later printings will reflect the change and make this note obsolete.

So, without further ado, I will end this mundane diatribe and move on to the tale I am certain you would much rather read.

Marc

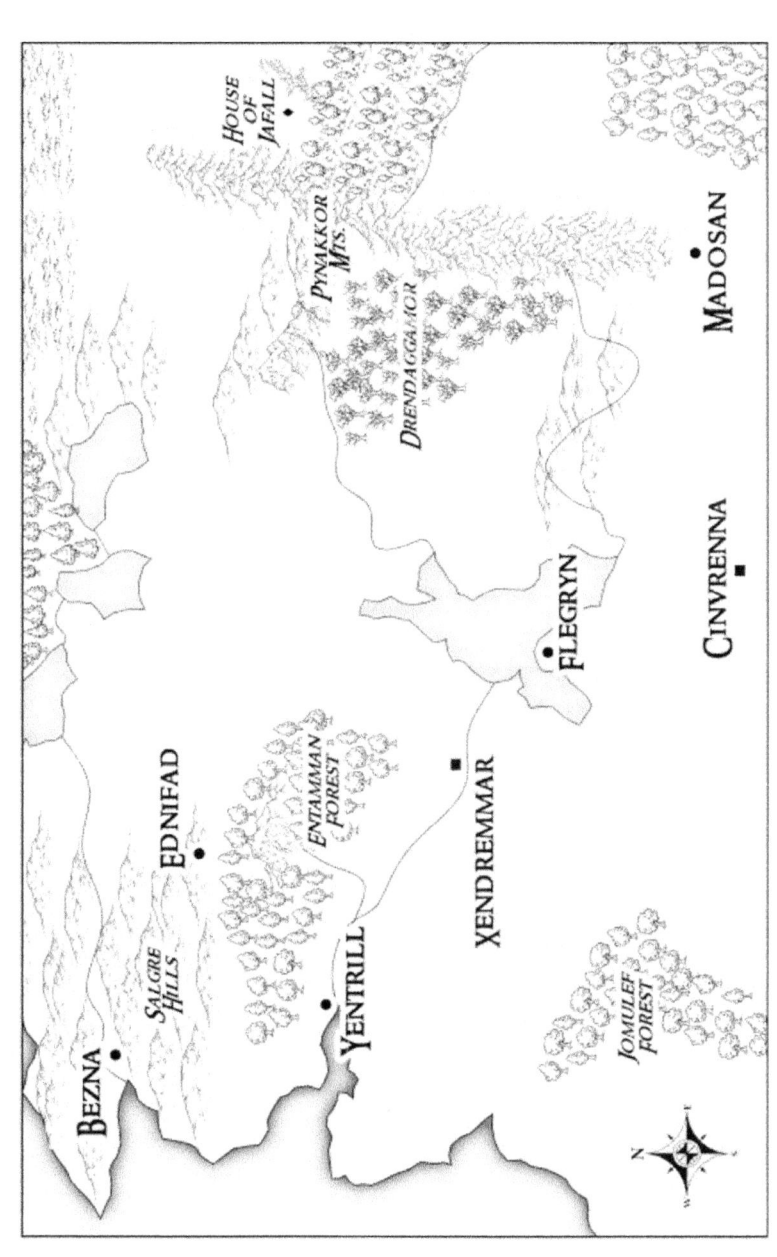

PROLOGUE

Lightning flashed, obliterating the sunshine that strove to enter the smoke-filled room. A young man's scream pierced through the clattering of falling books and overturned chairs. Blood splattered in an arc toward one wall.

"Where is he?" Caelynn asked. There were five other spellcasters clustered around her just inside the entrance to the large room.

"Precisely where I hit him," Grynvellon replied, his hand still extended forward. Slender tendrils of smoke rose from his fingers, where the bolts of lightning had erupted to smash into the intruder.

The vapour cloud concealing much in the room drifted to the ceiling, gradually revealing the result of the mage's attack. A man clad in black, his face veiled in the same dark fabric that covered the rest of his body, stood tall, a long slender blade in each hand. Everyone present in the room took in a quick breath, their eyes widening at the impossibility.

"Your spell seems to have failed." Sevellen stared in astonishment, not believing he would ever utter those words in regard to the other man's ability to handle the magic arts.

Daenar ignored the exchange between those five huddled by the door. He flung the now dead man off his chest, his previous screams still ringing in the spellcaster's ears. The poor fellow's blood soaked the floor, seeping from the long gash opened by the assailant's sword. He had been the closest thing the mage could grab to shield himself. Now, he was just in the way.

As soon as his hands were empty, Daenar raised his right, manipulated the needed components with his left and chanted strange words. A fireball shot from the palm of his outstretched hand and slammed into the stranger. The flames engulfed his assailant, once again hiding him from sight.

Chaos continued its reign as the man burned in the centre of the room. The five spellcasters near the door took a few more steps into the chamber, fanning out as they went. Four young acolytes wailed, as they had since the attack started, and scampered about in fear, not knowing where to go to avoid the conflict. Their eyes kept flicking to their two comrades who had already fallen. Daenar overlooked their panic and stared at the blaze, preparing himself as his brothers and sister no doubt were doing.

The fire soon subsided to reveal what the mages feared. The intruder still stood, unaffected by the magic that should have finished him.

"What do you want?" Grynvellon asked.

The veiled figure lifted one sword and pointed it at Daenar. The lone spellcaster sneered, flanked by the two innocents who lost their lives saving his own—though they had not volunteered.

"What has he done?" Grynvellon continued.

Daenar scoffed at the statement. Of course, the pompous Grynvellon would assume the worst of him.

The ebony-clad man remained silent, motionless until he sprang to action. Before anyone else could react, he threw one of his swords at Daenar. It took the mage the length of a short breath to realize he needed to do something. He lunged to the side, raising his left arm to shield his face. The blade embedded in the spellcaster's forearm, sending searing pain coursing through his entire body. Daenar grimaced as he continued to fall, managing to hold in the scream of agony that begged to pass his lips. When he hit the floor, the stone tiles dislodged the weapon from his arm. Blood gushed from the wound, turning the grey of rock to red.

Daenar's vision began to fade, but he would have none of

that. He covered the gash with his other hand and forced his eyes to lift upward. The assassin was already on the third step of his charge, his other sword raised to finish off his target. Before he halved the distance between them, the dark man staggered as a chair struck him. Daenar darted his eyes to where the projectile came from to witness Grynvellon concentrating, raising another seat to hurl at the interloper.

The warrior in black evaded the second chair, ducking under it with fluidity a cat would envy. He twirled around, flinging his free arm away from his waist. A small blade flipped through the air with such speed none witnessed its trajectory. In the span of a gasp, the hilt protruded from Grynvellon's stomach. The spellcaster slumped to his knees, both hands around the knife in a vain attempt to keep the blood from flowing.

Daenar took advantage of the distraction and followed Grynvellon's lead. As his attacker returned his attention to him, the magic-user hurled another projectile. Daenar was more pragmatic than his colleague, and much more callous. The assassin tried to duck under this missile, but its flailing arms and legs proved too much for him to avoid. The startled acolyte slammed into the veiled figure, sending both men tumbling to the floor. Daenar grabbed the other novices, who were even more frantic than before, and magically threw them on top of the tangled pair.

While the stranger struggled to free himself from the human net, Daenar hurried to combine two powders on the stone tile before him and chanted. *"Frentalin-malis drenfâllannâs komréllan posteriâs nô ménapôlâs! Hellanân vôrtellôn trennülümâs!"*

The tiles beneath the pile cracked, then fell away in a loud crash, taking everyone laying on them to the level below.

"What are you doing?" Ygrett asked, appalled.

"Saving my life," Daenar responded. "Do not disturb me with inane questions."

"You sacrifice innocent lives!" she persisted.

"Be content I do not sacrifice yours," Daenar retorted, returning to the task at hand.

He stood and made his way to the edge of the gaping hole. He leaned over to peer below. Five bodies writhed over crumbled stone, as was expected. Daenar recited his previous spell and mentally lifted a set of shelves lining the wall of the room. He tilted it horizontally so no books would fall off, then floated it over the open space. He stacked two more laden bookcases over this one, just for good measure. Then he sent his makeshift press flying to the storey below. He bent his will to add more momentum to the drop. The wood of the shelves splintered with the impact, but not before the flooring under the struggling bodies gave way, sending everything tumbling another level down.

Daenar stretched himself even further out above the hole and examined his work. This time, there was no movement. The spellcaster moved away from the ravaged edge and headed for the door leading to the stairs.

"Are you satisfied now?" Grynvellon asked through gritted teeth as Ygrett gently pulled the dagger from his stomach.

"Hardly," Daenar responded, not stopping on his way to the door.

"Let us hope you find what you seek before toppling the rest of the tower around us."

Daenar ignored him, exiting the room before making his way down two flights of stairs. The pain in his arm reminded him of his wound. He took the cloth belt tied around his waist and bandaged his forearm as best he could with one hand. Ignoring the blood seeping through the fabric to continue trickling down to his fingers, the mage raced through the door he needed to enter the room that no longer had a ceiling—or a floor you could see.

Daenar scampered over the mound of stone and paper. He ignored the outstretched hands protruding from the carnage, motionless. He would find what he sought beneath the debris, not atop it. Using his right hand, which was at the end of his uninjured arm, he grabbed a book and flung it to the side. He disregarded the thump the tome made when it landed and reached for the next volume to fling out of the way.

Two spellcasters appeared in the doorway. They were not present in the upper room during the attack, for Grynvellon, in his infinite wisdom, had dispatched them to find out how the intruder infiltrated the tower. They were surely returning to report what they discovered. One of them indicated the other should do just that while he entered the room.

"What has happened?" the wizard who remained asked as he sidestepped to avoid getting hit by the flying books.

"Ask the Head Mage," Daenar returned sardonically. When he did not hear the sound of retreating footsteps, he looked up to see the other spellcaster still standing where he was, perplexed. "I have no desire to explain, so if you are desperate for answers, find someone else to bother. If you wish to remain here, you can do so only if you help remove the rubble."

The mage stood for a few moments before deciding to mount the debris. "The name is Christoffen," he said as he settled himself to get to work.

"I did not care to know any of you when we first met. I still do not."

So the two spellcasters dug through the destruction. They used magic to clear the larger pieces of the stone floor too heavy for them to move the conventional way. Christoffen paused every time they uncovered one of the acolytes. His face remained emotionless, save to show the respect given to a colleague who had just passed. Daenar moved the carcasses out of the way, as if they were another slab of rock, so he could continue his work.

The six other mages entered the room as Daenar removed the last acolyte from the wreckage to reveal the assassin beneath.

"You could have saved yourself all this trouble by simply shoving the man out the window," Grynvellon said as two others helped him into the room. "It would have also saved more lives."

"The only life that matters is still striving," Daenar responded, not looking up from the man he stood over. "I still need answers."

"I did not know you dabbled in necromancy, Daenar." Grynvellon sat in a chair another mage somehow found in the destroyed room.

Daenar ignored this last statement, for he never acknowledged foolishness. If the old man wanted to demean himself with such childish pokes, he could do so by himself. Instead, Daenar bent down and tore away the cloth mask that covered his assailant's face. The mage's eyes fell on the large bulge and awkward slant of the assassin's neck. He placed his hand under the stranger's nose and waited until he was satisfied the intruder no longer breathed.

Appeased the threat was averted, Daenar took his time to

study the man. He tilted the head this way and that, opened the closed mouth and stretched the eyelids further back.

"He is half-elfin," Christoffen commented. He was the only one beside Daenar, as intent on the assessment of the body.

Daenar did not reply. Instead, he continued his examination. His hand went down to the collar of his black tunic and pulled it open. The bare chest of a fit man lay beneath. The muscles were hard and well-defined, the result of life-long training. Daenar was no expert when it came to physical betterment, but he knew how to distinguish a lout from a man devoted to fitness. The way the assassin moved in the room above proved he was one of the latter.

Daenar's eyes focused on the stone that lay on the chiselled chest. A black cord entwined the rock, then ran around the man's neck, keeping the unusual token close to his heart. The talisman was black like coal but seem much more resilient. Daenar lifted the odd pendant with the tips of his fingers. It was warm to the touch, much warmer than could be accounted for by its proximity to living flesh. Then the strange heat vanished, leaving an ordinary rock. Daenar would have sworn he felt a flicker of magical energy emanating from the pendant when he first touched it, but that was gone now.

Who sent you?, Daenar thought to himself.

"Great Pentaclin!"

These words caught Daenar's attention. He did not know who uttered them, but that did not matter. He released the pendant and stood. His eyes gave the body one last cursory glance as he did so, but nothing jumped up at him that would help him identify the man or his motives. So Daenar turned to the being that had summoned the spellcasters to this tower in the first place.

"Well done, my Chosen." Pentaclin spread his arms wide to show he was sending his praise to all present. The loose folds of the grey robes fluttered in a breeze that did not exist. His long, white hair also swayed the air current that was not there as his pupil-less white eyes took in every man and woman in the room.

After a moment of letting the mortals bask in his presence, the god of magic and knowledge slid his hands into the opposing sleeves of his robes and glided toward Daenar. His steps were indistinguishable, the hem of his vestment never leaving the floor to reveal even a single toe.

"What do we have here?" Pentaclin stopped beside the mage to study the dead assassin.

"I am certain you saw more than anyone in this room," Daenar sneered. He hated being patronized, no matter who was doing it.

"You missed nothing, I assure you." Pentaclin turned to face the spellcaster. "But a god need not explain himself to his worshippers."

"I do not worship you, Great Sage. You promised me vast knowledge if I helped you defeat the Great Beast before he tore the kingdom to shreds. You were quite emphatic you could not fashion this weapon of yours without my help. You sought me. I did not seek you. So start repaying me by telling me who this man is."

"I do not know who he is. And you were not the only one I sought. These other seven were as necessary as you in this endeavour. Without their aid, the Lance of Light would never have been fashioned. It took all eight of you to accomplish the task I set for you."

"We were honoured to serve," Grynvellon said, struggling to stand so he could show the god the respect he deserved. Daenar scoffed at the blatant flattery. Grynvellon ignored this and continued. "But I must ask. What happened to us during the enchantment of the weapon?"

Daenar stopped glaring at the pompous mage, for he too had felt a sudden shift in the energy they were pouring into the lance. Nothing was happening until something clicked within him. He now assumed the same realization came on all of them. It was almost as if someone lifted a veil, revealing how they should have performed the spells from the start. Daenar always suspected this particular part of his mind existed, but it continued to elude him—until this night.

Daenar cut off his introspection. He examined the other mages who had participated in the incantation that forged the only weapon capable of defeating the immortal Great Beast. They had indeed changed, and it touched more than their minds. All their hair now glistened the purest white. Their eyes, moving from one wizard to another, were now faded to a strange bluish-grey colour.

"I gave each of you incredible gifts," Pentaclin told them. "Do not be alarmed by the change in your appearance. Onlookers will notice the white hair and assume you have a great store of wisdom. They will not know the depths of your knowledge, but they will still show you the respect you deserve. The youthful complexion will confuse them, but they will understand you still possess strength and should not be trifled with."

Daenar grabbed a few strands from his shoulder and lifted them in front of his face. They too were white. "So you decided to shackle us together with intricate uniforms. You even went as far as giving them my eyes. How quaint."

Pentaclin scowled at the indolence. "The greatest gift I bestowed on all of you is the ability to see more than mortals are meant to see. It will take time for your minds to acclimate to your new sight. They have only begun to register all the extra information, which is why you do not yet perceive a difference. As time goes on, you will discover slight discrepancies in everything you have looked upon before. Not only will colours and depth expand, you will also come to understand how things are made and why they interact with each other as they do. This Enlightenment lightens the iris. You will bask in the wonders of creation at a level second only to the gods."

"Then why are his eyes white?" Caelynn asked, pointing at Daenar.

The mage whirled his head to glare at the god. "What have you done to me?"

"The same as all the others," Pentaclin reassured everyone present. "I told you the process lightens the iris. Daenar's eyes were light to begin with."

This explains why I have always seen more than all these idiots, Daenar thought to himself, still not wanting to divulge this fact. This was an advantage he possessed all his life, one he never admitted having to anyone. It was the ace up his sleeve. Now it appeared he must share it with these seven.

"What you should concern yourselves with now are the fates of the mortals," Pentaclin went on before the conversation continued down this path, one he clearly did not want to explain further. "The Great Beast may be vanquished, but he recruited five creatures as vile and almost as dangerous as he. These lieutenants still roam the lands of Kagendur and threaten the people."

"We have already done the heavy lifting by ridding them of the Beast," Daenar said. "The 'people' can take care of the rest themselves."

"You forged a weapon," Pentaclin reminded the mage. "Another mortal wielded it and drove it through the Great Beast's heart. An army followed him to ensure he got close enough to accomplish the feat. Still more kept the lieutenants at bay so this warrior could strike the final blow. According to my tally of events, you accomplished as much as anyone else, no more. So you can continue helping them."

"Your will be done," Grynvellon said. He turned to make his way to the archway leading to the corridor, leaning on the wall for support.

Pentaclin raised his hand. "You cannot travel the ways that are accustomed to you any longer." With his outstretched hand, the god of magic gestured to the lone window in the room.

The mages took the few steps to reach the opening. Daenar remained where he was, peering out the glass pane from afar. Bright stars sparkled in a clear night sky. The spellcaster's eyes narrowed as something dawned on him. It was still day. They should not be able to see stars for another few hours. And if, by some unnoticed feat, time had moved faster than it should have, the smoke of the many torches lining the streets would obscure the twinkling dots the slightest bit. Could the change in their eyes attest for the strange clarity?

"The city is gone," Sevellen gasped.

"We float among the stars," Helaenna clarified.

"I have transported your tower from its place in the Spellcasters' Guild," Pentaclin explained. "Here, in the heavens, nothing will distract you from your studies. You will forget the trivialities that bog down the minds of the mundane and concentrate on greater matters. Use your new sight to understand the wonders of this universe. Study all that the gods created. Learn the secrets of the cosmos. Devote yourselves to fulfilling the potential of mortal intellect.

"Along with the gift of expanded vision, so you may catch

what others miss, I also bestow immunity from the ravages of time. You will need eons to fully comprehend Everything, so I give you that time. You will not age, grow brittle with the years, or fall prey to disease. But make no mistake, I do not grant immortality, as should already be apparent." The god of magic gestured to both Grynvellon's and Daenar's wounds.

"The Great Beast was kind enough to bestow that privilege to his lieutenants," Daenar interjected.

Pentaclin turned glaring eyes on the arrogant mage. "I will not repeat that perversion," he hissed through clenched teeth. "True immortality is a state reserved for the gods. The Great Beast cast aside the warnings of Mother Fate and has paid for it. Though I bestow considerable gifts to you, you are still mortal and subject to death. Any violent act that would steal the life from a normal man will also do the same to you."

"All right," Daenar once again interrupted. "We understand. We will live millennia so we may learn all there is to learn as long as we remember how to use a knife when eating. It does not explain how you want us to help this glorious army of yours if you remove us from the world itself."

"I transported this tower for another reason. You will all wield immense power, power not meant to rule over others." Pentaclin's white eyes bore into Daenar's to ensure the mage was understanding every word. "You are my Chosen, my Munaedaar. Your task not only comprises learning all you can but includes preserving the essence of knowledge. So long as one of you continues to seek answers to questions, my legacy will persist.

"You are also the Champions of Order, the Keepers of the Scale. From this lofty vantage point, you will watch over Kagendur, catch any attempts to sway the Balance of Existence. And, from here, you will return to the world in times of need to rectify any tilt.

"You are forbidden from affecting the Scales in any manner save the rectification of an unbalance. Any direct attempt to do so will result in the instant disappearance of your power. You will lose all the knowledge you acquired and the magic will also escape you. You will revert to a regular mortal, with no skills to speak of, since you have all devoted your lives to the Art.

"To curb any temptation, you will refrain from interacting with the peoples of Kagendur. You will remain out of sight as much as possible. You will abstain from resolving conflicts. Mortal disputes no longer concern you. All that matters is the Balance. Only to right the wrongs pertaining to the Scales will I allow you to interact with the mortals."

"We are to do so now?" Christoffen asked.

"The Great Beast and his lackeys created a heavy unbalance," Pentaclin said. "Even with his death, the Scales of Everything lean too far to one side. The good in the world cannot counterbalance the evil of these five lieutenants that still remain. You must aid in their capture. Once that task is accomplished, your true studies may commence in peace."

"It is a shame Geneve, your mother," Daenar said, "does not simply lift the gift of immortality from these fiends so we could kill them."

Pentaclin lifted an arm and sent his will crashing into the arrogant mage. Daenar slammed into the wall behind him, toppling over the few books that somehow remained on their shelves after the collapse of the ceiling.

"You overstep, mortal," Pentaclin stated. "One day my patience will be spent and you will become nothing."

Daenar lifted his white eyes to glare at the deity. "Why do I have the impression I will never be nothing?"

Pentaclin whirled away from Daenar and motioned to the other assembled mages. "Follow me and I will show you how to travel from this tower to the lands of Kagendur."

The seven spellcasters followed their god out of the room, leaving Daenar alone, sitting on the floor. He remained there, looking out the window to the revealed heavens. One star flew across the opening, far off in the distance, not content to remain still like the others.

"Well," Daenar said as he stood, smoothing the folds of his robes as he did so. "At least he was good enough to keep his word. Let us commence in learning the secrets of the universe. Then we can find out who is attempting to end my life, so I may end theirs."

I

THE FIRST TASTE OF MAGIC

The sun appeared on the eastern edge of the Plains of Mandellon, beginning to warm the deep greens of the untamed grass. The deer and the elk of the free lands emerged from their dens, ready for the day. The birds took off from their nests in the branches of the sparse clusters of trees scattered throughout the vast expanse. The early light continued its slow crawl westward until it reached the Entamman Forest to give those birches and elms its warmth, after turning the white caps of the Qartyff Mountains nestled in the heart of the wood into blazing stars.

On the western coast of the continent, the tiny village of Yentrill stirred in the growing light. The family pets scurried along the mostly empty streets, lured home by the fragrant aromas of the various breakfasts being prepared. The silence began to recede as the children either rose of their own accord or fought with their mothers for a few more minutes of rest. Many of the men were already on the docks, readying their boats for the day's fishing expeditions. Their shouts helped to rouse those still trying to deny the arrival of morning and the need to get out of bed.

"Outta my way, twerp," a teen said as he pushed a younger boy aside. The tot staggered away from the older lad, his arms stretching out in hopes of finding his lost balance. All he found, however, was the unavoidable plunge forward as he failed to regain his footing. His brown eyes, naturally big, as was common in boys his age, grew even larger as he realized where he was heading. His arms flailed even more frantically as the swift waters of the Grannbellan sped toward him. His gaze flickered downstream, to the current that raced into the vastness of Vendetran Bay and the Elbatu Sea beyond.

"Easy now," came the most welcome voice of the lad's father. He grabbed the back of the boy's shirt collar and pulled him up. When he was certain his son could stand on his own, he turned his attention to the teenager who pushed him. "There was no need for that, Bren."

"We're going to be late and miss the tide, Father," the teen retorted without even looking back. He also sped on to avoid any other reprimand.

"One day, I'm the one who will push him into the river," the small lad snorted.

Hawer looked down at his youngest son, dismayed. "He's your brother, Raftennon. Brothers don't always get along. But they don't wish each other harm."

"Bren does." Raftennon crossed his arms and glared at his eldest sibling as he entered the town square just opposite the docks and the boats to which he was heading. The young lad's eyes continued to narrow as he remembered every shove, every elbow, every trip he had suffered in the first six years of his life. With every event recalled, his ire increased, and his father noticed.

"Listen to me, Raftennon," Hawer said as he knelt, blocking the boy's view of everything in front of him but his father's face. "Bren does love you, even if he doesn't show it. You'll learn when you get to be his age. He just acts without thinking."

"I hope he falls off the boat into the sea," Raftennon said, his words slightly muffled by the profound pout that distorted his lips.

"You don't mean that." Hawer ruffled the tot's hair, trying to cheer him up. "One day, believe it or not, the two of you will be closest friends, just like me and my brothers. Now, get back home. Your mother must have breakfast ready by now. I'm sure you'll want to eat that before it gets cold."

With a final pat on the lad's shoulder, Hawer straightened and started to walk toward the modest pier. He turned his head back once and Raftennon did his best to give the man a bright smile. The boy knew it fell short of appearing sincere, but his father returned the gesture, his much more genuine. Then the man followed his eldest son around the corner. He and Raftennon's other brothers would only return as the sun was setting, with an abundant catch, Roen willing.

Raftennon flicked a pebble with the toe of his boot. The small stone travelled the arc he almost did, straight into the flowing river. It disappeared under the swift running waters. He imagined Bren tumbling into that current, racing into the ocean, never to be seen again. His anger faded and he knew he would not be able to cope with such a disappearance, no matter which of his siblings it was.

Raftennon crossed the other side of the path and began his race home. As he was every morning, he was hungry. With the mention of breakfast, his stomach reminded him how famished he was. He only managed to make the first turn down a side street before he had to stop himself short.

A large dog started barking at him the moment it saw him. Raftennon tried to sidestep away from the animal but tripped over his own feet instead. He fell onto the dirt-covered lane, somehow managing to not scrape his hands. He scrambled into a sitting position, getting ready to back-pedal if need be. The mutt bared its teeth and growled, the heckles rising on the back of its neck but came no closer.

Three other boys, a few years older than Raftennon, added to the noise with loud laughter. One bent over with the force of his mirth, one hand on his knee, while the other pointed to make sure everyone knew who they were laughing at. Raftennon scrambled backward, still seated in the dirt, until he felt he was at a safe enough distance from the snarling dog.

"Look at this, guys," the boy standing in the middle of the trio said. "It's the demon child." He came forward the slightest bit and crouched down. "You don't look too scary to me, demon child. In fact, you look pathetic. I don't get why all the dogs snarl and back away from you, or why the horses rear when you get too close. You're not scary at all. If I didn't know any better, I would swear you were about to cry."

Raftennon was indeed fighting back tears. They were not borne of fear or embarrassment, as the ruffian seemed to think. They were the result of intense anger. Raftennon narrowed his eyes, not only to keep them dry but because his mind began to focus. It tended to do that of its own accord whenever he was really upset.

The older boy shot up straight and stumbled backward to where his friends were still standing. The bully's eyes widened in fright, a fact Raftennon ignored as he continued to stare him down from his seat in the dirt. The dog cringed, tail between its legs, before whirling around to bolt down the lane. The boys soon followed, leaving Raftennon alone, seething.

He watched them go, his breathing heavy. Only when the bullies disappeared around a corner did he close his eyes and concentrated on calming himself. He did not know why, but every time he got angry, people ran away from him. It was a strange occurrence that did not bother him. He knew it happened but gave it no more thought than that. He was usually preoccupied with trying to rid himself of his anger. He did not have time, or the inclination, to ponder the actions of others.

When he opened his eyes, after reaching the calm he sought, Raftennon caught a woman standing nearby, staring at him. When their gaze met, she spun away and resumed her walk down the street. Raftennon saw other villagers rush away when he turned his head in their direction. Only one old man kept his gaze on him instead of shying away. Raftennon could not read his expression, so he had no idea what the elder was thinking. He also did not care. The boy got up, dusted himself off and began the run down the streets again.

After a few more turns, Raftennon left the dirt track and ran across a sparse lawn. He did not slow as he rushed through the door, causing it to slam into the wall with the force of the push.

"Sorry," Raftennon muttered as he finally slowed and walked to his seat at the table. His three sisters were already eating their fried eggs and trout, as his father had guessed. They eyed him, no doubt reproaching him for his childishness, as they always did. He chose to ignore this insult, as he did the others.

His mother soon came to his side and stood over him, a plate in her hand. "So what's going on that merits our house suffering a pummelling?"

"Nothing," Raftennon continued in his abashed tone.

His mother stared at him for a few moments, then placed her youngest son's breakfast before him. She remained beside him and folded her arms as he began to eat, his first bites tentative. Raftennon knew she was guessing what had happened, for it had not been the first occurrence. So he forced himself to chew faster to appease the misgivings that were surely growing in her mind.

One day, Raftennon vowed to himself, he would do something that would end the teasing. One day, everyone would respect him.

The knock on the door startled her. She almost dropped the plate she was washing, managing to regain her grip on the wet crockery just before it left her fingers. She replaced the dish and washcloth in the basin, where they would be safe. She dried her hands on her apron as she made her way to the door. When she opened it she once again gasped in surprise.

"Tullae," she greeted the man in the doorway. "This is an unexpected visit."

"I apologize if I'm intruding, Melna," the old man said as he lowered his head in humble greeting.

"Oh, it's no intrusion," Melna responded while stepping back, inviting her visitor to enter.

Tullae tilted his head again before walking through the door into the small kitchen. A kettle-shaped wood stove and a large cupboard lined one wall. A long table dominated the room, with eight chairs surrounding it. The sunlight from the lone window provided soft illumination, making the space quite cozy. The old man waited for Melna to close the door behind him and gesture to a seat.

"Where are the children?" he rushed to ask before she commenced the pleasantries of inquiring after his needs.

Melna stammered for a moment, taken aback by the abruptness of the question. Even after all these years, she still forgot the man disliked interacting with anyone. He preferred to be left alone in his hut situated a short distance northeast of the village's unofficial perimeter. When he did venture into Yentrill's streets, the other villagers gave him a wide berth. They thought him strange, and Melna learned early on that was how he liked it. "Well, it's a lovely afternoon so the girls should be pestering Grampa Vernell's puppies."

"And the boy?" Tullae butt in, obviously not caring what her daughters were doing.

Melna could not understand his sudden interest in her youngest son. "Raftennon? He's around somewhere."

"I need you to be more specific than that."

"I can't be more specific," she shot back, returning the man's rudeness. She was not a woman to be pushed around, a fact she showed him when they first met. It was something she always made sure others understood about her, so they would not try to take advantage of her. "As long as he stays out of trouble, he can go wherever he wants within the village limits."

"I simply need to know if we may speak in private for a few minutes," Tullae said in a softer tone, his way of apologizing for any unintended insult.

"What is this all about?"

Tullae pulled out a chair and guided her into it before seating himself. The old man interlaced his fingers on the table and stared at the woman, his face a stern mask. "We need to talk about your son."

"What's he done?" Melna was now afraid. What kind of disturbance had her boy caused?

"Nothing." The old man continued to study her as she let out the breath she was holding. "Yet."

"I don't understand."

"I think you do. Otherwise, why would you assume the worst with the mere mention of him?" Tullae cocked an eyebrow, staring even more intently at the woman to catch every twitch in her face.

"Why are you here?" She shot back at him, her features hardening in anger.

"There is something unique about your boy. I doubt you know what it is, but I am certain you feel it." The old man explained himself without a single inflection in his tone to betray his thoughts.

Melna fidgeted the slightest bit. She glanced away, but caught herself and returned her gaze to the man sitting opposite her. His eyes told her he caught her slip, though. "Okay, I'll admit there's something. But that doesn't make him a bad boy."

"I make no such accusation. It makes him special."

This brought a smile to Melna's lips. She could never help but beam whenever one of her children received praise.

"And because of this," Tullae continued, "you need to take particular care with the boy."

"I don't understand," Melna said, her hands clasped on her lap, hidden under the table so the old man would not catch the fidgeting fingers.

"I sense great potential in him, a growing spark that needs to be moulded correctly lest it ignite and engulf the innocent."

"You're losing me, Tullae."

"Your boy is a bright one, is he not?"

Melna gave the man a questioning look, not understanding the reason for the inquiry. "I would say so."

"Does he know his letters?"

"Not yet. He's only six."

"You haven't started showing them to him?"

"He hasn't shown any interest in learning."

"That can change."

"Why is this important?"

"Knowledge, in itself, is important. I'm sure you would like all your children to better themselves."

"What are you getting at, Tullae?" Melna was now fed up with the man. She wanted him to get to the point.

"It's time the boy bettered himself."

"I still don't see how any of this concerns you."

"I wish to tutor him."

Melna struggled to find something to say. The old man sat in front of her, his hands still clasped on the table. The expression on his face revealed nothing. "You don't like children."

"I don't like people, in general," he corrected her. "There are a few I tolerate and their age has nothing to do with the choice."

"What makes Raftennon so special?"

"I never voice suspicion. I only point out facts."

"You want to test him?"

Tullae nodded. "Eventually. Don't worry, I will not hurt

him."

Melna let her eyes drift as far as they wanted to go this time. Why was he making this strange request? She spent years trying to figure him out, and these instances made it that much harder. "I need to know more," she said, returning her gaze to the old man.

"All I can tell you now is the boy seems to have a mental aptitude."

"What sort of mental aptitude?"

"Let me find out. And, in the process, get him off the street, away from those other children that want to tease him and do him harm for being different. They sense it as much as we do but don't know how to deal with the strangeness they feel."

Melna knew of the bullying, but still struggle to find a way to stop it. Now Tullae was offering her a solution, one she did not completely understand. Could she risk her boy's safety? Tullae did have a temper and showed it frequently, but he never raised a hand to anyone. But when they were together, he was nothing but a gentleman. How would he treat Raftennon? What was he planning?

"Why do I need to learn to read?" young Raftennon asked his mother. Melna took two days to think about Tullae's proposition and decided to give it a try. She could always change her mind later if need be. "None of the others read very well," Raftennon continued, referring to his siblings, "and it's not like there are any books on the boat."

"But being able to read would open many doors for you," she told him. Melna could not bring herself to say his chances of get-ting into the family business were all but nonexistent. The fish-ing vessel was small and his father and brothers already filled it. It would take the absence of one of them for Raftennon to get the opportunity he believed was a given.

"What do letters have to do with doors?" The crinkle of his nose as he tried to reason her statement almost made Melna snicker, which was a welcome distraction. Her latest chain of thought almost brought her to tears. Images of huge waves sweeping away one of her sons, or her husband, down to the depths of the sea invaded her mind. Raftennon's eyes saved her from that sorrow, as they accused her of being daft. She loved him the more for it.

"Never mind," she conceded, knowing he was still too young to grasp the concept of an alternate future for himself. She chose to try a different route, one he would understand. "Just think, if you learn to read you could do something your brothers can't."

That almost worked. Raftennon made a token effort the following day. It was not long before he started complaining about how hard the letters were to decipher, however. He grumbled about the uselessness of the lines and curves on the page. Melna encouraged him to continue but soon conceded to letting him return to learning the tricks of the fisherman trade. He was in such a huff she knew he would not learn anything.

Melna persisted, every day for the next week, coaxing her boy to sit at the table, promising it would get easier. Raftennon dragged himself to his usual spot and stared at the scribbling his mother penned on the two sheets of vellum they owned. He continued to make the merest attempt he thought would please her, but the sessions always ended the same. Fixing nets and rigging was simpler to master than trying to remember all the different lines on the parchment and what they meant. There were too many rules that complicated the language.

"Why is there an 'i' in 'fish'?" Raftennon interrupted as she finished writing the word in a corner of the sheet. That letter he grasped with little effort, but still on occasion confused it with an "l" or a "j". "There's no 'i' in 'fish'." He was referring to the sound of the letter's name not matching its pronunciation in this particular instance.

"Letters have different sounds depending on how they're used," Melna explained.

"Whoever invented this writing thing should have kept it as easy as speaking. 'I' should always sound like 'eye'."

"You're right, but they didn't. So we have to learn how the letters sound when they are put together."

"That's just stupid," Raftennon said before sitting back in his chair, crossing his arms and thrusting his chin onto his chest.

Melna sighed. Maybe Tullae's request to send her son to him right away was the better solution. But when she agreed to his proposal, those few days past, she insisted he let her introduce Raftennon to reading. It was prideful of her, she knew, but she wanted to impress the old hermit. If her boy arrived at the tutor's home with the basics already learned, Tullae would have to credit her for the accomplishment. And she could tell everyone she was the one to begin her son's education.

"Would you use the same knot to tie a lure onto your fishing line as you would to secure the boat to the dock?" Melna asked after a moment of thought.

"Well, no," Raftennon said, giving her that same stare that brought attention to her ignorance.

"Why not? A knot is a knot, isn't it?"

"You need stronger knots for some things. You also wouldn't use fishing line to anchor the boat."

"So, think of the different ropes as the letters." Melna grasped the new idea that just occurred to her. "And the knots are the way the letter sounds in the word."

"That still doesn't make sense."

"You use the same thick rope to hoist the sail as you do to batten it down, don't you?"

"They're called *lines*, Mother." Raftennon's sigh spoke volumes on his heightening exasperation.

"Do you used the same knots to do both jobs," Melna continued, ignoring the interruption.

"No, that wouldn't work."

"It's the same with letters."

"It's still more complicated that it needs to be. Can I go play now?"

Melna nodded, hoping her latest tactic would make things easier for him. Maybe some time to think it over would turn him around.

That night, Hawer came to the bed Raftennon shared with his brother Stamm. "Your mother tells me you don't want to learn your letters," he whispered, not wanting to wake the older of the two siblings.

"What good are they, anyway?" Raftennon asked, not taking care to keep his voice down. He was still too young to think of how his actions affected others and, therefore, did not consider the possibility of disturbing his tired brother. "They're way harder than they need to be. Talking works way better."

"What good are they?" Hawer forgot himself as well, answering his son in an equally raised tone. He caught himself when Stamm stirred the slightest bit. He continued in a subdued voice when the teen's movement stopped and the steady breathing of deep sleep resumed. "I tell you, if I knew my letters better than I do, maybe I'd become one of those magicians they have out there in Xendremmar."

"I thought you liked being a fisherman." Raftennon sat up, this time careful not to rouse his brother. He also whispered this statement, finally getting the point his father wanted this conversation to be a quiet one.

"Aye, I do." A twinkle appeared in the man's eye. "But that don't mean I don't dream of other things. If I was a magician, I would make wonderful things happen. I would make fish appear out of thin air!" Raftennon's own eyes sparkled in wonder as his father continued. "We wouldn't have to be on the water all day. I'd spend more time with you and your sisters. And we would still have enough food on the table for everybody."

"Do you really think I can be good enough to be a magician, Father?" The twinkle in the boy's eye became an all-out shine.

"You, my son, can do whatever your heart desires. If you want it enough, you'll find a way to make it happen."

With that, his father gave him a firm shake of the shoulder and left him to dream about magic.

The next day, Raftennon went to his mother, promising he would follow her teachings and make a true effort to learn. The lessons were long and arduous in the beginning, every letter a painstaking trial of memorization. His wandering attention also made things difficult, always returning his thoughts to the sea. But he did as promised and stuck with it.

As the weeks passed, his yearning for a fisherman's life waned as he began to understand the workings of the alphabet. Challenges changed from individual words to simple sentences. The smile his mother gave him when he managed to read a sentence without stumbling over the syllables made all the hard work worthwhile.

One day, a few months later, Melna took him by the hand and led him out of the house instead of waiting for him to take his usual seat at the table.

"Where are we going?" Raftennon asked as he walked beside his mother. He eyed the other children who stared at him as they passed by. Their glares still contained the same malice as always. The dogs still snarled at him.

"We're going to visit a friend," she told him, ignoring every-one around them.

When the pair reached the outlying houses of the village, Raftennon hesitated the slightest bit. He never crossed the peri-meter his parents established for him, so it felt strange to continue on. He quickly resumed his steps before his mother no-ticed his apprehension. She walked up a narrow path only wide enough for one person. The boy trod in grass that came to his waist, but he did not mind. He had spent a lot of time indoors lately, having the green blades brush against his legs felt good.

The trail wound around the few trees that sprung up here and there as they made their way further into the outskirts of the community. It also made sharp turns Raftennon did not under-stand. Why did nobody cut down the trees to make this a straight street like in the rest of the village? He glanced back to see the humble homes receding behind them. He marvelled at the thatched roofs. He had never seen them from above before. That was when Raftennon realized he and his mother were climbing a hill. He saw the track they followed veering to avoid the steeper inclines and the turns they took finally made sense to him.

The path led to a small copse of hardy elms. Almost hidden among the trunks stood a homely cabin. Raftennon stopped short when he saw the old man standing before the open door.

"It's all right, sweetie," Melna reassured him, with a gentle pull on the hand she still held to coax him to continue forward. "He's a friend."

Raftennon kept a close eye on the elder as he let his mother lead him toward the cabin. When they stopped in front of the entrance, both boy and old man studied one another.

"Raftennon," Melna put in, with the slightest quiver in her voice the tot did not understand, "this is Tullae."

Raftennon stared at the old man, taking a slow step backward to make it easier for him to duck behind his mother if the need arose.

"No need to be afraid of me, son," Tullae told him. His tone was not unkind, but the gruffness did not ease the boy's apprehensions.

"Say hello," Melna urged.

Raftennon mumbled his greeting before turning toward his mother, clinging to her leg. "I want to go home," he said, not caring if the old man heard him.

"Your mother tells me you read very well," Tullae interjected before the woman could respond to her son.

Raftennon eyed him for a moment before nodding his head.

"I have something for you, then." The old man took a step forward and stretched out his arm. Out of thin air, a rolled parchment appeared in his hand.

Raftennon inspected the offered vellum from the distance he kept between himself and the hermit. "What is it?"

"It's a story," Tullae told him, sliding to one knee to be closer to eye level with the small boy.

"What kind of story?" Raftennon turned toward the old man, but his hands remained tight around his mother's.

"If you want to know that, you'll need to read it."

"Tullae reads and writes better than anyone in the village," Melna explained. "He's going to teach you now."

"But you're teaching me," Raftennon protested.

Melna knelt before her son and brought her free hand to caress his cheek. "And I enjoy every moment of it. But you deserve the best, and that means me letting Tullae show you what he knows. There are things even I haven't learned yet."

"He's a strange man, Mother."

"That I am," Tullae agreed with a smile that softened his usual harsh expression. The old man placed the parchment on the ground in front of him before straightening up. "The story on that scroll is one I'm sure your mother has never heard before. There are words on there, mostly names of people and places, she would not know how to pronounce correctly. If you want to be able to tell her the tale, come inside so we may begin our lessons. Or you can go home. The choice is yours." Tullae turned and entered his humble cabin, leaving the door open.

Raftennon's eyes went from the scroll to the entrance, from the opening to his mother, before returning to the promised story. Otherwise, he did not move a muscle.

"Go on," his mother urged him. "I will walk you here every day and come get you once your lessons are done. You can tell me all the stories you learn every night before going to bed."

Raftennon hesitated a moment more before letting go her hand and bending to scoop up the parchment. He dragged his feet as he walked toward the door, looking over his shoulder at every step to ensure his mother still waited, in case he changed his mind. She stayed crouched where she was until he mustered enough courage to enter the strange home.

Thus started Raftennon's true lessons. Tullae was a patient teacher, never stern. He was meticulous and demanded perfection from his student, however. Raftennon almost gave up several times each day for the first month, wanting to beg his mother to resume teaching him. But the pride in her eyes when he came home and told her what he learned that day always pushed him to continue.

The months rolled on and the lessons became easier. Tullae praised Raftennon on his easy grasp of the Common tongue. The old man produced more complex texts every so often. The boy knew the hermit did this to stump him, but he always rose to the challenge and managed to decipher the documents. A year after their first lesson, Tullae brought out a parchment that finally stumped the star pupil.

"What language is this?" Raftennon asked after eyeing the scroll for a few moments.

"It's Elfin," Tullae told him.

"Why would I need to read Elfin?"

"There are a lot of documents written by elves," the elder explained. "Many ages of history passed by before humans ever thought of recording events or fancies on papyrus. So, while we stumbled about, forgetting everything we were doing, the elves were recording the important events that shaped those eras. Of course, they did so for their own benefit, not ours. But there are copies everywhere for anyone to study. Trust me, some of the best stories are written in Elfin. You'll want to learn this."

So Raftennon pored over the foreign scribbling on the page.

Elfin proved to be much harder to grasp than Common, a fact Tullae neglected to mention. At this point in his studies, the young boy had already discovered he possessed his mother's determination. He would overcome this new hurdle, as much for his own satisfaction as for the praise his mother would give him. It took several months of staring at the elegant script before the long flowing sweeps and tight rings started to make sense. The myriad intricacies of the complex language fell into place. Once he found this understanding, Raftennon wondered why it took him so long to grasp it. Before he knew it, he sped through words most adults did not even know existed.

One day, shortly after Raftennon's tenth birthday, the old man left the boy to practise reading an ancient Elfin scroll to get them something to drink. While he was in the kitchen, a parchment tucked under a ream of pages caught the boy's attention. The vellum was much older than the other documents in the pile. The once-black ink had faded to a dull brown. The script—that he could see—was more elegant than what was on the other scrolls. Raftennon carefully pulled the sheet from the stack, feeling unnatural warmth emanating from the page. The crisp Elfin calligraphy shimmered as the parchment moved over the table. This intrigued him, for he was certain the writing's glow did not come from the sun. The letters flared with some unknown, inner fire while the yellowed vellum stayed as dull as the old hide it was.

Raftennon mouthed the words inked on the scroll, trying to unravel the secrets of the ancient dialect. This was not the Elfin he had become accustomed to reading. It took a few moments, but the syllables began to fall into place.

"You can read that?"

Raftennon jumped in surprise and almost fell off his stool. So rapt was he in his work he had forgotten where he was and that the old man was there with him. The hermit stood in the archway to his kitchen, staring at him. One bushy grey eyebrow was cocked upward over a pale blue eye, which, with its twin, stayed locked on the young reader. The two cups of water he just got for them remained in his hands, forgotten for the moment.

"It's basically Elfin, Master Tullae," Raftennon said, not understanding the elder's surprise. "The wording is a little different and there are some vowels I don't know exactly how to say, but most of it is close enough that I can figure it out."

"It's the language of magic," Tullae explained. He continued to stare at the boy, much like he had the first day they met. "Most people, even those who can read Elfin, can't interpret the script. The differences in intonation and pronunciation are very difficult to grasp."

Magic? Raftennon could not believe he had heard what he thought he had. In the months leading to this day, the wish to become a magician still flared in his heart. His mother and Tullae had said he was progressing marvellously, but neither ever mentioned anything about magic. Raftennon did not dare bring up the subject with his teacher. He was sure the old man would glare at him and admonish him for his foolishness.

Tullae hurried to his seat beside his student, placing the cups of water in the safest place on the table to avoid any spills and made him read the entire scroll. He did not interrupt the youth, letting him muddle his way through the difficult language. The hermit had to admit the lad impressed him. When Raftennon finished his first attempt, Tullae corrected the few mistakes he made and taught him the correct inflections of the syllables. That task took more than two hours to accomplish, exhausting both teacher and student in the process. When he was satisfied, the old man placed a pouch beside his student's elbow.

"What's this?" Raftennon eyed the bag, a little wary of what was inside. After the latest exercise, all he wanted was to go home.

"Dried *prennenwood* leaves from the far east," Tullae explained. "Take one in your hand and crumple it while reading the scroll. As soon as you finish saying the last word, throw the pieces into the air."

Raftennon wondered why his teacher wanted all this done but decided to comply without question. He recited the words, stressing some vowels and cutting off consonants as instructed.

"*Imnâhalanee fentrôhnil mentânô silbynôvân jenrô / Imnâilanô venmayrennay drendânümâ kendré fâlloom.*" Raftennon crushed the leaves, making sure he did not drop a single crumb. Heat began to build inside his closed fist. He did his best to ignore the distraction and continued reading. "*Flaymmanâl kom-*

prénôr tenbâh sôronell!"

The recitation done, the boy tossed the broken pieces toward the ceiling. A bright flash flared mere inches above his hand. Raftennon flung his other arm over his eyes to shield them but was not quick enough to save them from the intense light. It took some time for him to regain his vision and understand what just happened.

"Congratulations, my boy," muttered Tullae, his tone much less gruff than usual. "You've just cast your first spell."

2

READY?

"Wait a minute!" Hawer was beside himself. His wife had just informed him of his son's first brush with magic. "You're telling me our son is a genius?"

"It would seem so." Melba's pride swelled as much as surprise overtook her husband.

"But we're not going to let him continue with this foolishness, are we?" He sat on the bed he shared with the woman he loved, staring at her in disbelief.

"What are you saying?" Melna tilted her head, her eyes widening to the point white showed all around the brown. "You're the one who put the idea of being a magician in his head."

"I did that so he would stop fighting you and learn his letters!" Hawer shot up from the soft mattress, taking a few short steps away before turning back. The expression on his face was both gentle and stern. "I don't object to him bettering himself, but becoming a magician is a little far-fetched!"

"Why 'far-fetched'?" Melna crossed her arms over her bosom, giving her beloved a derisive look. It was the glare she always gave him when he attacked whatever he did not understand. "Don't you think our son can do anything he sets his mind to?"

"How many magicians do you see in this village?" The man

brought his hands up to shoulder height, gesturing to the houses outside the wooden walls of their own humble home. "Who'll teach him? That old coot in his lonely hut? Is he even a magician? Can he fulfill our boy's dreams?"

Melna did not know the answers to these questions. It stood to reason Tullae knew at least a bit about magic, having taught that spell to Raftennon, but she never witnessed the old man perform any spells of his own in the long years she knew him. She did not know how skilled he was and what, exactly, he could teach her son. She was not about to admit this fact to her husband, however. "Raftennon is old enough to make his own decisions," was what she said instead.

"He's only ten." Hawer returned to the bed and plopped down beside his wife. She took his hand in hers.

"And when do you expect his brothers to cede their places on the boat?" Melna now peered into her husband's eyes with the abundance of love she felt for him. A confrontational stance would not win him over in this particular situation. "Bren and Stamm are old enough to wed and head their own households, but you know they won't abandon you until you have someone that can help with the lines when it counts most. With their uncle gone, they know there is no one else. They will stay on as long as you need them, which means there's still no room for Raftennon. What is he to do with his life?"

"If the hermit can't teach him all he wants to learn, are you willing to send him away?" Hawer said in a meek voice.

The question struck Melna like a stiff slap to the cheek. She had not considered this point. Indeed, if Tullae was unable to show Raftennon all he deserved to know, they would have to find someone capable of doing so. And, since there was nobody as versed as the old man in the village, they would need to turn to the outside world. That, or end his teachings and leave the boy with very little prospects in life. In Yentrill, men either fished or travelled to Entamman Forest to fell trees. That would still keep him away from home most of the time. And, after feeling the exhilaration he must have felt after casting that spell, no doubt Raftennon would never want to leave his studies. They could not shatter his dreams for a second time.

"If…" Melna stumbled over the words, trying to keep her

composure despite the prospect of the loss of her youngest son. "If we have to send him away to make him happy, that's what we'll do."

The couple did not discuss the matter further. They did not even bring it up with Raftennon. The boy continued his lessons with Tullae, learning Elfin dialects more ancient than the previous one. The old man put a lot of emphasis on pronunciation, sometimes spending the entire day on a single sentence. Raftennon felt silly enunciating the syllables, almost singing them it seemed at times. He did not understand why the first elves spoke in such a strange way.

"They didn't talk like that all the time," the hermit explained to him when Raftennon made a comment about the absurd fact. "These inflections were devised for the sole purpose of casting spells."

"What's the point?"

"The elves are the oldest civilized race remaining in the world." Tullae reached in front of his pupil and removed all the parchments that lay before him. The old man even turned the lad so they faced each other, instead of sitting side by side. "Among all the different peoples that lived all those ages ago, they devoted the most time bettering their minds. For this reason, the god of knowledge, Pentaclin, favoured them above all other races. The deity gave them the resources needed to cast spells. They were the first to receive the power, and they were the ones who developed the art.

"They used their own language for the incantations. The words helped them visualize what it was they wanted to happen. The properties of the components they handled contributed to the realization of the casting. But the most important aspect of any spell is the inflections. Each sound that comes out of your mouth affects the energy around you—in the air, in the ground, in your very being. The slightest error alters the essence of the flows and your spell fizzles away. Or, it may even backfire on you, causing great harm.

"Do you understand?"

"Spells are very picky and you need to sing them right for

them to work."

Tullae laughed at the juvenile simplification and ruffled the boy's hair before returning him to his studies.

To Raftennon's chagrin, however, the old man did not bring out the parchment again, nor did he teach him any new incantations. Whenever he mentioned his desire to explore more magic, Tullae told him what he was reading at that particular moment was the best text to help him learn. He simply needed to be patient.

Three months passed in which Raftennon's days consisted of breakfast with his mother, a day-long sojourn with the hermit and his never-ending store of scrolls, and a return home that gave him but an hour to spend with his family before retiring for the night.

On one sunny day, after a fortnight of dreary weather, Tullae came out of his bedroom after having slept in. Raftennon already sat at the table, labouring over the most ancient scroll he had handled to date. It was a transcript of the legendary birth of the Elfin nation of Lanasylnas in the lands far to the east. The old man smiled at the lad and went to his kitchen for a little breakfast without saying a word.

Raftennon continued to peer at the document, but his full attention was on Tullae. The student watched him from the corner of his eye until the elder disappeared into the other room. Only then did the boy reach out for the pouch that lay before him, teasing, since his arrival. With a quick tug at the pouch's lip, he peered inside and smiled, elated to see the dried leaves of the *prennenwood*.

Raftennon shot a glance through the open archway that led to the kitchen. Tullae was still nowhere in sight. The thump of a closing cupboard told the boy the old man was on the opposite side of the room. Raftennon leafed through the loose pages strewn in their usual disarray. If the hermit forgot to put away the little sack, maybe he did the same with the scroll. But it was not there. Raftennon passed through all the dishevelled piles, creating his own little breeze in the room.

"What's going on?" came a voice from the other room. The old man soon popped his head through the archway to see what the commotion was.

"I'm just looking for a scroll I read last week, for reference," Raftennon blurted out, quite pleased with himself for coming up with such a good lie on such short notice. He was even more satisfied when Tullae bought his excuse and returned to check on his frying fish.

Raftennon resolved to return to his studies, not wanting a recurrence of that near confrontation, but his eye caught the worn corner of the ancient parchment amid a stack he would have sworn he just rummaged through. He inched a trembling hand forward as if the paper was a hot coal. He pulled the vellum from under the thick pile, revealing the written lines in painstaking slowness. His heart pounded in his chest when he saw the familiar arcane scribble.

He raised his eyes, certain Tullae would be looming over him, ready to scold him. The hermit was not there, however, giving Raftennon the courage to go through with his desire. He placed the scroll before him and grabbed a handful of dried leaves. Heedless of everything around him, Raftennon read the strange language of magic and crumpled the foliage, each syllable and movement identical with those he performed the first time. The same spectacular flash rewarded his efforts. When the boy's eyes regained their focus, Tullae stood in front of him, his arms crossed over his slender chest. Instead of the expected scowl, a huge grin stretched his lips.

"I'm glad to see you remembered everything I taught you. Most novice students forget the inflections with such a long period away from the spell."

"You mean magicians forget their spells?" Raftennon's mind reeled with surprise at being caught and not chastised, as well as disbelief at his teacher's statement. His mother always told him magicians had infallible memories.

"The very inexperienced ones do, yes." Tullae held back a chuckle at the sight of Raftennon's bewildered expression.

"Then why did you keep the scroll away from me so long? You wanted me to forget it?" The indignation seeped into his voice, unintentional but not unwanted. Why did his teacher wish him to fail?

"Apprentices to the Spellcasters' Guilds are inducted when they are very young," Tullae hurried to assuage his student's mounting rage, "most no older than their eighth year. You've already passed that birthday, so you need an edge. Your skill at picking up ancient dialects would help you immensely. But I'd wager it still wouldn't be enough. But with this power of retention, they'll be hard-pressed to refuse you."

"What are you saying?" Raftennon was wary about Tullae's point. He was not sure what he was getting at. Was it was good or bad news?

"If you truly wish to become a mage, you'll have to go away and study with the Masters. I've just made sure they can't say no."

3

TO THE CITY

"You sure this is what you want?" Hawer asked his son, torn between convincing him to stay and ordering him to. "You know your mother will miss you a lot if you do this."

"I need to do this, Father. It's sort of like something is drawing me to the school. I read the words on the scrolls, and I'm someone else, someone with power. I feel important when I set the air on fire, Father. I feel like I can change the world for the better. Please let me go."

The determination in the lad's eyes and the longing in his voice were enough for Hawer to concede. The love for his boy shone in the gathering moisture that threatened to roll down his cheeks. Those same as-yet-unshed tears displayed just how proud the man was on that day. His youngest was becoming a man. "Fine, go become somebody. But don't forget to come back and visit your mother! I don't want to hear her crying over you for the rest of my life!"

Father and son embraced before the youth raced up to his room to pack.

The next morning, Raftennon gave a final hug to his mother, whose tears not only wet her cheeks but moistened his own. His sisters, downcast, forgo their usual teasing. They would miss their brother, but were not about to admit it. The men of the family were also there to see him off, foregoing the fishing for the day.

Tullae stood apart from them, tightly holding the reins of two pintos. For some reason, the horses were uneasy. The old man tried his best to calm them to allow the boy to say his farewells in peace. Raftennon faced his father last and clasped his arm, as men did. It took all his strength of will to fight back his own tears.

"Better listen to the teachers, boy. They know more than you. And remember," Hawer swallowed hard to hide the intensity of his emotions, "time makes you a man, but your actions make you a memorable one. Now go and make your mother proud."

Hawer gave his son a quick embrace before returning to his wife's side. Raftennon said goodbye to everyone one last time and met Tullae, who passed him the reins to his horse. The pinto's eyes widened in terror and reared before Raftennon man-aged to get a good grip on the proffered lead. Sensing its free-dom, the mount galloped away before anyone could grasp the flailing leather straps and trap it again. The other pinto tried to do the same, but Tullae had a better hold on his animal's bridle, as well as more body weight to keep the horse from rearing.

"Well, that was odd," the old man commented after his mount stopped trying to lift him into the air.

"Animals don't like me for some reason," Raftennon ex-plained as he watched the frightened thing gallop down the street, heedless of the people who scampered out of its way to avoid being trampled. "All my life dogs snapped at me and cats hissed. It's the first time I've been near a horse, though."

Tullae studied the lad for a moment while his family rushed over to make sure he was uninjured. The wrinkles on the old man's forehead doubled as his brow furrowed in thought. After a few moments, the hermit turned around and began leading his pinto toward the narrow lane to his secluded cabin.

"Where are you going?" Melna asked. "Are you cancelling the trip?"

"Not at all," Tullae shouted over his shoulder, never breaking stride. "Merely going to get us a safer mode of transportation."

A half hour passed before the old man returned to the waiting family, who were just about to return home. Tullae was leading an old ox cart dragged by an even older ox up the road toward them.

"What is that?" Hawer asked.

"Horses don't seem to like the boy, so he'll ride in the back of this cart," Tullae explained.

"Won't the ox bolt as well?" Raftennon wondered.

"This beast is so old it pays no attention to its surroundings. All it does is follow directions, so I am told by its owner. If you stay as far from the front as you can, chances are it won't even know you're there."

Every member of Raftennon's family shared the same doubtful stare.

"It's either this or we walk," Tullae told them, crossing his arms over his chest. "Would you truly force this old man to shamble all the way to Xendremmar?"

Raftennon shrugged and kissed his mother one last time. Then he walked to the rear of the wagon, giving the beast a wide berth so as not to chance to spook it, and climbed in. Tullae settled himself onto his seat before flicking the reins to set them off.

The cart rolled eastward out of Yentrill. Raftennon sat on the thin layer of straw that lined the bed of the rickety contraption, marvelling at what lay before him. Other children his age wandered a bit into the plains to play, no doubt following this very path. But he passed his time in the old man's home, studying. It was not like any of them would have asked him to join, anyway. Raftennon peered over the flatland, as rapt in their splendour as a wide-eyed babe watching the flicker of flames for the first time. The air was already strangely dry to his taste, so accustomed to the moisture of the sea was he. He turned his head to the left and saw the dark trees of Entamman Forest. In a mere half-day's ride, the tall sides of the Qartyff Mountains, nestled in the wood, began to come into focus and be more than shades of grey looming over the cedars, firs and spruce.

On their first night away from home, they made camp and Raftennon was pleased to find all his wilderness skills remained with him. Five years he spent learning to read, most of which under Tullae's tutelage. By the second year, the lessons with the old man were so intensive Raftennon no longer joined his family on the yearly excursions to the southern edge of Entamman

Forest. Tullae always told him he was free to enjoy the holiday with them. The scrolls would be there when he returned. But Raftennon felt compelled to stay. He could not explain the reason for this decision, other than saying he preferred to continue his studies over sleeping on the ground for two weeks. Four years it was since he gathered wood and readied a bedroll beside an open fire.

A day and a half later, as the sun began its downward descent toward the western horizon, the pair arrived at the shallow Bellyn River. They forded the calm waters where the woods met the plains, crossing without even a slip of a hoof or a wheel getting mired between the stones of the riverbed.

Two more days passed as the duo followed the southern border of the forest. A light rain joined them on this leg of their journey. The travellers did not mind, both accustomed to wet weather after having spent some time in Vendetran Bay. They came up on a road as sunlight struggled to pierce through the veil of dark clouds. It was mid-afternoon, but Tullae stopped them for the remainder of the day.

The old man retrieved a leather tube from his pack and tossed it to the back of the cart. "Study, my boy."

Raftennon did not feel like reading, the fresh air reviving in him the dreams he wished for when he was younger, in the days when literature was the farthest thing from his mind. The glare the hermit shot him would brook no argument. After heaving a sigh, the boy did as ordered.

Only when the sun's last grasp of the sky dwindled to nothing did Raftennon stop his studying. A meal of hot chowder followed before both travellers bundled themselves in bedrolls to sleep. Images of strange beasts in unknown caverns populated the boy's dreams that night, exciting him instead of frightening him, as one would expect.

"This soul should still remain in the Globe," the grey-robed figure huffed as he glided up the cobblestone steps that led to the raised dais.

"It is good to see you, my son." The woman sitting on the black throne atop the platform folded her hands on her knees, turning her emerald-green eyes from her work to her visitor.

"I apologize for my gruffness, Mother," the man stopped in front of her, placing his hands into the opposite sleeve of his flowing robes, "but this is a matter of utmost importance."

"I do not forget the value you place on this matter of yours. It is this very value that has created the predicament."

"A predicament that could have been avoided if the timing…"

"Do not lecture me on timing." The woman's gentle demeanour did not change, nor did the friendly tone of her voice, but the power placed behind those words made certain her guest knew she would not tolerate any reproach from him. "Time is my dominion if I remember correctly."

"No one is contesting that fact, Mother," the man replied, trying to calm himself and use the least confrontation tone he could muster. "I was merely under the impression this soul would be saved until the other ran its course."

"When did I give you that impression?"

The son stared at his mother, barely keeping the confusion he was feeling from his face. He was also finding it difficult to control his bubbling anger. The lady's nonchalance was quite infuriating considering the ramifications of her actions. "You agreed to keep them apart," he said through clenched teeth.

"And apart they stayed until their time came." The woman stood from her throne and took the few strides needed to reach her visitor. She placed a gentle hand on his shoulder and turned him to lead him down the steps of the dais. "You know everything I do, I do for a reason."

"I hope the price for this decision is not so high we cannot pay it."

Tutor and student travelled southward along the well-trodden path, pulled by the old ox that was proving it was still strong enough to do what was asked of it. It had not faltered or missed a step yet. They were presently exiting a small copse of birches as the day's light started to fail when a loud crash startled the cart's passengers. The beast continued to lumber forward as if nothing was amiss. The pair looked back to see two felled trees laying across the road, blocking any possible retreat that way. They turned around, Raftennon perplexed, Tullae wary. The boy's eyes widened as the old man's narrowed when they spotted the three men now barring their way ahead.

"What's going on?" Raftennon whispered after crawling to the front of the cart and leaning toward his teacher.

Tullae waved one hand, dismissing his question and instructing him to keep quiet, while the other pulled on the reins to stop the ox from advancing. Two more men emerged from the trees, one on each side of the path, to join the others forming the living barricade.

"Let us pass," Tullae ordered the strangers barring the only exit from the copse.

"You need to pay the toll," said the one in the middle of the line.

"Since when?" This was not Tullae's first voyage to the magnificent city of Xendremmar, but it was apparent to Raftennon this was his first encounter with this makeshift toll station. The youth studied the men, not knowing what to expect in this situation.

"Why do you care when the toll started?" asked the man standing to the right of the first speaker. Raftennon's gaze settled on the top of the stranger's ears, which were slightly pointed. The boy remembered seeing pictures on some of the parchments Tullae had made him read. They depicted some of the elfin heroes in the legends the scrolls recounted. The elves in those stories possessed longer ears, so either their descendants lost that feature or this man was only part elf. Raftennon concentrated so much on this anomaly he almost missed what the man said next. "It's today you should worry about because it's today you have to pay."

Tullae rummaged through the sack lying on the seat beside him, muttering to himself. After a moment that seemed as long as a lifetime, the leader of the ruffians began to lose patience. "Come on, old man! Just give us every coin you own, or you'll be paying us with your hides!"

"I'm sure we can find a use for the brat," another brigand chimed in, drawing laughter from the others that made Raftennon even more nervous.

The elder returned his attention to the self-proclaimed toll collectors and threw a pouch to the ground in front of them. The sack opened and a handful of small rocks fell out. The brigands' eyes widened until their whites reflected the moon that had begun its ascent into the sky. Raftennon watched in wonder as the men jumped onto the bag and scurried into the trees, fighting one another for the ordinary stones.

"They've all gone mad!" Raftennon stared in disbelief as his teacher flicked the reins to resume their way southward.

"No, they're just greedy." Tullae peered over his shoulder into the copse of birches so the boy would know the annoyance that crept into his voice was not directed at him. The highwaymen's gruff rebukes drifted from the growing shadows as they argued about who should get the bigger share of the take.

"Greedy for rocks?" Raftennon did not understand.

"Yes, for rocks. Of course, they don't think they're rocks." A slight smile formed on the old man's lips, replacing the scowl, as realization shone in the boy's face.

"It was another spell!" Wonder kept Raftennon's eyes open wide. Like his mother, he had never seen the hermit perform any feat of magic. It was clear the man knew the language and the actions needed in casting. But, until now, the student doubted the tutor could muster the power to cast a spell.

"What, you thought I would mutter to myself for nothing?" Tullae let his pent-up laughter finally escape his lips. "I made them believe the worthless stones were gold nuggets. They probably never saw such riches before in their pathetic little lives. That's why they're still fighting over the bag."

"You truly are a magnificent wizard!" Raftennon looked up at the elder with more reverence than he had ever before. What other marvellous feats could the old man accomplish, he wondered.

"What, that?" Tullae dismissed the entire occurrence with a wave of his hand. "That was but a minor illusion, boy, something you'll learn in the first month at the Guild. I am no wizard. If I were, we would still be at home. I would teach you everything you needed to know myself."

A dark realization doused Raftennon's wonder and admiration. "Just how long will this illusion last?" The boy whirled in the hay to stare back along the path, expecting to hear roars of rage as the unanticipated fortune turned back to ordinary pebbles. He continued to peer into the growing darkness, certain he would see the bandits running back toward them at any moment to slit their throats for the treachery.

Tullae snickered at his student's sudden panic. "Long enough for us to reach Xendremmar," he reassured him as he turned forward in his seat. "Don't worry. They won't be coming after us. We'll be safely within the walls before the spell dissipates, or close enough that they won't be able to catch up to us before we are."

On the evening of the next day, the travellers came up to the northern gate of the walled city. A high wooden fortification surrounded the numerous square blocks of tall buildings divided by the many streets that checkered the largest settlement on the Plains of Mandellon. Only the tiled roofs of the houses nearest the palisade peeked over the pointed poles, but Raftennon knew what he would find on the other side. A week before they left Yentrill, Tullae showed him a map depicting the avenues they would need to navigate to arrive at the Guild.

The pair made its way to a large door spanning the road, where the ox stopped when its horns touch the iron wrought wood. The old man bellowed as loud as he could to announce their presence. Raftennon managed to get his heart beating again after the unexpected scream before a panel opened and a set of darting eyes appeared in the narrow slit.

"Who goes there?" asked the man behind the wall, his voice muffled by the thick wood.

"We have business at the Spellcasters' Guild," Tullae informed him.

The eyes vanished before the crack of the closing peephole made Raftennon jump again. Silence fell on the gate's vicinity as the travellers waited for their admittance into the city. The boy started to wonder if that would ever happen. There was no sound of locks turning or pulleys grinding to open the door. The thought soon came to him that the guardsman decided not to let them enter and was now ignoring them. His apprehensions grew to the point where he was on the verge of saying something when the gate inched inward.

Tullae urged the ox forward and Raftennon peered at the guard as he began to close the wide door behind them. His head hung between his arms as he pushed the heavy door. A thick layer of mud hid the once-bright colours of his livery as well as the deep wrinkles that riddled his face. The man appeared much older than his strength indicated. It was obvious to Raftennon the man was suffering through a tough life. He should have been a fisherman. The fresh air would benefit him greatly.

Tullae steered the cart along the various streets and avenues. Some were wide enough to allow three carriages to rumble along side by side while others barely let the humble cart through. Raftennon soon lost his sense of direction, for the stars were often hidden by the high roofs of the buildings surrounding them. He marvelled at the stone structures, much different than the wood-constructed houses of Yentrill. He wondered at the complexity of the web formed by the crisscrossing streets and alleys, so much so his senses did not detect the less desirable aspects of larger cities. He did not see the filth lining the gaps between the myriad establishments or smell the human waste slithering down the gutters. Tullae also ignored all of this, for it was a scene with which he was familiar. Unlike the youth, the old man once travelled the Plains of Mandellon and visited their towns and cities. Everyone in Yentrill knew this of the hermit. The fact Tullae preferred to travel inland instead of sailing Vendetran Bay further alienated him from the other villagers.

The ox dutifully followed its given directions, including halting when bidden before a building that was as wide as it was tall, unlike its surrounding neighbours. Many windows shone from the four storeys, lighting the street better than did the lanterns hanging from lampposts dedicated for that very purpose. The shutters hung askew—those that still remained—revealing glass panes smeared with dirt and dust. Bird guano of various age and colour covered every window sill, masking cracks in the wood like plaster. The paint on the wall was cracked and so filthy one could not even venture a guess at its original tint. The roof was a hodgepodge of rotting planks and discoloured thatch. A wooden, winged reptile hung from an iron rod protruding from over the entrance. The sign was weather-worn and split halfway down the middle, the blue paint covering it mostly peeled away. In greying white, the words "The Blue Dragon" announced the establishment's name.

"This is where we're staying?" Raftennon asked, not able to hide his disgust. He had never seen such shambles and could not imagine anyone capable of letting their property reach this state.

"Only for tonight," the old man answered, understanding the boy's immediate distaste for the place. "Think of it as another night of camping, and it won't seem so bad."

They made their way to the stable attached to the left of the building. They found a stall and Tullae took care of the ox himself, for no one came out to do it for them. Raftennon stayed with the cart, gathering all their belongings. Their tasks done, the pair returned to the front door and entered the shambles of an inn.

The interior was as bad as the exterior. Cracks marred most of the floorboards, the walls were dappled with patches of missing paint and the decor was drab and unkempt. Many of the window coverings hung with filth so thick their original colour and material now lay lost under a motley of browns. A lone painting decorated the far wall, its image so faded it was no longer discernible.

Tullae led Raftennon through the crowd of surly men. Whenever the boy bumped into one of them, the man would whirl on him and scowl. Some even began berating him, but the old man always dragged him away before a real argument ensued. Reaching the bar, the elder banged on the chipped, wooden plank to get the barkeep's attention. It took a few tries to make the fat man acknowledge their presence.

"What do you want?" the barkeep asked with no fervour in his voice.

"We want a room for the night," Tullae demanded, his patience vanishing. Men like this one were the reason he avoided personal contact.

"I suppose you'll want food with that." The innkeeper mirrored the elder's irritation with his own sour tongue.

"You need not bother." Tullae gave him the phoniest smile Raftennon ever saw. "We'll be fine with just the room."

"It'll cost you two copper slips," the tavern's owner grumbled, his eyes returning to two men standing across the room. The patrons' argument now needed mugs slammed onto the table to emphasize each retort. Some surrounding drinkers turned their chairs to get a better view, on without the need to crane their necks.

Tullae rummaged in the pouch hanging on his belt and produced the pieces of copper. The bartender checked their validity without taking his eyes off the arguing patrons. His glare stayed fixed on them while he went to the other end of the bar. One of the arguers slammed his mug one last time before standing, his chair falling behind him with the force of his rage. The onlookers jeered him in disapproval as he walked away, forgoing the fight the spectators were hoping to see. The innkeeper watched him go before returning his attention to his work. Tullae glared at the man as he proceeded to fill a handful of drink orders.

Eventually, the barkeep did return to give them their room key. "Second floor, third door on the right," he instructed them, pointing to the far wall, where stairs rose to the upper levels.

Tullae thanked him sourly and led Raftennon through the throng of drunken patrons. They encountered more bumping and shoving, finally forcing the pair to separate. The boy yelled after his current guardian but lost him as the crowd swarmed around him.

At that moment, two more drunkards felt it was time to settle their differences with punches instead of words. The anger permeated the room like a volcanic eruption. Soon everyone in the common room was grabbing their neighbour and driving their fists into their faces. Raftennon fell to the floor as a large man shoved his way past him to reach his intended target. The lad scrambled through the forest of legs, not daring to stand.

Someone grabbed him by the collar of his tunic and yanked him to his feet. Raftennon closed his eyes, bracing himself for the blow that would soon come. Having never been punched before, he was not certain what to expect. The scuffles he endured with his brothers did not prepare him for this, for they had never intended to injure him. Brotherly love would not stop the blows this time, so he was doing all he could think of to lessen the impending pain. To his surprise, no one bloodied his nose or knocked him senseless. Not a single punch ever came. Instead, the student heard the muted voice of his teacher. Opening his eyes, Raftennon saw the old man as he started to pull him past the angry mob.

They reached the stairs and scrambled up to the second floor. Only when they got to the landing did the throng begin to thin out, permitting them to breathe once again. Tullae continued to drag Raftennon along the dingy hallway as if the fight were still raging around them. Thrusting the key into its hole in the door, he thrust the boy into their room. Only then did the hermit slouch onto a chair and relax. That was when Raftennon saw the blood trickling down the old man's temple.

"You're hurt!" The lad fell to his knees beside the elder, even though he had no idea what he should do to help.

"It's just a scratch," Tullae said, reaching for the desk of rotting wood flanking the only bed in the room. Atop it sat a filthy bowl filled with even dirtier water. "I'll be fine."

The old man proceeded to clean the wound and, to the boy's relief, it indeed was but a superficial cut. The hermit retrieved some herbs from a small pouch stowed in his pack, chewed them and spread the resulting paste onto the laceration. His administrations complete, Tullae took out a set of rations for their supper.

"Why can't we eat something from the kitchen?" Raftennon asked, tired of the dried fruit and meat. A freshly cooked meal would be nice after their week of travel.

"Because the kitchen is in worse repair than the rest of this place." Tullae did not even try to hide his disgust. "Would you trust food coming from such a hearth?"

Raftennon thought it over, attempting to reason why someone would let a building fall so much into disrepair. It could not be this bad in *every* room. His teacher must be exaggerating. He was not about to test this theory, however. "Probably not," he answered after a few moments. Raftennon took his share of the food and chewed, trying to imagine it was a leg of roasted chicken. "So if you knew this place was so bad, why are we spending the night here?"

"I'm an old man," Tullae explained. "I no longer have the strength to earn a living. And I've spent the last few months teaching you, at no cost to your parents. Don't misunderstand. I'm not bitter. I gladly pass my knowledge to you. But, because of this, I can afford no better. Don't worry, though. This will be the only night we stay in these shambles."

4

GAINING ADMITTANCE

The next morning, they entered the shabby stables beside the shabbier inn, half expecting to find their ox and cart stolen despite their obvious worthlessness. They were pleased to see them still where they had placed them. In fact, it was quite apparent no one even come close to them during the night. Everything was as Tullae left it, down to the overturned bucket he had knocked over and not bothered to right.

Navigating through the congested streets of the boisterous city proved to be a challenge. The further they made their way toward the heart of Xendremmar, the denser the sea of people became. Raftennon marvelled at the sheer numbers. He never imagined there could be so many people in one place. He knew the world was much bigger than his village of Yentrill, but he always thought all settlements would somehow be the same. Even the overcrowded common room of the inn did not prepare the boy for this.

While Raftennon stared at the multitude of strangers, none of them paid the travellers any attention—until they neared the Spellcasters' Guild. When the citizens realized where the pair was headed, they started to steal glances at them, differing expressions contorting their features. Some sneered at them, making their distrust of wizards unmistakable. Others ogled, wishing they had the gift of spellcasting, so Raftennon believed.

Still more, apparently educated in the art, by the snippets of conversation the lad could catch through all the other noises of the city, followed their path with surprise. They did not understand why a boy so old was heading to the Guild. There was no way the Tutors would admit him. Raftennon frowned at this. Everywhere he went, people judged him before even talking to him.

Tullae pulled the reins to stop before a large gate in an iron-wrought fence surrounding the complex of citadels that could only be their destination. Comprised of five towers amid beautiful gardens, the School took up four blocks of the city's tight grid. The spires reached high into the sky, as slender as wax candles. On cloudy days, the top of the centre-most tower no doubt disappeared into the grey heavens. This spire towered twice as tall as the others and stood in the middle of the cross the five structures created, each of the smaller towers pointing at a cardinal point.

"Close your mouth, boy," Tullae mumbled from the seat at the front of the cart. "This facade you see will soon be drab and mundane once you really delve into the depths of this place."

"There's more?" His mentor must be joking. What he saw towering before him should be more than enough to hold all the books in the world.

"Rumours tell of large catacombs hidden underground, spanning a few city blocks." The pair turned to stare at the man now standing beside their cart. They had both missed the signs of his arrival. "Some say these chambers are used for the intricate studies of the most advanced wizards and where they perform their uncanny experiments. They also say the hidden tunnels reached down to the very core of the earth."

"You are a magician here, then?" Raftennon asked.

The man shuddered and drew his grey tunic tighter around himself. "Me? No. Gods forbid."

"Then be off with your ramblings," Tullae ordered him. "Don't fill boys' minds with rubbish just to get a chuckle from their slack-jawed faces. Be gone!"

The man hesitated a moment more in defiance, but then left, muttering to himself.

"He was lying?" Raftennon's disappointment crept into his

voice. It would be something to discover all those mysterious places while he was here.

"The Guild does have secrets," Tullae said as he turned back to face the entrance, "which someone will reveal to you once they deem you ready to learn them. Until then, don't listen to the ramblings of idiots who don't know any better."

The gate swung open of its own accord, drawing a startled gasp from Raftennon. Tullae flicked the reins and the ox advanced into the garden, crawling along the main lane toward the central spire. Raftennon marvelled at the magical feat, wondering when he would learn that particular spell. It would come in handy when he wanted something but did not feel like getting up from whatever comfy spot in which he found himself at the time.

An elf in long, flowing, light-green robes walked toward them. The sun reflected off the sliver streaks in his otherwise long white hair. His clear blue eyes bore through the newcomers as he met them at an intersection of paths leading to the pair of smaller towers at the front of the complex.

"So, you have claimed an apprentice." The elf's dislike for Tullae was quite evident. The almond-shaped eyes peered past the old man to study the boy at the back of the cart.

"We both know I don't have the skills to properly oversee an apprenticeship, Teacher." Tullae bowed in respect, a sentiment not reflected in his eyes, which he kept downcast so as not offend the elf. Raftennon saw it, however, and decided he would be as polite as he could as well. "All I did was teach him to read the Script."

The elfin wizard examined Raftennon, taking in his stock from where he stood beside the ox. Only time for one breath passed before he shook his head. "He is too old." His tone was crisp, as was his turn to start back up the paved lane to the main tower.

"He's also more skilled than most of your enrollees," Tullae stated loudly enough for anyone around to hear. He straightened and stared at the elf, who turned back to face them.

"That is a bold statement coming from an usually soft-spoken man."

"I can't let the lad's talents go to waste," Tullae said with the most confidence Raftennon had ever heard from him. "You must, at least, test him."

The spellcaster returned his piercing eyes on Raftennon, to measure the boy's worth once again, it seemed. Raftennon sat up straighter and puffed out his chest, hoping it would make him seem more than he actually was. He did not know what the elf was looking for, but any little thing could help.

"How many spells does he know?" His wise eyes remained locked on the lad, but the Master Mage directed the question to his teacher.

"One." Tullae did not try to explain any further.

"But he reads the Script."

Raftennon started to inch his way closer to the hermit, getting increasing uncomfortable beneath the unwavering scrutiny from this strange wizard.

"Yes," Tullae reaffirmed, foregoing any sugarcoated words that might help. Then again, the old man knew what he was doing—Raftennon hoped.

The elfin mage continued to stare for long moments. Everything grew still around them. The ox remained motionless. Raftennon stopped moving so the planks beneath him would not creak in the growing silence. Even the hubbub of the cramped city seemed to slink away from them. Eventually, the elf whirled around to resume his way down the lane. "Bring him," he said over his shoulder.

Tullae patted Raftennon on the back, a broad smile on his face, before clambering down from his seat. Two young boys appeared on the path and one grabbed the ox's bridle without saying a word. Raftennon stared at his tutor for a moment, wondering what was happening. He lowered himself to the ground and watched the young pages lead the animal down a side trail into the gardens. Tullae wrapped an arm around Raftennon's shoulders and led him down the tiled lane to the central tower.

Arriving at the spire's base, the boy's jaw dropped again as he peered at the strange structure. The wall was perfectly round, with no proof of any mortar whatsoever. The building appeared to be one single piece of stone, instead of the expected layers of brick. Many windows spiralled up the edifice, as well as some doors opening onto narrow balconies. The tower reminded

Raftennon of a tall lighthouse that stood a few miles west of his home. Many times, he had gazed up at the balcony that surrounded the large lens that sent its light off to sea. He had marvelled at the height of that building. Now, he was looking upward at that same angle and was surprised to find he was only looking at what he thought was the tenth floor. By his estimation, the spire surely had at least a hundred storeys.

Tullae interrupted Raftennon's gawking by tugging on the front of his shirt, reminding him they were to enter.

Inside was an even more spectacular sight. The door opened onto a small tunnel about fifty feet long. When they emerged on the other side, they found themselves in the heart of the citadel. A stairway wound up the core of the structure, which was open from ground level to unseen ceiling. There was no banister to prevent the many figures walking up and down from falling to their deaths. Many doors lined the stairs, leading to the rooms used for study and research that lay behind the inner wall. In the centre of the first floor sat a large orb. A milky-white light radiated from within, illuminating the entire tower with the same intensity. Those at the top of the structure could see where they were going while the glow at the lower levels did not blind its occupants.

The elf was waiting for them. As soon as the travellers cleared the entrance, he led them to a door situated under the staircase. Raftennon let out a breath in relief, thankful they did not need to climb those dangerous stairs. They entered a moderately sized room without windows. The magical orb outside provided illumination, which seemed to radiate through brick and mortar to brighten everything, down to the points of the corners. Books covered three of the four walls, including the outer and inner curved ones. Shelves from floor to ceiling held tomes of all shapes, sizes and antiquity. A latticework of thin planks covered the last wall, holding various rolled scrolls, each of the holes filled to capacity.

The Master Mage went to these cubbyholes to retrieve one such parchment. Then he went to the desk that stood three paces away. Its twin mirrored it across the room, the pair the only furnishings. There were no chairs to sit in.

The elf motioned for Raftennon to come to his side. The boy

glanced at Tullae, who nodded his head to tell him it was all right. As the lad reached the Teacher, the wizard unrolled the scroll far enough to reveal the first few lines inked on the page and turned it toward him.

"Have you even seen this particular parchment before?"

Raftennon peered at the fine script for a few moments and admitted the content was new to him. The elf continued to stare at the lad, contemplating, validating the boy's words.

The spellcaster took his time, but eventually was satisfied and picked up one of the two small pouches he had placed beside the document. He opened it and rolled out two small, black rocks.

"I will give you only one chance to read this scroll correctly," the elf explained, unrolling the rest of the parchment. "When you reach this point," the Teacher pointed to the end of a line in the middle of the script and handed the second bag to Raftennon, "sprinkle a pinch of this onto both stones. Then take them in your hands. When you utter the last word, smash them together. Do not begin until I command you. Do you understand?"

Raftennon nodded and swallowed hard, his apprehension growing. Having little experience with tests, he did not know what to expect. The fact that Tullae's eyes betrayed the gravity of the situation did not help him either. He knew a failure here would end his dreams of becoming a magician.

The elf went back to the hermit and started mumbling something Raftennon could not catch. When he stopped muttering to himself, the spellcaster inclined his head.

Raftennon took one last deep breath and read the scroll. The text was an ancient elfin dialect he recognized, so he did as Tullae taught him and almost sang the syllables.

"Imnâ halônireey fandel-nôree mentânô silvenayrônân brentrol / Imnee hayleenôrayoo vendrâ mendrâ jenaylô-reefon fendrayee kendray fâlloom menteeüm / Kaffaynônâlee ventrâlü... "

Raftennon reached the designated spot and plunged his hand into the pouch, grabbing a pinch of the dark red powder inside. Without taking his eyes off the words, he sprinkled the dust onto the stones. Then he picked up the small rocks, surprised at their unexpected heavy weight. He did not let this strange fact distract him (he would not permit that to happen and disappoint the old man) and continued to recite the ancient script without losing a beat.

"*...jenmâllaynon fentâlee banjémônü!*"

As the last syllable left his lips, he struck the rocks together and a thunderous crash erupted in front of him. Raftennon jumped at the force of the noise. That astonishment was immediately replaced by another as he realized he remained unaffected by the blast. The expected ringing in his ears did not come. He still heard everything as clearly as he had just moments before.

A woman in velvet robes rushed into the room, clutching the sides of her head. The elf turned to her and put his forehead to hers. She calmed herself and glared at the Teacher, finally realizing what had happened. She almost raced out of the room after a glance at the lad from the corner of her eye.

The Master Mage then walked over to the table and rolled up the scroll. "What is your name?" he asked in a low voice.

"Raftennon," the boy stammered, looking over at Tullae, who was smiling with pride. "Will she be all right?"

The elf followed the lad's pointing finger and looked at the door, with a strange expression on his face. "She will regain her hearing in a few hours."

Raftennon stared at him, not understanding what was going on. The Master Mage seemed to be thinking a lot more than he had since their arrival, which should have been impossible. Was he not supposed to have managed the spell? It was simple enough. Or maybe the loud noise was not the intended result of the casting.

The spellcaster focused on the still grinning Tullae. "We will teach him. Bring him to the Eastern Tower."

5

TESTED

The first few months were hard going for the new student. The vast difference between his age and that of his fellow classmates (an average of four years, which was more than half the lifespan of the other human children) was the focus of the ridicule he received. Many comments about his late admittance implied a simple mind Raftennon did not have.

At first, being from the small town that he was, the jeering and laughter at his expense stung Raftennon much more than he would have expected—if he had taken the time to consider the situation. He tried to make friends, but the others did not want anything to do with him. In their eyes, he was a waste of space. Another student of proper age, one with more chance at becoming quite adept in the art of magic, would have benefited from the seat more than the preteen ever could.

Raftennon got the picture quickly enough, but he would still try to befriend a few of the boys his own age. A child could not cope with the world if it was devoid of others with which to play. When the other children rejected his attempts, and his status as a sub-par student emphasized, Raftennon turned his attention to the younger pupils in his own class. That proved to be even more painful as they teased him more ferociously than did the older crowd.

Finally, Raftennon dismissed them all and delved into his

studies. The other students' ridicule soon changed to envy and spiteful jealousy. Immediately, they saw his superior talent and hated him for it. He caught the teachers' attention, who would spend more time developing the boy's techniques. They knew he possessed something that would help him become a special mage if well trained, for they realized something highly unusual about him.

Every spellcaster drew energy from the air and the earth around him whenever casting magic. The joining of the universe's force and the caster's will made the spell possible. If the potential wizard failed to accomplish this drawing of power, he would never attain his desired results. This fact was so important the students spent the entirety of their freshman year at the Guild learning how to manage this feat. Many hours were devoted to heightening the pupil's senses so he could first detect the energy surrounding him, many more to learn how to transform it so he could use it. Only after the student successfully mastered this aspect of magic did he continue his education.

One year was all the Guild allotted to these rudimentary lessons. The teachers only expected the new pupils to grasp the basic collection of a small amount of energy at this point. The further one went in his learning, and the more powerful his spells became, he needed to draw more and more from his surroundings. If the pupil was unable to master this simple level of gathering by the end of the first year, the school dismissed him.

Raftennon did not need to worry about that particular situation. He spent only eight months accomplishing the yearlong work. This was the first sign of the boy's special abilities. The real proof came shortly after the latter half of his second year began.

The instructors prepared several demonstrations every term for the students to show their progress to the Guild's administrators, as well as the veteran wizards seeking apprentices. In each instance, the teachers pitted the most gifted of their respective classes against one another in different tests. This particular contest was Raftennon's first, and another special feat for him. No other student had ever participated in such a demonstration in the School's long history without first completing their sophomore year. On this day, the test was to determine who, among the participants, was most ready to fill a recently vacated seat in an advanced class.

Raftennon and seven of his classmates went to one of the eight small tables arrayed in a line in the centre of the grand hall of the North Tower. The pupils of the advanced class sat before them, as did all the Guild's teachers and most of its Master Mages. On each table lay a rolled-up parchment and three leather bags.

Raftennon's current teacher took his place before the assembled test takers and gave them their instructions.

"Before you is a scroll with a spell none of you have ever cast," the old man droned in his usual monotonous tone. "The components you will need are in the pouches which, along with the scroll, will remain untouched until the demonstration begins. You are to successfully cast the spell as quickly as you can."

The old mage studied the eight adolescents to make sure they understood his directives. When he was satisfied each was ready, he walked to the side of the room so the spectators had an unobstructed view of the competitors and gave the signal to begin.

The students hurried to unroll their parchments and read the instructions. Magic scrolls were usually divided into four sections (the exception being the test scrolls, like the ones Raftennon had used in Tullae's house and the one the elfin mage gave him to gain admittance into the school; these only had the last parts pertaining to the actual incantation).

The first part explained, in elaborate detail, what the expected result should be when one performed the incantation correctly, as well as whatever mishap could happen if done erroneously. Raftennon skimmed through the long sentences, immediately recognizing the spell. It was true he, like his peers, never actually cast it, but all of them perused the document in class. The boy knew what was expected of him, so he did not waste time reading the explanations again.

Likewise, he skimmed the next section, which described all the components required for the incantation. Raftennon only stopped his perusal of the ingredients' description, as well as where one may find them in the world, to peer into the pouches to ensure all he would need was there. He paid a little more attention to the sentences that followed, which explained when and how to use each particular item.

The third section held the steps to the actual casting of the spell (test scrolls began here, forgoing all details that came before it, because protocol dictated the teacher give the student that information and take all the necessary precautions). This part concerned the gathering of energy from the caster's environment. Depending on the power requirement, this step could be as short as two lines, or as long as several pages. This particular incantation had three verses, each syllable a phase in the gathering of the needed force from the mage's surroundings.

Raftennon skipped these instructions entirely. While some of the others began mumbling the words of preparation, he went directly to the last section of the document, to the phrases of the actual casting.

"*Immânümallâs ferbysôllâs...* "

"What is he doing?" asked one of the Master Mages looking on.

"He went straight to the casting," answered his neighbour, another veteran spellcaster.

"He really believes he can cast the spell without the proper preparation," commented another onlooker, already envisioning failure for the boy.

"He is the gifted one, is he not?" inquired yet another wizard, this one the oldest of the group.

The spectators turned to him in surprise.

"Since when do you bother to attend this most basic of demonstrations, Vendrammon?" asked the first man who had spoken. "You usually ignore the inexperienced, even if rumour circulates he may one day be as powerful as you."

Vendrammon ignored his colleagues and watched on as Raftennon took the green leaf paste from one pouch and rubbed it onto the rose petal from another. The lad disregarded the third bag, which contained an unnecessary ingredient thrown in to add difficulty to the test.

"...*mynaytrâl foorgôneea vrenlôh.* "

Raftennon brought the rose petal to his chest and pressed it over his heart, the green paste affixing it to his robes. The air around him seemed to flicker for a split second but returned to normal immediately.

Most in the crowd believed they imagined the sight and began to worry when the attendant, who had been standing off to the side up to that point, came over with a quarterstaff in his hands. The watching students wanted to cry out and warn the boy but quickly reconsidered. If his rash decision to skip the preparatory chant resulted in his harm, it was his own fault.

The attendant stopped behind Raftennon and spun around in a fluid motion, bringing his weapon down onto the boy's back. The staff splintered as it struck the blue robes. Raftennon did not move, showing no sign that he even felt the blow.

"He's done it!" cried one of the advanced students, not able to hide his astonishment.

Raftennon peered at the assembly, a slight smile forming on his lips. He was relishing the other competitors' stares of disbelief, for none of them had had time to even touch any of their spell components.

A group of pages came into the room to remove the tables and their contents in preparation for the second part of the test. The students switched the orientation of their line to face the side of the room instead of the gathered spectators. The instructors left their seats among the viewers to come down and place themselves along the wall beside the boys' teacher, who gave his pupils their next directives.

"We will now test your endurance. You are each to cast the deflection spell we have been working on for the past few weeks. You are to maintain it as long as you are capable."

The old man once again surveyed the testees to make certain they understood what they were to do. When he was satisfied, he nodded his head to signal for them to begin.

"*Immânilsülan ferbaysyllôsay myrnayfôrtrâl bynmôrvâl drenlôhay.*"

The students produced a small phial of honey and tipped it over an oak leaf. As soon as the single drop of sweet nectar touched the leaf, the boys placed it on their chest, right over their hearts, much like their previous spell. Like the other protective incantation, a burst of blue light engulfed the caster's body for the beat of an eyelash and then was gone.

The mage teachers thrust their arms in front of them, their own chanting already done. An unnatural wind blew up in the room, assaulting the youths, trying to push them to the floor. The eight students braced themselves for the impact and were happy their shields held.

The instructors' attack continued, the gale intensifying with every passing moment. One boy's protection soon gave way, and he fell backward, sliding halfway to the back wall of the room from the force of the gusts.

One by one, the competitors dropped in like fashion, each tumbling further back with the growing intensity of the magical wind. Raftennon remained standing, however. His strength did not wane as the others' did. The signs of fatigue or strain that slowly contorted his opponents' faces never touched his.

"Do you see that?" the same Master Mage that had initiated the first discussion began again.

"The boy is drawing the wind into him as it passes by," commented another.

"He is siphoning his energy from the teachers' own spell!" cried a third, not believing what he was seeing. The absorption of another incantation's power was something an aspiring mage learned after gaining an apprenticeship, not while he was still learning the rudimentary techniques in the general classes. And even then, only a scant few managed to master the skill. Though this fact explained why the lad was doing so well, it did not explain how he was accomplishing it.

Vendrammon looked on with interest as Raftennon continued to hold off his instructors' attack long after all his comrades had fallen. The teachers finally ended their onslaught when it became clear the student would not fall unless they put their entire strength behind the spell (so they believed). They were not about to do that, for it would certainly result in the boy crashing through the wall of the tower to his death.

Vendrammon got up from his seat and left the other wizards to gossip among themselves about Raftennon's feat and its ramifications. The Master Mage did afford the pupil another glance before exiting the room, quite intrigued with the lad.

He peered into the blue orb, wondering why it was showing him this particular, seemingly insignificant test. He watched with the same curiosity the Master Mages did as the student displayed feats that should have been impossible. How had this youth remained undiscovered until recently? He studied the boy's personal energy as he fended off his teachers' attack.

"He already knows to use his environment to fuel his magic," he marvelled aloud. He was alone in the room but did not even consider that point as he mulled over this latest discovery. "He may very well help us if the other's heart has truly turned as I believe it has."

6

TRYSTS

Three years passed and Raftennon's rapid mastery of the lessons and exceptional performances on tests propelled him into the proper class. He no longer needed to endure the ridicule of being the oldest in the room by several years, for now he was finally learning what the other young adults his own age were.

But another problem arose. His sixteenth birthday had passed a mere week before and Raftennon was finding it more difficult to concentrate on his studies.

Throughout his sojourn at the Guild, he never left to explore the city. Though the students lived on the premises and were required to remain on the grounds during the class terms, the Mage Dean did allocate blocks of free time. Some were only a day long while others lasted a few weeks. On the short breaks, Raftennon always remained in his room to work on projects that needed completing, or practise the various aspects of magic at which he wanted to excel. Only when the vacation was a month long did he leave the Guild. He would return home to visit his family and his old tutor.

The only interaction Raftennon had with living beings were his conversations with the other students. Slowly, they accepted him as part of the academy, even if most of them envied his skill.

Now, as he reached the middle of his teens, his hormones began to win the battle with his will. His eyes kept straying to this particular young woman. It did not matter whether she was across the garden, or beside him in their alchemy class, she would always pull him toward her without even intending to do so. He would spend countless hours admiring the slight golden hue of her long red hair. The bright glow of her emerald eyes always made his heart skip a beat. Her lips, oh those beautifully full, luscious lips, beckoned him to kiss them.

She did not seem to notice him, however, as much as the teachers did. On several occasions, they chastised him for his lapse of concentration, to the amusement of his classmates. They had new ammunition to throw at the small-town boy. The young woman merely smiled at him whenever the reprimand happened, and that would end the encounter—until the next one would arise. Everything changed, however, on the week after his sixteenth birthday.

The instructors dismissed their last classes and the students ran to their rooms to ready themselves for a two-day reprieve of study. Raftennon slowly walked toward his room, ignoring every bump from frantic pupils. Unlike them, he was not planning to go anywhere. With everyone gone, including her, maybe he could get some studying done.

His plans soon fell awash when a gentle hand touched his elbow. Raftennon stopped and turned to see the alluring figure.

"Jennalla!" The flame of red hair kindled his heart, robbing him of the ability to say more. Her shy smile sent shivers down his spine.

That grin widened at the sound of her name. She was pleased to find he knew who she was and did not just admire her for her appearance. "Hi, Raftennon. You headed to your room?"

"Yes," he stammered after an awkward silence as he tried to regain his breath.

"I was afraid you would deviate from your usual decision to remain behind while the others frolic in the city." She took another step toward him until only mere inches spanned between their hearts, his no doubt beating much more heavily than hers.

"Why?" This young woman was the only person—the only thing—in the school that confused him, and she did so tremendously.

"If you did, I'd be left all alone on the grounds." Jennalla raised her right arm at the elbow and brushed her fingers along the sleeve of his robes.

"You're not going to join your friends?" Her nearness made his head spin even wilder than it usually did when he was in her presence. He had never been so close to her as he was now. In fact, this was the first time he noticed the faint freckles that riddled her cheeks and the bridge of her nose.

"I was hoping we would be friends."

Raftennon's heart skipped a beat. He could not believe what he had just heard. He felt lost in a dream as she took his arm and led him toward her dormitory.

For the next two days, they spent all their time together, talking about where they came from. Jennalla was also from a fisherman family, from Bezna in the Salgre Hills. Raftennon was astonished to hear that fishing was possible on the western sea outside Vendetran Bay. She explained they accomplished the seemingly impossible feat quite differently than he was accustomed to. In her hometown, the boats were immense and needed to go far out into the ocean to find their catch. The fishermen braved the mighty waves until they subsided miles off to sea. There, they endured the pronounced rocking of the waters for weeks at a time before finally coming home.

Jennalla became sombre every time she talked about her family. Because of the long journeys to reach the reefs where the fish were, she did not see much of her father. She saw him even less after she began attending the Spellcasters' Guild. She broke into tears when she informed Raftennon about her father's abrupt death. A violent storm swept in and engulfed his boat before he and his crew had time to brace themselves. Massive waves assaulted the craft and her father fell overboard, disappearing in the churning waters. Jennalla never got the chance to say goodbye.

Raftennon held her tightly and consoled her, much as his mother had done for him as he recounted his terrible nightmares. The stroking of her hair was more tender, he felt, and his heart thudded in his chest. He was certain she could feel it too—and he was right.

Jennalla peered into his eyes when her tears subsided. Ever so slowly, she straightened up, while he bent down. Their lips met in the near darkness of the garden, the only light coming from the sliver of moon that managed to peek through the clouds.

This romantic encounter happened on their second night alone together. They parted company early, before the other students began returning to the Guild. They did this to avoid discovery; Raftennon did not want to ruin the moment with the teasing of their immature classmates.

Their clandestine affair did not go unnoticed, however.

The next six weeks passed by almost in a blur. Raftennon attended his classes, but could never recall what subject matter the teacher covered. He went through the motions of the assignments and sometimes succeeded. More often than not, the attempt ended in catastrophe, earning him stern rebukes from his teachers, which he never heard. His classmates skirted away from him during these tests, knowing full well there was a good chance they could end up on the wrong side of the botched spell. Raftennon never heeded the hurts he inflicted on himself from those errors. She overshadowed everything.

For the first week, they tried to keep their relationship secret. Jennalla never cared who knew she liked him, but Raftennon had no experience with romance and wanted to tread the foreign waters as carefully as he could. He did not want the rest of the school ridiculing him for not knowing what was expected of him, or worse, giving him advice on what he should be doing. He knew love had everything to do with the heart, so it was his heart he intended to follow. And his heart soon told him he did not care who knew he shared the same infatuation Jennalla felt for him.

The pair spent all the time they could together. Their teachers seated them at opposite ends of the class, for it was clear they distracted each other. The added distance did little to refocus the youths. Instead, their heads turned even further so they could stare into the other's eyes. A few magical gusts of wind pulled them apart, their interlaced fingers holding on until the very last moment before the invisible force separated them. Raftennon was so distracted he did not even think of trying to disrupt the spells. Instead, the couple reunited as soon as their chaperones lapsed in their surveillance.

The nights were the best. That was when they secreted themselves somewhere and spend time together without interruption.

The first of these trysts happened three days after their first kiss. Raftennon made his way to his room for the night, thinking of that experience and hoping a second would come soon. As he reached for his door, someone grabbed the back of his robes and pulled him back. He staggered as he struggled to turn while his assailant continued to drag him down the corridor. When Raftennon finally managed to take steps forward on his own instead of stumbling sideways to remain on his feet, he saw the golden-red hair. He grinned like a fool and his breath caught in his chest when Jennalla turned her head to smile at him. She let go of the dark blue fabric and took his hand instead, continuing the hurried pace down the hall.

She took him down corridors that were unfamiliar to him, turned corners so often he almost lost his bearings. But he kept enough of his wits to know they were heading toward the back of the tower, down a number of stories he neglected to count. They ended up on a floor just below ground level, in a square room with crates lined along two walls. Jennalla closed the door and took a lantern from where it hung beside the door. When her magical flame lit the wick, she took his hand and led him further into the room, behind the furthest stack of boxes.

She barely had the time to set the light down on a crate before Raftennon took her in his arms and thrust his lips onto hers. She took his face in her hands and guided him, showing him how she liked to be kissed. His sense of time eluded him, but he knew when they finally left the room it was too soon for him.

"Remember this room," Jennalla whispered, slightly out of breath. "This will be our place, where no one will keep us apart."

She would give him signs during the following days, telling him to meet her in the hidden room later that evening. Sometimes it was as blatant as her whispering her desire in his ear. Other times, it was as subtle as a knowing glance.

Raftennon actually missed the first of these stealthy signals. He spent the night in his room, wishing she was there with him. The next morning, Jennalla avoided him. She studiously sat at her seat, listening to the lectures, is if he no longer existed.

Raftennon ignored everything and everyone around him, save her, wondering what had happened, what he had done. Only at the conclusion of the day's lessons did she finally come to him.

"I waited for you for hours." She glared at him, her cheeks nearing the colour of her hair.

"You didn't tell me—"

"Don't you dare try to blame me!" Her raised voice drew the attention of everyone in the garden in which they now stood.

"I'm not—"

"This is your fault, not mine."

"I'm sorry."

"You better be." She stalked off, never looking back.

Two days passed before Jennalla came back to him and let him explain himself. He stumbled through his words, still not understanding how this was his doing. But all he wanted was for her to be happy, and he intended to do all that was needed to make that happen. He missed no more signals and made the gestures the other students told him he should show (advice they gave even though he still never asked for it). He did everything he could to make her smile. And she did. And Raftennon was happier than he had ever been.

At the end of those six weeks, Jennalla joined him as they walked to their alchemy class. "You know the tool shed at the edge of the West Tower's north garden?" she whispered in his ear.

"I do," Raftennon replied as he gently squeezed her hand.

"I'll be waiting inside." Jennalla stopped abruptly, their interlaced fingers forcing him to turn to her. "You better show up."

"I will."

"Good."

Raftennon did not even start to go to his room as he was expected to do every night. He did not attempt the pretense he followed every other night he snuck away to spend time with her. He did try to stick to the shadows and walk slowly, so as to not rouse any suspicion, but his strides were still too determined to be nonchalant. He almost ran through the garden to the small wooden shed hidden behind a tall hedge. He peered over his shoulder to see no one was around to catch him sneaking and entered the shack.

Jennalla lay on the floor, atop a large blanket. "Took you long enough."

"Sorry. I got here as soon as I could."

Jennalla stood and took the two steps forward she needed to reach him. She wrapped her arms around his neck and drew him closer for a deep kiss. It was long and sensual and left him breathless when she finally stepped back. Raftennon advanced toward her, wanting more. She outstretched a hand and firmly kept him away as she backed toward the blanket. When she was sure Raftennon would obey and stay where he stood, she raised her hands to the collar of her robes. Raftennon stared at her as her fingers worked the buttons down the front of her garment. He wondered at the pale, luxuriant skin usually hidden under the red fabric as the lapels inched open. His stare intensified when the garment slid down her body. He gawked at her nakedness, not knowing what he should do next. She came to him and showed him exactly what she wanted from him.

7

THE APPRENTICE

The following morning, Raftennon slowly gathered what he
would need for the day's classes. He was already late for his first
lesson, but the motivation to hurry continued to elude him. All
he could think about was Jennalla—and the things she did to him
in the shadows of that shed. He never knew one could feel as he
had at the culmination of their lovemaking. He replayed the
event in his mind, from start to finish, as he had done since wak-
ing. He shook his head in disbelief, still convinced some of it
was part of a dream. No words could describe what he felt when
Jennalla shuddered over him as he lost himself in her. He still
tingled at the memory of it. Already he anticipated the next
encounter.

Raftennon froze with his inkwell halfway into his pouch
when he saw the tall figure standing in his open doorway. The
newcomer's drab, grey robes flowed to the floor, completely
covering his form. The long, wide-hemmed sleeves hid the
man's hands, folded as they were over his slender chest. The
rising sun glistened on otherwise invisible runes embroidered
along the cuffs and the collar of the hood-less garb. To the
untrained eye, these marks resembled strands of stray cobwebs,
but to Raftennon's amazement, they made sense to him. Badges
of protection lined the stranger's neck, to ward off offensive
spells directed at him. Symbols of power were stitched about his

wrists to make his own incantations even more powerful. The visitor's dark, almost black eyes stared intently at the youth under bushy eyebrows. A thin leather thong, which matched his robes in colour, kept his long, pale grey hair out of his face. Raftennon gaped at the old man, unable to control his astonishment.

"You know who I am, it appears," the visitor said, finally completing his entrance into the room. The door slowly closed behind him of its own accord.

The awestruck teen bowed haltingly at the waist, not certain how to act in front of the great Vendrammon, reputed to be the most powerful spellcaster currently living.

"Do you believe what is said about me?" asked the mage, taking a seat on the only chair in the small dormitory room.

"That your magic is rivalled by none? That no one can defeat your spells?" Raftennon whispered the first words, but he regained his composure with every syllable, even though the reason for this visit still eluded him.

"Among other things." Vendrammon kept his arms hidden in the folds of his robes, his face expressionless.

Raftennon stared at the old man as he slowly straightened from his bow, trying to formulate his response. At length, he decided to go with brute honesty instead of transparent flattery. "I can't say. I've never seen you cast a spell, so I can't attest to your power. Frankly, I think some of the stories are pretty far-fetched. No offence intended, Master."

The aged spellcaster frowned at the student for a long time, clearly displeased by his answer—or so Raftennon thought. To his surprise, the old man's wrinkled face creased even more as his lips curled up at the corners. "That is good, my boy!" Vendrammon boomed in the quiet morning. "Never take words at their face value. Always question them until they are proven. Follow this advice and you will be caught off guard far less often."

"What brings you to my humble room, Master?" Though Raftennon gave the veteran mage the respect his reputation deserved, he was quickly losing patience with this strange conversation. The longer this encounter lasted, the longer it would be before he saw Jennalla again. And she was the only person he wanted to see at that moment.

Vendrammon leaned forward in the wooden chair and stared intently at the young man. All joviality left his features, replaced by stone-cold seriousness. "I have watched you for the past several weeks and am dismayed by your recent behaviour."

Raftennon shifted on his feet, not understanding why his conduct interested the most powerful man in the world.

"I know you are entering manhood, my boy, and with that come the distractions of the fairer sex. Believe me, I fought my fair share of battles with my yearnings as a lad." A slight smile tried to fight its way onto the old man's lips, but the noose-like grip his mind had over his emotions quickly put a stop to that. "I conquered those urges and concentrated on my studies, something you are not doing."

Raftennon began to reproach the comment, insulted that this stranger was meddling in his personal affairs. Vendrammon did not allow a single syllable to escape his mouth.

"I was never caught losing track of the lessons, stammering gibberish while trying to divine the answers to questions I failed to hear," the Master Mage explained, indirectly telling the youth his observations. "My learning never suffered. My academic performance never lapsed. My infatuations never kept me from performing my duties as an apprentice."

Raftennon stood before the old man, remorse for letting his attention slip from his studies battling indignation over the intrusion in his affairs with Jennalla. His warring feelings were so intense he almost missed the mage's last words. "I admit, my focus has been divided lately, but even you suffered the yearnings of the heart, so you say. As you mastered your emotions, so shall I, I assure you. When the time comes for my apprenticeship to start, I'll be ready and completely focused."

"Will you really?" Vendrammon said as he lifted his eyebrows in scrutiny. "You foresee this relationship between yourself and the young lady faltering at some point?"

"I...I...," Raftennon stammered, not understanding why the Master Mage would come to that conclusion. What he felt for Jennalla was the strongest feeling he had ever felt in his short life. He could not see it ending. Was it love? What else could it be?

"Now that you have experienced your dreams, finally touched her, fulfilled her, will your mind be strong enough to control your enlivened heart?" Vendrammon's stare became even more intense as he carefully analyzed the boy's every reaction, conscious and subconscious. "Will you be able to push her aside and subdue your yearning manhood to finish the task you gave yourself by coming here? Can you say goodbye to love so you may reach your full potential?"

Raftennon stared at the wizard, perplexed. What was the reasoning behind this line of questioning? He answered the revered mage in measured tones, carefully pondering every thought before revealing it. "In two years, when the time comes, Jennalla and I will part ways and concentrate on our apprenticeships. I've worked too hard to let my dream of becoming a spellcaster flutter away from me now." He knew Jennalla would say the same. He also knew they would find a way to spend whatever time they could together. It would be less than they were stealing now, but that was a sacrifice he would make.

"And if you did not have the customary two years, would you be willing to set aside your newfound feelings, shatter the heart of someone you hardly know but seem to care for so deeply?"

Raftennon still did not understand the old man. What was he driving at?

"My boy," Vendrammon continued, "you possess an extremely rare talent. As I said earlier, I have been keeping a close eye on you since your infatuation for the young lady surfaced. Truth be told, my surveillance of you began when I saw the remarkable skills you displayed during your admissions test.

"Do not fool yourself into thinking you are the first late bloomer admitted to this school. You are not. You were not even the most talented of the untrained to walk through that front gate. You are now among an elite group of students, granted, but you are on the brink, much as every child here is at some point or other. Many falter, not able to deny the pull of their hearts. Many leave to wed, to start a family. Most part from us after ten years of training, taking with them their limited knowledge. You studied under one such individual. He too showed much potential but lacked the determination to complete his arduous studies."

Raftennon never realized the extent of Tullae's talent.

Vendrammon got up from the chair and walked to the young man to place a hand on his shoulder. The elder's black eyes bore into the boy's brown ones. "I wish to save you from this choice. I will do all that I can to focus your attention on your current goal. I do not want to see your talent go to waste."

"I will not let love distract me, Master." Raftennon's conviction to continue his studies was fervent. At that moment, away from the woman who so distracted him, Raftennon himself actually believed he would accomplish the task.

"You say that now," the old man countered, taking a step back to get a better view of the lad's countenance, "but can you promise your emotions will not win you over in the years to come?"

Raftennon remained silent, unable to make that vow and keep it.

"I did not think you could," Vendrammon said. "That is why I am offering to take you on as my apprentice, at this very moment."

Raftennon's heart skipped a beat. Was the greatest spellcaster of the day really willing to take him under his wing at such an unheard-of young age? "I still have two years' study before I'm ready," he stammered.

"Most of your classes, at this point, are only meant to refine your reading, writing and pronunciation, my boy," the Master Mage said, clearly hating to explain his decision. "Your heightened skills in these areas are what facilitated your admission into the Guild in the first place. As for your other classes, like herbal lore, those are things I am certain you will absorb quite easily under my tutelage. I believe you are ready, or I would not be making the offer."

"I'm sure you have more important matters to attend to than waste your time teaching me what the other teachers are already charged to do."

"So, you are informing me you are not ready." Vendrammon folded his arms into his robes, his face as rigid as stone, revealing no expression whatsoever.

"I never said that," Raftennon blurted out, not wanting to ruin this incredible opportunity.

"It is your heart that is pushing you to refuse my invitation, then."

Raftennon lowered his gaze to the floor, his mind reeling with the battle within himself. He just recently found love. He was certain that was what he felt for Jennalla. Was he ready to give that up already? Could he go on without the feel of her, after what they shared the night before? Of course, they would both still be in the complex. It was not like he would not see her again.

"I know of the storeroom, boy," Vendrammon put in as Raftennon was about to answer. "I also know where you were last night. I keep a close eye on my apprentices; and you, I will watch even more closely. I will not permit you to fall to distraction. Keep that in mind before you decide. But make your choice quickly. I am a busy man. This offer I only extend once. When I leave this room, you either come with me or you never receive my tutelage."

It seemed like an eternity passed before Raftennon finally decided the fate of not only himself and his love, but, unbeknownst to him at that moment, the fate of his entire family.

"I would be honoured to learn from you, Master Vendrammon. You have my full dedication."

Raftennon never stepped into a traditional classroom again. Vendrammon instructed the teen to pack all his belongings immediately and waited motionless at the door while he did so. Then the elderly mage led his new apprentice out of the dormitory building to the South Tower. There was housed the spellcaster's personal suite, a set of rooms that would become Raftennon's home for the foreseeable future.

The boy's first lessons were obedience and blind faith. In no instance was he to question his mentor's orders; they were to be executed promptly, and correctly, on the first attempt. This proved to be a difficult hurdle, for the self-importance that always afflicted teenagers had a strong hold on Raftennon's pride. He also needed to content with Jennalla's image popping into his head at inopportune times, preventing him from listening or hastening to get a task done. He fought Vendrammon on a few occasions to get his way or to get some reprieve from reprimands that were clearly harsher than they required to be, in the teen's eyes. He never won these arguments, so Raftennon soon began to cede the power to Vendrammon and kept his defiant spirit under a tight leash. The Master Mage was, after all, his elder, and the man with the knowledge to pass down.

The next obstacle Raftennon had to face was his verbal speech. Vendrammon was a man gravely peeved by the shortcuts taken by the younger generation, especially with their use of contractions. Whenever his apprentice used terms as "can't", or "shouldn't", or even "I'm", the old spellcaster sent sparks shooting from his fingers onto the youth's flesh. Three months of shocks set his pupil straight.

As Raftennon learned these seemingly mundane lessons, Vendrammon also taught him the intricacies of herbal lore. He did not understand why his Master insisted on using the ancient terminology when the modern, shortened names made things a lot simpler. At first, the teen questioned these methods, but baleful glares from the Master Mage, accompanied by more magical lightning, soon quieted him.

When the studies became easier to grasp, and the squabbling of an immature boy finally subsided, the true learning began. The following months concentrated on the reading of scrolls, much to Raftennon's delight. He was returning to his specialty. He also learned to write these documents, to weave the magical energy within the letters. Up to this point, he never knew part of the spell's power came from the parchment itself. He always believed he was solely responsible for the feats of magic he was performing while reading the incantations. This revelation humbled the apprentice, to Vendrammon's delight. The old wizard kept these feelings to himself, of course, but was glad his protege was learning humility. It would benefit him in the end.

For eleven years, Raftennon spent every single moment in the private chambers in the South Tower. He no longer received the study breaks offered to the other students. Vendrammon did not believe in giving his apprentices any rest. If they truly wanted to become powerful wizards, they needed to make the appropriate sacrifices. Raftennon did not mind. He was so rapt in his studies he never noticed the missed respites. Jennalla disappeared from his heart within four months, and Raftennon even found himself forgetting about his family. He usually wrote his mother each month; but as his sojourn with the old mage progressed, when the spellcasting became more intense, he sometimes went a season before sending a letter.

In the spring of his twenty-seventh year of life, Raftennon was sorting some newly-arrived spell components and putting them in their proper places on the shelves that covered an entire wall of the small study. He performed this task once a month, supposedly to help him familiarize himself with everything pertaining to his craft (Raftennon believed Vendrammon detested this chore and that was the real reason he delegated it to his underlings).

As he placed a small phial on a shelf beside a large decanter, the door burst open and in strode a man Raftennon had never seen before.

"Who are you and what are your intentions?" Raftennon asked, turning to the visitor after placing his inventory list on the crate of supplies he still needed to sort.

The intruder simply raised a hand in Raftennon's direction and mumbled a few phrases as his other hand went into a fold of his dark robes. Raftennon immediately recognized the intonation of the words, though their sequence was unfamiliar to him. Reaching into his own hidden pockets, Raftennon began to recite his own spell.

"*Immânilsülan ferbaysyllôsay myrnayfôrtrâl bynmôrvâl drenlôhay.*"

The interloper extended his hands forward, rubbing them together as he did so. With his arms straight before him, he turned his palms out toward his target. A ball of fire the size of a large melon soared toward Raftennon, who calmly looked on as the familiar blue glow flickered around his body. The unnatural flames crashed into the unseen barrier, mere inches from the young man's face. The fireball dissipated, leaving Raftennon unharmed.

The apprentice reached into another hidden pocket and began reciting another incantation.

"*Drendaymônân symlôvaeelyay karnayjemô sreeznôvlanaee milônel revétômanaylâsim!*"

The intruder frantically rummaged through his own spell components to counter this unexpected attack. Before the man could manage to grab whatever he was searching for, an unseen force pushed him against the wall and pinned him there, unable to move.

"Again I ask; who are you, and why are you attacking me?" Raftennon began to walk toward the unknown interloper but stopped when he heard a sound at the door of the private quarters. The entry was empty, the door firmly shut.

"*Ventrâllaynus imânilsülan ferbaysylôsay myrnayfôrtrâllesis bynmâlloovaryan drenlôhaylan.*" Raftennon turned back to his trapped assailant to see the effects of the man's incantation. The dark-clad man lowered his arms and took a step forward, despite the force Raftennon thrust at him. The apprentice intensified his concentration, adding more strength to his invisible shield, but still the man passed through it as if it were not there. The energies that were supposed to immobilize the man simply dissipated as soon as they touched him.

Raftennon threw away the rosemary-covered twig he had needed to maintain his snare and flung himself behind the nearest desk. The trespasser began chanting again. Raftennon immediately recognized the attack. It was the very one he used to shove the man backward, the one that should have held him fast. Raftennon delved into his pouches for what he needed.

The desk started rising into the air and Raftennon sprang his trap. He focused on the floating piece of furniture, a new twig in his hand, and chanted the words. He bent his will on his former cover, which continued to float away from him, and pushed it toward his attacker. A battle of wills ensued as the young apprentice tried to drive the desk into his assailant, who in turn struggled to thrust it away from himself and his target. Eventually, the polished wood cracked under the strain, but the forces battling each other kept the splinters together.

The intruder slid a hand into his dark robes, obviously intent on casting another spell. Raftennon would not let him succeed. He sprang to his feet and rushed toward the man. The desk flew back as Raftennon stopped struggling against the other mage's will and drew his magic back. As the furniture splintered further as it crashed into the far wall, scattering books and scrolls with the impact, Raftennon bulled into the stranger, sending both men to the floor. The student lay on top of the unknown wizard, pinning his arm before he could remove anything from the hidden pocket.

"I will not ask again," Raftennon grunted as he straddled the man, immobilizing him. "I do expect an answer, however."

The interloper struggled to free himself, but to no avail. Raftennon shifted the magical force he still sustained back onto the intruder, pinning him where he lay.

"The moment I hear anything but Common come out of your mouth," Raftennon raised a balled fist, "I will knock you out. An explanation. Now!"

"Release him, apprentice," Vendrammon ordered in the calmest tone Raftennon had ever heard him use.

Without hesitation, Raftennon lifted himself off the spellcaster and dissipated both his magic spells—the one holding the man down and the one still protecting himself from magical attack.

"You owe me a desk," the Master Mage told his pupil as the stranger eased his way back to his feet.

"He is the one who tried to use it as a weapon," Raftennon pointed out, gesturing to the third man with his chin.

"It was in my way," the man said, smoothing his rumpled robes with his hands.

"What do you think?" Vendrammon asked the other spellcaster, completely ignoring the confusion plastered on Raftennon's face.

"I was not expecting that counter-spell."

"Which one?" A bushy eyebrow raised over Vendrammon's right eye.

"Either," the interloper admitted after a short pause. "I did not anticipate him casting his second spell so quickly. I certainly did not expect him to counter with the same incantation I used."

"You should have," Vendrammon chided the man he clearly knew. It appeared the Master Mage tolerated the shortcomings of his peers as little as he did those of his students.

"And I suppose I should also have anticipated him jumping on me like a common ruffian?" The stranger crossed his arms in indignation.

"We all know there are times when we should solve problems by other means than magic."

"Excuse the interruption, Teacher," interjected a perplexed Raftennon, "but may I get an explanation for these events?"

"You were being tested, my boy," Vendrammon explained, turning a smiling face in his direction.

"And you passed with flying colours," added the intruder, mirroring the elder's expression, all previous insult forgotten.

"This is Endrallor," Vendrammon introduced the attacker, sweeping a hand from its hiding place in his long, grey robes toward his associate. "He is another of the Teachers of the Guild. We act out this little charade to see if our students are as ready as we believe them to be."

"Ready for what, Master?" Raftennon, though quite sharp when it came to all affairs of magic, was still naive in the arts of interacting with living beings and sometimes found it difficult to follow the slight innuendos they used.

"There is nothing more I can teach you, Raftennon," Vendrammon clarified. "You have absorbed everything I have to offer; much more quickly than most, I might add. You need no more tutelage."

"You are sending me away?" Raftennon could not believe what he was hearing.

"Do you want to spend the rest of your life here at the Guild?" Vendrammon raised an eyebrow, once again defying the young man to challenge himself and give himself the credit he deserved. "If that is your wish, you may do so, but you will do so in your own quarters."

"There is much still to learn." Raftennon floundered, still struggling with the news. He always believed when his sojourn at the School came to an end his repertoire of spells would be full. He knew many, but he still felt ill-equipped to deal with what he could face out in the world.

"Of course there is," Vendrammon grumbled, displeased at having to point out this obvious fact. He started walking toward his apprentice. "My final lesson is this: there will always be something new to learn. You will never know everything. Even the Munaedaar, with the gifts bestowed to them by the god Pentaclin himself, are still learning. Keep your senses alert and you will find ways to quell that yearning you have for knowledge."

"It would be nice to visit my family," Raftennon admitted as his Master began to lead him to the door.

"You are now free to do so," Vendrammon informed the lad, fondly patting him on the shoulder.

"It would also be nice to learn how to hurl fire from my hands," said the young mage, grinning at Endrallor.

"The great Vendrammon neglected to teach you that spell, did he?" Endrallor chided the old wizard.

"The boy has learned to control fire," Vendrammon shot back.

"To light it, augment its strength, and extinguish it," Raftennon explained. "The act of actually throwing it has not yet been covered."

"There is a scroll in the Library Hall of the central tower," Vendrammon told him. "You may walk the stairs freely and study whatever you desire."

"That I shall do—after I visit my family and learn a levitation spell that will save me if ever I fall off the edge."

The three wizards exited the room, all equals now—to a fashion. The Masters could still best the new graduate, Raftennon had no doubt, despite the conclusion of this particular encounter. He suspected Endrallor held himself back during their confrontation. But the test was done, and Raftennon was now officially a mage, like them. He would soon go home to tell his family he had succeeded in becoming a magician.

8

GOING HOME

"He has the most potential to be the one we need, but his skills need much nurturing."

The black robed figure peered into the clear blue orb on its pedestal. Another man, similarly clad, entered the room and retrieved a volume from one of the many bookshelves lining the walls.

"Your misgivings are quite unfounded," stated the second person, flinging his arms off to his side. His ebony robes opened at his chest and flew backward. The clasp at his neck kept the garb in place as it changed into a flowing cape. The man slowly made his way to a window overlooking the stars. "We have sworn an Oath, which we cannot break."

"*We* cannot break it, no," interjected the first figure, still fixed on the images in the orb. "*His* devotion to our cause may not be so profound."

"In either case, we are bound not to interfere," continued the second, his eyes glued to the pages he held instead of the magnificent view outside. "Our role is to maintain the Balance, rectifying any tilt that occurs. We are not to influence the mortals in any other way."

"That is not my intention," explained the concerned, white-haired man. "All I am do is prepare for the event I fear if it ever comes to pass."

His companion nodded absently, so rapt in his reading he most likely did not hear a single word he just said. He intended to do as much as the Oath allowed to prevent a catastrophe without altering the ordinary flow of things, but no more. One possible renegade in their ranks was enough atrocity.

The sun shone brightly on the Plains of Mandellon, the tall grass mimicking rolling waves on the ocean in the slight breeze. The waters of the mighty Grannbellan rushed by him as he sat and enjoyed his lunch. Raftennon gazed at the trunk of a fallen tree as it sped away in the current, on its long journey to the sea, past his home. The newly appointed mage was on the northern shore because he chose not to take the road back home. He travelled that way many years ago and yearned to see more of the country. For that reason, he decided he would follow the river for the entirety of his journey. He also opted to go on foot.

At a leisurely pace, he set out from the city he never visited during his lengthy stay there. Before leaving, he inquired after Jennalla. He learned she left a few years back, one of those not chosen for apprenticeship. It seemed Raftennon's sudden disappearance, having had no chance to say goodbye, affected her deeply. She no longer possessed the drive to fully commit to her studies and soon departed from the Guild. Raftennon was surprised the lump in his heart was not as large as it should have been.

He was now two days out of Xendremmar, on a journey that should take him a little more than a week to complete. Raftennon's unhurried pace would no doubt prolong the trek, which did not bother the new mage at all. He had not written home to inform his family he was coming, so he could arrive whenever his feet brought him there.

After he finished his apple and shot the core into the flowing river, Raftennon gathered his bag, brushed the dirt off his dark blue robes and continued on his way. He admired the wild grass and studied the sounds of the plains. He gazed up at the stars at night, noting the positions of the constellations drawn by the gods, a figure devoted to each of them. Dyrlund's silver sun, Thorm's shield, Geneve's hourglass and, of course, Pentaclin's tome were all plain to see.

Five days later, he reached the Bellyn River where it churned into the Grannbellan. He stopped for another short rest, eating a serving of his travel rations before retrieving three pouches from the hidden folds of his robes. He extracted a raven's feather from one of the sacks, some black substance ground to powder from another and a small phial of green liquid from a third.

"*Lüvendrâmôllas silnévyndrâm silnébernümyl granvénooplay hendengyllôm.*" While muttering the arcane words that had been his life for the better part of his years, Raftennon drizzled the fluid onto the feather and sprinkled the black powder over it. The spellcaster floated off the ground, safely crossing the rushing river.

Another four days of travel through light rain, which did not bother the mage, brought him to the long unseen outskirts of a little town that stood unchanged since his departure. The villagers of Yentrill followed him with their eyes as the native stranger walked through the mud-covered lanes. None recognized the grown boy and he made no effort to reintroduce himself to them. The dogs remembered, however, greeting him with familiar growls and raised hackles he would never forget. The inhabitants stared at him as they tried to soothe their pets or gruffly quiet them. Raftennon ignored them all, his sights set on the small house near the mouth of the river.

There, he found the youngest of his sisters, all grown up now and as beautiful as their mother in her youth. He presumed it was Shenma because of the physical similarity, for the last time he saw her was on his last visit, more than a decade gone. She was ten at the time, still in the awkward, gangly stage every little sister had to endure in their big brother's eyes. She was hanging up the clothes to dry on the first sunny day after a short stint of dreary weather.

Shenma peered up at the spellcaster, recognition taking a few moments to set in. "Raf?" When he nodded, she squealed in excitement and dropped the sleeping shirt she had begun to affix to the clothesline to run to him. Raftennon needed to brace himself for the collision that almost drove him to the muddy dirt road.

"It is nice to see you too, Shenma," he stammered through his laughter.

"If it's so nice you could have come back a lot sooner." She shoved him away from her, a new smile fighting to overcome the scowl her lips now wore.

The door to the humble house opened and out strode an old woman. Her greying hair hung limply to her sagging shoulders. Her face was worn, creased more deeply than her years should have caused. Her eyes were tired and barely brightened when they set on her long-lost son.

"Mother." The mage pried himself from his sister's embrace and walked up to meet her. She waited patiently at the door, not quite believing he was home.

"Raftennon, my boy." The words came out the barest of whispers, something that disturbed the young mage greatly.

"What has happened?" he asked, keeping the extent of his concern hidden from the tired old woman that stood before him. He did not understand what had occurred to change his mother so. She was full of life when he saw her last.

"You've been gone such a long time," Melna managed to whisper between wheezes that further alarmed the spellcaster.

"I am here now," he told her, using the voice his father had whenever he woke from a nightmare as a child.

"Yes, you are."

Melna led her son into the house after a short fit of coughing. Raftennon found himself supporting her a great deal as they walked into the dark dining room. The magic-user could have sworn the house was brighter when he lived there. Leading his mother to the table, he helped her sit in her usual chair. Shenma stoked the fire in the hearth and put some water to boil. Raftennon took a seat next to his mother, letting his pack fall to the floor beside him.

"You look good, my son," Melna whispered, fighting to keep the smile on her face to hide a wince, its source still unclear to the wizard.

"And you have seen better days."

Shenma whirled around, not believing the gall her brother now possessed. A quick, tired glance from her mother kept her from snapping, however. Raftennon was right; her health had declined dramatically since his last visit from the Guild.

"We've had some hard years as of late," Melna said, barely

loud enough for the pair in the room to hear.

"You should have sent word," Raftennon reprimanded his mother. "I would have done what I could to help."

"You should have asked!" Shenma could not keep hold of her tongue any longer. The hurt and rage she felt for her brother's dismissal of his family during his apprenticeship finally burst from her heart and erupted from her lips. "When was the last time you even wrote?"

Raftennon bent his head in shame. He could not remember when he sent his last correspondence or what it contained. His learning shadowed everything else in his life, replacing his memories with thoughts of the future. His sister had a right to be angry with him. "I apologize for that. My studies take much of my time. However, I am here now, as I have said. Please tell me what has happened."

A dark cloud seemed to fall on the room, darkening it even further, as the two women lowered their gaze to the floor. Raftennon sat, unmoving, waiting for them to gather themselves. After a moment, Shenma broke down in tears and bolted from the room. His mother raised her head to peer into his eyes.

"A few years ago, I guess it was five—no, four, Shenma had just turned eighteen. That young lad living down the street, Davin, had just gotten the nerve to approach your father to get his blessing to propose to your sister." Melna trailed off, trying to gain a grip on her emotions. She blotted away tears with a dirty handkerchief before continuing. "Anyway, that's not what you asked me to tell you. The boys went out to sea as they did every morning. As soon as they unfurled the sails, a violent gust of wind blew from the east and hurtled them to the ocean."

She lost her composure and hunched forward, bursting into tears. Raftennon needed to strain his ears to catch what his mother said through her sobs. "I saw them leave. I started going to the docks to see them off like you did when you were just a boy. I suppose I sort of took your place after you left. One second they were fine, the next they were rushing into the high waves. Your father...your brothers...they were all gone! I couldn't see the boat as..."

Raftennon leaned forward and took his trembling mother into his arms. He said nothing for a while, concentrating on comforting her. She finally pushed herself away from her son, somewhat calmed.

"Your older sisters then, one by one, left town with their husbands." Melna shook her head as she recounted the destruction of her family. "Ezranalla and Gendan rushed their wedding plans, and they too are gone. It's just Shenma and me now. She turned down that nice boy so she could take care of me."

"Tell me of their families. Any nieces or nephews I need to visit and spoil?" Raftennon interjected before she continued, hoping the change of topic would cheer her. It did. They spent the rest of the evening talking about the letters she received describing the antics of said nieces and nephews. Raftennon promised to visit them someday soon.

While the night was still young, Raftennon led his mother to her room. The suffering she endured surprised him. She was in her midlife, granted, but even Tullae, the oldest man to ever live in the village as far as anyone could recall, was never so sickly. She should have lived more than another decade before this kind of weakness even hinted at threatening her.

Only when her breathing reached the even rhythm of deep sleep did Raftennon leave her bedroom door. He sought out his sister, finding her in the family room, mending a few dresses. "She has suffered greatly," he commented, sitting in the chair his father had favoured. He rubbed the wooden armrests, reliving many fond memories as Shenma put her work aside.

"It was a huge blow to all of us." She struggled to keep new tears at bay, taking a deep breath to steady her voice. "Blendalla left immediately afterwards, not able to stay in town anymore. She was lucky to find a good husband who was willing to take her away quickly from all of it. The others were quick to follow her example."

"You chose to remain." This was half question, half statement, for the mage felt confident he knew his sister's heart, even if it had been years since they last saw each other. But he still needed to hear it from her.

"Look at her, Raf!" she gestured to the closed door of their mother's room. "She needs someone to take care of her! When the boys died at sea, so did her soul! Someone has to make sure her body didn't follow!"

"Do you resent your predicament?" She skirted his unspoken question, so he came out and asked. His eyes conveyed his apologies for his doubt and for the situation his absence put the young woman in. "I hear you attracted a suitor. You should have your own family to tend."

"I love Mother."

"As do I. You could have still married."

"Not to Davin." Shenma stared down at the stitching she had resumed, the harsh pulls on the needle showing her frustration. "He didn't want the extra burden. He avoided the house because he didn't want to see Mother moping about. He made me choose between them. The choice was very easy to make. And it's the same choice I will continue to make until Mother gets well."

"I am glad she has you, little sister," Raftennon said after a short pause. He started to rise from the chair but stopped mere inches off the seat when Shenma looked at him more seriously than she had ever done. This was the moment he realized his baby sister had grown to adulthood and he missed all of it.

"You're not planning on staying, are you?" She held the dress on her lap, her deep brown eyes conveying the seriousness of the question. She was not reproaching him for any decision he may make, but she was making it clear she did not want him to patronize her in any way.

"I will remain for a while," Raftennon said, not able to help himself from sugarcoating the situation a little bit, "but yes, I will return to the Guild to continue my studies."

"Are you any good?" Shenma expressed conflicting emotions; all at once, she was a grown woman who toiled day in and day out to provide for others and the little girl he remembered, eager to see magnificent things.

Raftennon gave her a slight smile and rummaged in his robes. He took out a handful of grey powder from a hidden pouch, speaking what Shenma considered gibberish as he did so. "*Minalôren flaymmanüllüm wortellômen!*" The mage threw the dust into the air, causing colourful blasts of light to erupt inches over his hand.

The simple spell pleased her immensely, which made Raftennon loathe even more what he needed to ask next. He knew it would dampen her spirits again, but it was necessary. "I need to know more about the day the wind bore our brothers and father out to sea."

Shenma returned the dress she was working on to the basket, lacing her fingers on her lap. "I knew you would. But there's not much more I can tell you. I wasn't there. I was here, helping with breakfast. Mother told us a freak storm caught them and dragged them to the ocean. There was no way they survived. No one comes back from the Elbatu Sea."

That was common knowledge in Yentrill, but Raftennon had learned this was untrue. The villagers simply did not have the ships required to withstand the waves to reach the far regions where the surface of the water was calmer. Even if other memories of his time with Jennalla overshadowed all others, he still remembered all their conversations. This was not the time to educate his sister, however. Instead, Raftennon went to her and knelt before her, taking her hands in his before she could reach for another garment to mend. He required her full attention.

"Mother said the gust came from the east to blow them westward."

"Yeah, that's what she said happened." The perplexed expression on her face showed him she did not understand his statement.

"Does not a westward wind get caught in Entamman Forest?" The mage spoke softly, almost to himself.

"What's your point?" Shenma still did not know what her brother was implying. She was also getting agitated, having to relive the events that reduced their family by more than half.

Raftennon returned his attention to her, his new thought making his heart beat the slightest bit faster. "If a wind was coming from the east, or the north for that matter, the trees would have stymied most of its force. That is why the air currents we receive here come from over the bay or from Emnecron. Any natural gusts should have blown the ship back to the shore, if it were possible for them to gain enough strength—which it is not."

"You're saying this wasn't an accident?" She could not fathom what he was trying to tell her.

Raftennon did not try to convince her further. Instead, he turned the conversation down a more productive path. "Tell me everything out of the ordinary you can remember happening shortly before the accursed day."

"Nothing happened out of the ordinary." She was still reeling from the fact the loss of the family boat and its crew was not natural. "We just finished mourning the passing of the old hermit —"

"Tullae is dead?" the mage interrupted. This return home was quickly becoming the worst thing that had happened to him, far worse than giving up his first love. He was afraid his calm demeanour would soon crack and he would be unable to stop the flood of tears that threatened to burst from his eyes.

"I'm sorry, Raf." The pity on her face showed him the stoic mask he thought he wore was not as opaque as he would have liked. "I know you were close. He died peacefully in his sleep if it's any consolation to you."

It surprised the young wizard that fact did ease his sorrow just the slightest bit.

"Anyway," she continued, "that was the major event before… you know…"

Shenma trailed off, fighting another assault of sobs. This time, she pressed the index and thumb of her left hand to her eyes to prevent the outburst that would have surely lasted the rest of the night. "It's been a trying time for Mother, losing nearly everyone that was close to her all at once." Her control over her emotions slowly became more secure. She removed her fingers from her eyes and stared at the floor. Suddenly, her gaze shot up to the front door.

"What is it?" inquired Raftennon, having heard nothing from that direction. Then he saw the pensive expression dominating his sister's face.

"There was something else," Shenma eventually said, her mind still envisioning what she was about to relate, "just the day before the accident, or whatever it was."

"Go on," Raftennon encouraged after a few moments of silence as she contemplated what she was going to say.

"I was washing dishes when a knock came at the door," Shenma finally began. "Ezra answered it and I heard her talking to a woman. She was asking about you, wondering if you had returned here. Ezra told her you were still at the Guild, doing extremely well as far as we knew. Then she asked if you ever mentioned her."

"Who was she?" Raftennon asked, already suspecting the answer.

"I didn't catch her name, but I came over and looked out the door. She had long red hair and the most stunning green eyes I ever saw."

A lump caught in Raftennon's throat, vivid images of his first love invading his mind.

"Anyway," Shenma broke his reverie, "when Ezra said you hadn't mentioned her—which you didn't—she turned around and stormed down the street. What did you do to her to make her so angry?"

Raftennon shook his head in disbelief. Their relationship, though extremely enjoyable, had ended many years ago. Surely Jennalla no longer held a grudge against him. The mage sighed before giving his sister an answer. "I did not place her first among my priorities," he said, looking out the window to a far-off past.

"Would she be capable of doing it? I mean, is she strong enough to summon wind like that?" Shenma leaned forward in her seat and stared into her brother's eyes. "Could you really anger someone so much to push her to…?"

Raftennon did not have the answers to these questions, especially the unfinished one. When they parted, Jennalla did possess the power to cast such a spell. But a long time had past since then and only she knew the depth of her resentment.

Raftennon remained with his mother and sister for three more days, then prepared to journey northward to Jennalla's hometown. He made this decision while rummaging through his things after his conversation with Shenma that first night.

He perused the scrolls Vendrammon gave him and found a handful of offensive spells, as well as more defensive ones, to complement his existing repertoire. There was even a copy of the spell Jennalla could have cast to control the wind. With these incantations, Raftennon felt he possessed the means to subdue her, so he shelved his initial plan of returning to the Guild to muster more strength before facing her. The young mage spent every evening, after his family retired for the night, memorizing the new spells until he felt adequately ready.

"Do you really have to go?" his mother pleaded as he placed his possessions into his pack.

"Listen carefully to me, Mother." Raftennon left his packing, led his mother to a chair and gently sat her down. "I believe Father and my brothers were murdered to hurt me."

Melna stared at him intently, not understanding her son's reasoning. Shenma scowled at her brother for telling her this. Their frail mother did not need these events to resurface. Raftennon ignored his sister's baleful glare and continued.

"Someone cast a spell to send them to the sea. I am almost certain the caster is the one I set aside to further my studies."

"You're a nice boy, Raftennon," his mother told him, patting his hand as she did, "but you don't have to take this burden onto your shoulders."

"It was never yours to carry, Mother, yet you do so still." He grabbed her hands and held them in his. "I will confront her and find the truth. You need not worry any longer."

"You're a nice boy," she repeated.

"Mother." Raftennon's stern tone caught and kept her attention. He stared into her eyes, ensuring his words were getting through to her. "I hurt someone and she decided to inflict her retribution on my loved ones. I will set things as right as is possible."

"I don't want to lose my last son," she whimpered, her lower lip quivering with every syllable. A lone tear fell from her eye and quickly disappeared into one of the many creases on her face.

"You will not," Raftennon reassured her in a soft voice. "I was chosen to apprentice under the most powerful spellcaster in the land. Very few can claim to have that privilege; and according to my Master, I was one of his best." The young mage did not like to boast like this, but he needed to reassure her. "And by Shenma's account of what happened to our family, I know I spent more years learning my craft than the woman responsible for the tragedy did. I will not fall to her."

"There's been enough life lost over this," his mother continued to plead, a second tear travelling down the cracks on her skin.

"I do not intend to slay her," Raftennon comforted the woman. He was not certain what he intended to do once he found Jennalla. A part of him screamed for the opposite, to make her pay for what she did to his family. His heart still held a special place for her, however, and only wanted to discover the motives for her actions. He would have to wait to see her eyes, feel the soul hidden behind them, to find out which desire would overcome all others.

Raftennon reached out a hand and gently placed it against his mother's cheek. "I will be fine, Mother."

She smiled at her son, freeing her hands to wipe the tears from her face.

"I do have a request of you," the magic-user said to her.

"There is not much this old body can do anymore," she answered him, looking down at her wrinkled hands as they gently smoothed the folds out of her dress, "but if I can manage it, I will."

"You suffer much more than you ought to, Mother, and it is all because of the guilt you thrust onto your shoulders." Raftennon placed his hands onto said shoulders and gave them a squeeze. "Let all of it go. None of it is your fault.

"Mother," he made certain he had her undivided attention before continuing. "I want you to live."

9

A SLIGHT DELAY

Raftennon travelled in a northwesterly direction along the western edge of Entamman Forest. After consulting the two maps in the scantly stocked village elder's home—and listening to said elder's generous, yet uninvited, advice—Raftennon felt this course would save him the most time. Certainly, using the road that ran through the Salgre Hills from the border town of Ednifad to Jennalla's hometown of Bezna would have been the easiest path to take. Unfortunately, that plan meant adding weeks of travel to a journey that was already years overdue. The magic-user wanted the answers to his questions as soon as he could get them.

So the mage decided to take the more direct route, circling the forest's western tip before heading almost due north across the Hills. The rolling lands, according to the maps, were mostly grassy knolls with a few clusters of elm or birch. Some of the mounds were higher than most, but their sides rose gradually enough one did not need tools to climb them. Raftennon felt certain, despite his less-than-athletic youth, he could manage the ascents.

After kissing his mother and sister goodbye, the spellcaster began his journey under an oppressive sky. The grey clouds hung low over the lands, threatening to release their tears. The rain held off for a day, but the overall gloominess still bore down on Raftennon's saddened spirit. He begrudged this trip, but he had to know how deep Jennalla's scars ran.

The second day began a week of showers. The first four nights of his trek Raftennon slept under the protection of the trees of Entamman. Walking along the woodland's border, he would venture a little into the elms and the birches to make camp. On the fifth day, he reached the westernmost tree and turned toward the north, leaving the woods behind. That night he spent huddled up in a tight ball, having no tent to shelter him. He also could not light a fire to warm himself. All the scant scraps of wood he found were drenched through.

The next afternoon, the soggy grass under his feet began to rise. So rapt in his musings and continued mental recitations of the new spells he was learning, the newly-released apprentice did not even notice the change in terrain. Only after rising and descending the third hill did Raftennon finally realize he was in the land of Salgre. There was a slight tightening in his stomach as the apprehension of the impending meeting came to the forefront of his thoughts. He did not know what to expect, and that frightened him. Over the years, Vendrammon taught him to control his environment. Now, there were too many unknown factors he needed to learn about before he could even think about using them to his advantage.

After another two days of trudging through wet grass and softened earth, the sun finally reclaimed its reign in the sky and brightened the world. Raftennon's demeanour remained subdued. It seemed the clouds left the heavens only to enter his spirit. Try as he might to feel remorse for his choice all those years ago, he could not do so. Vendrammon was right to take him away from all the distractions. Raftennon now felt he would have succumbed to the weakness of the teen libido and would have destroyed any chance of attaining all that he had up to date. Jennalla and he were alike in many ways—or so he had thought. Why did she not understand his decision? Would she not have done the same?

On the first evening after the rain, Raftennon reached a clump of ash wood, nestled between two high hills. He slung his pack to the ground and set up camp. After a week of drenched nights, he finally found some dry twigs to light a fire and ate a properly cooked meal. The mage was preparing to lie down for the night when the depression flash flooded with movement. Before Raftennon knew what was happening, two figures jumped over his dying campfire and another hit him over the head from behind. The last image he saw before unconsciousness took him was the crooked smile of an unkempt man.

Raftennon woke the next morning with a splitting headache. He began to raise a hand to his temple but found his wrists tied together behind his back. Turning his head added to his pain— and dejection. His bindings were tethered to a spike driven into the earth beside the boulder he was leaning on. Closing his eyes, he tried to will away the throbbing between his temples. That brought only meagre relief, however, which the wizard believed he imagined rather than actually accomplished.

Movement to his right returned the mage's attention to his current predicament. He was in a camp of about a dozen tents. The shelters were bedraggled and offered little protection from the elements. Large holes punctured some of the canvases. Badly sewn patches barely covered the other defects. Their occupants were beginning to emerge from them, five or six per structure, each grumbling at another day of hardship, it seemed. Raftennon's breath caught in his throat when he realized what they were, though his outward demeanour did not show an ounce of his surprise.

Their faces ended in short snouts with orange-brown whiskers that formed a goatee under their black noses. Their equally black eyes were small and sunken into deep depressions under protruding brows. Long manes of strangely orange-coloured hair started at the top of their round heads, leaving the front half of their skull completely bald. The locks flowed down until they merged with the hair that entirely covered their backs, as well as the arms down to the elbows. Long, pointed ears twitched at every sound, sending the long tendrils of hair at their tips flailing to and fro. Long, yellowed fangs protruded from their lower jaws, flanking their snouts. Some had two of these tusks while others possessed as much as six, all ranging in length from stubs to daggers twice their muzzles' height. Crude tattoos of unrecognizable symbols decorated their hairless chests, as well as the equally bare forearms. Their loincloths were as filthy as their bodies, their feet as hairy as their back. They called themselves kroykl and were, as a rule, a vicious and sadistic people.

While Raftennon marvelled at the beasts he had only read about, the flap of the largest tent—which was also in better re-pair than the others—swept open and out strolled a filthy human. Of above-average height and muscular build, he was as dirty as the kroykl. The soil that covered his body hid all his features, turning the colour of his skin and hair the same matted brown. If the mage had had the privilege of travelling the world before his studies, he would have immediately recognized the distinct char-acteristics of the Plainsmen of the North. As it were, it took a few moments for Raftennon to put together the relevance of the chiselled features in his face and the broadness of his shoulders.

The man scratched his side through his dingy tunic as he walked toward the spellcaster to kneel before him. "Well, well, our guest is awake," he said before spitting off to the side.

Raftennon stared at the brute, studying him. He kept control of himself, not showing any sign the man's foul odour sickened him.

"What are you doing in my hills?"

Raftennon continued to scrutinize the ruffian, still unable to get a clean read on the man. It was apparent he preferred to im-pose his will on others, force them to do his bidding. What Raftennon wanted to know was the reason behind his actions, and what he expected of him.

"I was merely passing through to a destination that is none of your concern," the wizard answered, using a tone that clearly conveyed he would not be bullied into revealing anything he did not want to share.

The man burst out in laughter, first pointing to his comrades, then to his prisoner. "Do you hear that, boys?" the plainsman shouted at the kroykl so every one of them would turn to follow this conversation—another bullying tactic, Raftennon assumed. "What he's doing in my hills is none of my concern."

The brute stood and shot his leg out in a wide arc, striking his captive on the jaw. Raftennon blinked away the stars that began to form in his eyes and struggled to remain alert. The bestial henchmen mirrored their leader's mirth, glad he had another target for his rage.

The plainsman crouched down once again, grasping the magician's chin in a grubby hand to regain his attention. "I am Stav," he said slowly, making sure the prisoner was getting every syllable, "and these are *my* hills. Everything that happens in them concerns me."

"Very well." Raftennon did not feel like arguing with this wretch. There was no reason to keep his destination a secret. He did not even try to free himself from the filthy fingers. "I am on my way to Bezna to visit an old friend."

Stav released his captive's chin and crouched in front of him, an evil smiled forming on his lips. The wizard continued to glare in defiance, the ruffian's obvious attempt at intimidation having no effect on him. "Why didn't you take the road?"

"This route was faster," Raftennon replied, his tone conveying the plainsman should have known this fact.

Stav caught the sarcasm immediately. The corners of his mouth inched their way downward, his brow furrowed as his growing anger transformed his face. "But this route has a price." The smile slowly returned, but his eyes did not mirror the sign of happiness. Instead, they glinted of hatred and malice.

"I do not have much," Raftennon said, the brigand's expression failing to unnerve him in the slightest.

"We know. We've already been through your bags." Stav nodded to his right, showing his captive where his pack lay empty on the ground, all its contents sprawled around it. Most of the pouches containing his spell components were open, some of the lighter ingredients fluttering away in the slight breeze. The wizard returned his gaze to the ruffian, keeping the curses he wanted to utter to himself.

"So," Stav continued, ignoring the fire in his captive's eyes, "since you can't pay the tribute, you'll be staying with us for a little while. Maybe we'll find a way for you to work off your debt."

The plainsman stood and loomed over the magic-user for a few moments before turning to leave. As he did so, he kicked some sand into Raftennon's face, a final act of debasement. The mage did not flinch, not giving the man the satisfaction he sought.

For the rest of the day, the band of brigands ignored the prisoner. Raftennon continued to sit by the boulder, tethered as he was. He watched the kroykl devour a crude breakfast before scattering to the four winds, presumably out to find more victims. Even Stav went out, leaving only one henchman in the entire camp to guard him. The creature never even glanced in his direction.

Raftennon winced every time one of his spell components flew away in the breeze, his heart wrenching as they disappeared, never to be retrieved. To his surprise, a small figure he had not noticed before sprang from his hiding place and scurried after his departing things. The captive mage looked on as the stranger returned whatever components he managed to catch. The little man was barely over three feet tall, his pointed, dark brown beard reaching his belt buckle. His piercing, green eyes flittered about, noticing every one of the mage's possessions as they moved about the campground. Nearly as slender as a tree branch, he was clad in bright red leggings and a green vest over a white tunic. His clothes, including the light blue hat covering his head, were immaculate, unlike the rags the other beings in the settlement wore.

The small man looked up from his work and stared at the prisoner.

"A gnome," Raftennon marvelled. What was he doing here? Why was the kroykl not springing on the little fellow to capture him?

Before the mage could call out to him, he scampered away with all of Raftennon's belongings.

The thieves returned as the sun began to disappear behind the western horizon. They continued to ignore the wizard, so much so Raftennon started wondering if they intended to let him die of starvation. Only when the gnome came and brought him a bite to eat after the last ruffian scampered into his tent for the night did the spellcaster stop thinking about that slow and inevitable death.

"Thank you," Raftennon said between bites as the gnome fed

him. He was unable to do it himself since his hands were still bound behind his back. "What is your name?"

The gnome kept his gaze down at the bowl of stew he was holding, clearly uncomfortable. Raftennon did not blame him. If he lived in such a place, he would not trust anyone either.

"You need not worry, friend," the mage tried to assuage the gnome's fears. "Have you been ordered not to speak to me?"

The gnome remained silent, fidgeting with the empty bowl on his lap as he knelt before the captive, his eyes downcast.

"I understand," the mage said in the most reassuring tone he could muster. "I was simply wondering what a gnome was doing with this band of ruffians."

"I'm a fool," the gnome whispered so softly the magic-user was unsure he heard the words or if he imagined them.

"What do you mean?" Raftennon ventured the question, not understanding his server's meaning. "Do you regret the fashion in which you were captured?"

"Yes, I do regret that." The gnome wrung his hands as he kept whispering so low it was difficult to hear. "But I was referring to the job I've been reduced to. In exchange for my continued existence, I have to entertain this gang of animals. I am their jester." Intense loathing filled his last words. The gnome added something else under his breath, in a language Raftennon did not recognize (he had become quite the linguist during his tenure at the Guild, but this particular dialect was not among the handful he knew).

"I am sorry."

"I don't want your pity," the gnome growled, getting to his feet. "You may find yourself in a similar predicament if they find some use for you. If they don't, or you refuse to cooperate, they'll surely kill you."

"Not if we escape."

The gnome stared at the mage, not believing the man actually thought his idea was possible. His expression conveyed his belief those brutes had clonked the spellcaster on the head much harder than he first thought. "You can't escape them," he explained, making certain the prisoner was grasping the meaning of his words. "I used to try when I first got here. I learned pretty quickly that these vermin travel extremely fast over these hills.

You can't outrun them."

"We may not have to, if my hands were free and I had the proper spell components."

The gnome checked over his shoulder to assure himself they were still alone, which they were. He hurried to the wizard's side and crouched. Leaned toward the captive, he whispered with even lower volume than before. "Those things I was gathering up earlier today?"

"Yes," Raftennon responded in kind, leaning forward himself. "I would need to inventory what was not lost in the wind to discern which options are left to me. Above all, I must be untethered."

The gnome shifted from one bent leg to the other, clearly doubting the hope of any escape plan. "And you think you can get out of here with all that...junk?" He grimaced at the last word.

It became apparent to the mage the small man sampled some of the items after retrieving them. Raftennon struggled to keep the corners of his mouth from lifting at the sight of the jester choking on some of the more acrid roots he held in his many pouches.

"I am certain of it," the magic-user managed to say with conviction, and without any trace of amusement.

The gnome stared at him for long moments, a battle clearly waging within him. His mind calculated the risks. His heart fought with itself to determine if he should trust this stranger. All the while, his skin and muscles reminded him of what would befall them if they happened to fail.

"If I help you...," the gnome finally said, but trailed off, not daring to continue the question.

"I will take you away from here," Raftennon vowed, guessing his unspoken request.

A sound came from one of the tents and the gnome scurried away, clearly afraid of the consequences he would face if caught talking with the prisoner. Raftennon did not blame him, but he hoped he would come to agree to help him.

10

A Captive's Worth

The wizard did not see the gnome even once the next day, but he did receive a visit from Stav. The leader of the brigands came over a little after midday, the bright sun lending its heat to augment his bad odour. He sat down beside the magic-user as if he were joining a friend for polite conversation.

"Just how good are you at magic?" the thug casually asked, as if that were a question he posed anyone he happened to pass by during his excursion out of the camp.

"What do you want from me?" Raftennon wanted to get straight to the point. A severe distaste for the man overtook the mage shortly after they met. The first kick had steered his opinion in that direction while the second ensured he did not change his mind.

"I want to know if you'll be of any use to me," the plainsman continued in his nonchalant manner. He picked up two pebbles and began rolling them around between his thick fingers. The man was quite nimble, able to make the stones seem like they floated across his hand. With a quick flick of the wrist, he made one of them disappear. Only when one of the kroykl, a good twenty paces away, yelped and grabbed for an ankle while hopping on the other foot did Raftennon realize what the ruffian did with the missing stone.

"If you knew anything about spellcasters," Raftennon turned

his head to gaze into the dirt-rimmed eyes, showing the man how little his intimidation was working, "you would know we never reveal how powerful we are. Surprise is one of our greatest weapons."

"Of course I know that." Just in case his irritation at the magician's defiance was not apparent in the tone of his voice, Stav raised the hand holding the stone up to the mage's face. He squeezed for a few moments until both men heard the soft crack. The plainsman then opened his hand to let the two halves of the pebble fall to the ground. He then pushed his next words out between clenched teeth, so they were as sharp as the breaking stone. "But if you don't give me an answer, I'll assume you're no good to me and not worth keeping around."

Raftennon shifted his position, turning the rest of his body toward the ruffian to face him squarely. The restraints stretched to their limits, but the mage ignored the rope digging into the flesh of his wrists. A devilish grin formed on the spellcaster's lips as his bright brown eyes bore into the thief's dark eyes. "I invite you to slay me," Raftennon whispered, daring the brute to strike him by leaning forward and lifting his chin, exposing his throat.

Stav thrust his hand out as quickly as a viper strikes at its prey, clamping it around the magic-user's windpipe in the time it took to blink an eye. Raftennon tried to gasp, but no air came to his lungs. Stav's eyes shone with the realization he had taken his prisoner by surprise, relishing the feeling of superiority that coursed through his entire being. "Don't think I won't, mage," the plainsman spat, keeping his captive's face mere inches from his own. Raftennon gagged from the putrid odour of sweat and grime, despite the fact inhaling was impossible. "If you think I believe those wives' tales about the curse that befalls those who kill wizards, think again.

"Now, I'll ask again, but it'll be the last time, so don't waste any more of my time! We've lasted this long without someone with your gift, so we will have no problem with continuing to do so. Now tell me how good you are!"

The large plainsman released his vice-like grip on the young mage's windpipe. Raftennon gulped in as much air as he could, replenishing his empty lungs. His blurred vision returned to normal, the hatred for his captor radiating from his watering eyes. "I am but a newly-graduated apprentice."

"So you are worthless to me. You probably still stumble over your words."

Raftennon ignored the ruffian's mocking laugh and cleared his throat before continuing in a soft voice. *"Illimünisôl vindremôn*—Believe what you will."

The spellcaster studied Stav as he blinked a few times in confusion. If things were happening as he hoped, his voice had started to weave in and out of the plainsman's ears, each syllable more distant than the preceding one, each word more dreamlike. The only sure way to know if this was working was to continue.

"Illimünsalôn rengémenay—You do have a powerful mage in your midst."

The brigand stumbled to his feet, seemingly light-headed. From the stare his captor gave him, Raftennon knew the man still possessed enough sense to know he was being influenced. He also still had the presence of mind to get away before he lost complete control of himself.

Stav staggered toward his tent, never looking back, not giving his captive the chance to finish his enchantment. He was beginning to believe he was underestimating the man and vowed to rectify the situation in the morning. As he reached his humble pavilion, he felt his head clearing. Yes, he would rid himself of all worries as soon as the sun came up. The prisoner would die before he had the opportunity to bewitch him fully. For now, he would lie down and make certain he alone controlled his thoughts.

A soft rustling from the brush surrounding the camp caught his attention. The plainsman whirled around, intending to tear off the intruder's head. What he found struck him like a club to the stomach. A strange man stood amid the trees, the wind ruffling the hem of his black robes. His face remained hidden in the shadows of his hood, his posture unaffected by the approach of one of Stav's men. In fact, the kroykl did not even seem to know the trespasser was there.

The gang leader prepared to shout at his inept sentry but

stopped when something moved beside him. He turned, facing in the direction he just came from to see the smile on the captive wizard's lips widen. Stav stared at him, wondering what made the whelp so mirthful. Had the man managed to get inside his head after all? The plainsman felt more himself now than he did moments ago, so it had to be something else. That only left—

Stav whirled back to glare into the sparse forest that hid his gang's hideout. The apparition was no longer there. Frantically, he scanned the woods, standing still so as to appear as if nothing was amiss. The kroykl continued its rounds, still unaware someone was out there, somewhere. The hairy ears pointed forward, intently listening to its surroundings. But they did not move to catch sounds where the intruder should have been, or gone to. No one could disappear into thin air like that.

The plainsman returned his attention to his captive. Could the newly-graduated apprentice have made this stranger appear? Was this the hex the magician cast on him? Instead of trying to control him, was he meant to see things that were not there?

Stav told himself it did not matter. Come sunrise, he would deal with all his worries.

11

ATTEMPTED ESCAPE

The mage continued to stare at his captor as he flung the flap of his tent out of his way and stormed in. Raftennon was surprised his suggestion affected the plainsman so thoroughly. There was still another line to recite to complete the spell and have total control over his target. It lightened his heart to know it would be that easy to persuade the ruffian magically. It would help immensely in his escape. The spellcaster was now convinced he would come out of this predicament with his life. His newfound excitement kept sleep away.

Before Raftennon managed to nod off, but after the thieves were asleep in the rags they used for bedrolls, the gnome returned. The magic-user examined the small man as he approached, evaluating the slight swelling around his right eye and five new, circular bruises forming on his neck. It was clear the brute got over the implanted suggestion and made his jester pay for it. The gnome placed the mage's pack before him.

"You're sure you can get us out of here?" he asked in the usual hushed voice.

"Like I said before, it depends on what you salvaged," Raftennon again answered in kind.

The gnome opened the bag and tilted it so the wizard could take stock of its contents. After a few moments, the spellcaster nodded in approval. Half his components were gone, but there was still enough with which to work. "I can orchestrate an escape with these."

"But they will follow," the gnome grumbled. He did not appear to be afraid of the prospect, but more enraged at its inevitability.

Raftennon smiled. The jester glared, no doubt believing the mage was laughing at him. The magic-user had no idea what brought on this animosity, but he chose to ignore it. His mind was already plotting their escape from start to finish. "I certainly hope so," he whispered, still grinning.

"Okay, listen here, you fool," the gnome scolded the captive, almost forgetting himself and raising his voice. Fortunately, he lowered his tone to a hush before he managed to wake anyone. He also yanked the spellcaster's pack away from his face and closed it while returning it to his side. "If you think I'm going to follow you on a suicidal attempt at freedom, you're dead wrong! I won't risk my life for some half-baked scheme!"

"I assure you, my friend, I will not gamble your life. I would never ask you to jeopardize more than you were willing of your own volition."

"Are you calling me a coward?" The gnome was losing his temper, and forgetting the need to whisper.

"You are clearly a man who would do anything to survive," Raftennon explained, not wanting to lose this opportunity for escape. "That is a trait I can admire, as long as it does not include harming an innocent in the process. In the particular situation I now find myself in, you are but a mere bystander and should not suffer for my actions. For this reason, I will ensure your continued well-being. Come with me and your captors will no longer be of any concern. I give you my word."

The gnome stared at the wizard, his green eyes shooting to the shambles of a camp and back in indecision. He clearly did not like the prospect of putting his life in the hands of a total stranger. But surely he could see it was a much better alternative to staying in this prison.

When the gnome's determined gaze returned to the prisoner, he nodded his ascent and shuffled to the mage's back to begin untying his restraints. The gnome kept glancing to the tents as he worked, fearing a flap would fly open and one of their captors would discover them before they had a chance to even stand, let alone start running.

"You said you want them to follow us," the gnome whispered when he finished untying the last knot. He picked up the pack and handed it to the spellcaster, but did not let it go. Instead, he locked his eyes on the wizard's. "What are you planning?"

Raftennon's smile returned. He had something special waiting for the ruffians, something that would ensure their escape.

A couple of hours after the sun came up, Stav exited his tent and stretched the night's tightness from his limbs. Looking over to the boulder, he saw the magician sitting in the same spot he had been for the past few days, his head slumped forward. The long brown hair hung over his face, hiding his features. The gang leader motioned for one of the kroykl to go over and wake the mage. It was time for dying, not sleeping.

The henchman went over to the prisoner and grunted at him. When there was no respond, the beast thrust a crusty foot at his chest. The blue robes crumpled under the blow, falling into an empty heap.

After watching all this unfold, Stav ran up to the unbelievable sight and hurled the cloth away. All that remained of the wizard was a small mound of brown dust.

"What did you do?" the plainsman screamed, shoving the kroykl to the ground.

"I do what say!" the creature responded, snarling up at the human but choosing to remain seated in the dirt.

Stav repaid the insolence by drawing the long knife from its sheath affixed to the small of his back and hurling it into the kroykl's throat. It gurgled its last breath before slumping down to the earth in a growing puddle of black blood.

The plainsman began to return to his tent, leaving his weapon protruding from his former lackey's jugular, but a grunt caught his attention. Another kroykl hunched over the spot the captive had occupied, lifting a handful of grass to its snout.

"What did you find?" Stav hurried back to the scene of the disappearance. The tone of his voice warned the creature not to waste his time with any nonsense.

"Tracks. Medium an' small. Go dat way." The henchman pointed northward, its tiny, black eyes following the trail until the footprints disappeared into the thicket surrounding the camp. Stav, because of his long life with the kroykl, knew what it meant by the mention of the tracks' sizes. Small prints belonged to dwarves, gnomes, goblins, or other short races. These little tracks sprinting into the trees were clearly left by their jester. Medium footprints referred to beings of average height: humans, elves, and kroykl among others.

Stav bent down and examined the trails. Both were boot prints. Since the kroykl always went barefoot and he was the only human roaming freely in the hills, he knew exactly to whom these particular medium-sized tracks belonged.

"Gather the band, we're going after them!" The plainsman turned to return to his tent, already envisioning what he would do to the pair once he retrieved them.

"Why?" The tracker got to its feet and turned toward the human. "Dey no much use to us."

The kroykl hopped backward when the big man whirled on his heels. The fire in his eyes foretold a lesson in discipline that would make the last one seem mild in comparison. Stav snarled at his henchman but decided he would kill it after the gnome and the wizard were dead. "Get them!" he ordered through clenched teeth.

It took fifteen minutes to muster all the primitive kroykl, for they needed little preparation. Essentially, all they had to do was pick up their weapon and they were ready to go.

Stav sent his best pair of trackers ahead to lead the search. He followed close behind, with the rest of the pack close on his heels. The small copse of trees that surrounded the camp soon fell away behind them as they began the descent into the first valley. The sun shone down on the column of dark beings scurrying like ants up and down the slopes of the hills. As midday approached, they neared a thick cluster of aspen wood. Stav ordered a stop to consult his "hounds."

"Dey go in tree," conveyed the older of the pair, pointing a clawed finger into the heart of the thicket.

Stav directed his two trackers, with half of the crew, to split into two groups. They were to circumvent the patch of aspen, in either direction, searching for the point where the escaped prisoners exited the cover of the trees. Once they found the tracks, they were to call for the others to join them to continue the pursuit. If they met up on the opposite side before finding signs of exiting prints, they would send a different signal. Both halves of the gang would then enter the wooded patch to flush out the escapees. While the scouting troops made their way around the copse, Stav ordered his remaining men to fan out. Then they waited.

After an expectant half hour, the guttural whistle rang out in the otherwise still afternoon. Stav motioned his men to advance and entered the grove with them. The thieves inched their way forward, making sure the gnome or the wizard did not pass through their net as it got smaller. Eventually, the ring became so tight the kroykl began to walk in two separate ranks. Shortly afterwards, they reached the centre of the cluster and found their quarry.

Raftennon stood between two aspens as if waiting for a companion to arrive for a predetermined meeting. The gnome crouched behind the mage's left leg, glaring at his former captor. With his small arms folded over his chest, the jester stared down the plainsman, wordlessly daring him to try reclaiming his prisoners.

"Well, well, well! There's nowhere else to run!" Stav continued to approach them, brandishing his long knife, not phased by the confidence his quarry was exhibiting.

"Never did we run, Stav," Raftennon replied, keeping his hands hidden within the folds of his dark-blue robes. A slight smirk found its way to his lips. "Frankly, I am surprised it took you so long to catch up to us. This is the third stop we have made, readying ourselves for your arrival."

The smug smile on the wizard's face made the plainsman's blood boil. The man's arrogance was unbelievable. Did he not know in how much trouble he was about to be? Stav snarled as he and his followers tightened the ring around their fugitives. "You won't be so cocky when my knife is sticking out of your scrawny neck!" the plainsman screamed, not liking the way the wizard was looking down on him.

Raftennon closed his eyes and began to mumble under his

breath. The gnome glanced up at the mage, quite worried about the large mob advancing toward them.

"Invéktussaylâmôs nyrôvénosilvanâllas rendrâmôrnân vend-laynorégaya krâthlissaürem!"

"What in Necroma are you jabbering about!" the gnome exclaimed, getting even more agitated.

Stav did not understand the words either, but had no time to react. The spellcaster opened his eyes and strong gusts of wind blew around him. His robes flapped wildly as the air surrounding him became more violent, more turbulent. The gnome clamped onto the magic-user's leg, desperate to save himself from the unnatural whirlwind.

Stav tried to maintain his footing in the intensifying maelstrom, but eventually the magical force of nature got the better of him. He flew into the massive trunk of the aspen directly to his left. His head slammed against the smooth bark, but the plainsman managed to stay conscious long enough to see his men suffer the same fate. Soon the whirlwind swept up the members of the ruffian band to crash every single one of them into the trees. A circle of falling aspens widened around the former captives. Scattered among the debris were unconscious, or lifeless, bodies. Stav battled the growing darkness to see where his captives intended to go after this, but he succumbed while the wind was still decimating his band of brigands.

12

REACHING THE COAST

They spent a week walking through the Salgre Hills, for the gnome was unaccustomed to long travel. During his captivity, he remained at camp when the others went out for their "foraging", as they called it, gradually losing any endurance he may have once possessed. Having short legs did not help either. Both of them felt confident the maelstrom had taken care of their pursuers, so Raftennon did not protest to the frequent stops his travelling companion requested along the way.

Escaping the carnage left by the artificial windstorm proved to be the most difficult part of the journey for the gnome, who soon introduced himself as Denmur. That was the only information the newly-freed man would give Raftennon. Gnomes were not indigenous to the region, and the little man dismissed any inquiries about his arrival. In fact, he refused to answer any questions about his past.

Their trek was coming to an end, as the last ridge fell behind them and the ocean loomed in front. A moderately sized town huddled on the land that formed the eastern edge of Glanduran Bay. Many one-story houses lined the shore while taller buildings radiated inland from the curve carved by the waters. Many large vessels were moored among the waves crashing against the thick pillars of wooden docks. These immense ships impressed Raftennon greatly, having never seen boats of such size. He kept his awe hidden, however, appearing to give them but a quick glance.

The pair reached the road that led southward, all the way to Xendremmar and beyond. Stepping onto the packed dirt, they ended their voyage northward as the sun began to burn into the sea. Denmur took the lead and guided the spellcaster through the busy streets of Bezna. Raftennon looked around through the throng of townspeople returning home for supper, taking in the layout of the community. He wondered how the gnome knew the town so well but decided not to ask. Chances were he would be as close about this subject as with all the others concerning his life.

The travellers made their way to an inn a few blocks away. It was not the best-kept establishment of the community—from what Raftennon had seen from the hillside coming in—but it was not as run down as the tavern the mage frequented with his tutor, Tullae, all those years ago. A wooden fish painted a bright green hung from a small pole, proudly announcing patrons were entering the Green Mackerel Inn.

Raftennon lost sight of Denmur as a group of already-tipsy drinkers bumped into him. He scanned the room for his travelling companion as the townspeople came in for a drink after a long workday. The magic-user spent only a moment on his futile search before making his way to the bar, certain the gnome would find him when he was ready. For the moment, he needed some information.

"Excuse me," Raftennon called for the barkeep. The young man tending drinks ignored the wizard, too busy filling the orders of the very same men who had collided with him. The spellcaster tried again several times before managing to get the man's attention.

As the bartender took a step in the magic-user's direction, a large, burly man shoved his way in front of Raftennon, barking his order.

"Excuse me, sir." Raftennon kept his growing irritation to himself, succeeding in controlling himself enough to give the patron's shoulder a gentle tap instead of the shove he deserved. "I believe I was here before you arrived."

The big man continued to ignore him, demanding the delivery

of his drink, which the barkeep was hurrying to pour.

"Sir, I was here ahead of you."

The stern tone of Raftennon's voice finally caught the rude patron's attention. The large man turned to face the pestering wizard. "You got a problem, buddy?" His deep voice thundered through the room, catching every ear's interest. Conversations began to hush but continued without interruption. The townsfolk were not going to stop what they were doing and waste their time if this little spat proved to be nothing. They kept a fraction of their focus on the proceedings, however, just in case matters escalated to something interesting.

"Yes," Raftennon said, ignoring the crowd around him. "You forced your way past me, instead of patiently waiting like everyone else."

Shocked silence flowed away from the pair like the ripples that formed on calm water when a falling stone disturbed the mirror-like surface. Soon, the entire establishment was looking at the strange sight. The larger man loomed a full head and shoulders over the spellcaster and was almost that much wider— from all angles of view. Though Raftennon's gaze did not leave the big man's face, he still managed to see the sidelong glances the townspeople were giving each other. He saw some shake their heads while others let their eyes display the pity they felt for him. Clearly they believed the mage was getting into trouble he could not handle.

"What did you say?" The stunned expression on the man's face making it clear he was unaccustomed to confrontation.

Raftennon stared up into the man's eyes, ignoring the silence around him. He was well aware of the weight of baited breath, but the patrons' thoughts were of no concern to him. He prepared himself for any sudden attack while showing the brute he would not be cowed.

"I simply mentioned the fact you had no right to push your way past me as you did." The magic-user's demeanour did not change one bit, even when the large man puffed out his chest to intimidate him further. "I have been waiting to get a chance to speak to this gentleman. You, on the other hand, bulled your way in front of everyone. You should wait your turn as we all had to."

The regular patrons of the inn, down to the very last one, stared on in blatant disbelief. Some shook their heads again when they remembered to close gaping mouths. Others left their jaw where it had dropped.

"Is that so?" The big man inched closer to the wizard, imposing his girth on the smaller man. The gap between them was already almost nonexistent. Now the magic-user needed to crane his neck all the way backward to continue to stare up at him, unimpressed by his tactics.

"What are your intentions, sir?" Raftennon's calm still did not waver.

"I'm gonna ram my fist down your throat so I can enjoy my beer in peace." The bully spoke slowly, ensuring his target did not miss a single syllable. "Then I'm gonna pound on you s'more, so you learn never to bother me again!"

The brute raised a thick arm over the wizard's head, ready to drive it down between his shoulders. Raftennon closed his eyes and started to mutter. The large man arced an eyebrow, confused at the mage's behaviour. Then a broad smile formed on his lips, as he gained understanding. "The wimp's prayin' to his god for mercy," the ruffian pointed out to the inn's customers, laughing at the spellcaster's lack of courage. Some of the townsfolk laughed with him, their half-hearted mirth a clear display they were trying to stay on the bully's good side. Most turned around, but not far enough to miss the pummelling that was now sure to ensue.

Raftennon's gibberish stopped and he raised his brown eyes to glare at would-be assailant. The spellcaster drew his hand from inside his robes and blew grey powder into the man's face. The brute's surprised expression froze right after it formed. His arm even stayed risen in the air, huge fist poised to bash onto the top of Raftennon's skull.

Raftennon examined his handy work before giving the man's chest a gentle push. The bully slowly tipped over and fell to the floor, the position of his limbs not moving in the slightest. The man was as stiff as a statue. Only his eyes showed signs of life as they darted from one corner of the room to the other, looking for someone to help him. Unfortunately for him, no one dared to cross the obviously powerful spellcaster. The man remained sprawled where he lay for the rest of the night, until the effects of the spell wore off, at which point he skulked out of the tavern without saying a single word.

Raftennon did not wait for this to happen. He immediately dismissed the entire encounter and returned to the bar, glad to have the bartender's undivided attention (not to mention everyone else's in the room). "Now, good sir, I need some information."

"I-I'm s-sorry, M'Lord," the innkeeper stammered, terrified of offending the skilled wizard, "but I know nothing. I'm j-just a simple barkeep. A-All I d-do is serve d-drinks!"

It was clear Raftennon's spell bewildered the townspeople— all of them. He did not comprehend their astonishment. Yes, the incantation was complex enough it was only taught after one earned an apprenticeship, but this was by far not the strongest attack he possessed in his arsenal. Surely, in a town linked to Xendremmar by a well-travelled road, they should have seen such a feat before. Still, the patrons gawked at him even more now than when he started standing up for himself.

Raftennon shook his head and leaned against the counter, using his most reassuring tone of voice to calm the flustered barkeep. "Then could you serve me a glass of brandy and point out someone who can help me with my other need?"

The bartender nodded haltingly and hurried to fill his order. He placed the establishment's finest chalice on the bar, struggling to control his shaking hand and avoid an unwanted spill. Everyone in the inn waited to see if the wizard would fry the man if the order was not exactly right. Raftennon left his drink where it was, giving the barkeep a chance to fulfill his second request.

When it was apparent the mage was not going to take a sip just yet, and there would be no other amazing feats of magic, the throng of onlookers finally returned to their own drinking. The barkeep relaxed the slightest bit and pointed to a table in the centre of the room, where a group of men began to roar in boisterous laughter at an unheard jest.

"H-Hernam over th-there might be able to h-help you. He's in here e-every night and he remembers everything." The barkeep was pointing at the only man at the table that was not laughing.

Instead, he was staring at the spellcaster, obviously expecting to be called upon for the information the stranger was seeking.

Raftennon thanked him and fished out a couple coins from his purse. The inn's proprietor, a plump man who had clearly never worked a day in his life, jumped in to refuse payment. "I would be offended if a great man such as yourself refused the accommodations of this fine establishment, at no charge, of course," he said. It was more likely he did not want to risk offending the magic-user with what could be considered outlandish prices.

Raftennon once again thanked both men and, grabbing his brandy, made his way through the crowded room. His lips twitched at the corners as he tried to retain his stoic expression when the patrons cleared a path before him, some even spilling their own drinks in the process. The young magic-user enjoyed the spectacle the townspeople were making of themselves.

Hernam rose from his seat and walked to the back of the room. The bar regular led the traveller to a table where they would have privacy to talk. Raftennon sat in the empty chair opposite the one Hernam chose. The wizard studied the man, noting every single detail. Long hair fell over his shoulder under a wide-brimmed brown hat and a long beard reached the centre of his chest. Both were deep auburn with an equal amount of silver streaks. Wrinkles furrowed by the ocean weather crisscrossed his hard face, accentuating the piercing blue of his eyes.

"What do you want to know, Master Wizard?" Hernam said in a strong baritone voice.

"I am looking for someone," Raftennon started, placing his glass on the table. "A woman, with long golden-red hair and emerald green eyes. Her name is Jennalla."

"I don't recall that name." Hernam leaned back in his chair, intently studying the stranger.

"She is from this town." Raftennon began to think this conversation would prove to be a waste of time. Maybe the man did not know as much as the barkeep professed he did, or his information did not go back far enough to include Jennalla at all. Or perhaps he was one of these old men who knew all the histories of the town but did not care what happened in the present. Or there was nothing wrong with his memory at all. It could be he was choosing not to reveal anything. The magic-user decided to press on anyway. "She left for the Spellcaster's Guild in Xendremmar nearly twenty years ago…"

"And you expect me to remember the lass?" The man did not move, did not show any emotion whatsoever.

"I believe she may have returned here recently, no more than five years past," Raftennon persisted.

"I'm sorry lad, but no such lass has been here lately."

The wizard stared at the townsman, trying to ascertain his motives. He could not determine if he was being truthful or not. He opted for a different strategy. "Have any parents showed unusual glee as of late, speaking of a child they have not seen in quite some time?"

Hernam took off his hat with one hand to brush his hair back with the other. His eyes dropped to the floor while he replaced it on his head. "There's always someone cooing over their offspring who flew the nest. Off to the big city to make a name for themselves. Most of it is hogwash. Exaggeration to make themselves look like better parents. Wait a minute." Hernam's eyes flashed an even brighter blue as recognition slammed into him. "You said she went off to Xendremmar?"

"Yes, I did." Raftennon leaned forward in his chair, excitement making its first contact with his heart.

"Twenty years ago, you said?"

"Yes." Raftennon's heartbeat quickened, a fact that irritated him. The man had not yet given him any useful information and he was already getting excited.

"Still doesn't ring a bell."

The mage slumped back in his seat. He only now realized he had inched toward the table with every futile question the man had asked him.

"What I can do is narrow down the field for you, though," Hernam offered. "You see, there's not that many people that leave here to go to the school of magic. I can think of three families that sent their youngens around twenty years ago. You'll have to visit them yourself to see if they're the ones you're looking for."

Raftennon thanked Hernam for his help as the barfly recited the names, with directions to their homes, so the spellcaster could write them on a piece of parchment he produced from his pack. The wizard memorized the information as the bearded fellow said it, but he wrote it nonetheless, in case he would have need of it.

Raftennon rose from his chair when they were done and shook the man's hand while scanning the inn. "Now where did that gnome go off to?"

Raftennon spent another half hour searching the common room for Denmur, asking the patrons for assistance as he went. Most honestly answered they did not know his friend or where he was. When the magic-user found someone who noticed their arrival, the fellow's intoxication made his denial of that fact quite apparent. The spellcaster crossed his arms and motioned to the still-frozen brute sprawled on the floor. The liar's comrade blurted out the gnome never stopped walking, continued through the bar and exited out the back door. The barfly hurried to vow that was all he knew.

Raftennon left the two men, the first scowling at his companion for the pathetic display of cowardice, and headed for the back of the room. "What are you doing, Denmur?" he murmured as he reached the door, frightening the customers around him, who feared he was casting a spell on them.

The mage passed through the doorway and found himself in an alley filled with the refuse produced by the many drunkards inside the building. Raftennon looked to the right and saw a few figures pass by the narrow opening. Obviously, that way led to the street. He started walking in the opposite direction, going further down the lane. If the gnome left through the back door, he was no doubt headed to a place to which he did not want to be followed. Taking the back alleys would make remaining hidden much easier.

Raftennon trudged through debris and refuse, winding his way along an intricate maze of alleyways, ignored by many of Bezna's citizens. He would sometimes come out onto a street to regain his bearings before deciding where to go next.

An hour passed, wasted time that irked the usually patient wizard. The sun was letting go of its last grip on the sky, falling

completely behind the horizon to plunge the world into the darkness of night. At that precise moment, Raftennon heard boisterous laughter coming from somewhere down the darkened lane.
He followed the sound and soon found another inn. The sign
hanging over this door proclaimed this establishment to be The
One-Eyed Squid.

Raftennon began to walk to the door and stopped before
reaching it to let a dwarf tumble to the ground in front of him.
Two hobgoblins poked their upper bodies out the door and
screamed at the felled dwarf in their guttural tongue, informing
him of his doom should he ever return. One of them glanced at
the mage before dismissing him to rejoin the other, who was
already back inside the tavern.

The wizard returned his attention to the dwarf to see him
dusting himself off and wobbling down the dirt-packed road,
cursing at his misfortunes. Raftennon shook his head and entered
the Squid.

The air was thick with smoke. The laughs here were not as
jovial as the ones at the Mackerel. A chill ran down the wizard's
spine at the evil tone of the patrons' amusement. In one corner of
the room, a group of men of mixed race—humans, hobgoblins,
dwarves, even some sinister looking elves—were taking turns
hurling knives at a halfling. Raftennon's hands slide into the
folds of his robes, preparing for the horrible outcome that was
sure to come. He soon realized they were engaged in a contest of
sorts, in which the aim was to throw your knife as close to the
target—the poor soul of a halfling—without actually touching
him. The magic-user shook his head again in disapproval and
continued his scan of the patrons, wondering what happened if a
competitor hit the living target.

"Whattaya want?" someone screeched from behind him.

Raftennon turned to face an elderly woman tending the bar. It
was clear she once was quite lovely, but years of neglect and
poor hygiene had robbed her of her beauty. Her hair was
unkempt and dark. Whether that was natural or a result of infre-
quent bathing, he could not tell. The few remaining teeth still in
her mouth were crooked and rotten. Her clothes were so filthy,
the wizard hurried to raise his gaze back to her face, though it
was only marginally better. He did not want to think of what had

been done to get those garments so dingy.

"Whattaya starin' at?" she screeched again, her voice grating like fingernails dragged across slate.

"I am seeking a gnome," Raftennon said, his words almost drowned by the ruckus of the other customers.

"Git yer arse offa dat table, you ingrate!" she yelled to someone in the room, ignoring the spellcaster.

"What are you doing here?" someone asked at Raftennon's side.

The wizard started at the slight touch on his leg but, as usual, managed to keep his surprise to himself. Standing beside him was Denmur.

"I was looking for you," the mage stated. "You disappeared as soon as we entered the Green Mackerel."

"Yeah, sorry about that." The gnome turned his gaze to the group hurling knives as one of the hobgoblins yelled in triumph, the halfling fainting from fright. " I had some people to see. They were a bit worried about me, seeing as my departure was quite abrupt and all."

"I doubt the patrons of this establishment worry about anyone other than themselves." Raftennon scanned the room again, still disgusted by the flagrant disregard displayed by all for their peers.

"You shouldn't be so hasty to judge," Denmur chastised.

Raftennon snorted inwardly but decided to keep his mouth shut. He was not here to deal with the lowlifes of the community.

"So now you've found me," Denmur interrupted the mage's thoughts. "Now we have to find a place to stay for the night."

The wizard had to agree with the gnome. Finding the small man had taken too long. A visit from a stranger at this time of night would be quite inappropriate, so his search for the families he hoped would lead him to Jennalla needed to wait until morning.

Denmur rushed Raftennon out of the tavern, practically pushing him out the door, and led him back to the Mackerel. Entering the inn, the gnome stared in wonder at the still prone giant in front of the bar. Raftennon went up to the bartender, with no trouble this time as the other patrons gave way to him, and asked for a couple of rooms. The barkeep quickly provided keys and, to Denmur's growing surprise, still refused to take the spellcaster's money. Raftennon did not offer to explain what happened while the gnome went about his own business.

The pair walked up a flight of stairs and found the two adjoining rooms—the finest accommodations the establishment had available. A bed large enough for three tall men dominated each room, the mattresses and pillows soft and fully stuffed. A wardrobe covered half a wall, while a writing desk took up the space between the cabinet and the corner. A chest as wide as the bed sat on the floor against the footboard. The linens were slightly yellowed with age, but still in good condition and clean. A small window, set close to the ceiling so the alley that ran beneath it was hidden to guests, let in the moonlight. A bronze candelabrum with three thick candles stood on the mantle of the narrow fireplace in Raftennon's room.

The mage flung his pack onto the chest and turned to his companion. "I hope I will find you here in the morning."

Denmur ignored the comment and took the few steps to enter his own room, without saying a word or even looking back.

Darkness dominated the windowless cubicle. In fact, the space was so cramped it would have been more appropriate to call it a closet. The only furnishing capable of fitting within the close walls was a narrow stand carved to resemble two intertwined snakes. Their heads met six feet over their twirling tails, the forked tongues wrapped around a silver orb the size of a woman's fist.

An entire wall swung open (despite that fact, it was still more narrow than a regular door). Torchlight revealed the whiteness of the serpents, their scales intricately carved in their ivory construction. A shadow fell over the stand as a figure entered. The opening closed behind it, returning the room to total darkness.

Strange words clumsily filled the stale air, as if the speaker was not familiar with the language. The silver orb began to shimmer, its light intensifying until a cold glow permeated the cubicle. The man standing alone in the room stared up at the sphere, the eerie luminescence casting deep shadows on his harrowed face. He seemed uncomfortable being in this place and his voice quivered as he spoke to the metallic ball.

"A guy came into town today and he was asking about you."

He waited a few moments, as if for a response. When it was obvious none was forthcoming, he continued his report.

"This guy's a magic-user. He froze Guntram, turned him into a statue for the night."

The orb flashed, blinding the man. Then it winked out as abruptly, or so it appeared to him, for all he saw were red dots fluttering over the black walls. In truth, the sphere shone ever so slightly. A faint metallic whisper, which sounded as if it were coming out of a copper pipe, finally broke the silence of the room.

"Make sure he does not see another night in Bezna."

13

FINDING THE TRUTH

Morning came and Raftennon found Denmur still in his room. The gnome hurried to stuff a piece of parchment he had been writing on into his pack as the mage closed the door behind him.

"If you would prefer I leave the room to allow you to finish whatever you were doing, all you have to do is ask," the wizard stated, staying close to the door in case his companion decided to take him up on his offer. The little man was entitled to his privacy, even if he did appear to be involved, in some way, with what Raftennon considered the wrong crowd.

"That's all right. It's not important. I'll finish it later." Denmur shoved the shirt he slept in over the note and tied the bag closed before making his way toward the door.

"Last night you came looking for me instead of just getting your room," the gnome began as he entered the corridor. "What was the reason for that? I mean, I'm grateful you took me away from those thieves back in the Hills, but I don't intend to follow you until we find a way for me to repay the gesture. I have a life I would really like to get back to."

"I was thinking nothing of the sort." Raftennon grabbed his own bag from his room and caught up with his fellow former captive. "You seem to know this town and I need a guide."

"I haven't been here for years," Denmur said without looking back, hurrying down the stairs that led to the common room.

"All I require is help in my search for these three families." Raftennon gently grabbed the gnome's shoulder as they reached the ground floor and turned him around. "Do you recognize any of these addresses?" The spellcaster passed the list of names over.

"Two of these are on main streets and should be easy enough to find," Denmur offered after glancing at the parchment. "The other, if the stories I heard at the Squid are true, might be a problem."

"How so?"

"You may not need to find out." The gnome returned the vellum and headed for the front door. "Come on."

The two left the inn, and the mage surprisingly found himself hard-pressed to keep up with his guide. Despite his short legs, Denmur sped along the filling streets. A few times, Raftennon had to squeeze his way through a group of people and run to catch up with the gnome. The magic-user did not even have the time to take in his surroundings. If someone asked him later what the houses he passed looked like, he would be unable to give a description. He recalled every turn they took, so he could find his way back to the Green Mackerel, but that was all the information of the town he had time to glean.

Only when Denmur stopped before a wooden door of a narrow two-storey house did Raftennon have the time to look around. And that time was cut short by the prompt opening of that door after a sharp knock by the gnome. The man who answered was polite, if brusque, until Raftennon explained the reason for their visit. Upon hearing mention of Xendremmar, the woman who had come to the door to join her husband broke down in tears. The man quickly shooed them away, not wanting anything to do with the Guild that had taken their son away from them. Evidently, they blamed the boy's teacher for the tragic accident that had claimed his life. Raftennon apologized for disturbing them and let Denmur lead him away in that swift pace of his.

Their second stop proved to be just as fruitless. Denmur scowled at the old woman that now lived alone (her husband having passed away just last spring, Hanlon keep his soul), as she went on and on about her daughter's gifts. Raftennon sat down in the offered chair, ate the offered biscuits and listened to the childhood tales of the young lady. The mother was so proud of her child, stroking the air in front of her as if her little girl was actually sitting before her.

Raftennon gently interrupted the fond memories and inquired about the girl's current whereabouts. The old woman sighed and confessed her daughter had left for Ednifad with her spouse. She was quick to point out they had had the decency to marry in Bezna. She had been so lovely in her flowing pearl gown, the wind blowing the blond hair she had had since birth away from her shoulder to show her pretty face.

The wizard thanked the woman and tried to tactfully end the conversation. She seemed to not hear him and continued her tale. She finally mentioned her girl's name, but neither Raftennon or Denmur were paying attention. By the woman's description, the mage already knew she was not talking about Jennalla. It took a few more tries, but the spellcaster managed to navigate the woman to a farewell and led Denmur out of the house.

"That was a complete waste of time," the gnome muttered before the door finished closing behind them. "Two hours of listening to her yap about a daughter who clearly got fed up with her blabbering. How could you stand that?"

"I was being polite, something you should be." Raftennon smiled and nodded back at the woman, who was waving goodbye to the pair through her kitchen window. "I do not remember you being this crass back in the Hills."

"Back in the Hills, I was happy because I had finally found a way to end my captivity!" Denmur stomped forward, heading toward the northern tip of town.

"I suppose we will now discover if the stories you heard are true," the wizard commented, since only the last address remained.

They went down a few blocks, the streets getting narrower as they progressed, the pedestrians scarcer. The buildings made their transition from two-storey structures to their single-floor counterparts. The two men rounded a corner as the wharves became visible and walked down a narrow lane, much like the alley behind the inn, but this one was much neater.

Emerging from the confines of the cramped buildings brought

the travellers to a scene they were not expecting. Even Denmur, who had heard the rumours, was not ready for what they fell upon. In front of them lay a shallow inlet that should not have been there. Many partial structures jutted out of the water, shattered by the power of whatever had reformed the shape of the earth beneath it. Roofs were gone, walls had toppled over, and everywhere water covered the narrow lanes like a pall.

"They said the sea raised an arm and smashed into the town, taking everything it landed on with it to the ocean," Denmur stammered, repeating what was said the previous night.

"And there wasn't even a cloud in the sky," offered a middle-aged man standing behind the pair, "or the pulling back of the waters on the shore that usually happens before a tidal wave. There was no warning at all."

"When did this happen?" Raftennon asked, looking over the destruction.

"About two years ago, when that wannabe apprentice came back to visit her momma."

The wizard turned to face the man and took the steps needed to reach him. Denmur continued to stare at the devastation a little longer before following.

"Describe her to me, please," Raftennon requested.

"The momma or the girl?" The man raised a hand to shade his eyes from the noon sun's rays.

"The girl, and what caused this," Raftennon gestured to the unnatural bay, "if you do not mind."

"Well," the citizen backed up closer to the house behind him, into its shadow, and lowered his hands to grab his belt. "The wave sprung out from the sea like steam from a geyser. A thousand feet it soared into the air, then came crashing down onto the town. There was no splash. The water didn't spread to the other streets as it should've. Instead, it bore into the ground, making the big groove that allows the bay to stay exactly where it is. It was the most unusual thing I ever saw."

The man fell silent as his far-off stare told the mage he was reliving those events in his mind. Raftennon gave him some time to compose himself before clearing his throat to bring the townsman back to the present.

"As for the girl," the man continued, with a voice that shook just the slightest bit, "she was real pretty, just like her mother. A little pale for my liking, but that only made her green eyes shine even brighter."

Raftennon had his answer. He did not even listen to the man as he mentioned the red hair that now reached her waist. The spellcaster fell deep in thought, much as the townsman did, until Denmur's words caught his attention.

"I wonder what got her skivvies tied up in a twist."

"I can tell you that." The new voice came from the door of the building nearest the destruction. A woman, about the same age as the man, put away the broom she had been using to sweep her stoop.

"Sure you can," the townsman scoffed. "There ain't no power in the heavens that can stop you from spreading any rumour you happen to hear."

The woman gave the man a hard look and muttered a slight curse as he turned and left. Raftennon went over to her, intent on listening and judging the merit of what she had to say for himself. Denmur looked back the way they had come, at the part of town that was still whole. The gnome abruptly turned to follow the mage, his hands behind his back.

"Please go on, ma'am," Raftennon said, ignoring the man's even louder scoff as he entered his home.

"Well, she came home one afternoon to visit her mother," the woman gladly commenced. "Her father had been lost at sea, in case you didn't know. Anyway, she came home—her name was Jennalla, by the way—which just happened to be that house right there." She pointed to a pile of rubble in the middle of the destroyed lane, near the inland end. "So she came home and her mother—who was called Nennilla, if you didn't know—greeted her with her usual cold shoulder. You see, those two had never gotten along. That was one of the reasons she—Jennalla, I mean —went to that school. I thought it was a good idea as well. Maybe that's what she needed to take care of that terrible temper she had."

Raftennon was surprised to hear Jennalla described in such fashion. Throughout his studies in the classrooms, she had always been in control of her emotions. He quickly dismissed these intrusive thoughts, resolving to mull over them later, for the woman continued with her long-winded tale without skipping a beat.

"When she was a child—and I mean as early as when she was no longer on the teat—she would throw these terrible fits whenever she didn't get what she wanted. In my opinion, it's all the father's fault. I'm sorry, but I don't remember his name. He was gone so much that I didn't use it enough for it to stick with me. Anyway, without his firm hand to keep her in line, Jennalla became a spoiled brat. Her mother couldn't control her so she sent the girl away.

"I think that's what they were arguing about that night. I was at home, so all I could hear was screaming. I couldn't make out the words. Then Jennalla storms out of her house and stomps all the way to the exact spot you two are standing in."

Denmur looked at the ground around him, but Raftennon continued to stare at the woman.

"So she stops there and turns around to look back at her house. I watched her from my window," she pointed to the glass pane over her left shoulder. "She raised her hands, holding something I couldn't make out, and started screaming these words I had never heard before. For a moment there, I thought she had been possessed by some demon and was talking in their unholy language. Then the tidal wave came and barely missed my house! One minute, my neighbour's house is blocking the moon; the next, my home is oceanfront property! I mean, it was the darndest thing I had ever seen!"

The woman fell silent at that moment, her tale finished. She shook her head and clucked, still taken aback by the events of that day. She looked up and her eyes widened before she hurried to enter her house, bolting the door behind her.

Raftennon turned to see what had precipitated her strange departure. Behind him, spanned across the lane, was the band of ruffians who had been hurling knives at the halfling in the One-Eyed Squid the previous night. Denmur glared at the gang, the only people left in the alley. All the other sparse occupants had dispersed quickly upon their arrival.

"Looky here, boys," sneered one of the humans. "We got us a magic-user that don't know where to stick his nose."

"We're just gonna have to teach him," cried one of the two

hobgoblins, striking his open hand with a large club.

"Illünayminôr tenbâh rochenôltanâs fylnaymôrân sôron-ellômal!" Raftennon thrust his arm in the air and a bright light burst from his fingers, instantly blinding the thugs. Each of them frantically rubbed their eyes in a vain attempt to help regain their vision.

There were three elves in the group. Their pointed ears were the only ones to catch the soft words uttered from the direction the magic-user had been before the great light. At the last possible moment, they dove away from their comrades, narrowly escaping the trap. Everyone struggled with their sight, the red dots refusing to dissipate. Added to the blindness, the thugs found themselves huddled against each other, unable to move as some unseen force glued them together. Their arms flung about their torsos, but everything below their waist stayed as rigid as stone.

Denmur, seeing the elves rolling to their feet, free of the spell's effect, rushed to Raftennon's side. "Listen, I know I already owe you one, but I don't want to die today. I'd rather owe you two than not have a chance to repay you, if you know what I mean."

The mage ignored the little man and concentrated on another spell. Fiddling with a couple components in the folds of his robes, Raftennon thrust his arms out and bolts of white lightning crackled in the afternoon sun. The electricity struck one elf in the centre of his chest, leaving a wide, charred circle over his no-longer-beating heart. His other two cohorts sprung away before they became the next victim. Sparks still burst from the tips of Raftennon's fingers as he eyed the elves, who were skulking in opposite directions. The wizard only had enough charge for one target and was now deciding which one of them it would be.

The elf on his right made the choice for him when he feigned a lunge. That slight step forward was enough to trigger Raftennon's already taut nerves. The lightning bolt sparked from the mage's hand. The ruffian sprung back, ready for this attack, but miscalculated and landed in the inlet. The lighting crashed into the edge of the unnatural bay, still electrocuting its target, even though it had missed.

The last elf dove behind a large potted plant, hoping to find enough cover to save himself. He peered through the foliage, no doubt searching for some means to reach his target without getting fried. Raftennon studied his assailant just as intently, rummaging through his mental store of incantations. Before he managed to come up with something, however, a sharp pain shot up from his side. Looking down, the spellcaster saw the hilt of a dagger thrusting out from his darkening robes. The stain steadily grew as more blood seeped from the wound.

Raftennon slumped to the ground as Denmur folded his arms over his chest. When the mage lay on the cobblestones, his vision already failing him, the gnome reached for his weapon and pulled it out. Denmur wiped the blade clean on the wizard's sleeve. "Sorry about this, old chum, but a gnome has to earn a living. Thanks for rescuing me from those other brutes so I could meet up with my boys again, though."

He left the mage in the growing pool of crimson and joined the only surviving elf as he stood up from behind his hiding place. Together they made their way to their trapped friends to puzzle out how to free them.

The last image Raftennon saw was a dark figure staring at him from one of the rooftops surrounding him.

14

GETTING BETTER

The fragrant aroma of roasting onions found its way into his nostrils, making him realize his stomach was empty. The low rumble it uttered tore him completely from his dark, dreamless slumber. He tried to get up, but a great searing pain shot up from his side, draining all strength from him.

"You mustn't get up yet!"

Fluttering his eyes open, the mage saw a young man carrying a bowl of water coming to sit beside him. The stranger bent down to place the dish on the floor. He then straightened with the damp cloth in one hand. With the other, he lifted the sheets and examined the bandage, daubing the fresh blood that seeped down below the dressing.

"Where am I?" Raftennon croaked.

"You're in my home. You needed immediate treatment."

The dripping water thundered through Raftennon's aching head as the man wrung the cloth over the bowl.

"Thank you," the spellcaster muttered before succumbing to unconsciousness once again.

"You are approaching the boundaries of our allowances." The dark figure looked out into the starlit sky, his back turned to his comrade.

"As long as I do not cross them, you need not worry," retorted the second man, who ignored the errant silver-white locks that trespassed in his face while he peered in a heavy tome.

"Do you presume arrogance is the best path to take to placate me?" He turned from the window to glare at the man who continued to stare into his book.

"Why would I need to placate you?" Now the man looked up from his studies. "I have interfered in no way."

"You believe you have gone unnoticed?"

"Secrecy has never been necessary. Even you have appeared before the mortals."

"Do not question me, brother. I am First among the Original. I have lived by the Oath longer than you have existed. I perform my duties as ordained by the Great Sage."

"As do I."

A few tense moments passed as both men regained control of themselves, quelling the rage that was building within each man.

"You still surmise we need him to stop our brother, who has yet to be proven a renegade." The one by the window stated.

"I follow the evidence set before me."

"I know of your conversations with the others. You may have convinced some of them that observations are necessary. They do not share your misgivings. Do not delude yourself into thinking that. They are merely cautious and cannot counsel against anyone wanting to keep an eye on any situation that has the potential to affect the Balance."

"You are convinced I overreact."

"I listen to the theories and look at the lack of evidence you bring before us. I analyze them, as you should. None but you sees a pattern. You jump to conclusions."

"Where is our brother? When was the last time he stepped foot in the Celestial Tower?" The man leaned back in his seat and laced his fingers before him, elbows resting on the arms of the chair.

The man by the window seethed, barely containing his rage. He never liked being questioned by anyone. The seated figure knew this, so he continued before tempers escalated any more than they already had. "If I were wrong, do you not suppose Pentaclin would have reproached me for my error before now?"

The standing man turned to look out at the stars again. He took a long breath before continuing, finding his calm, yet stern, tone again. "That is not a certainty. The Great Sage may be waiting for us to rectify the situation ourselves. If we find your reasoning to be at fault and you have wrongfully accused one of our brothers, *you* will find yourself risking our retribution. Your human protege may also suffer the consequences, depending on how far you choose to take this."

A few hours passed before Raftennon opened his eyes again. This time, instead of trying to get up, he left his head on its pillow and scanned what he could of the room. A black cauldron hung in a large hearth across from him, the smell of roasted onions still seeping from the top as if they were just added to the broth. The roaring fire provided much of the light in the room, the sun only helping to illuminate the ceiling from a narrow window on a wall somewhere out of his limited sight. A small wooden table stood to the left of the fireplace with two matching chairs.

In one of these sat a man about Raftennon's age. His long, black curls bobbed every time he lifted his head, raising his eyes skyward, as if in reflection. They also bounced when he hunched back over the table, painstakingly scribbling on a parchment with a quill that had seen better days.

The man turned in his seat, hearing the soft rustle of the sheets as the mage craned his neck as far as he dared. "You've come back to us." The stranger came over and sat on the small stool placed beside the head of the bed.

"How long have I been unconscious?" Raftennon rasped, his throat dry from hours of forgetfulness.

"Since early afternoon. The sun has just set. Are you hungry?" The man rose to his feet and went to the fire. Grabbing a bowl from the mantle, he ladled in some of the roasted onion soup. He took only broth, deeming his patient not yet ready to stomach pieces of solid food.

"I should not be here," Raftennon stated, trying to get up. Once again, the pain in his side prevented him from accomplishing the task.

"If it hadn't been for the pouches hidden in your robes, you wouldn't be." Coming back to the stool, the man passed by the table and lifted two bags, both of which sported moderately large slits on either side. "It seems these stopped the knife from going in as much as that gnome would have wanted."

"The gnome…" Raftennon lowered himself back to a lying position, mindful of the darkness that wanted to retake him.

"Yeah, I saw everything. He played you, and you fell for it. I mean no offence. I was fooled by him too when I saw him stand by your side when the others arrived." He helped Raftennon to sit again, careful of the wizard's bandaged wound, and made him sip from the bowl while he continued. "But then I got a good look of his face and I recognized him right away. That band of thugs who were going to attack you are his boys. He's their leader. I never understood why those large brutes would follow such a small man. There are stories that portray the little guy as one of the most ruthless cutthroats in the land, but I never believed them myself. When he disappeared last year, I was sure someone called the bluff and did him in."

"I don't understand," the spellcaster gasped between forced swallows. His stomach was trying to reject the broth, but Raftennon knew his body needed the nourishment, so he mentally fought his innards for control.

"That's his greatest weapon." The mage's host held the bowl near his chest, waiting for the battle between mind and rising gorge to subside before offering another sip. "No one would suspect a shrimp like that to be so dangerous."

"Why would he attack me?" Raftennon tried to clear the clouds of anguish from his head. He needed to think straight.

"Money. I mean, that's what I think. It's the logical conclusion. It's the only reason people like them need."

The man took away the half-finished bowl when his patient waved it away, having had enough for the time being.

"You saved me," the mage whispered, finally looking down at the bandage around his waist. There was a tiny splotch of red in the centre of the white cloth. Fortunately, it was not getting any larger.

"Actually," the house's resident intruded on the spellcaster's examination of his wound, "I came out to get a closer look at you. After the gnome stabbed you, he and the elf went to the thugs you had trapped. The elf said something and the others fell to the ground, freed from whatever spell you had put them under. Then they left. I came out to see how badly he had stuck you. It's a sick fascination of mine."

The man returned to the stool, but chose not to sit down. Instead, he stood beside the bed, his hands folded behind his back. If there had been a mirror on the opposite wall, Raftennon would have seen the furtive twiddling of the man's fingers. "I like to study wounds, how they're made, how they affect the body. I'm studying medicine, you see, and understanding an injury helps me heal it. So I went to you to see what I might learn and found you still breathing. I dragged you here to dress the wound. Like I said before, you're lucky to be alive."

"Once again, I thank you...," the magician paused. The man caught the reason.

"My name is Cindran," he hurried to respond, trying to make up for not introducing himself earlier.

"I am Raftennon," the wizard replied, extending a hand.

"Nice to meet you, Raftennon." Cindran clasped his guest's forearm in greeting. "I'm glad I was able to do something to save you. I must admit, though, you still being with us is mostly your doing."

"What do you mean?" The mage dropped his hand to the bed's mattress to help support his upper body. He was still weak from his first real taste of betrayal.

"If it hadn't been for the herbs you had in your pouches," his saviour glanced back at the tattered bags on the table, still not believing the spellcaster's incredible fortune, "things would have gone a lot worse. These particular sacks hold potent curatives, some of which entered the wound with the tip of the gnome's knife. If it hadn't been for that good luck, there wouldn't have been anything I could have done for you." The host examined his patient again, a slight measure of awe in his eyes. "Some of the plants in your other pouches aren't found around here at all. Do all magicians practise medicine?"

Raftennon smiled at the aspiring physician, hiding the grimace as fresh pain shot up his side as he tried to switch to a more comfortable position. "We mages must all learn herbal lore," he said once he was certain no evidence of his soreness would creep into his voice. "I have studied long to memorize the plants' names and functions. I use most of them for my spells, not as curatives. My healing abilities are quite limited, I am afraid."

"Well, it's a good thing you were attacked in front of my house, then."

Raftennon spent the next week in bed. Cindran concocted herbal teas for the wizard to drink during the day while he was gone learning and performing his profession. When he came home, he would prepare the evening meals, light at first, but gradually gaining in substance. The magic-user was content to follow his doctor's orders, as long as he had his scrolls around him to continue his studies. Cindran moved a small table beside the bed and placed all the spellcaster's belongings on it, within easy reach. Only once or twice did the spellcaster defy his host's instructions, getting up to retrieve a parchment that had fallen to the floor.

During that week, Denmur's treachery occupied much of Raftennon's thoughts. How could he have allowed himself to be tricked so easily? According to his host, the gnome had a knack for gaining people's trust. But wizards were supposed to see through such lies, to focus on what lay behind the facade. The little thief was no better than his captors in Salgre Hills had been. In fact, the gnome was worse. The torture delivered by the plainsman and his kroykl did not wound him as the stabbing at the hands of a supposed friend had done.

Sheltered as he was during his childhood, while studying his letters, he had learned to rely on others. They had provided for him; his family gave him a loving home, the hermit gave him his first glimpse of knowledge. At the Spellcasters' Guild, everything the Teachers and Mentors said was to be taken as truth. You needed to trust them or your studies would have promptly ended.

It had been quite natural for the wizard to take Denmur at his word. Upon reflection, Raftennon realized most of what the gnome told him was indeed truthful. Never did he deny being a cutpurse. He never had to, as the mage never asked the question. The gnome always avoided the subject of his past entirely, and the spellcaster finally found the reason for the evasion.

None of that mattered, however. Though his flesh slowly recuperated, Raftennon's knife wound would never fully heal. He doubted he would ever trust anyone again.

Even Cindran began to raise suspicions. He said he was a student of medicine. Yet, where were his books, his containers of herbs, and other instruments? Now being able to turn in bed to get a good look of the room, Raftennon saw very little that proved the man's claims. Apart from the two tables, the two chairs, the stool and the bed, there was only one more piece of furniture in the room. It was a low cupboard, on which sat a water basin. Nothing adorned the walls and the thatch that covered the roof was plain to see over the rafters that sloped in only one direction. The only exit was a narrow door at the front of the room that led out to the street. The residence appeared to be a hut rather than an actual house.

Raftennon's thoughts suddenly left Cindran's questionable trustworthiness. The last thing Denmur told him implied the gnome would get paid for his treachery. The attack had been business, which meant someone wanted to hurt him. Someone wanted him to die in that street. Jennalla came to mind, but could she really have ordered his death? Was she that devastated by his sudden departure? What had happened to the lovely young woman who had cried at the memory of her father's passing, the woman he had begun to fall in love with?

For the next two weeks, Raftennon continued his recuperation. He was no longer confined to bed and took the first day of renewed mobility to explore every corner of the room. Without the limitations his wound forced on him, the search would have taken him less than an hour. Even the poorest of families in Yentrill owned more than what Cindran possessed.

One morning, the wizard followed his saviour, intent on learning something about the man. That was when Raftennon saw the outside of the house for the first time. It stood on the edge of the new bay, totally out of place. It was apparent it had not been here before the disastrous, unnatural tidal wave. Constructed of mismatched planks of wood, it was no more than a shanty. The builder had done a good job to cover every hole to prevent drafts, but the walls were still a patchwork of ill-fitting pieces.

Raftennon only took a moment to take in his shabby accommodations before following his host through a few back streets, steadily heading toward the centre of town. Finally, the supposed healer ducked into a building much larger than its neighbours. It was three stories high, with a tall iron fence surrounding a small patch of grass that encircled the structure. Raftennon came out of his concealment and, walking as if he belonged there, entered the edifice.

He found himself in a room that took up the entire floor. Many cots lined the four walls, while more formed a rectangle in the middle of the room, interspersed between thick columns holding up the upper floors. Most of the makeshift beds held sufferers of various ailments. Many clerics and what Raftennon assumed to be healers tended the patients.

"What are you doing here?"

The spellcaster whirled at the voice to see Cindran hurrying toward him. The wizard's natural emotionless facade masked all his feelings. "I needed some answers," he whispered, so as not to disturb the sick.

"I could have given them to you at home." Cindran took Raftennon's elbow and led him toward an unoccupied corner of the room.

"I wanted to see for myself," the magic-user stated, still without emotion. He offered no resistance to his healer's guidance.

"You doubted me?" Cindran stared into his eyes, the hurt from the mistrust already showing on his face.

"You must understand." Raftennon crossed his arms over his chest as soon as the pair reached their private corner, freeing himself from Cindran's grip. "I have been too trusting as of late and it almost cost me my life."

"That may be, but that doesn't give you the right to assume everyone is lying to you."

"You claimed to study medicine, but there is no proof of that in your home." Raftennon did not allow his host's feelings to sway his misgivings. He felt the man was not consciously trying to hide anything, but he was not yet ready to lower his defences.

"That's because I don't have any." Cindran mirrored the magic-user's posture, replacing insult with his own defensiveness. "You saw my house."

"Yes, it appears you are quite needy." Raftennon's tone was still flat, but he was beginning to regret being so harsh with the man. He had saved his life, after all.

"I am poor, I freely admit that, but I don't need or want your pity!" Cindran was furious now. He forgot himself and raised his voice enough to grab the attention of a few healers and afflicted. He took a moment to get hold of his emotions, but his next words still came out through clenched teeth. "I'm doing all I can to make something of myself. I can't afford books, so I read the ones that are kept here. I don't have the equipment to practise at home, so I spend most of my time in this building, using the tools that are here."

"And you starve yourself so I may eat," the mage interrupted, letting a little regret seep through his previous mask.

Cindran turned his head to stare at something other than his charge before starting to respond, but Raftennon cut him off.

"I have seen your wares, and you skipping meals for my sake. The nights you spend on the floor so I may have the bed are also taking their toll on your health. I will not permit that to continue." Even if he intended to become a more cautious person, Raftennon could never be a callous one.

"You think you have sufficiently healed to leave?"

When Raftennon nodded, Cindran motioned for him to take a bed. The man waved to another healer, an elf, to come examine the spellcaster. It was apparent the two coworkers had already discussed Raftennon's condition, for the elf asked no questions and immediately commenced his diagnosis of the mage's side. After the examination, he nodded and left without saying a word.

"You can go," Cindran muttered, still offended by the spellcaster's mistrust of him.

Raftennon returned to the hut without trying to clear up the misunderstanding. He regretted his behaviour, but he refused to forget the lesson the gnome had taught him. He needed to stop trusting people as soon as he met them. Many would have intentions not readily apparent on their first meeting. But upon retrieving his belongings, the magic-user prepared a few small sachets of those exotic herbs not indigenous to the Salgre Hills and placed them on the table as repayment for Cindran's goodwill.

Then Raftennon left the house, never to return.

15

REACQUAINTED

The air was thick with smoke, as it always was at this time of night. The ruckus of numerous drunkards also dominated the room as they washed away the woes of their days. A barmaid had the most distasteful task on that particular night: washing the blood that belonged to the halfling still attached to the wall. Apparently, someone had missed. But the mismatched group of cutthroats still prevented the removal of the corpse. They had yet to finished their game. One of the human males stared at the servant girl's behind as she bent forward on her knees to scrub the floor.

"Stop drooling, Marlon. It's your turn to get a round." Another man slapped him upside the head to make certain his statement had penetrated his companion's thick skull.

"Alright, alright!" Marlon got up from his stool and reached down to cup one of the barmaid's voluptuous buttocks in his rugged hand. "Hey, sweetums. We need another round."

The woman stood without acknowledging the order and made her way to the bar. The thugs leered at her as she went, except for the elf, another human, and the gnome. They remained deep in conversation.

"I say you still need more men," the human was saying.

"Then find some!" Denmur struck the table with his fist in frustration. "Those thieves have had almost a month to regroup!

Who knows how well Stav has replenished his ranks! There's no way I'm letting him get away with what he did to me!"

"Calm down, Denmur," the elf soothed. "We'll get him. The problem is money. We don't have the means to pay whatever mercenary we can pick up."

"What about our 'friend'?" The gnome glared at the human, for he was the only one who used the orb to communicate with her.

"She won't help you with this feud," the man stated, not daring to lift his gaze from his restless fingers.

"Figures! We do something for her, but she doesn't want to repay the favour!" Denmur crossed his arms over his chest and leaned back in his chair. "Would she be willing to conjure up some fool's gold?"

"What for?" the human inquired

"To pay the mercenaries, you idiot!" The gnome somehow managed to restrain himself from jumping across the table to slap his henchman on the back of the head. Gods knew, the man needed someone to knock the stupidity out of him.

"Are you certain you want to risk that?" the elf asked. "Most pyrite spells fade over time. The soldiers would surely come back for restitution."

"Instead of using your head to find flaws in my plans, Vrenfallan, why don't you come up with one yourself!"

Denmur hopped off his stool and stomped into the crowd toward the bar, nearly bumping into the serving girl, who was returning with his men's drinks. His departure went unnoticed by most of his band, and the two he had been conversing with kept their eyes downcast, trying to come up with a way of persuading him to forgo his foolish plan for revenge.

The gnome's trudge across the room was closely monitored from a table in a dark corner opposite the one occupied by the ruffians, however. The brown eyes stared intently at the small figure from under the hood of his blue robes.

The man walked down the dim street, brooding over the night's conversation. That gnome was mad! Since his return from the Hills, all he cared about was killing Stav. Nothing else mattered.

It had taken a great deal of work to make him focus on the attack on the mage. Even after all that effort to steer the boss in the right direction, that job didn't sit well with the ruffian. Denmur had corralled them away from the wizard way too soon. They did not even check the body and bypassed the looting altogether, which was unheard of in their band. All in all, the man was getting fed up with the gnome. He was longing for the days when the little guy was still captive in the Salgre Hills.

Now he made the ordered trip he never enjoyed. Every time he used the orb to communicate with the wizardress, it felt like he was losing a piece of his soul. And it was not in the way a righteous man slowly falls from grace. It was as if the contraption wrenched a bit of his life force from him, shortening his life and promising some unholy curse upon his death. The whole thing was unnatural and made him uncomfortable. But he was the only one of those that originally wanted to use the device with enough skill to do so. The elves (including the pair the magic-user slew) possessed the knowledge necessary to work the sphere, but also had the wisdom not to go near it. If he had only been less interested to see how the thing worked, he would not be on his way to have another soul-wrenching session with the snake pedestal. If he had been smarter, he would not be on his way to bother the powerful wizardress for a petty spell to fund an equally petty feud.

Walking through the back streets of Bezna, the thug found the dilapidated foundations of a ruined home in the lane of devastation the unnatural wave had dug into the town. He opened a set of cellar doors and went down narrow stairs. The waters of the magically created bay did not enter this entrance, protected by more spells. Down the steps he went, shivering in the strange cold that always chilled the living to the bone in this place, no matter the weather outside. His shoulders brushed the rough bricks of the walls, so constricted was the hallway that continued forward a few feet at the bottom of the stairs. The corridor ended in a pile of rubble. Timber, as well as stone from the foundation, cluttered the entire width and height of the passageway, sealing it from floor to ceiling. The thief heaved in a last, hesitant breath and began to reach for the centre of the debris.

His fingertips had barely brushed a protruding corner of a

wooden beam when he heard the shifting of stones behind him. The ruffian whirled around, reaching behind his back for the long dagger hidden under his shirt. He did not draw his weapon, however, for what stood before him was nothing more than a spectre. "We killed you," he gasped.

"Then you should ready yourself for death, for there is nothing you can do to prevent it," the robed figure replied.

"I don't think so." The human lunged forward, drawing his knife and swinging it as best he could in the confined space. All he saw was a bright light before his back slammed into the wall he was reaching for but a moment ago. A jagged rock threatened to pierce his flesh while the collision drove all the air from his lungs. He saw a cloud of fine powder collide with his chest, felt the grains of sand crash onto his exposed skin with more force than he expected. Then all feeling was gone. He no longer had control of his body below his neck. "I knew we shoulda checked you."

"You did not, however, and now we will aid each other," Raftennon said, placing his boot on the man's chest before leaning forward, crossing his arms over his knee. The blue hood hid all his features, but the thief would swear in future tellings of this encounter the wizard's eyes shone with some unnatural inner light.

"Why would I help you?" the man rasped, trying in vain to wiggle from under the magic-user's boot. Nothing moved save his head, which he turned from side to side—the only action he was able to manage while held by the spell.

"You wish to depose your leader, for he has clearly lost all focus," Raftennon reminded the man. The ruffian ceased his thrashing, surprised his captor knew this fact, for he had not mentioned it to anyone. "He will put all of you in unnecessary peril."

"That's none of your business." The thug managed to keep his composure despite the mind-reading skill the wizard apparently possessed.

Raftennon continued as if the man had said nothing. "I find myself wanting to repay the gnome for his treachery. But most of all, I would confront the one who wished for my death."

"I'm not crazy enough to defy *her*." The slightest quiver betrayed his attempted bravado, exposing the fear he was trying to hide.

"Oh, I know you would not do that. I had no intention of asking for your aid in that matter."

The brigand stared at the mage, who was now smiling down at him from the shadows of his hood. "So, what do you want from me, then?"

"You were about to contact your employer."

The thief glared at the spellcaster, not liking where this conversation was heading.

"I wish to speak to her." Raftennon's soft tone, intended to ease the lowlife's misgivings, did quite the opposite. The trapped henchman resumed his fight to regain control of his body and get himself out of the predicament.

"That ain't gonna happen," he affirmed between grunts of effort. "I'd be forfeiting my life."

Raftennon leaned forward even further, adding pressure on the man's chest. The thug began to have trouble breathing. It was as if the wizard were as heavy as an elephant, his foot applying much more weight than it should have. The ruffian stopped his flailing and concentrated on getting as much air into his lungs as he could.

"If you do not help me," the mage whispered, grabbing more of the thief's attention than the crushing force did, "you will not have to worry about what she will do to you, for you will already be a lifeless corpse."

The unnaturally bright gleam in the mage's eyes convinced the brigand the greater threat to his continued existence was right in front of him. "You said we'd be helping each other," the man gasped. "If I do this for you, what were you planning on doing for me? Because once she finds out I helped you, I'm as good as dead anyway."

"I will send you away from here." The spellcaster leaned back, relieving the pressure from his captive's chest. The man gulped all the air he could manage to inhale but still was unable to move a muscle. "Only I will know your destination. I would suggest you depart from that place as soon as you arrive. Go wherever you wish. That way, where you decide to hide will be unknown to all but yourself. I will not pursue you and she will have no idea where to start looking."

"But she'll look," the thief skulked, not liking his odds of coming out of this situation alive.

"She will be occupied with my search for her," Raftennon assuaged him.

That last fact convinced the ruffian. Indeed, she would be more interested in finishing off the wizard than chasing after him. And the longer that took, the more time he would have to escape.

He told Raftennon what he wanted to know, how to enter the serpent room and how the orb worked. The mage removed the thug from the pile of rubble and dragged him onto the floor of the narrow corridor, placing him on the bottom stair. As the lackey shook his head, still trying to regain control of his body, Raftennon felt for the hidden switch that would give him entry to the room.

"Hey, you said you'd send me away!" the scoundrel shouted, certain the wizard had tricked him. Not only was he still paralyzed, he was still in harm's way. "You use that thing while I'm still here and there's nowhere I'll be able to run to! She'll fry me before I even get a chance to take the first step!"

"I must first ensure I can operate the device." Raftennon turned and knelt before his captive. "If there are spells preventing another mage from activating the sphere, you will have to risk her wrath, I am afraid. Either way, I will speak to her, which should postpone her discovery of your presence."

Raftennon returned to the wall of debris and pushed on a small stone. The rubble swung outward as if fused together, forcing the magic-user to back away, dragging the thief up some steps to give the door the room it needed to open. Inside the small cubicle stood the twining serpents, ever holding the mystic sphere. The wizard said some arcane words and, when nothing happened, nodded in satisfaction.

"It seems I can use the orb without your assistance," Raftennon said before waving a hand in the thief's direction.

The thug fell backward and his arms flailed outward to cushion his landing. He shot up to a sitting position, bringing his hands up to his face to ensure he truly had regained the use of his limbs. Then he noticed he was amid tall trees.

* * *

The scoundrel transported away, Raftennon entered the cubicle and waited for the door to close behind him. As total darkness overtook him, a smirk formed on the mage's lips despite his adeptness at keeping his emotions hidden. It had been so easy to fool the thief into thinking his magic was more powerful than it actually was. No doubt the man thought the spellcaster capable of cheating death. There was no need to correct him, to tell him it had taken a healer being in the right place at the right time. Add a few details overheard in an inn to this confrontation, along with some obvious deductions, and the simpleton was convinced the wizard could read minds. Raftennon afforded himself another chuckle before getting down to the business that had brought him to this strange place.

He recited the communication spell, bringing the orb to life. Silver light shimmered in the sphere, swirling in all directions. He concentrated, forcing his will on the object, commanding the chaos to order. Finally, the images began to clear, showing him a large circular room atop a tall tower. There were no walls here, only a number of thick columns holding up the domed ceiling. Outside, the air crackled with the rage of a lightning storm, thunder shaking the edifice. Darkness oppressed the sky, the room surrounded by the swirling clouds.

Then the mage saw her face.

"Well, look who's still alive," came the metallic voice of a woman.

"It is good to see you as well, Jennalla." The truth behind the statement surprised Raftennon. Mixed in with the contempt he felt for the one responsible for his family's loss were the memories of that splendid six weeks they shared all those years—almost a lifetime—ago.

"I'm sure it is." The derision in her voice was unmistakable. It was apparent she was not reliving the same moments.

"You did not have to do it, Jennalla." Raftennon so wanted to forgive her, forget what she had done to his father and brothers, not to mention his mother. If she could just show some measure of remorse, it would make the task much easier.

"Yes, I did!" Her scream resonated off the close walls of the cubicle, her hatred shaking the foundations encasing the secret room.

"I never intended to hurt you," Raftennon continued in a calm voice he did not expect. Here was the woman who had destroyed two families. She deserved all his retribution, but the feeling all this was his fault kept rage at bay.

"Of course you didn't! All you were thinking about was yourself! What would help you advance faster than the others; make yourself look better than everybody else! Do you know what I did, Raf, after those wonderful weeks we had, finally together? I spent a whole week waiting for you, looking for you, trying to figure out why you were avoiding me! Then someone I didn't even know told me where you were! A total stranger had the decency to end my futile search!"

"It was out of my hands, Jennalla." The warmth in Raftennon's voice dissipated as an inkling of anger finally permeated his guilt.

"To Necroma it was!"

"You and I, Jennalla," Raftennon spoke through clenched teeth, now infuriated with the woman's self-indulgence. The man had not been responsible for the choices she made after he left her, after all. "We both knew the sacrifices needed to advance in the Art. You should have been ready—"

"How was I supposed to know you would be apprenticed two years before everyone else?" Her fury broke and a hint of sorrow crept into her metallic voice. Raftennon was not certain (because of the orb's distortion), but he thought he heard a few sobs between the words. "And even then, most say goodbye to their loved ones!"

"Jennalla—"

"No!" The possible tears were gone and the wrath returned with full force. "It took me a while to figure out what was going on, but I came to understand. You never had any feelings for me! All you wanted was someone to give themselves to you while there was still a chance! You knew apprenticeships would keep us both busy, so you made sure you got to have me before we were chosen. But you left the very next morning! I have no doubt you knew that night when you took me! You already had a reason to use me and then never see me again! You never had any intention of pursuing a relationship with me!"

"Come now, Jennalla—" Raftennon was fed up with her spoiled attitude. She viewed it as *he* had used *her*? That was absurd, but she forged forward before he had time to say so.

"That's okay, though, Raf! You wanted to know what it was like to shatter someone's heart! I thought you should also experience how it was to have your own smashed to pieces! How did it feel, Raf," now her tone was a mocking one, "to see everyone you cared about taken away from you? To find their lives snubbed to nothing, unable to do anything to stop their deaths?"

"That is enough, Jennalla!" Raftennon's ire burst from him, his yelling matching hers. "You had no need to injure my family as you did!"

"You still don't realize what you did to me!" A pause followed, and when Jennalla resumed, her voice was thick with grief. "For once in my life, after my father disappeared at sea, I was able to care about someone. I finally managed to bare my soul. But, just like my mother, you threw me away! You tore my heart to shreds, Raf!"

Silence blanketed the small room, darkening it even further. Raftennon pondered her words, not comprehending her reasoning. Granted, they had had much in common in those days and would have stayed close because of that fact. That same reason should have made his departure understandable to her.

"It's clear I haven't done enough to you, yet," the wizardress calmly stated, cutting into the mage's thoughts.

"You will not harm another soul, Jennalla!" Raftennon's voice boomed in both rooms, mirroring the thunder surrounding her. "You will end this madness, or I will end it for you!"

The orb hissed as if the two serpents holding it came to life and voiced their displeasure. Then the silver light winked out, leaving the mage in total darkness, which was still lighter than his mood. Raftennon had no desire to harm Jennalla, but it was becoming apparent he might have to do so. Her madness was deep and he saw no way of helping her out of it.

16

STOP HIM

Denmur rolled over onto his stomach, punching the slim pillow under his head, trying in vain to fall asleep. His rage continued to keep him awake. What had happened to his boys, who once followed him without question? Was he not the one who came up with the ingenious plans that permitted them to snatch the most valuable possessions in town? Was he not the one who devised cunning escapes that prevented their capture? So why would they not help him exact his revenge on the man that had insulted him so?

Finally, the gnome gave up and jumped out of bed. He went to the chest he kept in his room and rummaged through it, retrieving the notes he had taken concerning his plans to slay Stav. Closing the lid, he spread several pieces of parchment over it, carefully going over the possible ideas scrawled on them.

A bright light flashed, illuminating the room as if it were midday. The sudden change in lighting surprised Denmur so much he flung his scribblings to the ceiling. He quickly regained his composure and slowly turned around, ready to lash out at the intruder. When he saw the fury on the woman's face, he swallowed all his reproaches.

"You were supposed to kill Raftennon!"

"We did." Denmur did not shrink before the growing wrath in her eyes. In fact, his own anger began to grow at the implications of ineptitude.

"Then, explain to me how a dead man activated the orb to talk to me!"

"Hey, you're the magic-user. You're the one who understands these things."

The woman shrieked at the gnome, who was finally realizing he should be more polite.

"You will finish the job, or I'll make your stay in the Hills seem like an eternity in Paradise!"

The woman turned around and vanished, leaving Denmur alone among a sea of notes.

"I guess that means I won't be getting my fool's gold."

"Prantaktillômân vindirtis mendâllôm forkémôntrel." Raftennon finished chanting his spell while the farrier peered over his shoulder with anticipation. The enchantment would protect the blacksmith's tools, preserving them in pristine condition, no matter the number of steps taken by the mount. The wizard was doing this as payment for a horse. He wanted to reach Xendremmar as soon as possible. He needed to do some research.

Once the charm complete, the farrier almost fell over himself to test his equipment. He was so pleased he gave the mage his swiftest filly. Raftennon thanked him as he mounted the steed.

The magic-user trotted out onto the street, only to see his way blocked by the band of thieves that had become quite familiar to him. Denmur stood in front of his men, his arms crossed over his small chest, the knife he had used to stab the spellcaster in his right hand.

"Where are you off to, 'friend'?" The sarcasm in the gnome's voice was thicker than necessary.

Raftennon shook his head at the exaggerated bravado. "It has been such a long time," he responded with mock joviality.

"You could have always come back to the Squid. That's where I spend most of my time."

"Except when you visit the stables, it appears."

"I had in inkling to go riding today."

Raftennon took that to mean someone had informed the gnome of his whereabouts. The mage did not care who had passed on that information or at what cost. He had had enough of the forced banter. "What are your intentions?"

"Well," Denmur unfolded his arms and began playing with the tip of his dagger, "it seems you're not supposed to leave town."

"Your employer still has enough compassion to give you another chance?"

The smile on Raftennon's lips, as well as the derisive tone of his question, took all sense of humour from the gnome. The small man clutched his weapon in his hand and yelled at his lackeys. "Get him, boys!"

The thugs advanced on the wizard, who turned the filly around and galloped down the street in the opposite direction, toward the sea. He glanced over his shoulder to see the thieves scramble into the stables. He returned his attention ahead to make his first turn down a side alley. Whether the brigands owned mounts in that stable, or they would simply steal them, he knew they would be following shortly.

Raftennon's mount impressed him greatly, its speed indeed as formidable as the farrier had boasted. Weaving in and out of narrow alleys, constantly changing direction, the magic-user crisscrossed his way out of town, on the road headed southeastward. Immediately after passing the last house, Raftennon turned south, plunging straight into the hills. Up and down the grassy knolls he went, the steed effortlessly racing over the mounds.

For half an hour, the spellcaster fled in this manner, until he pulled hard on the reins. The young mare snorted its dismay at the sudden stop, exhilarated by the rare chance to spread its legs in such a vigorous fashion. Raftennon dismounted and led it to a clump of trees nestled at the base of a hill. This side of the knoll was steeper than the other banks, providing enough cover for the mage's plans. There he waited, preparing himself for what he had in store for his pursuers.

Raftennon did not wait long. Mere minutes later, the ruffians crested the rise. It seemed the thieves found horses already saddled and ready to ride. To the magic-user's delight, they were all huddled in a tight group. He immediately started chanting the arcane language that was his life.

"*Trémmelônysorâs filemonôrân verdrénnaymôr krünbellom*

direstôrylor!" Raftennon dropped to one knee, slamming the flat rock he had covered with bat guano onto the steep slope.

The ground trembled under the hooves of the ruffians' horses, which stopped their charge halfway down the incline. A low rumble shook the earth for a mile in either direction. The animals whirled in circles, frantic in their search for a means to escape the tremors. But they were surrounded by the ominous vibrations, the land shifting just enough to make footing precarious. Before anyone could decide what to do next, the top of the hill erupted and sent cascades of dirt flying into the air to double the knoll's original height. The hillside shifted downward like a carpet pulled from under someone's feet. The shallow valley between knolls shot up to create a second rising curtain of soil, obscuring everything from the wizard's view. Then the ridge fell into itself, engulfing everything that was on it.

When the dust settled, Raftennon peered into the newly created depression. It appeared as if the hill had been inverted, its top now pointed toward the centre of the world. Smooth sides of dark soil rolled down to the rounded bottom. No trace of the brigands remained.

Raftennon continued to stare, surprised. This was an incantation his mentor, Vendrammon, gave him when he left the Guild, one the mage had not used yet. The incantation's intended result was the creation of a landslide. The wizard had put all his mental strength behind the casting to ensure the slide was violent enough to engulf every member of the band. He never expected a cave-in of such magnitude. Raftennon had not thought he possessed such power yet. After another decade of honing his skills, it would not have surprised him to accomplish this feat. But he never believed it would happen this early after leaving his Master's teachings.

Raftennon shrugged and retrieved his horse. He would confer with Vendrammon when he arrived at the School. For now, he concentrated on calming the filly.

As the earth began to shift, the thieves flicked the reins and kicked at their mounts' flanks, trying to gallop out of the death trap. Some of the horses were so afraid they ignored the commands while others attempted to escape but stayed in place because they were unable to gain any footing. The more the thugs dug their heels, the more the mounts scrambled, the more the dirt gave way beneath them.

Denmur and Vrenfallan reacted first, the only two to realize the magic-user was casting a spell. Because of their attentiveness, they managed to move to the edge of the devastation, but it was still too little to save them. Try as they might, even they slipped into the trap and fell like all their cohorts, swallowed by the disappearing hill.

The gnome saw the futility of his actions, but he was not a man who ever gave up. He rose from his saddle and ran up the horse's neck, using its snout as a launching point to dive to safer ground. Drawing his knife in midair, Denmur stuck it into the outer rim of unmoving soil. Like a desperate swimmer hauling himself onto wet rocks to escape swift-flowing rapids, the gnome tried to pull himself to safety. His strength failed him before the landslide subsided and he disappeared into the engulfing earth.

He was fortunate, however, for his struggles lasted just long enough to save his life. The collapse ended seconds after dragging him in, only managing to cover him with a thin layer of dirt. Under this blanket, Denmur waited until the cursed mage rode away.

As soon as the wretched spellcaster disappeared behind the neighbouring hill, the gnome dug himself out of his shallow grave-to-be. "Keep thinking you've won, wizard. You don't know what awaits you in Ednifad. But I do. Vrenfallan told me. And when you find out, it'll change your plans. You're not as cold-hearted as you think you are. That's when I'll get you."

"You are correct." The black robed woman peered into the shining orb over her counterpart's shoulder. "This magic-user is definitely one to watch over."

The similarly clad man beside her nodded his head, but remained silent, his bluish-grey eyes locked on the crystal sphere.

"He reminds me of…well, that does not matter." She waved a hand as if sweeping the unfinished thought from her mind. "Whichever path he may choose, he will affect the Balance as few others have ever done."

The one standing directly in front of the orb hoped the other was right. Otherwise, their brother might very well succeed in his endeavours, whatever they would turn out to be.

17

REPAYING THE GESTURE

A three and a half days' ride brought Raftennon to the southern border of the Salgre Hills and the village of Ednifad. Evening was taking over the afternoon sky, the streets almost deserted as families already gathered around their supper tables. The wizard slowed his filly to a walk as he travelled along the only real street in the community. This road, which ran from Bezna in the northwest to the Mandellon Plains in the southeast, led eventually to Xendremmar.

Raftennon ensured his mount retained the careful pace as he scanned the buildings for any sign of an inn. They were all one-storey houses, of an architecture that reminded him of his hometown. One could have taken any of these dwellings to Yentrill and it would have blended right in. A striving tavern would most likely have a second storey, but there did not seem to be any such structure in town. And with the size of the humble community, any building of that stature would be easy to spot from anywhere along this thoroughfare. So the mage concentrated on searching for a sign that would announce the lodgings he sought.

Instead, he found the last thing he expected.

A woman came out of what appeared to be a bakery, or so he thought. There was no placard or banner showing the building held indeed such a business, but the delicious aromas that escaped the house when the door opened made a convincing argument to the fact. Raftennon stared at her, at her long, brown hair tucked in a bun, her slight figure and her deeply tanned skin. It took the magic-user a few moments to recognize who she was.

"Blendalla!" he called after his eldest sister.

The woman turned in Raftennon's direction, wondering who was trying to catch her attention. The spellcaster quickened the horse's pace and trotted toward her. She continued to stare at him until recognition finally set in. She had not seen him since his childhood, since his last visit from the Magic School, but she could not mistake the glint in his eyes.

"Raf! What are you doing here?" She put down her basket and embraced her brother as soon as his boots touched the ground after dismounting.

Raftennon clung to the reins to keep his balance. He had not even had time to settle himself after getting off the horse. He wrapped his other arm around her waist and returned the hug as best he could.

"I'm sorry," Blendalla continued, realizing how rude she was being. She let him out of the vice, but her hands kept hold of his shoulders, as if she was afraid he was a figment of her imagination and would disappear at any moment. "How are you? How's school? Did you visit Mother?"

Raftennon began to answer her questions, but she waved at him to stop and stooped down to pick up her basket. "We'll have time to talk later," she said, grabbing his hand to tow him behind her as she started down the street. "Right now, you must be hungry."

He had to admit he was, but he still stopped, pulling his clutching sister off balance in the process. Her eyes questioned him, wondering why he was resisting her. "I have to retrieve my horse."

Blendalla blushed, realizing she had dragged her brother away from his mount in her excitement. The filly had remained in the middle of the dirt track, patiently waiting for guidance.

Denmur spent the rest of the day after digging himself out of the destroyed hill returning to the road. Once there, it was easy enough to flag down a lone rider and dupe him off his horse. Then, it only took a quick slit of the throat and the steed was his.

The gnome was not as gentle with his mount as Raftennon had been with his. Denmur pushed the animal to its limit all the way to Ednifad. It fell dead from exhaustion as it neared the first house. The thief rolled to his feet and sprang for the cover of darkness behind an outer building of the village. He skirted around the back of a few houses, running as fast as silence would allow him. Finally, he squeezed between two structures and peered into the street. From this vantage point, he saw the wizard walking away with the woman.

A broad smile formed on the gnome's lips.

The moon shone bright in the sky, partially covered by wisps of high clouds. Introductions were made, supper enjoyed, and now Raftennon's three nieces were doing their best to postpone their bedtime.

"So your schooling's over," Ronnan, Blendalla's husband, said in the silence that followed the ruckus that left with the girls.

"My apprenticeship is formally ended," Raftennon amended, sitting across from the man at the dining table, "but I will spend the rest of my years learning. Even then, I will still not know everything."

"Listen to this kid!" Blendalla returned from the girls' bedroom. "All prim and proper."

The three continued their conversation well into the night, brother and sister relating all that had befallen them in the years spent apart. Raftennon did not mention anything about Jennalla, which included the fact she was the reason he was passing through town. He simply told them he was returning to Xendremmar for more studies. Blendalla avoided speaking about the night all the men in their family had perished at sea.

"Well, I'll be turning in," Ronnan stated after many hours of chatter. "I've got a dike to dig for old man Fragl in the morning. Nice meeting you, Raf." He shook the spellcaster's hand before giving his wife a gentle kiss and making his way to the couple's bedroom. Blendalla fondly watched him go.

"You are happy here," Raftennon commented.

"Yeah. I wish Mother would accept our invitation and come live with us. It's not good for her to stay..." Sorrow clasped her throat shut, preventing her from finishing the statement.

"She is in good hands," the mage interjected before the silence became oppressive. "Shenma takes splendid care of her."

"Speaking of Shenma," Brendalla's threatening tears dried up and her mood darkened, "she sent word about your suspicions. You think an ex-girlfriend is responsible for the wind?"

"She has admitted it." Since she already knew about Jennalla's involvement, Raftennon felt no need to hold anything back anymore.

"You've seen her?" Blendalla leaned forward in her chair, folding her arms on the table.

It was obvious his sister struggled to suppress strong emotions. Whether it was sorrow or rage, or a mixture of both, he could not tell. The spellcaster continued to sit back in his own seat, trying to maintain his impassive facade. "I have spoken to her through magical means. I have yet to confront her in person."

"I'm guessing, by the look on your face, that it didn't go well."

"No, it did not." Raftennon admonished himself for the lack of control over his facial expression. Despite their years apart, it was clear she could still read him much more easily than others could. The mage also held back a sigh, not wanting to show how much his failure to convince Jennalla to stop was bothering him.

"Should I have something to worry about?"

It was not just rage and sadness Blendalla was fighting to keep at bay. For the first time, Raftennon saw the fear. He should have caught that sooner. Of course, she would be afraid for the safety of not only herself but of her family.

Raftennon mirrored his sister's posture, leaning forward in his chair. He laced his fingers on top of the table and peered into her eyes. "You have nothing for fear." Confidence filled his voice. And why should it not? He had taken care of her brutes in the Hills, after all.

Raftennon stayed in Ednifad the following day. He did not know when he would have a chance to return, so he took full advantage of this visit. He spent the entire time with Blendalla and her girls, forgetting his current burdens. His nieces eagerly gave him a tour of the village, somehow succeeding to make something that should have lasted fifteen minutes go on for over an hour. And they did so while keeping it interesting. The excitement they exuded when telling their stories about what they did at every stop drew Raftennon in. Try as he might, the words to convey how much this time with his family pleased him continued to elude him.

That evening, he said his farewells to his nieces, promising to come back as soon as he was able, for he would be leaving in the morning. He could not tarry too long. There was no knowing what Jennalla was plotting now that he had disposed of her lackeys.

The sun had just peeked up from the eastern horizon the next morning when the magic-user placed the last scroll into his bag to finished his packing. Blendalla ordered her brother to make a final stop before leaving. She had arranged for the baker to prepare some bread for his journey. Raftennon voiced his appreciation and hugged her before exiting the house.

The wizard made his way to the bakery, only to find his gift was not yet ready. The proprietor apologized, saying he could not let the lovely Blendalla's brother leave until he received his bread. She had insisted. The man promised it would only take a few more minutes. Raftennon reassured him he was fine with the delay. It would not do to displease his sister, after all.

The spellcaster returned outside and stood in front of the building, taking in the fragrant aromas of various bread and sweet rolls. He watched the villagers exiting their homes and congregating in small groups. Some began conversations on some topic or other while others walked toward the southern edge of town. The mage's eyes followed these men as they passed between two houses to disappear behind one of the buildings. A moment later, they passed by the opening again, still heading out of the village. Now they carried what appeared to be axes, saws, ropes and wide straps of leather. Raftennon was uncertain those were indeed the sort of tools they transported, for his glimpse of them had been too short, but it was clear they were off to start their workday.

The baker came out, within the time promised, with a tightly packed bundle, steam escaping the gaps in the tight weave of the linen cloth hiding the loaves within. Raftennon thanked the man and went to his horse to place the package in one of his saddle-bags. As the magic-user was finishing to cinch the bag closed, one of his nieces came running toward him.

"Uncle, uncle, you have to come quick!"

"What has happened, dear?" the mage asked, placing his hands on her small shoulders.

She would not answer him, continuing to tug at his sleeve for him to follow. He did, the baker ensuring to look after his steed while he was gone. Running as fast as his blue robes would permit, Raftennon tried to keep up with the frantic child. He was not quick enough and sometimes stumbled, but managed to stay on his feet as his niece led him back to her home.

Bursting through the door, the wizard's breath caught in his throat, though his mastery of his outward expression kept the shock hidden from everyone else. Shards of glass littered the kitchen floor in front of the window that was no longer in its frame. Pieces of pottery also lay scattered throughout the room. The table canted to its side and the youngest of the girls shrieked at the far end of the room. Walking around the debris, Raftennon found Ronnan hunched over Blendalla. Her brown eyes stared up at the ceiling as a red pool steadily spread under her.

"What has happened?" Raftennon asked again, this time addressing the question to the adult who would hopefully be able to answer, despite his obvious shock.

"I don't know!" Ronnan screamed as he pushed a cloth onto his wife's chest, right over her heart. The strip of fabric was already soaked through, but still the man kept it over the wound. "I was in the other room when I heard the glass shatter. I ran in here and all I saw was the door closing. Then I saw Blendalla..."

His words trailed off into tears. Raftennon rushed around his brother-in-law and knelt beside his sister, trying to assess the damage. Ronnan would not remove the cloth, however, so making any determination was impossible.

Blendalla raised her arm, then let her hand fall into her brother's palm. He bent forward, placing his ear close to her lips to hear her whispers. "Gnome," was all she said.

At that moment, the door burst open and Raftennon's third niece ran into the room, followed by an elderly woman. "I brought the healer, Father!"

Raftennon sprang to his feet, giving the woman room to work. He turned away as she began her endeavours and rushed out of the house. Before reaching the street, the magic-user called to a neighbour who had stuck her head out of her front door. He demanded to know where the gnome ran off to. Thankfully, the old woman had indeed seen the strange little man running away and was glad to point out where he had gone.

Raftennon followed her directions, asking others as he went to ensure he did not lose the trail. Luck was with him, for there were witnesses all along the gnome's flight path eager to give the mage a helping hand. If not for his current state of mind, he would have heard the comments and learned the reason for the villager's generous aid. Most of them wondered what all this commotion was about and wanted to see what would happen if the two strangers met. Because of this curiosity, Raftennon gathered a mass of followers, each wanting the best vantage point to witness the events. Their directions led him out of the village, down the road that eventually brought travellers to Xendremmar, the very road the spellcaster had planned to use just minutes before.

Raftennon reached a long, two-storey building. The dull yellow paint was weather-worn but showed no signs of flaking. The wide steps leading to the main entrance appeared sturdy and in good repair, as did the wood shingles on the roof. Stables branched off to either side at the rear and a small wooden sign declared it the only inn for miles. A crowd of the curious was already growing around the building. It seemed the workers had left their woodcutting, or whatever else they had been doing, to see what was happening. The wizard stared at the structure for a short moment, his vision slightly blurred by oncoming tears of rage and grief, before taking a slow step toward the entrance.

"I don't think so, mage!" came a familiar voice from inside the inn.

"You attacked my sister!" the magic-user screamed back, barely keeping his wrath in check.

"Think of it as repayment for what you did to my men, and what you almost did to me!"

Denmur opened a set of shutters on the second floor to reveal himself. He was standing on an unseen chair, with his knife poised at an elderly man's throat. The crowd gasped at the sight. Most feared for the innkeeper's life while others pitied him. The villagers murmured among themselves, relaying how business had been so poor lately the innkeeper had talked about ending his own life. Maybe the gnome would be doing the man a favour by slitting his throat, as he had threatened to do so himself on several occasions. Raftennon heard all these soft-spoken comments but paid them little attention.

"You were the one who stabbed me to begin this confrontation," he reminded the gnome, still struggling to regain control of his emotions.

"It was only business, mage," Denmur chimed from his vantage point. "But you had to screw everything up by staying alive!"

"My sister still had nothing to do with any of it!" Raftennon roared, taking a step back in the battle to curb his fury.

"Hey, you're a powerful wizard, and a crafty bugger to boot! I needed any advantage I could get!" Denmur tightened his grip on the innkeeper's collar as the old man attempted to slink away from his captor. The gnome's green eyes never left the robed figure fuming in front of the building, however.

"And you believe anger will give you that advantage." Raftennon clenched and opened his fists, his fingertips brushing against the sides of his dark blue robes. His jaw was set and his eyes blazed with inner fire.

"Rage causes a man to make mistakes," Denmur explained, enjoying the sight of the flustered mage. "You're about to make one, and when you do, I'll be there to finish the job!"

"The mistake was made long ago when a young woman decided to take her anger out on my loved ones."

With a flick of the mage's wrist, all the windows and doors of the inn closed and barred themselves shut. Denmur's muffled shout seeped through the wooden shutters as he banged on them, ordering them reopened. Raftennon plunged his arms into his robes and began chanting some arcane spell. "*Entraylônnam krayllentraenol fôrnak! Kâllantrénnam fôrlan maytralnâk!"*

Pulling his hands out of a hidden pocket, his fingers covered with some unknown black powder, the magic-user added strange gestures to the droning incantation. A massive ball of flames burst from his palms, smashing into the front door. The spectators screamed in fear as the unnatural fire engulfed the building. The blaze spread over the structure at an alarming rate, covering all possible means of escape in mere seconds.

Raftennon stood silent vigil as the smoke thickened, billowing up into the sky. The inferno consumed every plank, every pole, every drape and carpet. The structure eventually crumpled in on itself, scattering what villagers had remained to witness the incineration. The mage stared on as the conflagration eradicated everything, and everyone, trapped inside.

18

LOCATING THE SOURCE

Raftennon passed beyond the southern edge of Entamman Forest, on the last leg of his journey back to the Spellcasters' Guild. The sun struggled to shine through the gathered clouds but failed miserably.

After leaving the wreckage that was once the inn, the wizard had trudged back to his sister's home, all emotion left at the destruction. As he entered the humble home, he knew right away Blendalla had not survived the attack. In fact, he had known before then, first suspecting that fate would befall her as he exited her kitchen to pursue the gnome. Now the healer confirmed his deepest fears, shaking her head in resignation as she passed through the door.

Raftennon stayed for the customary four-day mourning vigil, followed by the spiritual cleansing pyre. His emotionless eyes stared at the embers floating toward the heavens, taking his sister up to Hanlon's Gate, entrance to Paradise.

That regrettable task done, he departed to make his return to Xendremmar. He needed to find Jennalla and prepare to confront her. She wanted so badly to see this come to a fatal end. She would get her wish. He would make her pay for her treachery.

The weather complemented his mood—grey and dreary. The clouds overhead threatened to release a torrential downpour but decided to hold off. Raftennon never noticed. In his present state, an army of drummers could have rumbled past him and he would have never known.

Uncounted days later, the mage entered the large, walled city of Xendremmar. Seeing the familiar sights of the metropolis he had called home for most of his life, Raftennon began to regain some of his usual humour. He turned his thoughts from his departed sister to the task he had to perform. He had to discover Jennalla's whereabouts and devise a way to defeat her.

Riding through the front gate of the Spellcasters' Guild, the wizard continued to the rear of the complex where the stables were located. He handed the reins over to one of the grooms, not even bothering to give him any special instructions, before heading to the main library. Entering the central tower, Raftennon walked right into his old mentor. Vendrammon clasped the younger man's shoulders to make certain he did not fall over after their minor collision.

"You look terrible, my boy," the elder said with more feeling than he had ever used during Raftennon's sojourn at the school.

"I have endured very trying times as of late," Raftennon admitted, returning his teacher's embrace.

"I hope the scrolls I gave you were of some help."

Reminded of the gifts, Raftennon recounted his encounter with the thieves in the Hills and the exaggerated result of the landslide spell. The young spellcaster was unsure if it was the presence of his old Master or the ambience of the library, but his depression lifted enough for him to feel like himself again. Vendrammon led his former student further into the tower, nodding now and then as Raftennon relayed every detail of that ordeal. The Teacher failed to hide his surprise at the scope of the destruction.

"You brought the entire hill down atop their heads, did you?" Vendrammon rubbed his chin as he pondered the ramifications of the unexpected outcome.

"I was correct in assuming that was not the incantation's intended outcome, then," Raftennon interrupted his Master's thoughts, stopping their stroll at the foot of the winding staircase.

Vendrammon folded his arms into his robes (a gesture that warmed Raftennon's heart, bringing back memories of the years he had spent at the School) and turned to face him. "You knew the amount of soil affected depended on the will of the spellcaster?"

"Yes, I did." Unlike the test he had taken all those years ago, this scroll he read in its entirety. Not having cast the spell before, he needed to know every single detail before attempting it. The description on the parchment was quite clear on that particular fact, to the point of warning the caster to stand well back of the chosen target. "Are you saying I have more power than I suspected?"

"It appears you have more power than we both suspected."

The old wizard wrapped an arm around his former apprentice and guided him up the spiralling, banister-less stair. The elder struggled to keep the smile from forming on his lips, to keep his usually emotionless facade. His heart continued the fight, however, beating hard in his chest. It was not every day the greatest wizard to ever live received proof his protege would indeed surpass him. "You have come back to continue your studies," the Mentor stated after regaining complete control of his excitement.

"I need to do some research." Raftennon peered at the thousands of tomes lining the inner wall of the spire, afraid his task would take far too long.

"I have recently been apprised of the young lady's transgressions since she left us, as per the request in your latest letter." The elder's good mood vanished.

"What happened to her?" Raftennon stopped halfway up the stairs to the next landing. He waited for Vendrammon to turn to face him so he could see every nuance of his expression, hoping to gain as much information from his words as well as the slightest hint of emotion the old man failed to hide.

"I must confess something to you, my boy." The old man stared back, letting two emotions trickle past his mask. The first was admiration, no doubt for the attempt at reading his feelings. The second was impish glee, for the Master Mage knew the scrutiny would yield nothing. "Though the fear love would distract you was the main reason I apprenticed you so early, I was also afraid the young lady's emotional imbalance would have been detrimental to your own studies. We knew when she was admitted to the Guild she had a terrible rage she did not want to temper. Her mother insisted we help her, stating she would go mad herself if we did not intervene. The Mage Dean gave in to the woman's laments and permitted the girl to attend the School. Personally, I think he believed himself capable of calming her, teaching her the control she refused to learn from her mother. I wanted to save you from this kind of outburst from her."

"I appreciate that, Master." That was not really true. Raftennon did not blame his Teacher for anything that had happened. He was the one who had been infatuated with her. He was the one who had caught her attention. He was the one who had brought forth her anger.

"You should not," Vendrammon stated, letting a little regret show through his usual sternness. "It is apparent I was too late."

"We all know, Master, the Mage Dean succeeded in his efforts." Raftennon moved his eyes to every apprentice presently in the vast hall, studying each of them as they performed their designated tasks. "Jennalla has full control of her rage, using it as her strength. It has helped her gain her power. She has chosen to take out all her frustrations on me. I must find her and stop the madness."

The old wizard nodded and guided the younger spellcaster to a room halfway up the tall spire. It was like all the others above the ground floor, devoid of any furniture save for a stone table in the centre of the room. The unnatural illumination from the orb at the bottom of the tower permeated the room, shedding light on a pile of scrolls neatly placed at one end of the table.

"I thought you might like to add to your repertoire," Vendrammon said, gesturing to the mound of parchment.

"Thank you, Master." Raftennon unrolled the first scroll and glanced over the spell. "I will also be researching the place Jennalla is currently frequenting."

"You know her whereabouts?" Vendrammon started to take a step forward but another mage poked his head into the room. Before the newcomer had a chance to utter a word, the veteran spellcaster acknowledged him by raising a finger.

"The last time we spoke was through a communication orb," Raftennon explained, looking at the man still lingering in the doorway. "I caught a glimpse of the room in which her sphere was located."

Vendrammon nodded and started for the entryway. "I will

come see you when I have time to help with your search. For now, I have to attend to my new apprentice." The elder pointed to the young man still waiting on the threshold of the room. "He is as gifted as they come these days, but nowhere near as talented as you were when I first took notice of you. His accelerated path of grasping the fundamentals, compared to his current peers, is lacking when viewed beside your feats. I fear we will not see your like again for a very long time."

With a rare warm smile, the old magic-user left Raftennon alone in the study to pore over the material offered to him.

Raftennon spent two weeks memorizing his new ammunition, incantations the boy he was when he first arrived here, when his father said he could become a magician, never imagined existed. The rooms on the central stories of the main tower were for the practice of spells, hence the scarce furnishings. Powerful nullification enchantments were woven into the walls to ensure the safety of those not taking part in the learning process.

Despite all these precautions, the chambers surrounding the one Raftennon used remained empty whenever he was there. The mage soon became known as one of the most powerful spellcasters in history, for his incantations overwhelmed the shields and still shook the tower. A few innocents suffered muted effects from the attacks the wards only partially blocked. Only distance could ensure true safety, and Raftennon obliged the Teachers' request for him to perform his tests on the upper floors, where it would be easier to isolate him.

Raftennon ignored all the other talk, however. More than a handful wondered what he had done to attain such power, in such a short amount of time. Master Mages and Teachers gossiped as much as the students. But none of them could come to a consensus. Raftennon let them speculate and concentrated on his studies. He even retrieved more scrolls that lined the inner wall of the spire, adding weapons and armour he hoped Jennalla would not expect him to have.

In this manner, he learned a spell he had been seeking since his arrival.

* * *

Shenma neared the end of her packing while her mother still napped in her bedroom. A couple aprons and matching dresses remained on the table, beside the already laden packs. They lay there, forgotten for the moment. In her hand, she held the saddest letter she had ever received. In it, Ronnan explained Blendalla's passing and expressed his sorrow at her loss. The erratic writing revealed when his hands shook so much he could barely hold the pen. A blot of faded ink that made reading the words difficult showed her where a tear had no doubt fell from a grief-stricken eye.

The youngest of the sisters was preparing for the trip north-ward, so she and her mother could visit the grieving family. She placed the letter by the large bags, turned to grab the last of the garments, then yelped in surprise. "Raf! How'd you get in here?"

The wizard stood in the middle of the living room, his arms folded in his blue robes. Shenma marvelled at him, for she was certain he had not used the door. He would have had to pass by her to get from the front of the house to where he was now.

"Where is Mother?" Raftennon asked, ignoring the shock on his sister's face.

"She's sleeping…" Shenma started, pointing to the bedroom door with a thumb, but her confusion prevented her from con-tinuing.

"Where are you going?" Raftennon inquired, tilting his head toward the half-filled bags on the kitchen table.

"Oh, Raf! It's Blendalla! She's…" Tears filled Shenma's eyes, clenching her throat shut.

"I know, Shenma. I was there."

The young woman took the two steps to reach her brother and wrapped her arms around his waist. Raftennon embraced his sis-ter, letting her cry as much as she needed. "We're preparing to go see them," she said when she could manage it.

"Do you know where I may find Ezranalla?"

Shenma loosened her hold on her brother enough to be able to see his face, trying to determine why he was asking that ques-tion. "She's probably visiting Ronnan and the kids. She and her husband live on the northern edge of Entamman, and I'm assum-ing they got the same letter we did. And a lot sooner, too."

"That is well. Are you done packing?"

Shenma stared at the bags, wondering why they were there for a moment before remembering what she had been doing before her brother appeared in her living room and drove all other thought from her. "Ah, almost," she stammered. She started to ask him what was going on, but he slipped away from her and headed for their mother's bedroom. A few moments later, he returned with her. The old woman mirrored her daughter's bewildered expression.

"Raf, what's going on?" Shenma nearly screamed.

"The woman responsible for the wind that took our father and brothers was also behind Blendalla's death." The mage retrieved the closed sack from the table. "You are not safe here."

"Where else are we supposed to go?" Melna asked, leaning against a chair while her son slung the pack onto his shoulders.

"I have arranged lodgings for all of you in Xendremmar, near the Spellcasters' Guild, until all this is resolved." He reached for the second bag, but Shenma pulled it away from him, intent on carrying it herself.

"This is our home," Melna started, but Raftennon did not let her finish.

"I will not endanger the lives of those I care about any longer," the spellcaster stated, the determination in his eyes quieting his mother. "Once she is stopped, you may return."

"You said you could handle her," Shenma interjected.

"I did not foresee her treachery." The women could see the rage seething below the mage's attempt at a facade of calm. They could also see he would explain no further.

"So we're in danger," Shenma clarified.

"No one will harm you in Xendremmar."

Shenma stared at him, mulling over their current situation. As far as she could tell, there was a crazy woman out there willing to kill anyone close to her brother, just to hurt him. And this woman was smart enough to outwit him. Would they be safe in Ednifad, where her sister had lost her life? Should they risk it?

"Okay," Shenma conceded, seeing her brother's logic. "The horses are waiting outside."

"There is no need," the wizard said, before chanting words the women did not understand.

Moments later, they were in Ednifad.

* * *

Raftennon gathered the rest of his family and transported them to Xendremmar, where they settled in a large manor adjacent to the Spellcasters' Guild. The School owned the building and used it to house dignitaries who visited the complex but did not wish to spend the night within its fences. The Mage Dean offered to lend the empty house to them, as well as a watchful eye while Raftennon pursued Jennalla.

With his loved ones now safe from any further harm, Raftennon began his research. He spent many hours searching the many tomes of the vast library, trying to find the room without walls that housed the orb.

One night, three weeks after his arrival, Vendrammon finally returned to visit his star pupil. "I apologize for my rude absence," the old mage said as a form of greeting.

"I remember the countless hours you spent drilling your lessons into my thick skull," Raftennon replied, a broad smile on his face. "I have not been gone that long. I expect you treat all your apprentices with the same overbearingness."

"Do you finally see my motives behind all the apparently worthless nitpicks?"

"Yes, Master," the young wizard said, like a child who agreed with his mother only to get her to leave him alone. "You were correct."

The pair laughed, now that the teacher considered the pupil his equal, relatively speaking. There would always be the distinction the difference of age brought, and the respect that fact entailed, but their skill was quickly becoming quite comparable.

"How is your family faring in the drab manor?" Vendrammon hated the decor of the house outside their fences and shared that opinion with whoever was caught in the conversation. There were not enough exotic plants and objects of unknown origin in it to his liking. A home without mysterious artifacts was not worth having, as far as he was concerned.

"They all seem to be adjusting well to the boisterous life of the city." Raftennon put down the large book he had been reading, the passage in question giving him absolutely no insight on the room without walls. "All save Ezranalla's husband and their eldest son. They are woodsmen, most comfortable in the wilderness. The others are taking every advantage to visit the many merchants and to see the myriad of other wonders Xendremmar has to offer. My mother is even showing signs of renewed life."

"That is good to hear." The Master Mage picked up one of the tomes and thumbed through its numerous pages. "And while they are revelling in the streets, you are here, searching for... what, exactly?"

"A room with no walls, with pillars holding up a domed ceiling, located in a storm-filled sky."

Vendrammon frowned at the description, returning the heavy tome to the table.

"You know the room." Raftennon sat back at the furrowing of the old man's brow.

Vendrammon remained silent as he turned and hurried out of the study. Raftennon sprang up from his chair to follow his mentor up the spiral stair, all the way to the top of the structure. The old man took a book from one of the shelves lining the inner wall and entered the uppermost room of the spire. Raftennon went in after him, into a den with two plush chairs with a small round table between them. Vendrammon plopped down onto a fat cushion and opened the tome on his knees. Raftennon made his way behind the chair as his teacher leafed through the volume. The old man found the section he sought. Raftennon searched the pages for himself as the Master Mage turned them, so he saw the entry the moment the old man placed a finger on it.

In Mylnan Vinas, the Age of Darkness, the Vengeful God, Jafall, came down to the lands to bathe them with his hatred, to drench them with his vengeance. In the shadows of the Mountains Pynakkor, he erected his dwelling, ripping its foundations from the earth. Great rifts he created, taking stone to construct his edifice. Bottomless the crevasse became as the tower reached skyward.

The heavens he populated with the children of his aunt, Nemanta. Ever does the storm rage; ever does lighting lick the pinnacle of the spire; ever does thunder assault the senses.

There, Vengeance Personified looks down onto the world, from his vantage point atop the citadel. No walls obscure his vision, permitting him to fly to the borders of all realms, spreading the evil seeds that give him strength.

Pillars hold up the pride of his creation, the heart of his might. The Black Eye radiates its invisible light over the lands, spewing forth the words that invade the mind during the night, making one question the motives of their loved ones...

The entry went on, describing more of the ancient fortress.

"Jennalla is frequenting the House of Jafall," Raftennon said after a long silence.

"The god of vengeance may be giving her strength. From what I heard of the attack she made on your family, it is the only explanation. We would have never let her leave if we had known she was capable of such devastation. We knew she was not mentally fit to wield that much power."

Vendrammon closed the tome and handed it to Raftennon before getting up from the chair. "Read through that, my boy," the old mage gesture to the book as he made his way to the door. "There is much to learn about that accursed place before even contemplating a journey there. I will see what I can do to help you."

With that, the Teacher left the room, leaving his former apprentice in the magical light that could not warm the air.

Raftennon spent another week learning about the unholy temple. It took him that long because Vendrammon would come in every so often with a spell he thought the young mage would need, forcing him to split his time between his research and his memorization.

In this time, Raftennon learned the wastelands surrounding the tower were impenetrable. Not only did the perpetual storms ravage the earth between the ravines to the north and east and the mountains to the west, they also repelled all that tried to enter the land. Any attempt that succeeded to span the wide crevasse propelled the victim into a whirlwind that would tear him asunder. The hurricanes were so powerful even magic could not appease them. The murky lands to the south formed the last barricade.

The vast Swamp of Tears spanned the southern border of the wasteland from the Pynakkors to the ravine. At the northern edge of the mire, footing was impossible to find. It was like a lake of mud that sucked all those foolish enough to attempt passage down into its unknown depths, trapping them forever.

The only way one could enter was by invitation only. They would have to invoke the god of vengeance and plead for his favour. Only then could they safely travel the desolation.

That was the only way of entry—save one.

According to the tome Raftennon was currently reading—which happened to be the only copy in existence—one prisoner of the House managed to escape the clutches of the Vengeful God. He was an elf who had insulted the deity, slaying a man to save him from the god's wrath. The elf's punishment was imprisonment in the House, at the top of the central spire, where Jennalla's orb of communication now sat. For him, the sphere was one of sight, which showed him all the acts of revenge occurring in the world. Jafall gave the elf eternal life so his suffering would never end. The deity also removed the elf's eyelids so he would not miss a single second of torture.

It was not recorded how he accomplished this feat, but the elf fled the fortress, passing through its ravaged surroundings without the winds tearing him to shreds.

Raftennon read the entry the elf scrawled on a piece of bark from a tree deep in Drendaggamor, written in his own blood. The strange note somehow made its way into the hands of a travelling wizard, who then brought it to the Guild many years ago. Raftennon presumed the original crude document was stored somewhere in the complex, but looking for it was unnecessary since he already had its contents written before him.

Time unending I stare at the horrors until I couldst take nay more! While His attention is divert'd elsewhere, I make mine escape. Though His torture is dateless, the chains that keep me to the Eye art not. I make mine way out of the tower, past many atrocities that doth not affect me any longer. Out into the desert I go, expecting to fly into the wind I kept seeing between the columns. But hither, in the shadow of His House, the torrent dost not come. I follow the calm, which brings me to the foot of tall mountains. Along these I search, certain He will soon espy me and return me to the Eye. But He dost not find me and I fall into the stone. Bless'd darkness overcomes mine eyes and I stay hither f'r the first rest I hast had in millennia. Then I crawl, and crawl, and crawl, ev'r in blackness. Deeper into the earth I go, forev'r going down. The path veers upward and I climb, and climb, and climb. Eventually, I hear a sound I had forgotten. Only when I fall into the cold waters doth I recollect the noise of a birthing stream. Hither I rest f'r a while, relishing the sweet taste of the life-giving liquid, curing mine parch'd throat from its endless siege of wind. Finally satiat'd, I move on into more darkness, going down, and down, and down until I witness another miracle I had long forgotten. Light bathes mine face, warming it, returning life to it. Then shadows befall me, but I welcome them, f'r they come from memories of mine childhood. Leaves block the sun, but the darkness is not so deep hither. This will be mine home now.

Raftennon reread this letter, committing it to memory. Retrieving a map from the many shelves along the staircase, the wizard scanned the area surrounding the evil temple. He located the House of Jafall and the Pynakkor Mountains to the west of it. The mage trailed his finger down the pictured rocky ridge until it reached the source of the Masthoranin River. This must have been the water the elf found. Continuing south-westward, Raftennon soon came upon the dark trees of Drendaggamor, the Dead Wood. Was the elf still in the cursed forest? There was only one way to find out.

19

REUNIONS

"*Where* are you going?" Shenma demanded, not believing what she thought she heard. Surely, her brother would not be foolish enough to go *there*.

"Do not fret, Shenma. I will be safe," Raftennon said, trying to lessen her distress. He did not share her misgivings and tried to send some of his courage her way.

"Nobody's safe in the Dead Wood, Raf!" The young woman was nearing hysterics. Raftennon was thankful his mother was out with his other sister and her grandchildren visiting the Animal Pens. "They say the trees eat people and the sun doesn't even dare shine there! Evil things make that forest their home and whoever goes in never comes out!"

"That is obviously rubbish," he interjected while she paused to take a breath. "Someone managed to escape it. How else would I have received my information?"

That did not assuage her, but she did begin to breathe a bit more slowly.

"Listen, Shenma." Raftennon took both her hands in his, catching her eyes with a grave stare. "I must do this."

"Why?" She almost screeched the question. Her apprehension was regaining its strength, but she did not try to withdraw from her brother's intended reassuring grasp.

"The family cannot stay in Xendremmar for the rest of their

lives and they cannot leave until Jennalla's threat has been elim-
inated. If I do not go to Drendaggamor, I will never be able to
reach her."

"I don't want to lose the only brother I have left!"

The young woman whirled around, yanking her hands out of
Raftennon's gentle grip and fled the room. Her cries echoed
through the empty halls, each of them sticking an insubstantial
dagger into the spellcaster's heart. Memories of Blendalla's
wound came to mind and the mage hurried to quash them before
losing his resolve.

*He grows quickly, but his anger is becoming an issue. Then
again, it is giving him strength. Let us hope he masters the emotions that threaten to wrench his power from him, as it did her.*

*Once he does that, we will commence his true training. I can-
not wait for the others to conclude their lengthy investigation.*

"So you think you can save your family by keeping them near
the school, do you?"

She glared into the orb atop the twining vipers, akin to those
in the ruined neighbourhood of her old home. These snakes were
black obsidian, not white ivory as were their counterparts. The
sphere was also larger than the silver ball and was bluish in colour. She had replaced the orb of communication used to confer
with the thief with the one of sight Jafall had employed to torture
the elf. Through this focus, she followed all of Raftennon's
deeds, all his efforts to keep his loved ones safe.

"Nothing you can do will save them," Jennalla whispered, her
words losing themselves among the raging wind. "You wanted to
toss me aside and leave me behind to lose everything. You will
learn what it is to have nothing."

Raftennon entered the room, one he had not seen in months.
Everything was as it had been when he left: every phial in its
designated place on the numerous shelves, every scroll in its
proper cubicle. The wizard took in the familiar sight of the desk

and the array of herbs suspended in pots over it, remembering his first lesson in herbal lore. The small alcove set off to the side was as empty as it ever was, ready for the students to practise their spellcasting—all under Vendrammon's severe scrutiny, of course.

Before the door could close another man brushed past the mage, his arms filled with numerous scrolls. "I'm sorry, sir." He dropped his load onto the table set under the window. While the documents settled themselves on the polished wood, the flustered youth stretched an arm outward to reach for the few parchments that threatened to roll to the floor. "I mean, I *am* sorry, sir."

Raftennon smiled, not able to keep the change of emotion hidden. He remembered his first lessons on pronunciation and the grilling to never use contractions. The young mage had slipped up on numerous occasions himself during the first few months of his private studies. "You must be Master Vendrammon's new apprentice."

"Yes, sir." The teen straightened from his work and finally saw to whom he was speaking. "You're Raftennon!"

"That is correct." The spellcaster bowed, more to hide his growing smile than to show respect. The novice's awe was more than the magic-user could handle. He inwardly reproached himself for losing control of his emotions in such fashion. It was more than refreshing to have someone think so highly of him, even though he had no idea what he had done to inspire this level of reverence.

"They say you're fast becoming the most powerful mage in all of history!"

"If he is, it is because he has forgone all shortcuts, like the contractions you feel compelled to still use."

Both men turned to the new voice. Vendrammon slowly walked passed his former apprentice and went to the table to his current student. "You may retrieve the rest of the materials."

The awestruck novice bowed at the wizards and hurried out of the room, slamming a shoulder in the door jamb on his way. He grunted in pain and whirled a full turn before regaining his footing. Then he disappeared down the hall.

"You must forgive the lad." Vendrammon frowned at the disarray formed of his precious scrolls. "He may be skilled, but he still has much to learn about the Art. Are you ready, my boy?"

The Master Mage left the mess to return to his guest. Raftennon checked his pack one final time before nodding, signalling he had all he needed.

"Very well then, let us begin, and add another stop for your own castings." The old wizard was referring to the limitations of the teleportation spell Raftennon had recently learned and used to gather his family to the safety of Xendremmar. The caster could not transport himself, or any other, to a place he had never physically visited beforehand. Therefore, the teacher would be sending the star pupil to the next stop of his journey.

Raftennon stood motionless as the old wizard handled the spell components and recited the prescribed words. The air crackled around him, faded, and the younger spellcaster found himself in the middle of an unknown street. Three women stared at the mage, who had appeared out of nowhere in front of their eyes. It took a few moments for them to regain control of themselves, and when they did, they ran around the corner, screaming in terror.

Raftennon forgot about the encounter almost immediately, trying to get his bearings. He knew he was in the village of Madosan, nestled at the southern tip of the Pynakkors. In fact, it was because of these peaks he could figure which way he now had to go.

The magic-user made his way toward the mountains, studying his surroundings as he went, burning the image into his memory (he would need it to travel here in the future). Once he branded the mental picture into his head, Raftennon ignored everything and everyone around him, including the murmurs that were spreading about his abrupt arrival—until he ran into an old "friend."

"Well, well, look what we have here."

A large man stood in the middle of the street, flanked by five equally massive brutes, blocking the mage's way out of town.

"It is nice to see you have survived, Stav," Raftennon said, betraying no emotion. Truth be told, the plainsman's presence stirred no feelings within the mage. He was not surprised the ruffian managed to live through the whirlwind in the Hills; the gnome had found a way out of the cave-in, after all. At the moment, the wizard had much more important things to deal with than an old dispute.

"Sure it is." Stav sneered, directing two of his lackeys to advance on the spellcaster. It was clear the thug felt they had not resolved their differences.

"As far as I am concerned, we settled everything in Salgre," Raftennon said, unimpressed by the muscular pair stomping toward him.

"You took out most of my men!" The plainsman's veins throbbing on the sides of his neck as he yelled.

"Call it repayment for your 'generous hospitality'." Raftennon folded his arms into his robes. His lips seemed to quiver, a sight Stav did not miss.

"Oh, if that's the case," the ruffian said, a sneer curving up one corner of his mouth, "I owe you some change."

The thugs, one at either side of the wizard, reached out to grab him. Their hands recoiled almost immediately, each of the brutes fanning their aching fingers. As they touched the flesh under the blue robes, intense heat burned through their own skin, searing the muscle beneath.

"I would not attempt that again if I were you," Raftennon advised in a nonchalant tone, ignoring the lackeys and keeping his eyes locked on their leader.

Stav ignored the warning, sending the rest of his band. The three thugs only advanced a few steps before Raftennon cast a curtain of fire in their path with a sweep of his hand. The flames leaped up as high as the brutes' chests, barring their way.

"Do not sacrifice the lives of your men again, Stav. All I desire is to go on my way, undeterred. What you do after we part company matters not to me."

"And where, exactly, do you think you're going?" The plainsman fumed, furious he could not get his hands on the spellcaster yet again. "The roads out of town lie behind you. The only things in front of you are the mountains and the..." Realization overtook the thief's face, replacing his rage with bewilderment. "Why are you travelling to the Dead Wood?"

"That is none of your concern." Raftennon stared at the ruffian, becoming irritated at the unnecessary delay of his journey.

"I know what's going on." Stav waved his finger at the mage. "You intend to find that elf and steal the secret of eternal life from him, don't you."

"My intentions are my own." Raftennon did not know what the thief was talking about but was becoming quite interested in what he had to say. The magic-user was under the impression not many knew of the elf's existence.

"That story's a wives' tale," the plainsman continued, seemingly unaware the magician had spoken. "There's no truth to it. There's no way an elf can live forever. It's probably just an old elf who's exaggerating his age."

"What do you know of him?" Raftennon dissipated his magical fire and walked toward the brute.

One of Stav's lackeys took the opportunity to grab him, only to suffer the same burns as the others. The last two unharmed brigands wisely stayed away from the wizard, who continued to walk forward as if nothing had happened.

"Why would I tell you anything?" The plainsman returned his attention to the advancing mage, readying himself for any possible attack. "You and that cursed gnome did away with the best posse I've had in years! Where is the shrimp, anyway? You planning another ambush? Maybe finish the job you failed to do in the Hills?"

"It appears I was a pawn in his escape." Raftennon stopped a few feet in front of his former captor and slid his hands into the folds of his robes.

"Yeah?" Stav mirrored the mage's action and crossed his own massive arms over his rock-hard chest. "Why should I believe that?"

"He attempted to slay me—twice." Raftennon's demeanour did not change one bit as an invisible vice seized his heart while his next thought came into his head. There was no way the spellcaster would show any weakness to this ruffian, and weakness would be exactly how the man would take the display of emotion. "When that failed, he took my sister's life."

"Serves you right for trusting the twerp." A rare immature tone crept into the plainsman's voice, making certain the mage caught the implied I-told-you-so meaning.

"I repaid his gesture by ending his existence." Raftennon's

rage toward Denmur, still hot in the pit of his stomach, warmed the coldness of his usually indifferent inflections.

"You killed the gnome?"

The grave expression on the mage's face answered the thug's question. Stav nodded his head, impressed the man actually had what it took to take care of a problem—permanently. "Okay, I guess that's ample payment for the loss of my men." The plainsman gestured to his men to stand down, to relax from the offensive posture they still held against the wizard. "Go on to the Dead Wood, if that's what you want. But, if you want some advice, I'd change my mind if I were you. No one who sets foot in Drendaggamor ever comes out alive."

The mage stared at the thug, the hint of a smile forming on his lips, so minute no one caught it. Raftennon knew better than the common peasants of this land the forest's fantastic, eerie tales were highly exaggerated. A wizard had left the wood with the piece of bark, after all. "I will take my chances."

Raftennon took the few steps needed to pass by the brutes. None of them attempted to stop him, a fact that pleased him greatly. Too many useless deaths had already occurred on this journey. The spellcaster walked a few feet toward the edge of town before Stav called after him.

"If you really insist on looking for the immortal elf, I may have some information for you."

The wizard turned to face the ruffian, who still stood with his arms crossed over his chest. His men scowled beside him, their disappointment clear on their faces. It was apparent the plainsman had mentioned the magic-user to them. Raftennon could only imagine how twisted his version of the events had become.

"Of course, I don't do anything for free," Stav added, his own smirk lifting the left corner of his mouth.

Raftennon sighed and rummaged in his robes, producing a small leather pouch. He threw it to the thief, who caught it as it threatened to pass over his shoulder. Stav hurried to untie the thong and opened the bag.

"What in Necroma is this?" he yelled, not liking the prank being pulled on him.

"I have no need for currency on this journey, so I carry none," Raftennon explained. "What I give you is dragonwing.

Many apothecaries would pay dearly for so much of the herb. Once you have sold that, you will find I have compensated you rather generously."

The plainsman examined the strange leaves, then stared at the mage, and finally stuffed the payment into his belt pouch. "Look for a patch of black poplars surrounded by dead elm trees. The elf is supposed to haunt that place, so the old wives say."

20

CRUSHING BLOWS

Five days Raftennon marched northward along the western edge of the Pynakkor Mountains. He walked in shadows every morning until the sun finally freed itself from the rocky peaks. Ever on his right, the massive stone of the earth rose, almost as sheer as a fortress wall. Narrow trails appeared here and there where, presumably, goats and other rock climbing animals came down to the plains to graze. Raftennon studied the winding tracks, wondering if he would have to climb one of them eventually.

As the fifth evening inched to twilight, the wizard reached a canyon opening in the mountain ridge. The sheer, stone wall veered toward the heart of the range at an almost perfect right angle. From the depth of the ravine flowed the Viprennys, its source secluded somewhere in the Pynakkors.

Raftennon set up camp on the southern shore of the Snake River. He peered across the waters to the dark elms and birches of Drendaggamor, their branches seeming to swallow the moonlight almost entirely. There was his destination. Hidden in the shadowy depths of the large forest lay his quarry. How he would find the elf, he did not know.

Tomorrow, the search would commence. In the morning, he would cross the river.

* * *

"That's it, Raf, sleep tight. Don't let the serpents bite!"

A maniacal cackle resonated through the room, mingling with the shattering boom of the thunderous storm mere feet away. The laughter lasted no longer than the first thunderclap. Jennalla returned her attention to the sphere showing her every move her former lover made.

"Who is this elf, Raf? I thought it was me you wanted. I don't know any elves, not anymore. What are you up to?"

The moon had made its journey through the sky and now set beyond the western horizon, giving the burden of illuminating the heavenly darkness over to the stars. They shed little light, which suited the creature perfectly. Its dark eyes peered from the mouth of the ravine, scanning the southern shore. They could not see much in the shadows of twilight, which pleased it immensely. If its vision was this impaired, the human was most likely blind.

The summons had surprised it, to say the least. It was not the first time someone had offered it prey. In the past, it had always been to save their own skin. This time the woman was nowhere near its lair, in no danger whatsoever of being eaten. But she still pointed the finger at someone else to satiate its hunger.

The fact she delivered the gift through words spoken in its head also astonished the beast. It did not know how that was possible, and it did not care. Having the morsel where the woman had promised and as vulnerable as she said, that was what mattered. It had been a long time since a fool ventured this close to its home.

Other images invaded its mind, making the message much longer than it needed to be. The woman proceeded to show it feats of magic, in great detail. These were tricks the beast had already encountered. She was warning it to be careful, that this prey would be dangerous. It decided to listen, for it knew the strength behind these spells. It had lived many decades, a feat accomplished by being wary and not letting its morsel get the better of it.

Slithering along the shallow waters of the river, it approached the campsite, the embers of the fire shining in the creature's eyes, which were now seeing in a different light. Instead of trying to pierce through the darkness, it was picking up the warmth emitted by the coals. In this fashion, it also found the outline of the mage's sleeping body, radiating intense heat compared to the rest of the landscape. He was prone and unaware, as promised.

Slowly, it slunk onto dry land, parting the tall grass as it inched its way closer to the slumbering spellcaster.

Raftennon heard the shifting blades near his ear but shrugged the sound away, certain it was part of a soon-to-be-forgotten dream. The clenching of his chest, however, was not something he could ignore. His eyes shot open as he gasped for breath.

The large anaconda from the mountains tightened its grip on the mage, squeezing the life from him. A mere fraction of its total length was all it needed to entirely engulf its prey. Its triangular head hovered in front of the man's face, appearing to relish the slow departure of his last remaining breath. The black eyes glistened ever so slightly in the starlight as the forked tongue flickered in and out of its eager mouth.

Raftennon desperately searched his repertoire for a spell that would get him out of the predicament. As whatever air he could manage to inhale burned in his lungs, his salvation came to mind —he hoped. Rummaging through the hidden pockets of his robes he could reach, he felt for the components he knew were there. The serpent's increasingly tight grip made the task that much more difficult and his compressed chest reminded him he did not have much time.

The snake felt the magic-user squirming to delve into his garments instead of trying to free his arms and recognition flashed in its black eyes. It almost seemed as if it knew the man was searching for what he required to work his magic. Raftennon grunted in pain, his ribs nearing the breaking point, as the anaconda squeezed even further. Thankfully, he found what he wanted: crushed mustard seed and some greyish-black powder. He blended both ingredients in his palm, ignoring the searing heat that shot through his hand. He then smeared the makeshift paste onto the beast's dark green scales.

The reptile released its prey, hissing in agony, moving away before it had finished uncoiling itself. Raftennon knew the sensation of burning flesh coursing through its long body would be much worse than what he now felt in his hand. The serpent whirled on its intended morsel for a second attack, however, instead of slinking away to nurse its wounds as the spellcaster had hoped. For some reason, this creature was intent on finishing him off before he could regain his breath. The creature's sluggish mobility on land gave Raftennon the time required to take in a much-needed gulp of air before striking out with his burning hand. His palm covered one of its glaring eyes, blinding the creature and finally driving it back to the river.

Raftennon watched it slither away in the dim starlight, marvelling at its magnificence, despite its desire to kill him. Mountain anacondas were rare to begin with, but this specimen was no doubt unique. The beast appeared to be at least forty feet long, but in the poor light of the moonless night, one could not be certain. A good two feet in diameter, he could not believe he had not heard the giant reptile sooner. Its girth left a deep impression in the tall grass, a vivid reminder to the wizard of his narrow escape. Raftennon's admiration of the beast heightened when the sluggish undulating curve of scales disappeared into the dark waters and swam away with alarming speed.

Confusion invaded his rambling mind, perpetuating the whirling of his thoughts. Why would a creature, clearly made to hunt in water, crawl out of its element and attack him? The answer to that question came to him almost as soon as he finished thinking it—someone sent the reptile to stop him.

The magic-user gathered his belongings and ran to the bank, where he stopped to survey the evidence of his assailant's dive dissipating as it flowed downriver. He was certainly not going to wait for the serpent to regain its composure and return to finish what it had come to do, but he would foolishly venture into its comfort zone even less. He had to traverse the river, nonetheless. He could no longer put off his trek into the forest until morning.

Unable to see anything, Raftennon rummaged in his robes for the proper components and cast the spell that had introduced him to magic. The light he conjured was much brighter now after his long years of training, almost rivalling the intensity of the sun. With the help of this magical glow, he scanned the slow current, finding safe passage to the other side. He waded through the waters as fast as his sodden clothes would allow. The splashing he produced was loud enough to wake any animal sleeping nearby, but he did not care. He needed to cross before the anaconda decided to return. His enchanted light faded out when he reached the northern bank, since the incantation only lasted as long as its components did. His crossing done, the mage forgo calling more illumination to save his store of ingredients for a later emergency.

Before him loomed the feared trees of Drendaggamor. Below their boughs lay perpetual night. Even when the sun shone with all its strength, under the leaves it was merely dusk. Dark things lived within the forest, their evil permeating the earth, twisting the plants, spoiling the air. The Dead Wood merited its name, not only because the trees seemed to have no life in them, but also for the fact whoever went in was never seen alive again (save for the one wizard who brought back the piece of bark).

Raftennon had no time to ponder these wondrous details as a rustling from the river startled him back to his present predicament. He whirled around, only to see the darkness of the night. Ripples on the water's surface distorted the reflected stars, betraying the passing of—something. The spellcaster knew it was not the last effects of his frantic fording.

He scanned the riverbank, trying to see through the tall grass and reeds lining the waters like a wide hedge. He was not about to be surprised as he was earlier, but he still could not see the anaconda. Closing his eyes, he slowed his breathing, straining to hear everything, down to the slightest movement. He was not an adept hunter, so he missed all the noises the snake was making as it slithered, ever so slowly, nearer to him. Raftennon, knowing this fact about himself, only appeared to be concentrating on listening to his surroundings. What he was actually doing was handling more spell components within his robes, muttering the words of magic that were now his life.

"Nighe-oollanômay blaynâdémor flaymaynôlan..."

In this manner, he prepared himself for the attack, which was slow to come. The wait was so long Raftennon began to suspect he might have imagined the rustling after all. The snake proved that false when it lumbered from between the elms nearest its target. It actually moved faster than expected and once again coiled its massive serpentine body around its prey.

Raftennon was ready for this attack and wrapped his arms around the wide body before the creature's vice could trap them. The mage's fingers grasped the serpent right below its triangular head with its one remaining baleful, black eye. He spoke the remaining phrase of his spell while the mammoth reptile squeezed the air out of his lungs.

"...*dürnaymôlâs fortâs!*"

When he shouted the last syllable, blue light slashed out from Raftennon's hands, like ethereal scythes reaping long stalks of wheat. The magical blades swung outward into the night sky, taking the serpent's head with them. The living coil released the wizard, dropping lifeless around his feet.

Raftennon slumped to the ground, sitting on the dead snake, wishing this was the last time he would need to gasp for air—ever. When the white spots relinquished their hold of his vision, the mage retrieved a knife from his bag and began gutting the reptile, chopping the flesh into manageable pieces. Then he spent the rest of the night smoking the meat, glad for the added provisions.

The spellcaster was so rapt in his work he did not realize a cloaked figure stared at him from the top of the southern ravine in the mountains. The silver-white hair flowed in the slight breeze as the man watched the labouring wizard. The fading darkness as night succumbed to morning hid the hint of a smile on the stranger's lips.

"Ugh! This can't be happening!" Jennalla stormed around the circular room without walls, raging as violently as the torrent in the sky surrounding her. "What does it take to kill this guy?" The wizardress forced herself to calm down and returned to the orb atop the serpent pedestal. "That snake should have swallowed him in one gulp!"

She peered into the sphere, which illuminated everything it showed in a bluish colour, enabling her to discern every little detail despite the twilight. Her eyes traced every curve of his body, every toned muscle as he chopped his intended assassin. She saw the determination in his eyes, the unflinching realization some things needed to be done, no matter how gruesome. Unwanted, some of the old passion that had drawn them together warmed her heart, hastened her breathing.

"No! I will not be distracted like that! You need to pay!"

Jennalla wrenched her eyes from the sphere, and the attractive man within, and walked to the southern edge of the room. Planting herself between two pillars, barely out of the reach of the hurricane winds, she stared over the mountains.

"Why are you seeking an elf that's supposedly hiding in Drendaggamor?"

21

ENTERING THE DEAD WOOD

Raftennon finished his work an hour before sunrise. He had to rush the smoking of the meat to reach this deadline, so the provisions were of lower quality, but they would suffice. He then took advantage of the last remnants of darkness to catch a bit more sleep. He used the anaconda's head as a vessel for a detection spell this time. Nothing, or no one, would be creeping up on him again that morning while he rested.

A few hours later, he woke, the heights of the Pynakkor Mountains still hiding the sun, which would have trouble showing itself that day through the gathering clouds. Raftennon assembled his growing possessions and took one last, deep breath before stepping into the shadows. The air under the dark leaves of the elms, birches and poplars was oppressive as soon as he passed the outer trees. Raftennon's lungs laboured harder than usual because the shade beneath the branches was thick with unseen pollen, or some other substance. He could smell ages of decay, rotting fruit and an unfamiliar mouldy odour. Within all these cloying scents, the wizard detected the faint aroma of moss, wildflowers and mushrooms. His heart started to race, not because of his difficulty breathing, but the possibility of finding rare and exotic spell components.

The spellcaster walked on, further into the darkness. He began to breathe easier, growing accustomed to the atmosphere of the ancient forest. The silence that prevailed here disturbed him. He could not hear any sign of life. No birds flew from branch to branch, chirping to their mates. No small animal scurried along the underbrush. In fact, the only sound was the dried leaves crushed under his deliberate steps.

He crept forward, intensively scanning for any signs that could guide him in the right direction. The Dead Wood was an immense forest and he did not have the rest of his life to search for the elf. He was hoping luck would be on his side and he would quickly stumble on the cluster of black poplars Stav had mentioned. Raftennon continued northward, keeping close to the mountains. If he did not manage to find the elf, maybe he could find some clue about where the mountainous passage of his escape entered the forest.

A slight dimming of the eerie woodland's gloom marked the coming of evening. Raftennon paid it little mind as he kept a keen focus on the obstacles in front of him. He was making his way through the thick underbrush, for there were no trails to speak of since the woods were devoid of life.

The mage stumbled on a protruding root. He had tripped so many times already he had now lost count. Usually, his flailing arms prevented him from falling to the ground. This time he dropped to his knees, unable to stop himself. He stared at the black earth under the leaves he had just disturbed. The grains of sand appeared to be moving, like a teeming colony of ants. The wizard leaned forward the slightest bit for a better look to make certain it was indeed the dirt that was shifting and not his imagination playing tricks on him. As he concentrated on the strange movement, he felt something brush against the nape of his neck, under his long, brown hair. Whirling around, afraid of another unexpected attack, Raftennon tried to rise to his feet and catch whatever had touched him. All he managed to accomplish was trip on another root and fall on all fours again, his bag flying off his shoulder. Before he could do anything else, the roots started wrapping themselves around his wrists and legs, pinning him down. The earth beneath him began to give way, slowly drawing him in.

Then the voices came, invading his turbulent thoughts, driving any idea of escape out before it had a chance to develop completely. "You…belong…to…us…now…"

The words came in slow syllables, drawn as thin as possible as if brought by the air that could not move in this stagnant place. Raftennon gasped for breath, vivid memories of the anaconda coming to mind. Then a low hiss came from behind him, with the same far-off quality as the unknown voice. He intensified his struggles to turn to search for the source of the new sound, but he was held fast. His hands were already covered in dirt.

"You…will…nourish…us…"

Raftennon felt his strength sapped from him, drained by the roots that twined up his arms. The birches shuddered with ecstasy, relishing the stolen life coursing through their branches. The wizard continued his fight until the forest began to dim. He saw welcoming darkness, a place where there were no anacondas trying to crush him. He felt warm, heat provided by a thick blanket of dirt. He had never known such exquisite comfort. He would not need to think any longer, feel any longer, want any longer. The trees promised.

I cannot permit my task to end this way.

Raftennon summoned all his remaining will to reclaim the energy stolen from him. An evil wind sprung up around him as the leaves thrashed in rage. The roots struggled to keep their hold on him. The mage sought his already-claimed strength from them and fought to take it back. Eventually, the roots started to loosen as Raftennon's life force trickled back to him.

"You…will…give…us…what…we…need…"

"I will not!"

The wizard's outburst broke the spell and the snaring roots disappeared. Raftennon found himself on all fours, the strap of his pack still around his wrist. The earth beneath his hands was normal dirt, unmoving, no longer covering his fingers. The fallen leaves that peppered the ground were in the same spot they had been before the altercation began.

Had it all been a dream? No, it was not. He was still kneeling. Was it another of Jennalla's attacks? That notion did not feel right to him. He had not sensed any malice behind the assault, only hunger. Maybe this was the fate that befell travellers who entered the Dead Wood—they were consumed to feed the darkness.

Raftennon slowly rose to his feet, brushing the ordinary dirt from his robes. The leaves swayed over his head in defiance, despite the fact there was no wind to propel them. The mage stared at the branches, mentally conveying his strength of will. Soon the rustling subsided and the spellcaster resumed his search.

Days passed. How many he could not tell from the virtually unchanging light in Drendaggamor. Mornings were as sombre as evenings and no creature came out (through its expected nocturnal habits) to indicate what time of day it was. He would eat whenever he was hungry and his rations, even the newly obtained anaconda, were slowly dwindling to nothing. A few days back, the underbrush had been so thick he could go no further unless he turned westward. This course brought him deeper into the forest and away from the guiding mountains. Now, Raftennon had no idea in which direction he trudged.

One night (he guessed the time of day from the degree of gloominess), while he rested, eating a chunk of freshly roasted anaconda, something broke the silence of the Wood. In the distance, Raftennon could not guess how far, something howled at the unseen moon. The spellcaster's muscles tensed as he strained to hear any hint of its whereabouts. He stopped chewing the reptilian meat, concentrating solely on the search for the ululation's source. The sound was not repeated, neither did the animal show itself. Raftennon spent the night in uneasy slumber, trying to remain as alert as he could while still getting some rest. He succeeded in doing poorly in both endeavours, but a second howl never pierced the quiet, nor did anything decide to visit.

"Where is he?" she roared, frustrated at the orb's refusal to follow the mage into Drendaggamor. "What's he up to? Why can't I see him?"

"He is within the Dead Wood," came a voice from over her shoulder.

"I know that!" Jennalla screamed at her unseen companion. The strange occurrence did not surprise her, as if talking air was a norm in that surreal room atop the mystical House of Jafall.

"The Wood has a life of its own and is much older than the device I graciously allow you to use. The trees prevent all magic from crossing their borders." The steel in the voice reminded the woman she was here only as a courtesy and that fact could change at any time.

"Ugh!" she exclaimed as she turned away from the sphere. "How am I supposed to know when he's dead?"

Raftennon was exhausted. He had no idea how long the animals followed him. The eerie howls came now and then, reminding the wizard he was no longer alone in the forest, robbing him of whatever sleep he tried to get. After a few hours of trying to avoid the sound, he gathered his courage and headed toward where he believed the ululations originated. It would be better to face the beasts now and deal with them while he still had some energy, rather than let them choose the time of their attack, which would certainly come at the spellcaster's weakest moment.

Around he went in the Dead Wood, not knowing in which direction he travelled, a fact that did not bother him in the slightest since he was already lost. As he trudged through the underbrush between the lifeless trees, the mage prepared the components for several spells, having enough time to change his mind numerous times on which incantation he would use.

Finally, not being able to go on without significant rest, Raftennon plopped onto the ground, his pack slipping off his shoulder. He closed his eyes, sleep quickly stealing over him.

Some time passed—how much, he did not know. The spellcaster was startled awake by the rustling of leaves not far to his right. His eyes flew open, but they only caught a glimpse of shadows darting from one tree trunk to the next. Gathering his belongings, he once again failed to locate the foreboding noise as it returned, this time to his left. Something was definitely in the Wood, near at hand.

Despite his heightened senses due to the warnings, Raftennon did not see the attack come. The shadow shot out from a thicket, sprinted past the magic-user and knocked him off his feet. Another ran from the opposite side, pounced on the wizard and sped off after leaving a large scratch on his hand. A third sprang forward and chomped at the mage's side, thankfully only catching the blue robes. Raftennon scrambled to stand, desperate to regain control of his racing heart and fleeting thoughts.

After regaining his footing, he finally saw what had stalked him for the past few days. Nearly a dozen black shapes inched their way through the trees, their hungry, black eyes fixed on the mage. The taut muscles of their powerful shoulders flexed with every deliberate step. Long, yellowish fangs glistened with saliva as the animals longed for the feast they would soon receive. Raftennon studied the beasts. Though he had never seen one in the flesh, he had come across depictions of the noble timber wolves of Dombellarr. Granted, that forest was days to the north, but there was no mistaking the heritage. These wolves, though smaller than their northern counterparts, were definitely blood relatives.

One of the creatures tilted its head to the sky and howled, sending a shiver down Raftennon's spine. Usually, he would have been able to keep his emotions in check, but fatigue had set in. He fumbled for the proper spell, but nothing would come to mind. He was not drawing a blank—he had not forgotten a single incantation in his vast repertoire. He simply could not find one that would deal with all the members of the pack at the same time, surrounding him as they were. Whenever he thought of an attack, he immediately realized at least one of them would get through and rip his windpipe from his throat.

So, he did all he could. Muttering the spidery language of magic, Raftennon flung his hand in front of him, palm out. An arrow of flame shot out, leaving a widening streak of burning grass and leaves behind it. The growing cone of fire caught three of the wolves, extinguishing their lives. A fourth barely escaped, the fur on its right flank gone, the skin underneath already beginning to blister. The other animals hesitated at the sudden, unexpected attack, giving Raftennon enough time to prepare his other surprise.

The beasts quickly regained their composure, however, once again catching the smell of blood from the wizard's scratched hand. They pounced on their prey—who was no longer there. Raftennon reappeared outside the closing circle of wolves and set off running. Hearing the rustling of leaves, the animals whirled to begin the chase.

The pack weaved through the trees in tight formation, making turns together as if sharing a single will. In this fashion, they by-passed the fleeing wizard and made their way ahead of him. Too late, Raftennon realized what they were doing and slid through the dead leaves to a halt.

The wolves launched themselves at the magic-user, who had brought another spell to mind. He ignored the pain in his arm as a wolf rushed by him and nipped at his flesh. All that mattered was the proper chanting of the mystical words. Even the agony of the next wolf's attack meant nothing. It was difficult, more so when the sharp teeth clamped onto his other forearm and started to fling it wildly, trying to wrench it from its socket. The assault ended abruptly, however, when the energy field took form around the caster, repelling the other wolves that lunged at him. The one clutching his arm fell prone to the ground, severed in half where the invisible dome materialized.

The beasts continued to crash against the magical barrier, testing its strength. One of them smashed into it hard enough to crack its skull, ending its life. After that, the others opted to wait for the man to weaken.

They did not know about Raftennon's special gift of replen-ishing his magic's energy. They could not fathom their wait could potentially last for the rest of their lives. So, when the wiz-ard slumped his shoulders and the barrier winked out, the pack attacked again, convinced their prey was theirs.

This time, the wolves found the earth sliding under their paws. Maples and elms toppled over, losing a grip in the soil that should have lasted forever. Instead, animal and plant rushed to the bottom of the pit forming around the mage. The beasts scrambled to flee the unnatural slide, much as the thieves' horses had done in the Salgre Hills. And like the steeds, the canines fell, drowned by the sliding earth. Only four wolves succeeded in es-caping the trap. They eyed the spellcaster, crouched, alone, on the other side of the shifting ground. One of them howled in rage, ignoring the torment its burned flank no doubt caused it. The other members of the pack voiced their own fury until the oppression of Drendaggamor echoed with the cacophony of anger.

The collapsing earth settled and Raftennon dropped to one knee, trying to regain his strength. He may have been one of the most powerful mages in the world, with the unique ability to supply his magic solely from the energy surrounding him, but he was still human. The precious few hours of furtive sleep he was forced to live on for the past few days were taking a heavy toll on his body, not to mention the effects of the wounds he recently suffered. The spellcaster desperately needed to patch himself up, then get a good night's rest.

The wolves studied his slow, deep breathing, his slouch and the life fluid trickling down his arm. They knew the man was weakening. The apparent alpha, the timber wolf with the burned flesh, tentatively stepped onto the shifted earth, testing its stability. When it realized the ground no longer engulfed whatever ventured on it, the animal snarled its discovery to the others.

They rushed the magic-user, eager to finish the hunt and get the morsel they longed for. Raftennon saw them coming and pulled one more trick from his sleeve. He rose to his feet, as if hauled up by invisible strings. His hunters quickened their pace, hoping to catch him before he cast another spell. They were too late, however, as their prey continued to rise into the air. One wolf leaped after him as he floated toward the sky, barely miss-ing the sole of the soft leather boot. Raftennon levitated into the branches, eventually to settle onto one of the uppermost boughs of a huge elm.

As unconsciousness took over, one last thought came to him. *I hope they cannot climb trees.*

22

MEETING THE FUGITIVE

He had no idea how much time had passed. He awoke to find himself still in the branches, blood trickling down his arm, all the way to the earth where the four wolves remained with salivating maws. Raftennon tore a piece of fabric from his robes and crudely bandaged the wound before returning to peaceful oblivion.

Another undetermined amount of time slipped away before the wizard revisited to the land of the living. When he opened his eyes, the perpetual gloom remained, but, thankfully, the beasts had not. Their patience exhausted, they had no doubt returned to whatever place they called home, leaving their intended prey to rot for all they cared.

The weak magic-user rummaged through his pack and retrieved some of the scarcely remaining snake meat. He gnawed at it thoughtfully, pondering his next move. Had the wolves truly gone? Should he chance climbing down the tree? Of course, he would not, not with blood still trickling from the vicious bite. The loss of blood would certainly cause a tragic fall and his struggle would be for nothing. So, in the elm he stayed, regaining some strength to float back down, much as he had gotten here in the first place. Here, in this dead tree.

Raftennon sat up, almost losing his balance in the process, and took stock of his surroundings. Despite the ever-present darkness, it was not as oppressive here as it had been on the ground. The mage glanced upward to see the sun shining in the sky, though it did so through a haze that dulled its brightness. But even that was an incredible feat in such a horrible place. The branches above him were bare. Not a single leaf grew in the vicinity. He lowered his gaze to finally notice the bark of the bough he was sitting on, as well as the trunk he had been leaning against, were a greyish colour. It was clear no life flowed from its roots to the tips of its branches—its bare branches—its bare, dead, elm branches.

Raftennon surveyed the location, grabbing onto the lifeless trunk as he began to slide off his equally lifeless perch. All he saw were the darkened leaves of live elms and birch between which he had run to escape his hunters. From here, he also regained his sight of the Pynakkor Mountains. He had travelled nearly a three-day hike into the heart of the forest. He did not dwell on this discovery, however, as what he sought was not in that direction.

He searched northward (thanks to the peaks, Raftennon reestablished his bearings) and found what he was desperate to find. More dead elms and birches lay before him, the bare branches giving him an almost unobstructed view of the trees beyond. Even from this distance, the wizard saw they were poplars. Their bark was darker than usual, and their leaves were almost black. He was getting close.

Raftennon wolfed down his morsel of anaconda. He then recited his levitation spell once again and lowered himself to the ground, making certain to keep his destination in front of him. It would not do to lose his way now that he knew where he had to go. It would not do at all.

Stumbling as quickly as he could due to his wounds and prolonged lack of sleep (his unconsciousness had helped, but it would take another few good nights' rest to recover fully from the stalking of the wolves), Raftennon made his way to the strange trees. Examining the peculiar species of flora, he found the unique plant quite fascinating. You could not find black poplars anywhere else in the world, which made them one of the rarest plants in existence. Raftennon plucked some leaves and a bit of the dark bark and stowed them in a small bag, which then went into the hidden recesses of his robes. Who knew, maybe he would need them for a spell he had yet to learn. If not, he was certain Vendrammon would find a use for them, even if they simply ended up becoming part of his vast collection of exotic plant specimens.

Deeper into the cluster of unique trees he went, collecting more of the curious flora of the area. As he finished gathering a handful of large mushrooms, something caught the wizard's eye. One of the poplars appeared to have one side paler than the others. In the growing gloom of the intertwined leaves, the lighter patch seemed to gleam with some unknown inner light.

Raftennon crept up to the tree, not certain of the reason behind his actions, for there was no need to sneak up on the plant. His heart sped up in his chest, rendering him light-headed. Culminated with his previous loss of blood, the mage stumbled over his own feet and fell to his hands and knees, his nose stopping inches away from a protruding root. The spellcaster lifted his head to see a splash of bright colour in an otherwise bleak landscape of blacks and greys. Around this side of the trunk lay a bed of *pennlannae*—bloodflowers. Blooming only where blood had spilled to the earth, the vibrant red petals drooped toward the tainted ground, as if bent in eternal mourning.

Raftennon raised himself to a kneeling position, wiping the dirt off his palms. He stopped in mid-stroke when he saw the exposed trunk of the poplar. A large piece of bark had been removed and the wood underneath still remained bare, even after all these years. He had found it! Here the elf had torn his makeshift parchment and had opened his skin to write his message, to document his anguish, finally to have a chance for his screams of torment to be heard.

With renewed strength, Raftennon scanned his surroundings. Many tightly spaced black poplars populated the vicinity, shrouding it in the forest's usual gloom with their thick leaves. Dark shrubs spanned the gaps between them, leaving only a few narrow paths one could use to navigate through the thickets. Here and there, one of the poplars stood, lifeless, as grey as the elms fencing the area. Branches were missing, and some were torn asunder. Lightning strikes, most likely.

Raftennon began his search for the entrance to the elf's adopted home. The discovery of the diary tree lightened his spirits, which remained so even as time passed without any sign of a dwelling. The wizard did not know exactly what to look for. Never during his research did he come upon a description of the elf's hiding place. He squinted as he focused on the distances revealed between the trees for any hint of a possible structure. He looked up in the branches, for it was common knowledge elves built many of their dwellings among the leaves. Still there was no evidence anyone lived, or had dwelt, in this forsaken Wood.

Despair once again assailed Raftennon. How could he find a being who had no doubt perfected the art of hiding during the long decades after his escape, when he did not even know what to look for? What made it worse was the fact this place needed to be so well hidden even a god would have trouble finding it.

As Raftennon pondered this, a chilling sound stole his breath from him. Fear clenched his heart. He had hoped to discover the hideout before this happened. Another howl broke the silence of the forest, much closer than the first one had been. The wolves were returning and this time Raftennon was not sure he had enough to keep them at bay, for certainly they would be coming back in greater numbers.

The mage stumbled backward before turning to flee. His first running step trod into a thick bush, causing him to tumble forward toward a dead poplar. He raised his arm to stop his fall. Instead of bracing himself against an unforgiving trunk, his hand fell into darkness, taking him with it. Blackness soon engulfed him as he tumbled downward, rolling head over heels along a steep slope. Roots scratched his face, trying to catch him, trap him in the gloom.

Eventually, Raftennon did stop. No light found its way to him, so he had to feel his surroundings to determine where he was. Obviously, he was somewhere underground. The tree had been hollow and the shrub effectively hid the access to this narrow tunnel. He knew it was narrow because he could touch both sides with his outstretched arms.

Could an elf really live below-ground? Granted, no one would ever think of looking in a place like this for one of the nature-loving race, for he would never see the rays of his beloved sun. But would he actually do such a thing? Did it really matter? Going back to the surface, to where the wolves no doubt now waited for him, was suicide. It would do him far less harm to search this place and see what he could discover.

Raftennon started to inch his way down the shaft. Using his hands, as well as the slight slope of the floor, to guide himself, he made his way toward what he hoped was the heart of this underground complex. The passage wound its way deeper in the bowels of the earth. There were so many twists and turns Raftennon lost all his bearings—again—but the path never branched out in front of him. The corridor had no offshoots, gave him no choices, a fact for which the spellcaster was much grateful. All he had to do was continue along the passageway's course.

After countless hours, when Raftennon's throat cried for water and his stomach grumbled for food, the wizard sighed in relief when he saw light in the distance. He continued to stumble forward, expending most of the strength remaining to him to reach the illumination. Finally at his destination, Raftennon's step faltered and he fell to the ground on the threshold of a large cavern.

The mage had no energy left to notice anything save the fresh blood seeping through the bandage on his arm. Forcing his body to withstand the threatening unconsciousness, Raftennon rolled onto his back. He wiggled his uninjured hand into the folds of his robes, retrieving a short length of *ghensen* root. He shoved it into his mouth and chewed, each bite clearing his vision.

The herb gave him enough strength to examine the room, something he regretted immediately. Another wave of vertigo assailed him. This time, it was not due to his injury, but to the appearance of the cave. A fire burned in the centre of the cavern, casting eerie shadows and illuminating disturbing images all over its sides. A small forest of painted trees covered the walls, their trunks twisted and gnarled beyond recognition. Depictions of birds flew between the branches, their beaks large and lined with sharp fangs. A green sun burned atop the fire, its rays sending forth unnamed shadows among the monstrous forest.

Raftennon tried to pry his eyes from the demonic pictures to inspect the many tunnels leading away from this place, but they would not obey his thoughts. He stared at a black representation of a tall tower with twisted spires, like skeletal fingers, reaching for the sky. His gaze remained locked on the House as all else faded, returning the spellcaster to blessed oblivion.

Raftennon woke to the smell of roasting meat. He opened his eyes and saw the animal on a spit over the fire—it was a large timber wolf. He nearly gagged at the sight, not ready yet for another confrontation with the beasts, no matter if this one was dead.

Beside the magic-user lay an earthen bowl filled with clear, cold water. He gulped it down to assuage his thirst, letting the cool wetness wash away all his worries, and attempted to still his rushing thoughts.

As his senses returned to him, Raftennon inspected his arm and found a clean bandage now replaced the filthy, torn piece of his robes. The wizard hurriedly scanned the room to discover who had done this.

An elf crouched in the entrance of one of the many tunnels branching out from the cave. His long, matted hair was soiled so deeply its original colour was no longer discernible. His only garment was a long tunic made of what appeared to be wolf pelt. A crude rope of intertwined roots served as a belt to hold the garb closed. The elf's skin was stained a brown almost as deep as his hair, his complexion hidden behind a mask of filth caked on over decades, even centuries, of forced existence away from civilization.

Raftennon only gave these images a fleeting glance. His attention soon locked on the elf's clear blue eyes, the only thing about him that had not faded during his captivity and subsequent exile. They stared, unwavering, into the mage's brown eyes, showing no sign of insanity. The spellcaster began to wonder if the elf's madness was but a misguided rumour.

" 'Tis quite a pleasure to finally receive some company in this…" The elf looked up at the ceiling and grimaced at the images he had drawn there. His gaze drifted to the black tower and remained there as he forced the rest of the words out. "…place. It hath been far too long."

Raftennon struggled a bit with the elf's ancient accent of his native tongue, even though Elfin had been the wizard's strong suit at the Guild. Some parts of the dialect were strange to him, so it took the mage a few moments to decipher what the elf had said. But in the end, he managed to understand the meaning of the statement, if not the individual words. And that was all that mattered.

"How long have I been unconscious?" Raftennon inquired in Elfin, though with a much more current dialect. He might be capable of following what his host was saying, but that did not mean he would manage correctly responding in the same vernacular.

"What is time to a being such as I?" the elf asked before snarling at the twisted images on the wall.

"So," Raftennon attempted to ignore the sudden display of madness, wanting to continue his conversation with the sane part of the fugitive, "it is true you have lived longer than the years that were originally intended for you."

"Who knows what the gods intend f'r the petty mortals with whom they toy?" The elf strode further into the room, going to the fire to retrieve a charred haunch before retreating to his original crouching place. "If thou hunger, feel free to englut until ye are satiat'd," he offered between tearing bites of his morsel.

Raftennon gagged at the mention of the wolf. All he wanted was to forget his encounter with them. He tried to find distraction by concentrating on testing his head's fortitude. He eased himself to a sitting position among the furs piled up under him, serving as his bed.

"If I were to ask how long you have been hiding here, you would not be able to tell me, would you?" The wizard managed to push his words through his clenched teeth as he battled with vertigo that threatened to overtake him. The dizziness soon passed, permitting him to concentrate on the elf's answer.

"Of course I couldst," his host almost shouted, spewing small chunks of meat with every syllable. Raftennon could not comprehend his sudden anger. "I hast dwelt hither since the human ran off with mine journal! He is the reason I anon live like the worm, continuously shunning the sun! *He* peers through the mountains, past the trees. *He* continues to hunt me. *He* will not allow me peace!" The elf babbled something Raftennon did not understand before glaring at the wizard. *"He* sent thou, did *he* not? The human hath betray'd me! *He* hath reveal'd to thou the way the other had taken, after his betrayal!"

"I assure you, the one you speak of did not send me, and he still does not know your location." Raftennon assumed the elf was referring to the god of vengeance, Jafall, who had imprisoned him for so long. The human must have been the mage who had left the Drendaggamor with the piece of bark.

"Shadows touching thou, always shadows touching thou, telling thou thy brother hath lain with thy sister."

Raftennon stared at the elf, who was rocking on his heels, staring off into the distance. A small tendril of meat hung from a corner of the fugitive's mouth as his eyes peered through the image of the House on the cavern wall. What was he saying?

"Mother left thou in a blanket, in the midst of twilight, so thou couldst perish, so the lady couldst continue frolicking with the lowlifes of the slums. Pass the victory fingers of wood."

"Excuse me?" Raftennon had trouble following the babbling. He was sure there were fragments in that growing sea of madness that could make sense if he had enough time to puzzle them out.

"Thou lie!"

The elf lunged at the magic-user. Thankfully, the room was large enough to give Raftennon the time needed to overcome his initial surprise and ready his defences. The elf leaped over the fire, missing the wolf on its spit by the breadth of a hair, his eyes filled with unexplained rage. His attack went no further as a strange wind gusted from the mage, crashing the elf against the stone behind him. There the captive screeched and cursed, trying in vain to free himself from the force that held him fast.

"I knew the human would betray me, sending *his* servants to retrieve me! 'Twas quite apparent when he took mine journal! 'This is part of history' he told me. But I knew better! I knew he would find the dragon wings and betoken *him* the way!"

The elf continued to whimper, though his struggles ceased. His eyes flittered from one edge of the cave to the other.

Raftennon tried to calm him, knowing the longer this bout of madness lasted the less he would be able to get useful information from the fugitive. "If the human's intentions were truly to reveal your position to his 'master', surely his forces would have come for you before now."

"Nay, nay, they would not!" The elf snapped his head downward, his whimpers forgotten, his eyes expanding to reveal much more white than was normal. "F'r thou see, I did not wait f'r him to return to find better hiding! Thou know that! Did thou discov'r the entrance beside the taken materials f'r mine journal? Nay, thou did not! Thou came across the forest, knowing exactly whence to go! Like I once did, thou follow darkness that is forbidden."

"To tell you the truth, though I *was* searching for you, for different reasons that you currently assume," Raftennon was quick to add, "I came upon your hiding place quite by accident. It was cleverly hidden. I would never have found it if I had not stumbled in my haste to flee the wolves."

"Those accurs'd monsters, so much like their brothers and sisters in the northern forest, but yet so diverse. I once sympathiz'd with them, each of us taking the same path into the darkness, forsaking our people. But *he* show'd me the errors of mine ways. Oh ay, the treachery, the betrayal, I saw it all." Tears trickled down the ageless elf's face, which softened with every drop, relaxing with resignation. "I saw a family torn asunder because a wretch manag'd to steal the heart of the righteous daughter! The maiden did not know better, but I did! I saw *his* nightly visits, sowing the doubt the maiden soon felt toward her father's wishes. Still, I cannot close mine eyes to the image."

Raftennon finally noticed the missing eyelids. The elf's skin ended above the eye, instead of folding inside as it should have. Even the eyelashes were gone.

"I need your help," the mage whispered after a few moments of silence.

"I attempt'd to help, once." Again, the elf's emotions changed instantly. The sorrow disappeared, replaced by apathy. His eyes betrayed no emotion as he stared at the floor at the spellcaster's feet. "In *his* service I was, hoping *he* would aid me right the wrongs that had been done unto me. But the payment *he* demand'd was too high and I forsook *him*! I hid mine failure and aid'd the ones *he* had deem'd indign. But *he* found mine treachery and I suffer'd greatly f'r it! I will help nay longer."

Raftennon was losing him and did not know what to do to stop it. How could a young human counter centuries, or even millennia, of desensitization?

"If you do not assist me now, more innocents will suffer," was all Raftennon could think of saying to persuade him.

"They know not the meaning of the word," the elf countered, still emotionless. "Whatev'r petty fate they hast drawn is a blessing in the greater scheme of things. F'r them, at least, there is an end to the pain."

The tears resumed. The elf's shoulders would have heaved if the mage's spell was not still pinning him against the wall. Raftennon pitied him but did not allow emotion to cloud his judgment. He let his invisible grip dissipate but kept his guard up. The elf slid down to the ground, not taking heed to his surroundings or what was happening to him.

"I cannot return to *him*! I cannot endure the newly conceiv'd evils *he* hath devis'd since mine departure!"

Raftennon stared at the distraught elf, not knowing what to say to gain his trust.

"I will go without you," the mage told him. "All I require is the way to reach the passage in the mountains."

"*He* will find me! *He* will retrace thy footsteps!" His hysterics were returning, first showing up in his furtive eyes.

"Find another place to hide." Raftennon hastened his words, desperate to keep his host calm. "Wait until I leave and when his eyes are on me, flee. He will be too occupied with my approach. He will not see your escape. I will not know where you are going and will not be able to lead him to you."

The elf lifted his gaze to the wizard, all trace of insanity gone from his eyes. Raftennon drove the feeling of déjà vu out of his head and concentrated on his current task. It would do him no good to reminisce about a scoundrel he did not care to ever meet again. He did wonder if this very plan had worked the first time.

"Wherefore doth thou undertake this foolish endeavour?" the elf asked him, not catching the human's distraction.

"He has enthralled someone I once cared for." Raftennon swallowed the lump in his throat, uncertain if it was caused by fond memories or sour ones.

"Thou wish to prevent this fate from befalling thy companion." The elf pointed to his unblinking eyes, referring to the centuries of torment he had suffered.

"Yes." Raftennon was still not sure what sort of punishment Jennalla deserved, but he felt the elf's doom was much too excessive for anyone.

"Tis too late! *He* snares his victims 'ere taking them to the accurs'd spire! Thy companion is already doomed—past the night of the earth! There is nothing thou can doth!"

The elf rose and skulked into the nearest corridor, leaving the mage alone in the strange room. Raftennon sat there, not knowing what step to take next. The elf's voice came bouncing off the rock walls from deep within his complex.

"Turn back, while thou still can! *He* will englut thou as *he* did me!"

23

FOLLOWING THE SIGNS

Raftennon remained in the cavern for another two days (he did not know this fact, having no way of telling time this far underground), mending his wounded arm. The elf had used his people's expert healing arts before their conversation, so the bite closed quicker than expected and infection did not attack the exposed flesh. Two hours into this recovery, the magic-user got over his revulsion of the cooked timber wolf and ate. He then carved it and replenished his dwindling provisions, for the elf did not return to claim the remaining meat. At the rear of the cave was a well, which the spellcaster used to fill his water skin.

When he was well rested and his wares restocked, Raftennon took the tunnel that would take him out of the subterranean complex. Or rather, he meant to. During his ministrations, the elf moved the wizard to a more comfortable spot while he was still unconscious, which disoriented him. He no longer knew which corridor he had fallen down to enter this place. He tried a few times to find it again, for there were numerous passageways that began to ascend from the large room before delving deeper into the subterranean complex. But he did find the correct way and finally crawled through the shrub hiding the hollow of the dead tree.

Raftennon climbed the elm next to the one he had just exited, using the conventional way this time, pulling himself up with his arms. It would not do to use up his spell components on matters he could deal with by other means. He was glad to see his wound did not reopen and the pain was almost nonexistent. From the barren branches, he found the mountains to regain his bearings.

Once that was done, the spellcaster headed eastward toward the Pynakkors. He would discover the secret passage himself.

As he began the journey, a shrill cry came from behind him. Turning, Raftennon did not see the elf as he had expected to, so near the scream had sounded. The forest was barren, devoid of any sign of life.

"Thou forsake thy soul! *He* will take thou!" The elven voice resonated in his ears, repeated for a long time as the mage quickened his pace to reach the rocky peaks.

More immeasurable time passed in the Dead Wood and Raftennon was still no closer to finding the elusive hidden passage. He came to the foot of the Pynakkor Mountains after a two-and-a-half day's hike, as the sun finally appeared in this part of the world after half the day was gone on the range's eastern border.

Upward he bent his gaze as he walked, searching for any indication, however slight, of parting rock denoting a path through the high peaks. As expected, he did not see anything. If the trail were that easy to find, Jafall, or one of his servants, would have found it by now and destroyed it. Maybe that was what had happened and the wizard was now on a futile search. It had been many centuries since the elf's escape and he had not come back to that hidden path, so he would not have known of its destruction, if that were indeed the case.

Raftennon shooed these thoughts from his mind. He had to continue with the premise the passage still existed. It was the only way he could end Jennalla's vendetta before she harmed any one else he cared for.

A full week passed while the magic-user waltzed up and down the western flank of the mountain range, and still the way eluded him. After so much wasted time, he decided to return to the elf and try once more to persuade him to help. Raftennon turned into the forest, starting his trek back to the thickly bunched poplars, darker in bark than their counterparts outside

Drendaggamor.

On the afternoon of his tenth day out of the underground complex, he sat down at the base of a tall birch, its leaves obliterating the sun's rays, and drank from his water skin. He took a few moments to rest his weary legs before climbing the tree, hoping to see a sign of the dead elms. Raftennon had a sneaking suspicion he was heading in the wrong direction. Getting lost in these woods—again—was something he wanted to avoid. Almost as much as another encounter with his least favourite canines.

In the boughs of the birch, his heart sank. He had veered toward the north and there were no dead elms anywhere.

"This is proving to be quite the dilemma," Raftennon said to himself. "Jennalla seems to have chosen the perfect place to make her sanctuary. Wait a moment. What is that?"

The spellcaster squinted as he gazed westward, focusing on a void in the dense forest. A long hole broke the otherwise thick roof of foliage. Raftennon climbed down the birch and headed in that direction.

As Drendaggamor's eerie gloom began to darken, the first subtle warning of the coming evening, the mage found the curious expanse. The trees dispersed in front of him to reveal a wide aisle of black earth. Nothing marred the smoothness of the area. The elms on the opposite border formed a straight line parallel to those on Raftennon's side. The other two sides of the unnatural clearing were so far away he could not see them. Raftennon peered at the strange phenomenon, wondering what could have caused it. The soil had an unusual sheen to it, slightly reflecting the darkening rays of the setting sun, which could now reach him since there was a gap in the forest's canopy.

Raftennon reached down, meaning to scoop up a fistful of the dirt to examine it more closely. Instead, his hand passed through the black substance and whatever he managed to grab soon oozed out of his hand between his fingers.

"Mud," he concluded, "very diluted at that. It explains why it shines so in the failing light. There is more water here than earth."

Raftennon contemplated his next move for, even though this discovery was quite interesting, it did not help him return to the elf, or guide him toward his ultimate goal. But he could not think for too long, as branches cracked behind him. The mage whirled around just in time to see the baleful gleam of two black eyes. The next moments were a blur as a large, furry creature soared toward him. Long teeth parted, aimed for his throat, and he barely had enough time to duck out of the way.

A desperate howl shattered the relative silence of the Dead Wood and Raftennon lost his footing. His boot plunged into the dark mire, unbidden, and was immediately caught in its grip. It took all his strength to overcome the intense suction of the quicksand and save his only footwear (he had neglected to pack a spare pair, not accustomed to these long travels as he was). That minor crisis averted, Raftennon returned his attention to the doomed cries of the creature. It was another annoying timber wolf, who had made one last attempt to avenge its brothers, but its leap propelled it into the bog. Its thrashings for escape quickly covered the animal in mud, snaring it, dragging it down into the earth. Soon, it was gone, swallowed, to be forgotten beneath a mirror surface of darkness.

Raftennon watched the failed attempt for freedom, apathetic to the creature's mewling, having lost all compassion for the wolves of these woods. "I hope you are the last," he told the van-ished beast, cleaning his boot the best he could. "Back into the shadows of the night you go..."

The elf's words resonated in the back of his head.

...past the night of the earth...

The clearing did look like a starless night. Was this what the elf had meant? Did he give him signs to follow? Did he even realize what he said? Was this actually tied in with the secret passage through the mountains?

There was only one way to find out.

Raftennon got to his feet and brushed the dirt off his blue robes before heading toward the northern end of the deadly bog. The next morning he came to the border of the elf's "night". The black earth tapered to its tip, mingling with firmer sand until the ground was safe to walk on wherever one tread. Raftennon stopped at this point, not knowing where to go next. He turned in a full circle, trying to decide in which direction he should now travel.

All around him stood tall elms, rife with their strange, darker-than-usual leaves. The foliage was so thick Raftennon almost missed what he was looking for. In front of him rose a massive tree whose trunk split four feet over the ground. The two arms of this elm were as large as the trunks of the surrounding trees, sporting as many branches as its brothers. The wizard marvelled at the symmetry of the plant. It resembled the sign the children made with their index and middle finger back in Yentrill, when they would win one of their many games—games he was never invited to play.

...pass the victory fingers of wood...

The elf's words rushed back to the forefront of his mind. Was this what the mad fugitive meant? As with the mud, Raftennon only had one option. He made his way to the large tree and examined it. There was no bark where the twin massive trunks met. Instead, the heart of the wood was exposed and was still charred black. The spellcaster surmised that a powerful thunderbolt must have been the cause of the tree's separated growth.

The mage tightened the strap of his pack and laboured up the eastern trunk, thankful for the numerous boughs that enabled an easier climb. Three-quarters of the way up, he peeked through the leaves, deeming this vantage point to be high enough for his purpose—the branches above began to thin dramatically, making any further ascent treacherous. He scanned the mountain range, while he searched his memory for anything else the elf might have subconsciously divulged during his ramblings.

...the dragon wings...

The elf had mentioned dragon wings. What did that mean?

Then Raftennon discovered the relevance. Scanning the peaks of the Pynakkors, he saw the expanse of mountains to which the elf had referred. The sun appeared over the crests at that moment, in a gap between two smaller ranges nestled in the larger chain. The sunlight radiated off the snow-capped summits like fire, emphasizing the form of the skyline. The elf remembered dragon wings because that was the exact impression the range gave its onlookers. The sun added the effect of a flaming head, the creature soaring straight up into the sky.

Raftennon took note of his bearings and the direction he was now to take, then climbed down the forked elm.

Three days it took the mage to reach the base of the peaks. Once there, he found an impassable wall of rock. In fact, he had walked by this very spot during his futile search after leaving the elf's cave. He searched the stone, frantically searching for—and almost pleading to find—the path that would permit him to continue his journey. Without it, he could not reach Jennalla and end the threat to his loved ones. Then he stumbled upon what had eluded him for so long.

In front of him, directly below where the sun had positioned itself at the base of the dragon wings, was the way forward. A dry stream bed wound its way from the heart of the Pynakkors to the Dead Wood. The cold water from the snow-covered pinnacles no longer flowed to Drendaggamor, leaving a rocky path up the steep slope.

Raftennon laboured up the secret trail, at last free from the cursed forest.

24

NARROW FLIGHT

"There he is!" Jennalla cried as the orb finally showed her an image of the wizard. "He's going into the mountains. What does he think he's doing?"

"He must know something we do not," her invisible companion said.

"You're a god! You're supposed to know everything!" she screeched, turning her head to direct her anger back over her shoulder.

"And I am not obliged to explain myself to one of my worshippers!" The air trembled with the deity's wrath, the lightning crackling with every syllable.

Jennalla returned her gaze to the blue sphere, fuming at the ineptitude of the forest. The Dead Wood should have taken care of him. Her frustration grew even hotter when the sense of admiration for the man crept once again into her heart, warming it. She quickly banished the feeling and calmed herself. She knew what she could do.

The walls of the Pynakkors pressed in on either side of the mage as he scampered up the steep slope, following the path of the dried-up river along the bottom of the narrow crevasse. The rocks under his feet were loose and treacherous. Several dislodged from their places of long slumber and rolled down the foothill to the edge of the woods. Above him rose the mighty peaks, gaining height quicker than he was. Raftennon eventually found himself in a deep, narrow ravine. Darkness shrouded his path, for the high rock walls shielded the sun all but one hour each day.

Upward he laboured, scraping palms and shins as he climbed the memory of a rivulet. He began to wonder if this ghost of a waterway even had a source, and if he would have to follow it into the heart of the mountains.

The elf's journal had mentioned an underground stream. Did this brook flow when he escaped his captivity? Raftennon resigned himself to a long search for the water's fountainhead, but dismissed that thought when he came up to the foot of a sheer precipice. The peaks shot straight up to the sky in front of him, blocking any advancement.

Raftennon inspected the uneven sides of the ravine for the opening that would permit him to continue on the uncertain path the elf had set for him. All he found, however, was a hole so small even a mouse would not have been able to pass through.

Despair tried to grip Raftennon's heart, draw all the strength from his spirit. The wizard scolded himself for giving up so easily and began the search of his surroundings. What he saw were more rocks. Three walls of stone encircled him, devoid of any form of life. No plants clung to the small ledges strewn here and there up the precipitous slopes. No birds felt the cliffs good enough in which to build their nests. The only flaw in the relatively uniform facade was a small shadow over a narrow ledge a few feet over his head.

Raftennon struggled up the sheer slope, taking several minutes to climb the dozen feet that separated him from the shelf. He reached his destination after much effort to find the black eye of a slender cave staring out at him. Barely three feet in diameter, the hole seemed to delve deep into the heart of the world. This fact Raftennon soon confirmed as he scampered up onto the lip and crawled into the passageway.

Countless hours passed as the mage continued to crawl along the cramped passageway. It abruptly sloped upward and the going became even more difficult. The stones here did not dislodge as easily as they had in the stream bed, but soon the mage's elbows and knees were quite sore. Several sharp-edged rocks lined the walls and floor, forcing Raftennon to tread carefully so as not to seriously injure himself. The total darkness that engulfed him after entering the shaft made the crawl even more dangerous.

Eventually, the ground disappeared in front of him. At least, that was what Raftennon thought when his hand did not strike stone as he had expected. In truth, the bottom of the tunnel was still there but was a span lower than it had been previously. The unexpected change in terrain caught the spellcaster by surprise and sent him rolling forward. Something thin and sticky coated his face as he fell. As soon as the unanticipated roll ended, Raftennon brushed away the unknown tendrils covering his skin with quick swipes of his sleeved arms.

When he succeeded in slowing his flustered heart, he sat up and found he could do so without having the ceiling directly overhead. Rummaging through his many hidden pockets, he retrieved the spell components he needed and spoke into the darkness.

"Illaymânal komprénôrralay tenbâh sôrônayllymônâs flaym-môran."

A ball of bright blue light formed from tendrils of flame shot from the mage's fingertips to hover an inch over his hand. Raftennon lifted his hand to look at his surroundings. He found himself in a small cave. It was large enough for him to stand in, but he remained seated, giving his agonizing knees and elbows a rest.

Looking around, the mage felt like he had been here before, even though that was impossible. Several tunnels ran out from the room in all directions, just like the mad elf's home in Drend-aggamor. So the fugitive had actually buried himself to hide, instead of finding concealment. It seemed this room had been his inspiration, and that was the reason it looked so familiar. How long had he stayed here, and what happened to him to make such an impression? And was it good or bad?

A slight breeze came down the tunnel he had just fallen out of, swaying strands of cobwebs that barely stuck to the walls of rock, no longer like the thick meshes that obstructed the other openings. Raftennon examined his clothes, realizing the sticky substance he had rolled through was the missing spider webs. He tried to brush the cobwebs off his garments with his free hand, but gave up once they covered his skin, not having done anything to improve the state of his clothing. He rubbed the cobwebs off his hand on the stone floor as he considered the tunnels in the magical light.

Each of them sported a thick wall of web that covered its opening. The silver strands were so dense the conjured illumination could not penetrate them and reveal what lay beyond. The wizard studied every blocked path in turn, pondering his next move.

Then his eyes came upon a tunnel where the curtain was not as opaque as the others were. The spellcaster leaned forward for a closer look and saw what he believed were patches of the obstruction that had lost their hold on the rock, much as the ones in the opening he had created when he tumbled into the cave. These did not sway while he moved in front of the gap, for other, newer strands covered them and held them in place.

All this meant one thing: the last person, or beast, to enter this room had done so from this tunnel. This was the path the elf used to escape from the House of Jafall. This was the path Raftennon needed to take to reach his destination.

The magic-user uttered a few words, handled the proper spell components, and flames shot out from his fingertips, engulfing the spider webs blocking his way. Soon the obstacle was no more and Raftennon began his trek down the new tunnel. Thankfully, this passageway was large enough to allow him to walk upright.

More immeasurable time passed, a fact the mage disregarded. A swift strike on the wizardress was no longer in his plans, nor was a quick return home for his family. All he cared about now was reaching Jennalla.

The spellcaster stopped twice on this leg of his journey when his stomach's laments were too much to bear. Only at these points would he allow himself to eat a small portion of his provisions, for he had no idea how long he would wander in the bowels of the Pynakkors. Truth be told, he had lost his sense of time. He did not know if the sun was up or if the stars were shining in the sky. He did not know how many days he had spent in the darkness. All he knew was the course he currently followed was still climbing up toward the mountaintops.

The magical light still guided his steps, showing him all the sharp rocks protruding from the floor in several places. Raftennon pitied the elf, who had to crawl through this tunnel in total darkness. He must have been quite bloody at the end of the ordeal. Truth be told, the spellcaster believed if it had not been for Jafall's curse of immortality, the elf would have never survived the escape.

The conjured torch also revealed the moving shadows around him. Now and then, something would scurry along the wall. Before the wizard could cast the light on it to see what it was, it would return to the blackness, not to reappear for hours. What was important was the fact they did not dare come out of the dark to attack him—yet.

"Something definitely dwells in these tunnels," Raftennon commented aloud. He needed to hear something real in this place, where echoes of unseen scurrying played with the mind. Without a companion, his own voice would have to do.

He knew the noises could have been tricks of his imagination, but the numerous cobwebs that lined the walls of the tunnel, as they did in the cave, were a sure sign of life. Living spiders made these and were continuing to make more. Raftennon reached out a hand and touched a patch that glistened more than the others around it. The sticky strands came away on his fingers, obviously not affected yet by the dry air.

While the magic-user studied this new discovery, he felt a prick on the nape of his neck. Tiny legs ran down his back, and when he whirled around to catch a glimpse of his attacker, he saw only darkness. Another sting burned his unlit hand, causing him to lose his concentration. The magical flame winked out and the shadows came alive. Raftennon felt thousands of soft, miniature steps all over his body, along with stinging pricks all over bare and covered skin alike.

Soon blackness overwhelmed his awareness to accompany the darkness without.

He did not know how long he was unconscious, but a few things became apparent to him as he regained his senses. Upon opening his eyes, he found narrow strands of moonlight pushing away the gloom of the tunnel. Glancing up, Raftennon saw a sliver of a bone-white crescent shining through a slit in the rock ceiling of the cavern he was now in. A thick coat of spider webs also covered this cavern's sides, much like in the passages leading to it. Unlike the other recesses of the underground maze, these meshes teemed with life. A multitude of arachnids scurried along the sticky network, entering and exiting the room through numerous holes in the walls.

Raftennon looked down at himself and saw a number of the spiders flitting over his abdomen, adding more strands to the cocoon of silk trapping him against the wall. The critters, their bulbous bodies as large as his closed fist and as black as the closed-in tunnels, laboured to cover him. His legs and torso were almost completely enveloped, and the magic-user found his arms already affixed to the stone. He wanted to brush away one of the arachnids making its way up to his face, but his wrist moved not a whit inside the weaved manacle.

Despair rushed in to overwhelm his resolve. He needed his magic to get him out of this predicament, and he needed his components to perform the arcane art. But not only could he not move his hands to handle the materials, he could not even reach the hidden pockets of his robes because the thick cobwebs covered them. It almost seemed as if the creatures knew what he was and how to stop him.

Raftennon drove away the growing depression and forced his mind to concentrate on finding a way to get out of the quandary. He went through his repertoire of magic that needed no components. Though most incantations required the handling of the proper ingredients, there were a few one could cast using words alone. Unfortunately, the only spells of this sort that Raftennon knew were mental suggestions and tricks of the mind. He surmised the arachnids' limited brain capacity would render any of his attempts utterly useless.

The spider scurrying up his chest reached his left shoulder and stopped. It appeared to study him for a moment before plunging its mandible through the man's robes to the flesh beneath. Raftennon felt the venom enter his veins. The numbness, which had already taken all feeling from his shoulder, raced to the rest of his body. The spellcaster could not help but envision the end of his journey.

Unexpected warmth washed over him, beginning from his toes and rising up his legs. As it moved up his torso, the sticky strands melted off him to fall in a large heap around his feet. Soon the two forces invading him met and struggled against each other, the heat overcoming the poison and eradicated it.

With the cocoon gone, Raftennon knelt in the moonlit cavern, shaking off the last remaining tendrils of paralysis that had begun to expand from the arachnid's bite. Around him crowded the horde of its brothers and sisters, millions of faceted eyes staring at him. The wizard glared back at them and heard an unfamiliar voice, which seemed to originate from somewhere deep within himself.

You are needed for a great deed after this ordeal is overcome. You must not fall now.

Raftennon did not know what the voice meant and had no time to ponder the strange occurrence further. The spiders began to inch toward him, closing the semicircle in front of him. He straightened up and leaned against the stone wall behind him, using it to support his still weakened body. Rummaging in his uncovered robes' pockets, he retrieved the items he needed and recited the words not many others in the world could pronounce.

"Entraylônnam krayllentraenol fôrnak! Zellentrénnam fôrlan maytralnarnâmak!"

A wide cone of flames rushed out from the palm of his outstretched hands, reaching the far wall of the cavern. Many small bodies screeched in pain, as more scurried in all directions for the tiny recesses leading out of the cave. The sound resembled a human's scream as much as it did a viper's angry hiss, filling the darkness with an unholy shriek the mage would never forget.

Raftennon continued to carpet the floor and walls before him with the flames, showing his captors no mercy. Only when his concentration wavered as the mysterious warmth vanished from his body did the torching end. Not a single arachnid within sight remained alive. The putrid smell of burned spider flesh filled the spellcaster's nostrils, but he ignored it.

He slumped to the floor to regain his breath. The fire had

been stealing the oxygen in the room and the air was now very thin. He fought the dizziness that tried to return him to oblivion. When he began to breathe easier, replenishing his twirling mind as the cracks in the stone permitted the refilling of the atmosphere around him, he heard the scurrying within the fissures in the rock. The spiders were overcoming their fear and coming back to finish him. And he had nowhere to go. While the unnatural fire lighted the room, Raftennon had searched the walls for any way out. All he saw was one tunnel large enough for him to pass through, but the sounds of the returning arachnids were loudest in that direction.

The back of his head thudded against the cavern wall behind him as he let it fall backward in frustration. He blinked as he saw the opening in the ceiling once again. There was his only means of escape. The spellcaster dove into his hidden pouches and prepared himself. Moments later, he was on his way up toward the sliver of moon, floating to the small, starlit crack.

The black robed figure peered into the crystal-blue sphere, shaking his head in dismay. This situation was getting out of hand. Not only did he have to deal with their suspect's unknown whereabouts, now he had to confront his brother about this unauthorized meddling. And then there was this spellcaster who…

The air rustled behind him as another cloaked figure appeared.

"You have reneged your Oath," he stated to the newcomer, absolutely no trace of emotion in his voice.

"It does not appear so," the newly arrived man responded just as flatly.

"You blatantly interfered in the fate of a mortal," the first said, turning to his comrade.

"It does not appear so," the second repeated.

"We are not to affect the Balance—"

"Correction," the silver-white haired man interrupted, passing by his colleague to look into the orb, "we cannot sway the Balance, unless it is to amend a tilt."

"What are you getting at?" The first scrutinized the other, not liking the change he had undergone since the onset of his suspicions against their brother.

"If the mortal was destined to perish under the mountains, I would not have been able to save him."

The skeptic stared at the other, unable to dispute his logic. This made the spellcaster very special indeed and portended to some grave event the Chosen could not handle themselves. That was quite a disturbing possibility.

25

RETURNING TO SHADOW

"Why is he not dead?" Jennalla struck out at the orb atop the twin serpents. The magic holding the sphere in place prevented it from falling to the floor, where it would have surely shattered. This thwarting of another of her actions only heightened her anger.

"It appears your faith in the arachnids was misplaced." The strange voice of the air was still with her, still mocking her.

"I'm really getting tired of his dumb luck! He's so despicable!" Jennalla crossed her arms over her breast, the perfect image of a spoiled brat who did not get her way. Her bright green eyes shone in the crackling lightning that surrounded the tower, reflecting quite the opposite of her words.

"Is that so?" The god teased, for he could sense her innermost feelings. She was remembering what had drawn her to the young mage during their tenure at the Spellcasters' Guild in Xendremmar. Those same features were warming her heart once again, despite all her efforts to dismiss them.

"If you think you can do any better, go right ahead." She sulked in the desolate room, alone with the spectre.

"I will not lower myself to your level and take part in this petty squabble."

"Lower yourself?" Jennalla's fury returned as she wheeled around and glared at the ceiling. She could not see where the deity had manifested himself, but she felt he preferred the apex of the dome, directly below his beloved Black Eye, so she aimed her reproachful stare in that vicinity.

"This mage means absolutely nothing to me." The air trembled with his annoyance at his worshipper's insolence. "I have better, and more important, things to think about than the ones who squander my love. You want to make him pay for what he did to you all those years ago, you do so. You will have no help from me."

The sky surrounding the tower crackled and spit its lightning as if to accentuate the departure of the godly presence. Once the sudden outburst from the heavens subsided, returning the storm to its usual turbulent whirlwind, the wizardress knew she was alone in the room without walls.

Jennalla turned her gaze back to the crystal-blue orb, which was now showing her Raftennon's landing on the peak of the mountain, over the spiders' cave.

"He wants me to do this myself. That's fine with me!" The derision in her voice was unmistakable. "I'll show him." She lifted her eyes to the ceiling, hoping the god heard her, before returning her attention to the sphere. "And I'll show you too exactly what I can do!"

Jennalla strode to the southern edge of the room, mere inches from the blustering winds, and called out with a voice aided by magic.

Raftennon inched his way down the rocky slope. His levitation spell had brought him to a lonely ledge at the summit of one of the Pynakkors' peaks, one never before visited by anything that could not fly. For that reason, there was no path leading down from it, so the wizard had to blaze the trail. Carefully placing one foot below the other, gingerly adding his body weight onto the new step, Raftennon descended the face of the mountain. Occasionally, the ledge he chose as a foothold rolled away, cascading down the slope. The mage would soon follow, careening down the steep incline until he could grab a protruding stone or the scraggly branch of a dead, forgotten bush.

In this fashion, he left the roof of the world to reach a

sheltered ravine nestled between the towering heights of the Pynakkors. The moon had passed beyond his sight to the west by this time and the stars shone their brightest before the time of their waning came with the lightening of the sky. Raftennon found himself a shallow nook and settled down for the rest of the night, confident he was far enough from the spiders' lair to discourage any pursuit.

He constructed a small fire as close to the rock face as he could manage, hoping to hide it from anything wanting to spy him, before sitting down and heating a piece of wolf meat. His stomach, finally relaxing from the shock of the flight, grumbled to remind him it had been a long time since his last meal, so long he could not remember when it had occurred.

Raftennon also took the time to ponder what had transpired in the cave. He believed his journey had come to an end. The spiders had subdued him and he had no means of countering the poison that flowed through his body. The heat had not come from him, nor did the voice that spoke in his head. It was unknown to him, he was certain of it. Where had it come from and what had it meant when it said he was "needed for a great deed"?

Raftennon eventually pushed the matter aside, resigning himself to think on it more when he returned to Xendremmar after he accomplished his current quest. For now, he had to focus on reaching Jennalla and figure out what to do with her when he got there.

It was mid-morning when Raftennon awoke after a bout of furtive sleep. He turned in his bedroll and his closing eyes shot open when they fell upon the wisp of smoke rising from the dying fire. He scurried out of his blankets and rushed to gather his belongings. He did not know if anything, or anyone, had seen the result of his blunder, but he was not going to chance a confrontation in the mountains. He had had enough encounters already on this journey.

When all his things were in his pack, and his pack on his shoulders, Raftennon made his way northward. He was not sure where he was going, but north was the general direction he needed to take. He did not know how far his crawl underground had taken him, but he was fairly certain he was still south of the House of Jafall.

His progress was sluggish and treacherous. The fishing trade that surrounded him in his youth had not prepared him for a trek through the hard mountainous terrain, not to mention its thin air. In fact, the only peaks near Yentrill were the Qartyff Mountains nestled in the centre of Entamman Forest, a good six-day march from the village, along two rivers. He had never travelled that far from his home until he came to Xendremmar for his formal schooling in the arcane art of magic. His inexperience in mountain climbing, and lack of general wilderness survival expertise, cost him many hours of retracing his steps, trying to find an accessible path through the wild crags of the Pynakkors. He also paid for his naivete with many cuts and bruises resulting from the numerous trips, falls and slides he suffered along the way.

Even though it was slow going, Raftennon managed to make some progress. The peak over the spiders' lair receded—or so he believed. The terrain was monotonous. Each summit was the twin of the last and the far-off sun was no help. Its arc remained the same as it made its way to the western horizon, pointing out how short his strides downhill actually were.

Evening replaced afternoon, the fading light of the setting orb tinting the undersides of the gingerly floating clouds the colour of roses. Some of them happened to resemble the flowers, their puffy petals blooming toward the people of various towns and villages, whose inhabitants were no doubt closing up shop or hurrying to loved ones for a freshly prepared meal. Raftennon's stomach chose that moment to remind him he should also be thinking about supper. His choices were not as appetizing as the lavish feasts the townspeople were certainly enjoying, but his travel rations would have to do. The wizard did not light a fire that night, not chancing a second mistake that would once again reveal his position.

He did not have to worry about that, however, for the shriek that pierced the evening sky proved that the smoke was unnecessary. He was already discovered.

The first sharp cry was answered by another, then a third, a fourth, until the mountaintops reverberated with the shrill cries of an immeasurable hoard. The din was so oppressive it drove all thought from the mage's mind, preventing him from figuring out what was happening.

Raftennon clutched his pack close to his body and shrank against the rock face of the peak looming over him. Then he saw the sky darken to the north, a black carpet streaming in his direction. The shrieks grew louder, and not just because their source was getting closer. The darkness was gathering more black shapes as it travelled southward, growing in size in front of his gazing eyes.

Soon Raftennon could make out what the creatures were, but could not believe what he saw. The beasts were common mountain hawks. He had read about the birds during his studies at the Spellcasters' Guild. Native to the Pynakkors, they built their aeries at the most extreme of heights, in small groups for added protection. But never was it documented they flocked in such numbers. There were thousands of them soaring toward him, if not tens of thousands. What force could be driving them together, and for what purpose?

The answers to those questions became clear when the flock swooped down and streaked past his position. Some of their talons found their mark, scratching the wizard's exposed skin or ripping his blue robes. Raftennon crouched onto the stone ground and covered his face, lest one of the hawks managed to fly away with one of his eyes.

The onslaught lasted for long minutes until the last bird finally passed the spellcaster. Raftennon gasped, for the ocean of flapping wings drove the air away from him, preventing normal breathing. He did not have much time to collect himself, however. The mountain hawks were already turning to make another pass. They moved as if with one mind, their actions precisely choreographed. Raftennon was certain Jennalla had sent them and was now controlling their every action.

As the avian army began its second attack, the magic-user hurriedly retrieved a few items from his pack and handled them in the proper fashion as he murmured the incantation. "*Invéktussaylâmôs nynôvérolisnâl vendrânôrân vend-laynorégaya krâthlôsseerâm!*"

The hawks charged him, their shrieks once again piercing the otherwise silent dusk in the mountains. Their beaks sought the warmth of his blood, strove to please the will of their master.

Their eager cries soon became gargled screeches amid the cracking of bone as the birds smashed into the mountainside. Raftennon stood in the eye of a freak whirlwind, concentrating on maintaining the violent force of the twirling winds. More hawks tried to dive through the magical barrier. The maelstrom swept them away too, crushing them against stone. The wizard mourned every single death, knowing full well they were only doing as they were commanded, feeling no malice whatsoever toward the man.

He almost lost his concentration, and his blustering protection with it, when one of the raptors caught in the wind disappeared into the rock wall. Raftennon steadied his thoughts and forced them back to maintaining his barrier. Only when the faltering winds returned to their full force did he investigate what had happened to the hawk. The rocks in that area were dark, shadowed by a massive boulder that blocked the light of the setting sun. Try as he might, Raftennon could not make out any discerning features in the darkness.

He was so intent on trying to see through the shadows he missed the relative silence that came over his perch. The assault had ended and no more hawks hurled to their deaths. Instead, the flock circled overhead, well away from the destructive winds of the spellcaster's making. The masses waited for the mage's defences to crumble, as surely they would after some time. There was no way he could maintain this forever.

Raftennon smiled, knowing full well the thoughts Jennalla was feeding their small minds. She still did not know of his special ability, of how he drew strength from the air around him to fuel his magic. Let her continue to think that. He was not going to reveal this little advantage of his just yet.

Raftennon widened his whirlwind, forcing the flock to retreat even further. When he was satisfied they were far enough, he dispelled his protective maelstrom, grabbed his pack, and ran for the shadowed spot between the large boulder and the rock face, where the hawk had disappeared. There he felt, rather than saw, the opening that loomed at the base of this section of the peak. He ducked into it before the hawks could reach him.

He only managed to take a couple steps before he found the

way before him blocked. His toe caught on a protruding stone and he stumbled forward, an almost vertical slab keeping him upright. His cheek crushed small bones as he fell into the soft remnants of the doomed hawk that had shown him the way into the alcove. He brushed away the bloody feathers that stuck to his skin and desperately sought the way out of this predicament. It could not be that this was but a shallow niche in the mountainside. He could not return outside to the waiting horde and hope to vanquish them all.

Raftennon rushed to feel the entire wall in front of him, as well as the ones to his side. He was indeed at a dead end. But, he was certain he could hear something echoing from somewhere above him. He to reach the ceiling, and only found it behind him. At the back of the shallow alcove, there was no rock overhead. Here was escape. Raftennon scampered up the steep incline. He could already hear the approaching horde, their shrill cries of revenge filling his ears with promises of a slow and painful death. Mountains hawks knew nothing of vengeance, but there was no mistaking the emotion in their shrieks.

The wizard felt time slipping away from him, for the hand- and footholds were sparse and narrow, but he finally got off the ground and commenced his ascent. He did so just in time, for as he removed his foot from the floor a hawk entered the niche and smashed into its brother, adding more feathers and gore to the already coated wall. If the spellcaster had not been forced to move to the right to find proper footing, the bird's beak would have impaled him in the back. A second raptor crashed where his legs had just been, so he would have lost an ankle as well.

Raftennon scrambled up the sharp incline, sending pebbles and small stones tumbling down onto the carcasses. This, much to the mage's dismay, alerted the other birds of his position. They slowed their charge and flapped their wings to rush up the dark tunnel. Their eyes, like the wizard's, were made to see in daylight, so they did not see the top of the passageway. Many of the vanguard slammed into the alcove's ceiling then fell, taking some of their brethren with them. This gave Raftennon some needed time to add to the lead between himself and his pursuers. He scurried up the obscure passage, sending more debris falling to pelt the struggling flock.

Raftennon's heart skipped a beat when his hand, while feeling for something to grab onto to pull himself up, did not find solid stone where there should have been some. Instead, it continued forward until it found a ledge. The mage doubled his efforts to reach it, sending even more rocks rolling down below him. He inadvertently dislodged enough debris to cause a landslide, which obliterated the entrance to the tunnel, and all the hawks that had been scrambling to follow their quarry.

Raftennon finished his ascent and slumped against the wall of this new passageway, catching his breath after the most gruelling climb he had ever done. Invoking the magical light once again, he took a quick look at his surroundings. The shaft continued in a more manageable slope, with jagged rocks protruding from every stone surface. Thankfully, the passage was large enough for the magic-user to walk through it. All he had to do was maintain the flame and keep a close eye on where he stepped.

But first, he had several cuts that needed ministering.

Jennalla slumped to the stone tiles of the room without walls, her strength all but drained. How could he have survived her latest attack? She had summoned every single hawk that called the Pynakkors home, and still he found a way to escape.

Why was he in the mountains anyway? What could he possibly gain from trudging around in the rocky peaks? What did he know that she did not? Could there be a secret passage that would permit him to reach her?

If there was, she would be ready. She knew what she would do. But first, she required rest.

After the tedious work of bandaging all the small nicks that covered his entire body, Raftennon changed into fresh, intact robes. He then ate a leisurely meal of dried fruits and a slight piece of jerked wolf meat before lying down for a long nap.

When he awoke, the magic-user set off deeper into the tunnel. Casting a new light to float over his outstretched palm, he made his way through the jutting rocks, taking care to not worsen his already ravaged body. The passage continued to climb, the incline so slight Raftennon did not notice it until breathing became laborious, the air around him thinning the longer he went. Countless hours passed and the journey grew more arduous. The atmosphere could not supply the oxygen the mage's aching muscles demanded. More and more frequently, it seemed, he needed to stop to catch his breath.

On one of these stops, in between pants, a noise reached his ears after echoing off an unknown number of rock walls. At first, he thought he imagined it, but it soon came again. Something in the distance was gurgling as if trying to cough up water from its lungs. The sound was sporadic but was definitely there.

Raftennon gathered his belongings, as he had done countless times since leaving the Spellcasters' Guild in Xendremmar, and continued on his way. Thankfully, the passageway began to slope downward, returning heavier, more breathable air to ease his aching chest and legs. The protruding shards on the subterranean walls smoothed away as the incline steepened. He no longer had to mind his step for sharp rocks anymore. Instead, he had to be careful not to slip on the increasingly slippery floor. The air became damper as he went and the dripping sound multiplied, the increasing sources reverberating off the stone.

Soon, Raftennon's magical light reflected off large drops of water as they fell from long stalactites to gather in small, clear pools. Was he nearing the birthing stream the elf had encountered during his escape? The answer came when the wizard's foot splashed into water instead of landing on solid rock. Raftennon lost his concentration and the blue flame over his palm extinguished. He slipped and soon found himself sitting in the shallow pool of ice-cold water that had reflected the light so well it had appeared to be part of the floor.

The noise that attracted his attention came again, this time to his left and without the distortion of echoes. He felt a slight current pass by him, presumably from the water rising from its underground source. Now that he was no longer concentrating on seeing where he was going, Raftennon could hear the growing river gain strength to his right. Somewhere, far off in the distance—he assumed, since the reverberations inside the network of tunnels and caves made judging distance impossible—he heard the waters falling from some height to fall into an unseen lake. By the sound of it, the subterranean waterfall must have been quite a sight to see.

This must be the source of the Masthoranin, a river the mage had seen depicted on maps he had studied while at the Spellcasters' Guild of the continent's eastern half. This was a good sign. The Masthoranin ran eastward until it surged into the Lake Crystalac, in Rond Thora—the strongest kingdom of the continent. By the flow of the current, he deduced he was facing northward. He was still headed in the right direction.

Of course, two other rivers cascaded from the mountains: the Viprennys and the Haun. Both waterways meandered into Mandellon, toward the west. If this wellspring fed one of them instead, then the mage's bearings were inverted. But he was certain he had not travelled far enough to find either of these sources. The Viprennys spilled from the southern tip of the mountain range. The Haun ran from the western branch of the peaks, a distance that should have taken him much longer to travel, at the slow pace he had been managing.

Raftennon shook his head, driving the doubt from his mind. This had to be the Masthoranin. He was still on the correct path. He had to be.

The magic-user crawled across the shallow stream to the other bank as quickly as he could. The water was chilling him to the bone. Once he was on dry land again, he took the opportunity to refill his waterskin with fresh water. That done, he summoned his magical light once again, at half strength this time, illuminating only the floor on which he was about to step onto, and resumed his trek through the darkness.

"I hope these tunnels end soon," he said to himself. "I may just run out of fire grass. Then, I will be forced to continue on my way without the convenience of light."

26

AWAKENING THE EVIL

The tunnel continued for a little way at a level angle, something Raftennon had not expected. The elf's message, which the spellcaster memorized before setting off on this journey, mentioned he climbed a long way before falling into the stream like the mage had just done. Maybe his exhaustion had made this even stretch of the passage seem like a continued climb, or maybe he had been too tired to care and had simply forgotten to add it to his log. Either way, Raftennon anticipated every step to be the first one leading back down into the bowels of the earth. He would not consider he was on the wrong path. He was not anticipating what he encountered next, however.

Much as had happened when he walked into the pool of ice-cold water, his foot did not land on solid stone as he expected. Instead, it only found open air. Raftennon tumbled forward and mercifully landed on a ledge but a foot below. The wizard laboured to catch his breath after his heart leaped into his throat, willing it to slow down. Thankfully, he managed to keep control of his magic flame this time. It still hovered over his upturned palm to show his immediate surroundings.

Raftennon found himself clinging to one jagged side of a large cavern. The expanse spanned much farther than his magical light could illuminate. The rock wall went off for immeasurable distances at either side of him. He stood at the top of a massive cave, the ceiling within easy reach of an outstretched hand if he had still been standing at the mouth of the passageway. The bottom of the cavern lay hidden in the blackness of the subterranean night.

Raftennon rummaged through his pack and retrieved a small glass orb about the size of an apple, with a leather strap thread through its centre. He murmured a sentence and passed the globe through the brilliance hovering over his other hand. The light entered the sphere and remained there. The spellcaster begrudged the used of the receptacle, for it muted the illumination slightly and did not help to maintain the glow any longer. The orb would also be useless after this single use, the glass blackened from the inside.

Raftennon tied the ends of the cord together behind his head like a necklace, freeing both his hands for the descent that was to come. The elf mentioned he climbed for some time, but the magic-user assumed it was in an inclined tunnel, much like the ones he had travelled up to this point. If he had known to expect this huge drop-off, he would have waited to ration out his fire grass until after passing this juncture.

Raftennon bent over the edge of the ledge as far as he dared, letting the orb dangle in the vast, dark expanse, hoping to reveal a way down the jagged cliff. There were many narrow hand- and footholds, but it would have required many years of experience to manage to scale down that rock face. Raftennon realized this right away and was in no way inclined to end his journey in this cavern.

With a sigh of resignation, he rummaged through his spell component pouches. If this kept up, he would have to use his feet to dodge Jennalla's attacks instead of using his vast repertoire of protective barriers.

A draft from his right made his robes ripple in a room that, up to that point, had offered only stagnant air. He stopped moving, keeping absolutely still, waiting to feel the breeze again to make sure it was not a trick of his imagination. The intrusion proved to be quite real when a low growl echoed off the unseen cavern walls. Raftennon tried to pinpoint the source of the menacing sound, but the ricochet effect the rocks gave the noise made the task impossible.

He gazed up to the tunnel entering the large cave, contemplating turning back. He disregarded that thought quickly enough, remembering his family, still trapped in Xendremmar, unable to return home unless they wanted to chance another surprise visit from Jennalla. Raftennon returned his attention to the darkness in the depths of the cavern, steeling his heart to whatever was waiting for him down below.

Taking the dove feathers from the pouch he had barely managed to open before the interruption, the wizard pronounced the appropriate incantation and threw the feathers into the void. He stepped off the ledge after them and floated down along the jagged rock wall.

The cave was quite deep, the seconds ticking away like hours as he descended into the mountains' depths. Eventually, the cliff behind him did curve inward until it became a manageable gradient, but he maintained his spell and kept floating downward. He did not intend to risk a slide down this slope. There was no telling if there was another precipice waiting to appear in his magical light, this time causing a much more serious, maybe fatal, fall. His doubts proved unwarranted, however, as the incline continued to decrease until he landed on the cavern floor.

Raftennon examined his surroundings, seeing nothing but darkness beyond the limited glow of the orb hanging from his neck. Inside the ring of light, around his feet, old bones carpeted the floor, the remains so thick the stone underneath never peeked through. He bent down and picked one of them up, not recognizing to which species it belonged. It had been a large being, judging by the size, but he could discern no more. It was no animal, he soon found out. He lifted another bone that lay right beside the first one, and this one had a piece of torn rag still wrapped around it. Whatever this thing once had been, it had clothed itself.

Raftennon rummaged through the gruesome remains, gathering all the flammable material he could find and placing it in a neat pile. Retrieving the tinderbox and flint from his pack, he lit the heap, shedding a little light in the large cavern. He then went to another section of the room and repeated the process. When his work was done, he had three reasonably sized bonfires, evenly spaced from each other to illuminate the entire base of the cave.

Raftennon's breath caught in his throat as he surveyed the area. He knew there were many dead bodies underfoot because of the ease he had had of finding fuel for his fires, but he had not expected this. The carpet of ageless skeletal remains ran from slanted slope to slanted slope. As Raftennon stumbled through the room, his hopes of discovering a spot clear stone diminished as the darkness decreased. But thinking about a room filled with skeletons and actually seeing it were two completely different things. Many carcasses were animal, or at least not humanoid. Some were so old they had crumbled to dust beneath the weight of the added bodies. Some still showed the marks of gnawing teeth. Others were splintered into millions of tiny shards, the crushing blow that had caused the damage quite considerable. But none of them had any remnants of flesh or sinew keeping the form of the skeleton, to help identify the victims.

When Raftennon finally managed to tear his eyes from the horrible sight, he took in the rest of his surroundings. The bottom of the expanse was shaped like a bowl, the walls curving inward as they neared the floor. The stone was smooth, almost as if polished by something to render them impossible to scale. The wizard ran a hand on the nearest wall and found it to be quite slick. Two tunnels led out of the spacious room. The larger one, directly in front of the mage, was level to the floor and immediately turned to the right, preventing one from seeing what lay further within. The other, smaller tunnel ran off to the left. Its mouth was roughly eight feet from the ground, and with the smoothness of the wall could prove difficult to reach. Raftennon could see from where he was standing that this passageway led downward, deeper into the bowels of the mountains.

The magic-user returned his gaze to the lower opening when he heard a much louder growl than the one that had caught his attention at the top of the cavern. Slowly emerging from the passage was a large creature, its short, black fur engulfing the firelight sent its way. The long, thick legs flowed under the monster's massive girth, propelling it forward as if it were floating on air. The paws were more like hands, save for they only had three fingers, or toes if you will. The body, tubular in shape, was as muscular as its limbs. In fact, its torso was so like its legs in dimensions it appeared to be a fifth appendage linking the other four together. The creature possessed no tail, but it did have a head, and quite a head it was. Pointed ears, the size of an elephant's, pivoted on the beast's temples, taking in every crackle of the fires around the room. Where its eyes should have been was a huge maw, so large it took the entirety of its face. Another loud growl travelled past several rows of razor-sharp fangs before echoing off the rock walls.

Raftennon's blood chilled in his veins as he watched the thing searched for him with its giant ears. He remained as quiet as he could, having no desire to confront this monster.

The image of the Spellcasters' Guild in Xendremmar came to mind as he remembered where he had seen this beast before. It had been during one of his lessons on the Ancient World, before his apprenticeship with Vendrammon.

"Before the taming of the lands by the various young races of Roen's second attempt at creation," his instructor had been saying on that particular day, *"many different species of beasts roamed freely in the forests and the plains. The avian fauna was very different from the birds you see flying today.*

"However, the most ancient of the beings, and the most dangerous, could be found under the earth. Many of these fearsome and powerful specimens were bred by the gods of evil, their forms twisted, their will broken until they only serve their new masters. Their sole purpose became the destruction of all that was good in the world."

The instructor opened a tome sitting on a large podium at the front of the classroom. He then invited the students to come forward and take a good look at the portrait that was on the displayed page. The picture was an intricate depiction of the creature that now stalked the mage. It hunched on its powerful legs, ready to strike. The huge maw was gaping wide, revealing several rows of small, razor-sharp teeth nestled in the gums behind the first row of larger, curved fangs.

"This," the teacher continued, *"is the nennbak, one of the eldest of the perverted races. Once a majestic animal, the gods Jafall and Nemanta collaborated on its transformation. The god of jealousy was envious of what the young dwarven race was beginning to extract from the bowels of the mountains, so he be-*

seeched his aunt for aid. The goddess of devastation jumped at the opportunity to further destroy what Roen had created.

"The nennbak soon became the bane of anything that aspired for any sort of subterranean glory. Those that dug for riches were hunted and ground into their treasures before taking their last breath. Those who only wanted to explore the subsurface wonders were permitted to do so, but would never have the chance to share their discoveries. You see, because of Jafall's influence, the nennbak became very intelligent beings. They constantly devised more sadistic ways of torturing their victims before giving them the luxury of death.

"Their entire physique was conceived to give them stealth and ease of transportation in the many tunnels they conquered. Their slender, supple bodies enabled them to almost slither through tight fitting openings. Their legs were powerful enough to propel them over wide chasms and sustain falls from tremendous heights. Their paws, with their three claws, could crumble the strongest rock and render them to dust in mere seconds. The nennbak burrowed through solid granite as if it were loose beach sand.

"Because of their subterranean existence, eyes were useless to them, and evolution soon took care of that problem. Nature continued what the gods began, enlarging the ears, along with their sensitivity, even further. The eyes, which had been reduced in size during their corruption, disappeared after a few generations of disuse.

"The nennbak's primary means of attack was its giant maw. One bite could sever a man's torso in two, but the creature seldom used that tactic. First, it would stalk its prey, playing with its mind with strategically timed growls that would echo off the walls of the caverns it called home. When the confusion set in, with the target going mad because it could not find the source of the sound, the nennbak came out of hiding and continued the stalk, using its intimidating physique to further terrify the hapless victim. When the last vestiges of courage finally slipped away and the prey bolted for any promise of safety, the nennbak, with the aid of its tremendously honed hearing, pounced and tore away a leg, right from under the fleeing man."

The class had gasped at the gruesome description. Even the most steel-hearted of the group could not believe the beast capable of such atrocities.

"Do not fool yourselves, students," the instructor continued, seemingly reading their thoughts. "The nennbak did not usually kill for nourishment—they did so for sport. Though they did need to feed, a single meal of one average-sized human male could sustain the beast for many months. Some even surmise it could live off rocks and mushrooms alone. The killing of an entire party of dwarves, let us say, was unnecessary for the beast's survival. But the nennbak would commit that very atrocity quite frequently when they first appeared. If the reason for the death was not nourishment, then it was clearly malice. They did serve the god of vengeance, after all."

"Do these things still exist?" one of Raftennon's classmates asked.

"Some suppose so, but most historians believe them to be extinct, for one has not been seen in quite some time.

"The dwarven race was nearly annihilated by the creatures. The scarce survivors scurried to the surface and travelled vast distances from their old homes in hopes of escaping their demise. They passed many centuries living above ground, gradually losing their heritage and old way of life. Eventually, they returned to the darkness under the mountains but did so in ranges far away from their original homeland. They also do not delve as deeply as they once did, save for their great subterranean kingdom beneath the Divirion Mountains. There, the nennbak never entered, for the range was sacred to Flonn, the forger of the gods, and he permitted none of the twisted beasts to enter."

"Couldn't the dwarves defend themselves?" another student asked.

"The nennbak's hide, while supple, was as hard as the rocks it inhabited. Though it was not impossible, steel seldom sliced through the skin, axes never hewed a tendon, and hammers never made a dent. The only means of defence the peoples had was escape."

"If the creature could leap across wide chasms and burrow through the earth as if it weren't even there, how could one run away from it?" inquired yet another pupil.

"You had to deafen it," Raftennon whispered. Because of the rapt audience, the room was silent and everyone in attendance heard his comment.

"Correct, young sir," the teacher affirmed. "The nennbak relied solely on its hearing to find its prey. The creature's ears were so fine-tuned it could hear a feather land on a stone slab in the centre of a hurricane. Create a loud enough noise and, theoretically, you could 'blind' the beast for quite some time, enabling easy escape."

Raftennon returned his attention to the present when the creature reached one of his fires and dispersed the tattered clothes and other flammable materials, extinguishing the light and quieting the crackle of the flames. It then pricked its ears and located the other fire that was closest to it. Mercifully, that campfire was on the other side of the cavern, away from the spellcaster, giving him the time to prepare himself.

Rummaging through the hidden pockets in his robes, Raftennon retrieved the spell components he would need and brought them out, only to have them thrust out of his hands by a massive paw. The nennbak, having heard the rustle of the clothe as he searched for his ingredients, leaped across the cave and landed on the magic-user, pinning both his shoulders to the bone-covered floor.

Raftennon did not even try to free himself from the powerful grip. Instead, he reached out with his right hand and grasped the nearest large bone, for the nennbak had decided to deviate from its routine. It was foregoing the usual maiming of its victim. It opened its massive jaws and aimed for the wizard's head, intent on ending his life with one swift bite. Raftennon thrust his chosen weapon, a femur of an ogre-like being, in front of his face. The nennbak's many teeth clamped down on the bone, easily splintering it. The manoeuvre succeeded in saving the mage's life—for the moment.

The beast tilted its head to spit out the shards of bone from its mouth, clearly not what it had intended on eating. While its head was turned, Raftennon took the opportunity to scream into the exposed ear. The results were quite unexpected, even to one who had studied the beast and some of its habits. The nennbak leaped clear off its prey, roaring in frustration and pain, to land halfway up the wall. The massive claws dug into the rock and the monster remained there for a few moments, like an insect, waiting for its ears to stop ringing.

Raftennon scrambled to his feet to retrieve the dropped sachet, but the rocks he had been carrying with him were now lost in the sea of bones. The scuffle had pushed them down into the thick layer of death on the floor and the mage did not have time to look for them now. He searched the area around the fire nearest to him and took two small skulls, ignoring the fact these could have belonged to dwarves that had once called these caves home.

The nennbak inched its way down the smooth wall, showing no sign of slipping. Its hearing seemed to be returning, for it began to gain speed, intent on finishing this quickly. Maybe it was too hungry to play games. Or, most likely, it did not want to chance another earache. Either way, Raftennon ignored the beast's descent, calmly chanting and sprinkling the powder from the pouch onto the skulls.

"Kaffaynônâlee ventrâlü jenmâllaynon fentâlee banjémônü!"

The nennbak reached the floor and rushed the wizard, its jaws wide open. The firelight gleamed off the hundreds of sharp teeth as the beast crashed through the burning rags, barrelling toward its prey.

Raftennon grabbed the skulls and bashed them together. The bone splintered in his hands, decimating the last remnants of the long forgotten pair. A loud, thunderous bang echoed off the stone walls, resonating all the way up to the unseen ceiling and through the two tunnels that marked the only exits from the subterranean pit. The nennbak shrieked in pain before plopping to the skeletal carpet, lifeless. The only remaining fire shone off the black blood that trickled out of the creature's ears.

Raftennon slumped to the ivory-covered ground, the first assault finally registering in his mind. The adrenaline from his initial furtive plight for survival left his veins, leaving throbbing muscles in his arms where the monster's claws had dug into his flesh to pin him down. He took a few moments to catch his breath and rub some feeling back into his biceps. Then he retrieved all his belongings, which had been shoved to the side when the nennbak made its first leap on top of him. The spellcaster looked over at the ancient horror to make certain it was dead. It remained motionless, much like the air. In fact, the cavern was so calm it made the magic-user uneasy. For some reason he could not grasp, it was not safe to linger here.

Not wishing to discover the source of his apprehension, Raftennon examined the pair of possible exits again. The larger, and lower, passage was undoubtedly the easier of the two choices, being at floor level and the part he could see even and smooth. Of course, this was the way the monster had entered the cave and, logically, would only lead further into the depths of the mountains—probably leading him straight to the heart of his worries. So, he turned to his only other option.

Looking up at the lofty entrance, Raftennon contemplated the means to gain access. Granted, the opening was only two feet above his head, but the wall sloped outward as it rose from the floor, augmenting the distance almost twofold. The mage had devoted his life to expanding his knowledge, not enhancing his physical strength. He never attempted a leap like this before and was not certain he could accomplish it.

"Well, there is no other way to find out if I can do this than try it," he told himself in hushed tones, wary of other finely-tuned ears somewhere deeper in the cavern system under the Pynakkors.

Raftennon dashed through the morbid remains and tried to continue running up the incline. His feet slipped down the slick surface, but Raftennon pumped his legs to take advantage of whatever slight purchase he could. His first attempt brought his fingertips to the lip of the tunnel, but he could not grab hold to haul himself up. He slid down to land among the dried bones, his moderately heavy pack dragging him all the way to a sitting position. There was no way he could make it to the passageway with all the added weight of his provisions.

Raftennon took aim and hurled his possessions toward the narrow opening. A loud thud resonated off the walls as it slammed into the top edge of the entrance. The magic-user backed up a few steps and tried again, hoping to augment his chance of success with a more direct trajectory. Once again, the bag thudded against the stone wall, this time hitting just below the small hole. The third throw finally found its mark, the pack barely squeezing into the constricted space.

With his possessions in place, Raftennon made a second attempt to reach the passage, this time starting his run near the centre of the cavern. As before, only his fingers rose above the lower edge of the opening and, for an agonizing short moment, managed to maintain their grip on the rock. But, as was expected of a man not conditioned for physical endurance, his strength quickly depleted and he repeated the slide down the slippery slope.

The feeling in the pit of his stomach, warning him trouble was brewing, intensified with every second he fought to free himself of this place. Not wanting to waste another attempt at freedom, Raftennon resolved to use another tactic. Kneeling, he spread his arms wide and pushed as much of the debris beneath the opening as he could. Back and forth he went, adding more and more bone and tattered cloth until a small mound stood under the elusive exit in the otherwise impassable wall.

His work done, Raftennon returned to his previous starting point in the centre of the cave. His ears caught the slightest hint of claws scratching on stone somewhere down the large tunnel to his right—at least, he thought he had heard something coming from that direction. He had no intention of waiting to see if it was only his imagination. After taking a deep breath, he sprinted toward his makeshift ramp. Two steps brought him to the top, bones tumbling down to the ground with every push of his legs. A few more shattered as he leaped for his goal, crumbling what remained of the heap to the floor.

Raftennon finally saw the inside of the passageway as his arms made it inside. His legs dangled from the lip of the hole, trying in vain to find purchase on the slick surface. The mage struggled to pull himself up, using his upper body to haul the rest of him into the passage. An eternity seemed to pass before Raftennon managed to inch his way into the tunnel.

He had to push his pack farther into the darkness to give himself enough room to drag his feet out of the massive bowl. The shaft was so narrow he could not even get onto his hands and knees. The only way he could advance was to wriggle forward while pushing his bag before him. There was no space for him to sling his possessions onto his back, or to look back to see what was happening in the cavern behind him.

His boots had barely disappeared into the darkness when a second nennbak entered the cave, roused by the sounds of the previous battle. It pricked its ears at the sound of the wizard's scrambling. It took a step in his direction, even though he was in a shaft too small for its body. Its paw brushed against its fallen comrade and the creature turned to feel what it was. When it realized what it touched was a carcass, the beast abandoned the noise and delved into the fresh corpse to quench the hunger that had assailed it for such a long time.

Jennalla smiled as the orb on the serpent pedestal showed her Raftennon crawling up the narrow tunnel.

"So he thought he could do better. That'll show him!"

She was referring to the awakening of the nennbak and the only being who would have bothered with the task, the god of vengeance, Jafall. It seemed the persistent luck that enabled Raftennon to continue toward his House was finally beginning to irritate the deity. That was the reason he had left her, so he could rouse the hibernating beasts without her knowledge. She was not fooled, however. She knew the god was the only being capable, and inclined, to perform this summoning.

"Raf's pretty resourceful, I'll give him that. But he's really starting to anger me!"

The wizardress looked out of the open room to the tall peaks of the Pynakkors. It was time to begin her preparations for the final obstacle. He would surely fall this time.

27

INTO THE WIND

With his arms and legs aching from the climb up the winding tunnel that seemed to go on for eternity, Raftennon stared in awe at the devastation beyond the confines of the Pynakkors. The sky rushed past as he peered upward from the opening of the passageway. The black clouds barrelled along with the strong winds that buffeted the mountains. Small pebbles and large hailstones crashed into the rock wall to his left. Other stones were plucked from their resting places on his right to disappear into the massive twister.

While the torrential gusts stormed about ten feet overhead, and an equal distance to either side of the burrow opening, the air in the strange continuation of the tunnel was quite calm. Not a grain of sand stirred, not a weed swayed. It appeared someone had erected an invisible field to prevent the tornado from touching down along the chosen path. Only in this expanse could Raftennon see the ground. A few small pockets of crushed stone lay atop naked rock. The dark grey plateau was flat and even, with cracks zigzagging across the pathway at irregular intervals.

Focusing on the small patch of visible horizon at the end of the calm, Raftennon saw a faint glimpse of darker shadows against the blackened sky. He could not make out any of the details from this distance, but his memory of the descriptions written in the many tomes he had read, as well as his imagination, told his eyes what lay in front of him. Black, fang-like spires reached for the heavens, surrounding a single twisted spire that loomed over the wastelands around the structure. Atop the central tower sat the fabled Black Eye, radiating its hatred and jealousy throughout the world. A massive, blackened stone gate, formed in the likeness of a skull's open jaw, admitted the House's invited guests. Raftennon had always wondered why such an entry was needed since no one could travel through the raging hurricane that continually surrounded the House. Anyone answering a summons from Jafall would surely be transported before the god of vengeance by magical means, most likely in a chosen room in the depths of the contorted minaret.

Of course, Raftennon was not summoned. In fact, he was certain he would be quite unwanted. None of the obstacles he had come across in the mountains were coincidental. The last thing that could be attributed to happenstance would be meeting Stav in Medosan, but even that encounter might not have been chance. He could only see that conversation as a boon to him for without the plainsman's advice, the spellcaster would have never found the elf. But Raftennon would not put anything past Jennalla's twisted mind.

Something bothered the magic-user, however. Casting spells from vast distances took immense power. Had Jennalla become that powerful? Could she have controlled all those creatures? If she had discovered the means to bend even the ancient nennbak to her will, she would be more of a challenge than he first anticipated. Surely she was not that strong. But if this was the case, it meant someone was aiding her.

Raftennon crept out of the narrow tunnel and stretched his aching muscles, finally having enough room to do so. He wolfed down a morsel of what little provisions he had left as he stared down the strange corridor. He could only think of one being who would help her, in this place. And if he was correct, this encounter would become extremely difficult.

The wizard pushed aside this train of thought to dwell on other matters. The mad elf had mentioned this calm area leading away from the House in his diary, but he had failed to mention where he had exited the dark tower. Was Raftennon expected to follow this path to a secret entrance, a path that was so obvious he could not fathom how the god of vengeance could have missed it for so long? Or was he to simply enter the complex through the front door?

Raftennon could not ponder this issue further, however, as the mystical passage crumpled under the power of the supernatural storm. Violent gusts shot out from the path's walls and ceiling, shoving the mage back against the steep slope of the mountain. There they pinned him, crushing him into the ageless stones. Raftennon's mind raced to find a way out of this predicament. With each fraction of a second that passed, the sudden onslaught ground his body into the unforgiving rock. The force of the hurricane prevented him from rummaging through his many pouches of components. The winds were stronger than he was and pinned his arms as effectively as manacles would.

Here he was again with the dilemma of coming up with a spell that required only words to cast. The problem here, as with the spiders, was the only spells of this type he knew worked exclusively on beings with a conscious mind. None of his choices could affect the forces of nature itself, even though this particular attack seemed to have some intelligence behind it. The storm would apply more pressure to whatever limb he was trying to free at that moment, instead of continually applying the same amount of force over his entire body...

"As if someone was controlling it," Raftennon whispered, barely able to push the words out in this grinding wind.

The mage ignored the pebbles that assaulted him, scraping his face and smashing onto his closed eyelids. He isolated his environment, forgetting his predicament, focusing only on what he needed to accomplish to save himself. He sent his mind into the maelstrom, searching for what should not be there. Almost immediately, he found what he was looking for. It was a minute trace of rage, but it was strong enough for him to see and latch onto. His will refused to let go as the consciousness became aware of its discovery and attempted to flee. Raftennon tightened his mind's grip on the anger as it turned to fear and tried to scamper away. The spellcaster's will not only held on but hauled itself along the thread that would certainly lead to the source of the emotions, as a normal person would pull himself along a rope spanning a tumultuous river to cross it.

The winds assailing the wizard receded, but he did not notice. All his attention remained bent on the pursuit of the desperate feeling, which he permitted to return to its owner at a pace with which he could keep up. Eventually—mere moments for the observer, had there been any, an eternity for the young spellcaster —the chase revealed his assailant. The desperation flew up the side of the House of Jafall, snaking between small balconies and openings—which had no railings to prevent falls—to the top of the centre-most spire, all the way to the room with no walls.

"Jennalla," Raftennon growled, not at all surprised at the discovery.

He bent his will to keep hold of her, to impede her casting of more spells to hinder his approach to the mystical fortress. The wizardress, having gotten over the initial shock of being discovered as the source of the storm, struggled to break Raftennon's resolve. The mental battle lasted only a few short moments before the link broke under the strain of the two powerful combatants.

Raftennon slumped onto one knee, gasping for breath. It felt as if he had been holding it for quite some time and now could not get enough to enter his lungs to fill his body's need. The mage glared at the barren path, nestled in the middle of the perpetual storm, to the horizon where his final destination lay. There he would put an end to all this foolishness.

Jennalla finally succeeded in severing the bond forced on her. She could not believe how strong he had become. Contrary to Raftennon's belief, she did know of the special skill that enabled him to draw strength from the air around him, but surely, that could not compare to the power she had received from the god of vengeance himself. There was no way he could be that...

The rest of the thought flitted away as she slumped to the stone floor of the keep's highest chamber and succumbed to darkness.

28

Payment from the Uninvited

Raftennon peered into the winds that zipped past over him at speeds he had never seen before. If he had had any doubts this maelstrom was indeed not natural, the force of this vision would have quickly swept them away. Here, in the centre of it all, the gusts were so violent they appeared not to move at all. It seemed as if a thick fog surrounded the massive structure erected by the god's will, so fast were the stones and other debris flying around it.

The mage pondered what to do next as he looked over his surroundings. He was still expecting an attack from the keeper of the tower. His arrival was surely not wanted. There was no logical reason Jafall would want him this close to Jennalla, who was becoming quite apparent to be the deity's favoured worshipper. He sensed the divine power in the woman's struggles during their last mental confrontation, confirming Vendrammon's suspicions. He felt the twisted hatred in her attempt to yank his mind out of his head.

But, underneath it all, Raftennon thought he perceived a small amount of the old love that had brought them together all those years ago, alone in the Spellcasters' Guild in Xendremmar, while all the other students left the complex on a much-deserved vacation. There was still hope he could talk some sense into the enraged woman—a hope Jafall most certainly wanted to quash. So where was the welcoming committee to dispose of him?

While he pondered this fact, Raftennon surveyed the black wall looming over him. The jagged rock, ripped from the earth by celestial hatred, shot up into the tumultuous sky, much like a steep, narrow mountain. There were no signs of mortal masonry work whatsoever. No bricks could be made out, no mortar to show where the stones were fused together. The very structure of the building was unstable. Numerous towers narrowed in some places before widening again in their higher reaches, making the entire complex seem like it was about to collapse in on itself, the heavy weight of the summits shattering the slim expanses underneath. But the House did not fall, and never would, as long as hatred and jealousy found themselves a place in the mortal heart.

Amid the raging storm, immune to the forceful winds, a strange blackness that almost appeared to have substance came oozing down the sides of the fortress. The darkness made Raftennon's blood boil and his pulse race. Nothing had provoked the intense anger that overtook him, yet he was enraged than he had ever been. The feeling was so strong he almost threw himself against the wall, intent on tearing the ancient edifice down with his bare hands. He craned his neck back to roar at the sky, hoping the release would help him regain some composure. The scream allowed the spellcaster to calm himself to a point he could resume some form of thinking. That was when he felt Jafall's minions, living inside the House, were the ones influencing him.

To aid his concentration, Raftennon turned his back to the blackness. Maybe the serenity of the magical tunnel would set the example for his emotions. What he saw there nearly sent his heart beating at a frenzied pace once again. The passage was gone. Replacing the clear view of the Pynakkor Mountains was the uniform wall of flying rock caught in the mystic twister.

"It appears there is no turning back," Raftennon stated with a hint of apprehension. Though he did not intend to leave before confronting Jennalla, he would have liked to still have the option.

As he started to turn back to the oppressive House, a ripple distorted the flying debris that now blocked his path back to the mountains. Intrigued, Raftennon took a step closer to the whirlwind and inched his hand toward the maelstrom. Instead of the expected assault on his flesh, the pebbles and larger rocks passed right through his fingers.

"An illusion," the wizard mused. "Could it be possible the god does not see through this trick? It would certainly explain how he could have missed the elf's flight." It did not solve the puzzle of how Jennalla found him at the mouth of the tunnel, however.

Raftennon stored this new discovery—and new question—into the recesses of his mind for further analysis once he returned home. For now, he turned his gaze up to the black wall, through the black mist, fighting another volley of black thoughts. Now that his eyes were no longer as easily drawn to the unnatural darkness, he found a light shining just below the grey haze of the storm, which blew fifteen feet off the ground this close to the structure. A narrow balcony protruded from the wall, where it bent inward before disappearing into the torrential winds. The glow was seeping through an open door barely under the curtain of debris.

"Perhaps the elf did not exit the House through a secret passageway, after all," Raftennon wondered. Maybe he had fallen out that very window to this very spot. It would have been quite easy for him to forget such a trivial detail amid all the other ordeals through which he had gone.

Raftennon examined the side of the edifice once again, this time paying closer attention to the stone. It was roughly hewn, and though the many edges were rounded by time, he believed he could still manage to scale it. That was good. He was not sure he had anything left in his hidden pouches with which to cast the levitation spell.

Raftennon took one last look at his intended hand- and footholds and began the fifteen-foot ascent. He was only halfway up when his arms started to ache from the strain of keeping hold of the scant purchase the warped surface afforded him. Several times, he lost his footing, adding more agony to his already aching limbs. Raftennon never once looked down as he struggled upward. He kept his eyes on the opening, convinced every second that passed would be the one Jafall's henchmen would scamper out to whisk him away, never to be seen again. The words of several protective spells ran through his head, taking his focus off the growing pain in his muscles.

After a long uninterrupted struggle, the mage pulled himself onto the small balcony. He looked into the room while rubbing the exhaustion from his biceps. A lone torch hanging on a sconce on the left wall illuminated the empty, misshapen room. The walls bulged inward here and there, and corners did not exist at all. The ceiling drooped in several places as if the entire structure had been hastily constructed in clay by a child aspiring to be a sculptor, but without a lick of talent.

The only fact Raftennon concentrated on now was the absence of the welcoming committee. Could his arrival truly have been missed? He doubted that very much. It was the god of hatred he was thinking of, after all. The deity was supposed to be all-seeing, all-knowing. Missing the appearance of someone whose purpose was to thwart the plans of his most devoted worshipper, if not his own, was surely not a sign of his omnipotence. Where were the House's defences?

Raftennon was certainly not going to shoot a gift horse in the mouth. He crossed the room and cracked open the only door to peek at the corridor beyond. All he saw were shadows. Faint light seeped down from the upper levels, turning everything into shades of grey. A roughly-hewn catwalk ran along the wall on either side to join more passageways that spanned the expanse that was the centre of the structure. These narrow bridges filled the inside of the tower like many strands of a spider's web, crossing each other at differing heights to create countless junctures. Some intersecting paths met at large balls of rock, presumably more rooms somewhat like the one he was in right now.

Raftennon raised his gaze to the grey shadows shrouding the higher reaches of the spire, apprehension clamping his throat shut. The fact the House was devoid of life was quite disconcerting on its own, but the complex maze of bridges and catwalks looming above him fed the spellcaster's worries even more. He could easily lose his way in this strange network, and the longer he remained trapped in the core of the House, the greater chance Jennalla and Jafall would have to find a way to dispose of him.

The door flew open as Raftennon dropped to his knees before falling onto his side, grasping his head with his hands. Fear clamped down on his heart even further as a strange sense of danger came over him. An extraordinary rage came over him. He was not the one who was angry. It was the air around him that appeared to loathe him. Centuries of hatred flowed through him in a matter of seconds, and the intensity of the attack took the breath from his lungs. The spiritual assault was so strong an actual punch to the chest would have been a welcome replacement, even if it came from a member of one of the mighty ogre races.

Raftennon felt accused of countless affronts, hundreds of deaths, thousands of betrayals, millions of lovers' affairs. He forgot his surroundings and the purpose for being here. All he could focus on was finding a reason why he was blamed for all these slights.

Concentrate, young one.

The words squeezed in between the crowding emotions, coming from somewhere within the mage's consciousness, but not originating from there.

You have the strength to overcome this ordeal. These are only impressions forced upon you. Shut them out and they will hold no power over you. Regain mastery of your mind. It will show you the way.

Again, the message cut through the overwhelming emotions, demanding Raftennon's complete attention. He focused on this strange voice, blocking everything else out, struggling to find his usual calm inside the turmoil. Slowly, the accusations from the House dissipated, leaving the magic-user with his own thoughts, and only his own thoughts.

His breathing slowed to its regular rhythm. The pounding in his chest eased. Clarity returned and he could finally ponder what was happening to him. This was the second time the outside voice had come to his aid. In the mountains, it had freed the mage from the thick spider webs and countered the venom that coursed through his veins, threatening to seize his heart. Who was helping him, and what was the motive behind it?

Raftennon stared up into the gloom of the strange structure, up at the myriad of passageways that led to unknown sections of the House. To his surprise, his quieted mind indeed showed him the way to the room at the structure's summit. A trail of faded greyness ran along certain dark bridges and up specific spirals as if the hatred and jealousy had parted to let someone pass through the House's emotional defences. As far as Raftennon knew, Jennalla was the only mortal with permission to currently reside in this place. It appeared, even with the god's blessing, his guests were not immune to the onslaught of feelings the tower exuded. A path needed clearing for them to reach their specific destination.

Raftennon walked up the winding way, the darkness lightening as he went. The shadows did not dissipate as he ascended the many stories, per se. It was more as if the wizard's sight rid itself of an unnatural haze when he fended off the last attack. The negative feelings no longer burdened his spirit and he seemed to understand his environment a bit better. The voice had made him concentrate to a point where he could fully comprehend his surroundings.

More emotions attacked the intruder as he progressed up the magically constructed structure. He witnessed the results of jealous rages, of unfounded revenge, of wars without reason. Each attack was more gruesome, more perverted than its predecessor was, but they affected Raftennon less and less. Unlike the elf, who had built up a wall of indifference because of centuries spent watching the atrocities, the magic-user's defences were the result of a mind now focused on his goal. With the voice's help, Raftennon discovered a way to repel the images the House used to try to destroy his resolve.

Up winding stairs he went, following numerous ramps and spanning countless bridges, and still Raftennon remained alone in the vast chamber. He followed the path of least emotion, shrugging off all the mental attacks hurled at him. Still, the Vengeful God's henchmen did not come to stop him.

"Jafall will have to get that window sealed up. But why isn't the House stopping him? Why is he being allowed to continue on his way up here?"

Jennalla paced in front of the orb as it showed her every move Raftennon made inside her current home. She had seen him crumple under the initial attack, but could not understand why he had been permitted to get up. When she had first visited the House, she had had an invitation, and still the rage of the spirits dwelling within almost drove her mad. Jafall's arrival had saved her then, and an added charm from the deity had made her immune from any future onslaught, as long as she remained in the areas he designated to her. Raftennon had neither of these things, but still he managed to get to his feet. That was impossible—unless the man had struck a deal with the god.

Jennalla dismissed that absurd notion almost immediately. There was no way the righteous hypocrite would ever side with evil like that. He would foolishly throw his life away instead of embracing his dark side.

She had no time to waste debating the possibilities any further. Raftennon continued to climb the winding path that would lead him to her, and it was clear nothing would hinder his progress. The House was powerless against him, and Jafall, for whatever reason he decided to keep from her, was not even stepping in to defend his keep.

The wizardress went through the numerous pouches hidden in the folds of her blood-red robes. Finding everything satisfactory, everything she would need in its proper place and in adequate supply, she relaxed the slightest bit.

It had been years since she had last set eyes (physically, not magically) on the love of her last years at the Spellcasters' Guild. He seemed to be quite handsome still, from what she had seen through the orb.

She brushed aside the fond memories and reminded herself the man had deserted her. Now was the time for her revenge, the time he would pay for humiliating her when he chose to discard her without a second thought, like a parchment with a large inkblot marring its intricately scripted words. Tonight, his suffering for the loss of his family would end. Tonight, Raftennon of Yentrill would learn the true meaning of a woman's scorn and would learn nothing more afterwards.

29

ATOP THE TOWER

Raftennon's head popped through the hole in the floor of the up-permost room of the tallest spire in the House of Jafall. A sudden flurry of lightning flickered between the large pillars, bathing the area in an eerie yellow light for a fraction of a heartbeat before returning it to its usual gloom. Thunder rocked the room with the force of its crash.

Raftennon noticed none of this. His full attention was on the woman standing beside the crystal orb on its serpentine stand in the centre of the room.

"So you finally made it." Jennalla greeted her old "friend", the annoyance with his arrival quite apparent in her voice. A gust of wind blew across the room, swaying the bottom hem of her blood-red robes. She ignored it. The only thing that seemed to exist for her was the mage finishing his ascent into the room.

"I wish it were under different circumstances, and a different locale." Raftennon took his last step off the winding staircase that finally brought him to the end of his long journey. The mea-gre meals he was forced to endure to ensure he had enough to last the entire trip, the numerous assaults he had to fend off, the trials he had to surmount, they were all forgotten the moment he set his eyes on the source of his hardship.

"You should have thought about how your disappearance would have affected me before choosing the magic over what we had." A sudden silence in the raging storm let Jennalla's words, spoken through clenched teeth, waft clearly to Raftennon.

"What we had was developing fondness." He tried his best to remain calm, but her arrogance already began to wear away at his resolve to give her another chance to explain herself.

"Fondness? That's all it was to you? You think I give myself to every guy I'm fond of?" A crash in the distance fought with the wizardress' angry screech—and failed.

"It was six weeks—"

"You think I hadn't noticed you before then?" Jennalla's fury had complete control of her. "You think I didn't see all those glances you tried to hide from everyone? I knew you were in-fatuated. I knew because I was sneaking peeks at you too! It may have started as a teenage crush, but I only sleep with guys I love!"

Raftennon lowered his gaze, taking a submissive posture to mask his growing rage. He could not believe her. She had des-troyed his family, and all she continued to think about was a failed infatuation. What infuriated him the most was the fact he had no sympathy for the woman. He should have felt remorse for breaking her heart, but her actions had driven all compassion from him.

"I sincerely apologize. I did not realize." Raftennon kept his tone tranquil and soothing. He needed to calm her down, or things would certainly go awry. Despite what she had done, he still did not want to take her life (though she could change his mind quite easily). The apathy he felt was bad enough as it was. He did not want to risk adding remorse to it.

"Of course you didn't!" Jennalla screamed at him, not noti-cing his jaw set and his eyes gleam with sudden anger. "You're a man! All you think about is what's best for you! To Necroma with the rest of the world! To Necroma with those that love you!"

"You never loved me," Raftennon whispered, just loud enough for her to hear. His brown eyes glared at her while her green orbs flared in rage. A large crackle of lightning blasted just outside the room.

"How dare you tell me what I feel!" Each word was a sen-tence, each syllable an intended blow. Raftennon stood unaffected by her anger. The hurt in her heart had changed her so much he no longer saw the woman that had first introduced him to the possibilities of a shared life, all those years ago.

"You do not know what love truly is," he said without a trace of emotion. The oppressive air in the room without walls seemed to part to let the words drift to the crazed wizardress.

Jennalla could take no more.

"Entraylânnem kraylentra fôrnak! Kâllentrannem fârlan maytralnâk!"

Orange flames engulfed Jennalla's hands as she thrust them in front of her. When her arms completely extended, the fire shot out from her fingers and barrelled toward Raftennon. The fireball grew in size and intensity as it sped toward the mage, who crouched down and covered his face with his forearms. The fire swallowed him, intensifying even further until the man disappeared in the crackling inferno. She gave the flaming orb a moment to consume the wretch, then clapped her hands together. The conflagration erupted in a bright flash, its shock wave shaking the open room from pillar to opposite pillar.

"And you were supposed to be so gifted," Jennalla sneered, convinced she had done in her enemy. Disappointment also tinged her voice. She had much more rage to dish out.

The smoke in the room cleared, whisked away into the whirling wind of the perpetual twister surrounding the tower. Jennalla gasped in disbelief when the figure of a kneeling man appeared through the mist. Steam rose from his dark-blue robes, which miraculously remained unmarred. There was no sign whatsoever the blaze had even touched him.

Raftennon slowly stood, glaring at the woman he once believed he could love. "You have grown powerful in the years you have spent resenting me for something you would have done yourself."

"Oh," Jennalla shook her head, believing his insolence even less than his impossible survival, "I'll show you exactly how powerful I've become."

More arcane words echoed between the pillars, turning the room into a war zone of unreality. Lightning flickered from the stone columns, rivalling the ones forking in the sky beyond the missing walls. Raftennon used the natural electricity in the air to draw away the magical current before it could touch him. Jennalla then sent water sprouting from the previously barren floor. The unnatural fountain engulfed him, as had her flames, with much the same result. Raftennon encased himself in an invisible barrier, letting the water gush around him until Jennalla grew tired of the torrent.

Then she surprised him by speaking words he never imagined he would hear. He was not familiar with the spell, but the few syllables he recognized sent chills running down his spine. Before the apprehension could subside, her casting was done and the blood from the self-inflicted cut on her palm splashed onto the tiles before her feet. The black, stone-like surface glowed a bright red for a split second before bulging upward. The rock oozed down to reveal the horrific demon Jennalla had summoned.

Raftennon stared into the fiery eyes that glared at him. Small, bat-like wings flapped from shoulders twice as wide as the thing's torso. It hopped on short legs, its hooves clanging in time with the storm outside. Arms ending in three-fingered hands as big as wine casks swayed, long talons scraping the floor tiles. Its grey skin appeared to be stone, down to puffs of dust falling from its joints every time it moved.

The spellcaster had just enough time to thank the gods she had only managed to call forth a minor fiend. The beast charged and the mage dove to the side to avoid being impaled by the long horn protruding from its forehead. With surprising deftness, Raftennon rolled onto his feet and attacked. A beam of white light struck the creature in the chest, charring flesh and driving it back to the edge of the room. Raftennon glanced at Jennalla, hoping she was overconfident. To his satisfaction, she simply looked on in shock and rage rather than preparing to attack him while he was occupied. The wizard rushed to finish the demon before either of them recovered. A concentrated gust of wind sent the abomination tumbling out of the room and into the arms of the hurricane.

Jennalla screamed in frustration and resumed her assault. Raftennon kept on deflecting her spells, letting the wizardress exhaust all her resources. He could tell her strength was waning, despite the stream of energy supplementing her. For a moment, while a torrent of crystal knives threatened to shred his magical barrier, he had seen a red river of mist flow from the centre of the ceiling to surround Jennalla's head. Her attack had intensified at that moment, so Raftennon knew something, or someone, had just given her a boost. The magic-user changed his tactic and began flinging the knives back at the woman instead of just blocking them. This ended that barrage before she could fully use her new advantage.

Eventually the wizardress let up her onslaught, staggering back but refusing to show any more sign of defeat. She screamed at the storm, her green eyes smouldering at the man who refused to go down. Raftennon was glad for the respite. His components were almost depleted, which meant he was running out of tricks to save his hide.

Jennalla raised her left hand and traced a set of arcane symbols in the air before her flushed face while her right hand did something within the folds of her red robes. She intoned the words with a weary voice. *"Frentaylin-mallis drenfâllannâs komréllan posteriâs nô ménapôlâs! Hellanân vôrtellôn trennülümâs!"*

The floor began to quiver and rattle, its creaking all but drowned out by the wailing of the whirlwind surrounding the room without walls. The whole tower seemed to moan in pain. Raftennon ignored the strange sound and continued to stare at Jennalla, keeping all emotion from his face. He had an idea what this spell would produce, but it was an incantation that conformed to the caster's will. He needed to wait to see what she planned next before deciding how best to defend himself.

The stone at her feet broke free and shot up before her, creating a wall between the two combatants. The tiles rose like the birth of a tidal wave. And, like a tsunami, the rising rock sprang forward, rolling in on itself, much like a parchment furled to enter its case, crushing everything in its path. The serpentine pedestal crumbled under the weight of the coiling slab, its orb lost in the curl of rubble. As soon as Jennalla disappeared behind the growing curtain, Raftennon rummaged through his pouches.

Jennalla thrust all her fury into the furling tiles, which now spanned the entire width of the room. The floor rolled until it had nowhere else to go. At that point, the curled stone crashed through the supporting pillars on that side of the room and was instantly engulfed by the hurricane outside. The winds did not hesitate to begin tearing the massive roll of rock to pebbles, along with everything it had taken with it.

The wizardress stood before a wide precipice. Only a ledge spanning less than a third of the room remained. Before her loomed a large hole that revealed the innards of the House. One step forward would have plummeted her to the depths of the keep, with several deviations and crushing obstacles along the way. Only two-thirds of the pillars still stood to hold the domed roof aloft. The crown of the tower did not seem to realize it was missing supports, the magic in the structure enough to prevent it from falling.

Jennalla sighed in relief—and sorrow. The emotions played out their war on her face. Her heart was heavy, and that made her angry again, and confused. She should have been happy, having just defeated her foe. Raftennon's suffering and death were all she wanted.

"That is what happens when one is consumed with her object-ive. Once it is complete, there is nothing left to turn to."

Jennalla whirled on the voice, her rage obliterating any other emotion she had begun to feel. Raftennon emerged from behind the sole pillar that stood between them, where he had teleported before the rolling floor crushed him. Small tears lined his blue robes, especially around the ankles and left sleeve, for he had not been quite fast enough. Pieces of rock had dislodged from the larger mass and flew at him, like spray from a wave. The bottom hem of his garment had been caught under the stone when he fin-ished casting the spell and he had raised his arm to fend off the strange tsunami, as futile as that seemed now. So those scraps of cloth now rushed within the hurricane, but it was a small price to pay for not being in that storm himself.

"I will kill you if it's the last thing I do!" Jennalla shrieked, lunging at the man she had apparently loved.

She slammed into him, her fingers streaking upward, striving to reach his eyes. Raftennon's quick reflexes enabled him to catch her wrists before she had a chance to blind him. The attack surprised him, despite the fact he should have expected it. Her magic had failed so far, so why should she not try a different tactic? But this was so—feral. No person, no matter how infuriated, would act like this.

The pair struggled for long moments, each draining the other's physical strength until Raftennon succeeded in pushing her away. Jennalla stumbled backward and hit the pillar with her shoulder. The impact spun her around, sending her to the edge of the sliver of floor remaining in the room.

Raftennon ran to her before he could think to do otherwise. He reached out to grab onto her as she lay less than an inch away from the precipice. Jennalla took the proffered hand and let him pull her away from danger. When she was safely away from the brink, she wrenched her arm out of his grip and swung her free hand at his face. Raftennon tried to withdraw, but her long nails still drew blood. Three shallow, crimson furrows appeared on his cheek, sending waves of painful heat coursing through the mage's face. Raftennon's reflexes made him thrust the wizardress away, this time toward the widest part of the floor, safe from any fall. He brushed his fingertips over the scratches, knowing they would heal quickly enough. How long would it take his heart to follow suit? Despite all his efforts, his feelings for the woman, both love and hate, were leaving deep scars on his soul.

Jennalla glared at her past lover and rummaged through her robes, not even bothering to get up. Raftennon rushed to do the same, preparing himself for her next attack. The wizard plunged his hand into an empty pouch. There went the protection spell he had first thought up. Into another pocket his hand went, and still nothing. He hurried through his other pouches, ignoring the woman sitting in front of him, who was rubbing her palms together.

Finally, Raftennon's hand fell on something. It would not help him ward off her spell, but it would give him more time to think of something. He retrieved the dried prennenwood leaves and crumbled them between his fingers.

"Flaymmanâl komprénôr tenbâh sôronell!"

Instead of throwing the crushed leaves straight up into the air as he always had, he threw them at Jennalla, who was turning her palms in his direction. The dazzling flash exploded between them. The bright coloured lights had no effect on Raftennon, for he had learned to protect himself during all the years he had spent perfecting this particular spell. Jennalla, however, brought her hands up to cover her eyes and screamed in pain. Large blisters of heat bubbled all over her face, her intended attack evidently another fireball.

The wizardress writhed in agony, trying in vain to alleviate the torture of her blackening skin. She rolled on the floor in her anguish, unknowingly nearing the pillar behind her. Raftennon jumped after her, diving to grab her as her feet swung out beyond the edge of the room into the torrential winds. Jennalla flew away from his reaching grasp. All he could do was watch her fly away from him.

She did not go far before crashing into another column, the force of the collision spinning her like a newly-spun top. The impact sent her twirling on the inner side of the post, toward the centre of the tower. The strength of the unnatural winds cast her across the ledge, straight into the hole she had created in hopes of destroying her enemy. Despite the anguish of her burned face and the ribs that were certainly broken, Jennalla still had the presence of mind to fight for her survival. She groped for safety, somehow finding the lip of the still-existing tiles and latching onto their edge.

Raftennon walked over to her and peered down at the swelling, charred flesh of her face and the burned eyes that stared up at him.

"You...must...be...relishing...this." Each syllable she forced out of her swollen lips was a battle against excruciating pain, but still she made herself say them.

Raftennon could only stare at her and shake his head. What was he to do? Should he save her, so she could continue tormenting his family? Could he actually let her plummet to her death? Did she want to be saved? The damage to her face was extensive, and only she knew how severe her crash against the pillar had been. Maybe letting her fall would be the merciful thing to do.

"You...watch...me...die." Somehow, her burnt eyes still shot her hatred at him.

"No." Raftennon turned and walked to the far side of the floor, not looking back as she lost her grip and plummeted to the black bowels of the House of Jafall. Was his act one of mercy, or revenge? He did not know—or care. He currently felt nothing.

30

LEAVING THE HOUSE

The stars shone into the lonely room atop the mystic tower, shedding their brilliant, unfiltered light through the only window. Two robed figures continued to peer into the crystal-blue ball, one impassive, the other concerned for the mage's safety.

"You feel too much for this mortal," said the first, and senior, of the pair.

"We need him."

"That is yet to be determined."

"It has already been resolved." This new voice came from behind them.

Both men turned to the newcomer, bowing to him. His long, white hair swayed in the breeze that surrounded only him, in time with the folds of his grey robes. His white eyes looked over his students.

"Divine Pentaclin," the elder of the black-robed figures whispered.

"Your brother has indeed forsaken his Oath, and I fear he wishes for a most atrocious conclusion to his plans." The Celestial Mage informed them.

"We must prepare to counter his actions," began the first of the ebony-clad pair.

"We must prepare the mortal for his Enlightenment," the second interjected.

"Hush," the first admonished in a low voice.

"I am afraid Arramen is correct," the deity chimed in. "Though I have much faith in you Chosen, your centuries of remote study and apathy toward mortal life have rendered you inadequate for the task. We cannot afford to spend days reflecting on a decision, contemplating every possible ramification. We need someone who will act quickly. We need someone skilled enough to learn the Sacred Art, but rash enough to not be hindered by the heightened discipline.

"I have also obtained new information that forces our hand. We need a new weapon, and we need it now if it is to be ready in time. You have my blessing to recruit him."

Arramen bowed to his god, hiding quite well his ecstasy at the prospect of mentoring a newly Chosen. After a moment of unspoken communication between himself and his master, Arramen disappeared from the room, leaving the Celestial Mage with his senior Munaedaar.

"I hope this mortal is capable of overcoming what he is about to face," the black-clad wizard said.

"We will see." This part of the future was hazy to the god, a fact that disturbed him immensely. He had seen what would happen if they did nothing, but the consequences of his current actions were not revealed to him. "For now, please contact Sedrill in Crystalmyre and make the arrangements."

The mage slumped against a pillar, the raging winds outside coming into the room slightly to push his long, brown locks into his face. He sat there, not caring about the flailing strands. His blank stare took in none of the destruction that surrounded him. His mind blocked out the results of the decision he had made all those years ago. His eyes never turned to the gaping hole in the floor. He did not want to see the place where he had lost the person he had given his heart to—at least partially.

The wind picked up and blew his hair clear off his face. That was when the spellcaster finally realized he was no longer alone. He lifted his eyes to gaze upon the manifestation that stood before him, at the point where the edge of the mutilated floor met the last pillar standing at that end of the room. The deity wanted the mortal to take in this image, to remember it for the remainder of the time he would allow him to have. Let him take in the robes, the colour of coagulating blood, rustling in the gusts the storm tried to force into the room without walls. The lightning flashed off the silver chain hung around his neck, with the form of an angry fist dangling at the centre of his chest. His hands he hid in the folds of the garment, as he concealed his face in the shadows of the hood pulled low over his head. These features he would reveal shortly and he would relish the added shock when the worm finally knew before whom he grovelled.

"I have no quarrel with you, priest of Jafall," Raftennon said with resignation.

The hands left their concealment and drew back the blood-red hood. His complexion was as ashen as the surface of the moon, so drawn over his bones they showed through, almost as if they were not covered at all. The sunken eyes were as red as the robes and he made them flare just the slightest bit. His long hair was as devoid of colour as his skin, which made him look more dead than alive. "On the contrary, mortal, I take the defeat of a devoted follower quite personally. And we both know what I stand for."

"Jafall," Raftennon whispered.

"The god of hate, jealousy, and most importantly at the moment, vengeance!"

The spellcaster looked up at the deity with no trace of fear in his eyes, his heart empty. "Then go ahead and finish me." He returned his gaze to the tiles before him.

Jafall started to laugh but clamped his jaw shut. He stared at the mage, not believing what he saw. All the man felt was resignation. The mortal truly did not care whether he survived this night. Jafall growled in frustration. The mortal's lack of regard for his life took away all satisfaction from the kill. He would not let that stop him from exacting his revenge, however.

The god reached behind him to draw a massive crimson broadsword. He twirled the weapon around his body with ease, demonstrating his proficiency with it. The dread the display should have instilled in his victim did not assail the magic-user, who continued to stare at nothing. Jafall snorted in disgust and took a step toward the spellcaster.

Another man materialized across the room, where the floor was no more. He stood atop the battered wall, his feet firmly planted on the split rock. His black cape rippled wildly in the storm, his hood flattened against the side of his face. He held his arms together behind his back, the black fabric of his pants and tunic flapping as maniacally as his cloak. But there he remained, entrenched in his position, defying the unnatural maelstrom.

"You have no business here," Jafall informed the Munaedaar, not caring which of the Chosen dared to encroach his domain.

"Actually, I do," the newcomer said, his calm voice drifting into the room despite the howling of the raging wind, and pointed out Raftennon with a nod of his head.

"Your kind are not supposed to meddle in mortals' affairs," the deity snorted, a sneer stretching the skin over his mouth even tighter. "That's the chain your precious creator shackled to your ankles."

"Be that as it may, but we must amend a transgression we have allowed to happen." The Munaedaar kept his precarious perch on the top of the tower wall, unaffected by the torrent trying to whisk him away.

"How does that make this mortal so important?" Jafall stopped his advance and turned his gaze to Pentaclin's Chosen.

"Because of our 'chain', as you quaintly put it, he will be key to the success of our endeavours."

"None of that concerns me." The deity returned his attention to the brooding wizard and took another step toward him, raising his broadsword for the only, and fatal, strike.

"If we do not succeed," the intruder continued, his voice still emotionless, "you will have dominion over nothing. For only oblivion will remain."

Jafall turned to the figure, pointing the tip of his crimson blade at the black-robed chest. "I've seen what concerns you, and all I see is someone who's chosen the winning side."

"He plans on awakening one of the Five." The newcomer conveyed flatly.

"Another magnificent weapon added to my brethren's cause." Jafall beamed, thinking of that group of powerful creatures that had wreaked havoc on the lands all those centuries ago. That had been a wondrous time in this world's long history.

"He will do so by creating the Daemon Warrior," the robed figure persisted, still attempting to get through to the god.

"Again, another magnificent weapon." The deity was finally grasping the motives behind this visit. The feeble Celestial Mage sent his lackey to help prevent the massing of these mighty evil forces. Pentaclin should have known this attempt would be futile. How could Jafall not reap the benefits of the strife this union would cause?

"The damage to the Balance will be catastrophic," the Munaedaar continued, cutting into the god's reveries.

"Which will make you very busy trying to rectify the hopeless situation."

The god of hate had had enough with this pointless discussion. He turned his attention back to the mortal, who still slouched against the pillar, oblivious to what was happening around him.

"And when there is nothing left, who will you hate?" The Munaedaar's words retrieved the deity's focus.

"No one is powerful enough to shatter the Scale." A slight tinge of worry crept into his thoughts, a feeling the deity shoved away as soon as it was formed. No being, even one divinely chosen, could manage that feat.

"Once he acquires all the pawns he requires to execute his plan, he will be."

Jafall stared into the darkness of the stranger's hood, delving into the being's mind. He sensed the sincerity behind the words and the worry of the otherwise unshakable figure.

"Bah!" The god dismissed the intruder and focused once more on the spellcaster, who had finally gotten up and was now standing at the lip of the shattered floor. The mage looked down into the formidable House, maybe contemplating following the woman to a quick end. The deity looked into the man's soul and still felt the emptiness inside him.

The god of vengeance rushed forward, his crimson eyes turning to the Munaedaar, who remained perched atop the marred wall. A sadistic leer crept onto Jafall's lips as he watched the figure stare at him while he slammed his shoulder into Raftennon's back. The wizard flew off the edge and disappeared into the gloom that was the House of Jafall. The Munaedaar shook his head and vanished.

The deity laughed at his triumph. He had lost one of his most devoted worshippers, but she had been much too needy anyway. As consolation, he had struck a blow against one of his celestial brothers. Jafall felt he had received the better half of this exchange.

His mirth shattered when he first sensed, then saw, what was happening.

Raftennon saw the black-clad man appear across the room and wondered who he was, what he was doing here. When he began to speak, the mage immediately recognized the voice as being the one that had twice invaded his thoughts, offering him help and support. He had not imagined it. There was truly someone looking out for him. At that moment, Raftennon's self-loathing and apathy vanished. He needed to survive this ordeal if he was to find this stranger and get some answers.

The magic-user blocked out what the men were saying to each other, turning his concentration inward. He required full control of his entire being. He did not want the god to sense any aspect of his plan. He buried all hope the newcomer gave him and replaced it with the emptiness he had felt after leaving Jennalla to fall to her death. That image actually showed him his next course of action. If the deity decided to do anything other than what he expected, however, it would mean the end of his life.

When he was ready, Raftennon rose from his seat at the base of the pillar and walked over to the edge of the floor. Jafall and the black stranger had concluded their conversation. This was it, the moment that would decide his fate. Would the god of vengeance be true to form, or would he suppress his malicious instincts?

Raftennon blotted out all thought, keeping his mind blank. He needed to concentrate extra hard on keeping the excitement from sprouting in his heart when Jafall pushed him into the void. The spellcaster had counted on the god's delight in tormenting his victims. He gave the celestial being a chance to sentence him to the same fate his enemy suffered, and he had taken it.

Now, as Raftennon plummeted through the gloom to the bottom of the tower many stories down, he put his scheme into action. The time for subterfuge had passed and he had to work fast to save his life. Retrieving the last of his remaining dove feathers, he clasped both hands on them as he fell by a stone bridge, missing it by mere inches. He willed the shock of the near miss away and whispered the appropriate words.

"Inmellan thôrnadayleemôn jemboeelaynü fellüm."

He had to use considerable force to throw the feathers far enough in front of him to be effective. At the speed he was now falling, they would pass him by before he knew it and be useless. It would do him no good if the spell took effect above him. Thankfully, his attempt succeeded and the magic caught him, letting him float safely to his destination.

Raftennon saw the window he used to enter the House rise past him, and still he descended. He was sure it was that exact window, for no others appeared afterwards. He glided further down, deeper into the hidden bowels of the deformed tower. He finally landed on a narrow bridge another fifty feet below. If it had not been for the incantation, he would have shattered the span as if it had been constructed of beach sand and his bones would have surely suffered the same fate.

The mage took in his surroundings, safe for the moment. He needed to climb back up to his exit. Fifty feet was not that far to go, but if you had to do it using an intricately woven web of bridges and ramps, it seemed more like fifty leagues. Who knew how long it would take him to find his way. All he knew was Jafall would discover his deception in time and could navigate this maze much more easily than he.

The discovery proved to be immediate. The god appeared in front of the wizard before he decided to take his first step. The blade of the broadsword lay nonchalantly on the deity's shoulder while the bony fingers of his right hand drummed on the long hilt. The red eyes smouldered, but the rest of his face conveyed no emotion.

"You have the gall to deceive me like that?" Jafall's voice resonated off the twisted walls, dispersing the House's phantom feelings from the pair as if they feared their master.

Raftennon stared at the god, knowing his struggle was over.

There was nothing left in the hidden pouches of his robes for him to use. He had no more tricks to save himself. He stood up straighter and prepared for the inevitable swing that would lop off his head. To the mage's surprise, Jafall put away his weapon.

"I admire fearlessness in a man, especially when he has a goal he wants to achieve." Raftennon blinked at the deity, not believing the jovial tone of his voice. "I do not know what your goal has become, but you surpassed many obstacles to get here. Then you stood there and let someone you once loved fall to her death. That is the kind of attitude I demand of all my worshippers."

"I will never worship you," Raftennon whispered, not caring if this slight brought the retaliation he still expected.

"Never?" There was no anger in Jafall's response, only amusement. "Who knows what the future may bring. I am a god. I have an eternity to wait."

"I do not know where this conversation is heading, but I would prefer to get on with my death if it is to happen." His lack of fear surprised the wizard. He did not wish to die, but he would tolerate mockery even less.

"Luckily for you, I've decided to let you live." Jafall pulled his hood over his head, returning the skull-like face to shadows. "Think of it as your reward for defeating my most gifted worshipper."

Raftennon continued to stare at the god as he and his keep started to waver like images seen in the distance on a desert horizon. The magically constructed stone walls fell away, replaced by the blackness of night. The bridge disappeared from under his feet, and the mage found himself floating inches above the tops of many poplars. He had time to blink once before the magic holding him up let him go. The spellcaster tumbled down through the thick foliage, snapping small branches as he went. Twice, he nearly stopped his fall by grabbing one of the thicker limbs. Both times, he lost his grip and continued down through the leaves. These near stops, though they did not bring an end to his plunge, did save his life.

Raftennon plopped onto the leaf-covered ground and struggled to keep his consciousness, a battle that lasted a couple of shaky breaths before oblivion overtook him.

31

Revisiting the Forest

He returned to reality with the sound of low growling all around him. Clarity trudged to his muddled mind and the wizard's heart began to race. Before his descent through the trees, he had noticed the tall peaks of a long mountain range to his left. Far ahead of him, nearly at the horizon, a narrow band of blue wound its way across his vision. Then he saw the familiar leaves before they became a blur whizzing past him as he crashed through them. Now, with the well-known sounds surrounding him, he knew exactly where he was, and what he would see when he opened his eyes.

He did so ever so slowly, wishing he was wrong. But he was still surrounded by the black poplars of Drendaggamor and the noise coming from the small group of ragged timber wolves interspersed in between the trunks.

Raftennon chuckled despite the pain it brought him. Jafall had let him go from his grasp, only to throw him to the wolves—literally. The deity must be splitting his sides with laughter.

The wizard struggled to his feet, using the tree beside him for support when a bout of dizziness assailed him. While his left shoulder scraped against the coarse bark, the fingers of his right hand squeezed even tighter around the dead branch he had picked up. This meagre club was the only thing he would have to fend off the beasts. One wolf inched forward, its one good eye radiating the hate it felt for the man. The other orb was cauterized shut amid burned flesh rimmed by singed fur.

"Well, you seem to remember me as much as I remember you. And it appears you have had no luck replacing your fallen friends." Raftennon continued to stare at the same wolf that had led the pack the first time they met in the Dead Wood. The other three that had survived the encounter positioned themselves at equal intervals to surround the mage. "Did you not learn your lesson the last time?"

The alpha seemed to shake its head as if to answer negatively before leaping for the magic-user. Raftennon tensed to jump out of the way, but it was too late. The animal's paws already lay on his shoulders, pushing him to the ground, its fangs inches away from his throat. Right after contact, the timber wolf whimpered in pain and turned its head. When the pair landed on the leaf-covered earth, the animal rolled off the man. The feathered shaft of an arrow protruded from its neck.

Raftennon scurried away from the slain beast, his brown eyes scanning the woods around him. The other wolves twirled as well, desperately trying to find the source of the projectile. None of them located the shooter and another canine lost its life as a second arrow found its mark in its flank. The remaining pair leaped into the forest, getting out of harm's way as quickly as their legs could take them. Only then did Raftennon's saviour reveal himself.

"Did you come out of hiding for the sole purpose of saving me?" The spellcaster marvelled at the sight of the strange elf, wondering what could have compelled him to leave his haven. The mage started to get up, brushing dead leaves off his robes as he went.

"I was sent to aid thou." The fugitive slung his bow over his shoulder and walked over to the lead wolf.

"You were *sent*?" Raftennon stopped in mid-swipe. The elf was here on someone else's behalf? Was it the black-cloaked figure?

"Ay, I was sent. And now we wilt be off. Art thou capable of carrying one of these wolves? Meat like this cannot go to waste."

Raftennon still felt weak from his fall through the trees, but he still managed to do his part. He took the smaller of the two animals and followed the elf back to his lair.

He spent four days in the hidden cavern under the dead pop-lar, regaining his strength. The elf helped him prepare for the journey home by scouring the forest for some much-needed spell components. He knew Drendaggamor better than any other liv-ing thing and was the only one who could find the exotic plants. Furthermore, in Raftennon's current weakened condition, he would be quite susceptible to the forest's spiritual attack.

On the day Raftennon began his journey home to Xendrem-mar, the elf showed the mage the quickest route out of the cursed woods. He did this from the confines of his sanctuary below the earth, still refusing to go with the spellcaster. *He* was still out there looking for him.

"But you came out to save my life," the wizard pointed out.

"A man in black came and implor'd I go out to aid thou. I couldst sense he was a very powerful being, and he promis'd he would watch ov'r me while I did this errand f'r him. This forest also defies *him*, preventing *his* prying eyes from peering under its canopy. And I know some secrets not shar'd by any other. So I did what the man in black asked, and now he is gone. He is nay longer hither to help protect me, so I will return to protecting myself."

Raftennon did not ask for more details. He knew who the man in black was. His name still eluded him, as did his purpose, but the magic-user knew it was the same man who confronted Jafall in his own House.

The two men said their final goodbyes, both certain they would never see the other again. As long as the god of ven-geance still existed, it would never be safe for the elf to venture out of his hiding place. The mage watched his host scurry down one of the many tunnels he had dug deep into the earth, then turned to scamper up toward the exit.

It took Raftennon two days of laborious trekking through thick underbrush and closely placed tree trunks to escape the Dead Wood. The setting sun shone in front of him as he looked over the Plains of Mandellon in the direction of his home. He took in a deep breath, cleansing his lungs of the stifling air he had been forced to breathe inside the forest.

After basking in the view of the cheerful land for a few moments, he handled his newly acquired spell components and spoke the words that would send him to his family.

32

A BRIEF REUNION

Raftennon washed up and headed to the dining hall in the manor beside the Spellcasters' Guild, where his loved ones waited for him. Mother, sisters, brothers-in-law and nieces, each greeted him with warm hugs and strange looks. Apparently something had changed in him, but they could not put their finger on it. He assumed they meant the melancholy that still refused to leave him. Though finding the black-caped man preoccupied the mage the most, Jennalla's death still troubled him. He did not want to talk about it, however.

During the meal, Raftennon steered the conversation to other matters. The women recounted all the wonders they discovered in the vast metropolis of Xendremmar, of the grand festival he had just missed and all the new wares they had purchased. They had had such a good time that Raftennon's mother and his youngest sister Shenma had decided to stay. All that remained in Yentrill for them were bad memories, which ate away at his mother's soul. City life seemed to agree with the older woman, rejuvenating her and giving her the will to keep living. The other members of Raftennon's family were eager to return home.

When they finished recounting all their adventures, Ronnan asked the wizard if it was safe to return home. He wanted to resume his life in Ednifad with his daughters.

"You are no longer in danger," the mage assured them.

They pressed him for more details of his trip.

"The important thing is we are all free from harm, and each of you can return to your ordinary affairs," was all Raftennon would tell them. "The threat has been dealt with."

Ezranalla began to ask that he elaborate—again—but the sound of someone clearing his throat resonated through the large room. Everyone turned to the archway that served as an entrance at one end of the hall to see the hunched figure of the Master Mage Vendrammon. Raftennon wordlessly thanked his teacher for the interruption.

"I apologize for the intrusion," the old man's respectful tilt of the head was aimed at every member of the family, "but may I have a word with my most gifted of apprentices?" Vendrammon directed the question at Raftennon's mother, who smiled at him and nodded her consent.

Raftennon rose from his chair and walked over to his mother to give her a kiss on the cheek before exiting the room with the older spellcaster.

"Thank you," the younger mage said as they rounded the first corner out of the room.

"I presumed you did not want to divulge any of your trials on the way to the House." Vendrammon turned his black eyes to look at his former student without moving his head.

"Not to mention those inside the keep." Raftennon kept his gaze forward, ignoring his teacher's stare. In fact, his thoughts were turned inward, so much so he did not notice any of his surroundings as the pair made its way through the manor.

"I hope those experiences will not affect you too gravely." The elder continued his sideways scrutiny as surefooted as if he were looking forward.

"Every experience changes the man." Raftennon's tone was cold, dispassionate.

"How one deals with atrocity determines the strength of his will," the old man responded, concern creeping into his voice just the slightest bit.

Raftennon caught the emotion and turned his head to his mentor, flashing him a warm, reassuring smile. "I will be fine, Master."

"Learn from your experiences, my boy, but do not let them

define you." Vendrammon stopped in front of the wide doors that served as the manor's main entrance. The old mage squinted as he stared into the other wizard's eyes. "Some changes you cannot control. Those you must accept. Do not permit them to alter who you want to be, however."

"Is this why you interrupted dinner?" Raftennon returned his teacher's stare, perplexed. "I assure you, I am still myself. I simply need to process a few events."

Vendrammon continued to study his protege for a moment before lowering his eyes and nodding his head. "I came for another reason. Word of your adeptness in the Art has travelled to the far reaches of our land, and beyond. Even the great Mage Dean of the Spellcasters' Guild in the Crystal City has heard of you."

"Frenmallos of Crystalmyre?" Raftennon had been reaching for the door to open it for the old man but stopped before his fingers had a chance to even touch the brass handle.

"You have been summoned to the capital of Rond Thora," Vendrammon explained. "You have an audience before a Conclave of the most powerful members of our order. They wish to ascertain your true power."

"Why?" Raftennon did not understand. What could the group of highly respected spellcasters want with him?

"You will receive all the information you seek in the Crystal City."

Vendrammon motioned for the stunned wizard to let him out of the guest house. As the old man crossed the threshold, he instructed his former student to ready himself for another long journey. The next day he would travel to a kingdom he had only read about in the scrolls of the Guild.

That night, as sleep struggled with the mage's anticipation for the trip, Raftennon could not help but think this had to do with the man in the black cape.

ON THE LANGUAGE OF MAGIC

As described in the *Allamyrantha*, Pentaclin first revealed the powers of magic to the Elfin Nations. The first elves to practise spellcasting needed a means to focus the energies required to fuel their incantations. They found characteristics in certain plants and other materials affected the flows in deferring ways. They also realized sound played a large part in the proper execution of their spells.

Since they were chosen by the Great Sage, and no other race could yet wield magic, the mages wove the language of the Arcane Arts using their native tongue. Some altering to the recitation of the words was vital to properly, and safely, gather the power needed. Inflections were augmented or diminished while new syllables were created.

The Elfin script consists of elegant strokes difficult to reproduce by even the most gifted penmen unless they understand the origin of the alphabet. These letters have been described as "curves of clouds flowing down into branches of slender trees, finally parting into strong roots."

Unlike in the English language, each group of graceful lines represents a sound. Instead of having two letters indicating the *ch* sound in the word "**ch**ariot", elves have one symbol.

For ease of reading, a phonetic translation is used in this volume, utilizing the alphabet we mere non-magic-wielding mortals already know. Unfortunately, to attempt to recreate the correct pronunciation, the use of unusual characters was needed for some sounds while the expected combination of two letters appears to represent others. What follows is a guide to help the reader grasp—as much as possible—the intricacies of the Elfin language.

Vowels
a — as in m**a**n
â — as in p**a**lm
ay — as in d**ay**

Vowels (continued)

e — as in d**e**ss

ee — as in s**ee**

é — as in prot**e**ge; it is closer to the sound the letter represents in the French language

i — as in k**i**t

o — as in l**o**t

ô — as in b**oa**t

oo — as in t**oo**l

u — as in b**u**t

ü — as in **tu** in French

y — as in **eye**, no matter its position in the word

Neighbouring vowels are voiced in separate syllables unless grouped together above.

For example:

- *ay*, as aforementioned, is pronounced h**ay**.

- *oa* would be said like "**boa**," in two syllables. They are not to be confused with *ô*, which represents the sound those letters make in the word b**oa**t.

Consonants

ch — as in **ch**ariot, no matter its placement in the word

g — as in **g**old, even before a vowel

gh — as in fo**g h**orn; these letters never form a single sound, as seen in English; this combination also denotes a change in syllable

h — as in **h**elp, even at the end of a word; no *h* is ever silent

s — as in **s**ee

th — as in **th**eatre

Consonants not mentioned above are pronounced in the expected fashion (for example: *b* as in **b**ed and *p* as in **p**irate).

Double consonants, like *ll* and *nn*, are spread across two syllables. Think of the words "royal liege". You would pronounce *ll* as if saying these two words, but there would be no gap in between. The sound is sustained from one syllable to the next while still maintaining a distinction between those syllables.

It should also be mentioned this transcription does not take into consideration the differing inflections of syllables. Only the sound of the letters are shown in this text. The same grouping of letters may appear in different words and must be recited differently for the spell to work. In the Elfin tongue, these accents are denoted by dots or apostrophes interspersed in the writing. These symbols are placed between any two letters and at any height in the line. It can vary from a "star" hovering above the "clouds" to a "seed" buried beneath the deepest "roots." The placement of the identifier denotes the type of inflection used. For simplicity's sake, these symbols have been omitted in this work.

Glossary

Balance, The: also known as the Balance of Existence. All creation must maintain an equilibrium in order to function. For every positive there must be a negative. Any shift in this Balance would have dire consequences, ranging from catastrophic storms to the very destruction of Everything.

Bellyn River (BEH-lin): A small river in Mandellon flowing through Entamman Forest, from the Qartyff Mountains to the Grannbellan River.

Bezna (BEHZ-nah): A large fishing village in the Salgre Hills, on the western coast of Mandellon.

Black Eye: A divinely crafted gem that sits at the pinnacle of the House of Jafall. The god's influence radiates from the dark stone, turning all mortals' hearts against one another. The effectiveness of the Eye's corruption depends on the strength of the individual's will. Some barely feel the pull from the gem, while others mistrust everyone and seek to repay every slight.

Blendalla (blehn-DAH-lah): Raftennon's eldest sister. She marries Ronnan and lives in Ednifad with him and their three daughters.

Bren (BREHN): Raftennon's eldest brother, a fisherman by trade.

Caelynn (KAY-lin): One of the Munaedaar. She is one of the Original Eight who enchanted the Lance of Light.

Celestial Tower: A spire formerly part of the Spellcasters' Guild in the old Crystalmyre, before the capital was rebuilt in its current location. Pentaclin elevated the structure into the heavens and gave it to the Munaedaar for their use to further their studies without distractions from the mortal world.

Christoffen (KRIS-to-fehn): One of the Munaedaar. He is one of the Original Eight who enchanted the Lance of Light. A scholar at heart, he devotes most of his time gathering notes on all aspects of subjects that interest him.

Cindran (SIN-dran): An apprentice healer in the town of

Bezna.

Daenar (DAY-nar): One of the Munaedaar. He is one of the Original Eight who enchanted the Lance of Light. He left shortly after his Enlightenment to pursue his own objectives. The enchantment of the weapon that fell the Great Beast was his only collaboration with the other Munaedaar. He also has done nothing to fulfill his obligations to maintain the Balance of the Scales.

Davin (DA-vin): A young man from Yentrill, who had wished to wed Shenma, Raftennon's sister. He ended the relationship, unwilling to care for Shenma's ailing mother.

Divirion Mountains (DI-vi-rion): A mountain range split down the middle when the main continent of ancient Kagendur was ripped apart in one of the many battles between the gods. The Great Divide now spans the gap between the two sides of the vast range of peaks. The god Flonn favours these mountains and the dwarves revere them. In the bowels of these peaks the dwarves constructed the vast complex of their main kingdom.

Dombellarr Forest (DOM-behl-lar): Vast evergreen forest to the north of the Mandellon Plains. Home to a noble species of large timber wolves known throughout the northern regions of the continent.

Drendaggamor (DREHN-da-ga-mohr): Also known as the Dead Wood. A forest nestled at the western foot of the Pynakkor Mountains in Mandellon. The wood is cursed, half its trees dead, but never decaying. It is said one who enters the Dead Wood never comes out.

Dyrlund (DEER-lund): God of Light, Truth and Justice. He presides over the deities of good. His holy symbol is the Silver Sun.

Ednifad (EHD-ni-fad): Small town in western Mandellon, nestled between the Salgre Hills to the north and Entamman Forest to the south.

Elbatu Sea (EHL-ba-too): Sea to the west of Mandellon.

Emnecron (EHM-neh-kron): Region to the south of Mandellon.

Enlightenment: A magical process in which newly initiated

Munaedaar gain their longevity and ability to see what other mortals cannot, so they can learn what is beyond the reach of normal minds. The process turns hair white, complexion so smooth that no one can put an age to the mage, and lightens the iris to a bluish-grey colour.

Entamman Forest (EHN-ta-mahn): Forest to the north-east of Yentrill, in Mandellon. The woods surround the Qartyff Mountains.

Everything or **Existence:** The collection of all the worlds and planes of existence connected to each other by the Void.

Ezranalla (EHZ-rah-NA-lah): Raftennon's sister. Lives on the edge of Entamman Forest with her husband and children.

Flonn (FLON): God of Manual Skills, Invention and Progress. Patron deity of dwarves and journeymen. Also referred as the Celestial Blacksmith. His holy symbol is the Hammer. At the behest of Dyrlund and Geneve, Flonn orchestrated the creation of the world and the heavens.

Gendan (JEHN-dan): Ezranalla's husband. Lives on the edge of Entamman Forest with his wife and children

Geneve (JEH-neev): Goddess of Fate, Life, Death, Birth and Time. Patron deity of seers and other fortune tellers. Also referred as Mother Fate. Her holy symbol is the Hourglass. Geneve judges the fate of the departed, sending souls to either Paradise or Damnation. Though she does not lead the gods of neutrality, the other deities would defer to her judgment if a unified front is needed.

Glanduran Bay (GLAN-dur-ran): Small bay on the eastern shores of Elbatu Sea. The fishing town of Bezna is nestled at its point inland.

Grannbellan River (GRAN-beh-lahn): A large river flowing from Lake Nenamyd to Vendetran Bay in Mandellon.

Grynvellon (GRIN-veh-lon): One of the Munaedaar. He is one of the Original Eight who enchanted the Lance of Light. He took leadership of the group upon its inception and no one has contested his authority.

Guntram (GUN-tram): Bully who frequents the Green Mackerel Inn in Bezna.

Hanlon (HAN-lon): Keeper of Paradise. A mortal appointed by Geneve to watch over the entrance to Paradise, greeting those worthy of eternal bliss.

Hanlon's Gate: Spiritual gate souls pass through to enter Paradise, where they spend eternity existing in pure bliss; entrance to heaven.

Haun River (HAH-oon): A river flowing westward from the Pynakkor Mountains to Nenamyd Lake in Mandellon.

Hawer (HAH-wər): Raftennon's father, a fisherman by trade.

Helaenna (HEH-lay-nah): One of the Munaedaar. She is one of the Original Eight who enchanted the Lance of Light.

Hernam (HƏR-nam): Know-it-all in Bezna.

House of Jafall: Fortress situated in a wasteland to the northwest of the kingdom of Rond Thora. The magically constructed towers sit in the middle of a perpetual whirlwind. At the very top of the tower sits the Black Eye, the physical manifestation of jealousy, forever turning mortals' heart toward vengeance. No one may enter the God of Vengeance's home without a divine invitation.

Jafall (jah-FAHL): God of Hate, Jealousy and Vengeance. Also referred as the Vengeful God. His holy symbol is the Clenched Fist.

Jennalla (JEHN-nah-lah): Mage from Bezna, learning the craft at the Spellcasters' Guild in Xendremmar. She shared classes with Raftennon before he gained his apprenticeship, as well as a short romantic relationship.

Kagendur (KAY-jehn-dewr): The enchanting world in which these stories take place.

Kroykl (KROY-kəl): A species of vicious, sadistic brutes. Of average human height, the creatures possess tusks flanking their snouts, long pointed ears and small black eyes under protruding brows. Orange-brown hair covers their chins and the back half of their head, all the way down their backs and to their elbows. Crude tattoos cover their forearms and bare chests.

Madosan (MA-doh-SAN): A town nestled at the southern tip of the Pynakkor Mountains in Mandellon.

Mandellon (MAN-deh-lon), Plains of: Plains west of the kingdom of Rond Thora, bordered by the Pynakkor Mountains to the east and the Elbatu Sea toward the setting sun.

Marlon (MAR-lon): A human male thief; one of Denmur's crew in Bezna.

Master Mages: Each Spellcasters' Guild has a faculty of Master Mages who take on apprentices to teach them the advanced aspects of the art of magic. Customs vary across nations, but the standard is one apprentice to a Master Mage at a time, so the most focus can be put toward proper learning.

Masthoranin River (MAS-thoh-ra-nin): River flowing from the Pynakkor Mountains, eastward in the kingdom of Rond Thora to empty into Crystalac Lake.

Melna (MEHL-nah): Raftennon's mother.

Munaedaar (MOO-nay-dahr): A group of mages selected by Pentaclin, God of Knowledge, entrusted to ensure the continuation of learning. The deity gifted them eternal life to fulfill this goal, for a single lifetime is not long enough to accomplish the task. They are also entrusted with maintaining the Balance, charged with rectifying any tilt to the Scales of Everything.

Mylnan Vinas (MILL-nan VEE-nas): In the Old Tongue: Age of Darkness. A bygone age where the world was covered in darkness, oppressed by Helkree, god of shadows.

Necroma (neh-KROH-mah): The realm of Damnation for the souls deemed worthy of eternal suffering; Hell.

Nemanta (neh-MAN-tah): Goddess of Storms, Destruction and Disease. Also referred as Stormbringer. Her holy symbol is the Flail.

Nemmbak (nehm-BAHK): An ancient, subterranean creature, thought to be extinct.

Nennilla (NEH-ni-lah): Jennalla's mother, now deceased.

Pennlannae **(pehn-LAHN-nay):** Known as bloodflowers. These red flowers only sprout from ground which have soaked up blood from the wounded. Their petals droop downward, which gives the illusion the plant is bent over as if mourning the loss of life.

Pentaclin (PEHN-tah-klin): God of Magic, Knowledge, Wisdom and Language. Patron deity of mages and scholars. Also referred as the Great Sage or Celestial Mage. His holy symbol is the Tome.

Prennenwood (PREH-nehn-wuud): Large trees only found in the northern regions of Rand Thora.

Pynakkor Mountains (PEE-na-kor): Mountain range delineating the Plains of Mandellon to the west from the kingdom of Rond Thora to the east.

Qartyff Mountains (KAR-tif): A small range of mountains nestled in the centre of Entamman Forest in Mandellon.

Raftennon (RAF-teh-non): A young mage believed to have the potential to become one of the most powerful spellcasters ever known.

Roen (ROH-ehn): God of Agriculture, Nature, Animals and Healing. Patron deity of druids and elves. Also referred as Shepherd of the Gods or the Great Herder. His holy symbol is the Stag. Roen creates all form of life in Kagendur, from plants, animals, to the races of mortals.

Ronnan (ROH-nan): Raftennon's brother-in-law, married to Blendalla. He lives in Ednifad with his wife and three daughters.

Salgre Hills (sal-GRAY): A range of grassy hills in the northwest region of Mandellon.

Scales of Everything: A celestial construct that measures the Balance of the universe. Unseen by the mortal world, the Scales tilt depending on the acts of mortals and gods alike. Too much evil, or too much good, causes an imbalance that can adversely affect the world. If the Scales lean too far or too long to one side, the world will suffer catastrophic consequences. The shattering of the Scales will result in the destruction of all realms of Existence.

Sevellen (SEH-veh-lehn): One of the Munaedaar. He is one of the Original Eight who enchanted the Lance of Light.

Shenma (SHEHN-mah): Raftennon's youngest sister.

Spellcasters' Guild: A school where the gifted learn the art of magic. Mages teach the initiates the basics they need to control their power. Master Mages then takes on apprentices for more intense learning. These guilds are spread across Kagendur, in every land, mostly in large cities so the students can be condensed into classes and more easily sorted according to their talent and power.

Stamm (STAM): Raftennon's older brother.

Stav (STAV): Human barbarian who leads a band of criminals kroykl based in the Salgre Hills.

Thorm (THORM): God of Honour, Valour, Protection and Bravery. Patron deity of knights of honour. Also referred as the Platinum Knight. His holy symbol is the Shield.

Tullae (TOO-lay): An old man who shelters himself away from the other villagers of Yentrill. He teaches Raftennon to read and introduces him to magic.

Vendetran Bay (VEHN-deh-trahn): A narrow bay on the eastern edge of the Elbatu Sea. Grannbellan River flows into it.

Vendrammon (VEHN-drah-mon): Master Mage of Xendremmar. He was the most powerful mortal mage of his lifetime until Raftennon came into his full strength.

Viprennys River (VEYE-preh-niss): A river flowing westward from the Pynakkor Mountains to Nenamyd Lake in Mandellon. It is known as the Snake River because of its winding course through the Viprennys Hills.

Void, The: The ether regions connecting the different planes of existence.

Vrenfallan (VREHN-fa-lan): Male elf thief in Bezna; Denmur's second in command.

Xendremmar (ZEHN-dreh-mar): A city on the northern bank of the Grannbellan River. It is the largest settlement on the Mandellon Plains.

Yentrill (YEHN-tril): A village on the shores of where Grannbellan River flows into Vendetran Bay, on the western border of Mandellan.

Ygrett (EE-greht): One of the Munaedaar. She is one of the Original Eight who enchanted the Lance of Light.

THE STORY CONTINUES IN...

THE DAEMON AND THE LADY

Tentative Release
FALL 2016

Visit
www.lupynebooks.com or www.MarcLabelle.com
for updates

ABOUT THE AUTHOR

Marc Labelle was born and has spent most of his life in Sturgeon Falls, Ontario, Canada. He currently shares his home there with his wife, Sheena, and the eldest two of his four children.

You can visit Marc on the web at the following addresses:
    Author website: www.MarcLabelle.com
    Blog: www.MarcLabelle.com/wordpress
    Facebook: www.facebook.com/authorMarcLabelle
    Twitter: @MarcJLabelle
    LinkedIn: ca.linkedin.com/in/marcjlabelle

www.ingramcontent.com/pod-product-compliance
Lightning Source LLC
Chambersburg PA
CBHW060531180626
46817CB00002B/516